I0770058

"Dufrain's characters leap off the page
and into your heart."
— Carole Stivers, Author of The Mother Code

"Historical fiction that feels both
intimate and expansive, with prose
that lingers like a haunting melody."
— The Indie Lit Lounge

"It feels like To Kill a Mockingbird
collided with Almost Famous and
then aged into a noir confession."
— Lyrics and Fire

"A stunning coming-of-age novel
about grief, friendship, and the
search for closure set against the
politically charged backdrop of 1970."
— Reader Views

The Blues and Billie Armstrong

ROY DUFRAIN JR

Boodwater Books LLC
bloodwaterbooks.com

ISBN: 979-8-218-82335-1

Printed in the United States of America
Cover and interior design: Casanova, Bloodwater Books
Fractal Art Background: Blair Gibb / blair-gibb.pixels.com

To my father,
*for the ink in my blood and
the conviction that words matter*

"The blues is the truth.
If it's not the truth, it's not the blues."

— *Willie Dixon*

The Blues
and
Billie Armstrong

UNEASY LISTENING

The first time I heard the blues was a gray rainy Wednesday in September of 1969. I was sitting with my mother in our house on Fourth Street. I was twelve years old, almost thirteen; she was thirty-two and quite dead.

This was up in Lupoyoma City, a small-minded town next to a big muddy lake in the hills of Northern California. Earlier that day I'd walked out the front door under a clear sky. I was halfway across the lawn when my mother hollered, "Your lunch!" I jogged back and she handed me the brown paper bag, the top folded over twice with a sharp straight crease and my name printed neatly with black felt pen on both sides. She wore a sundress with blue flowers on a white background, and I didn't think to tell her how pretty she looked.

That afternoon the sky crowded up with gray-bellied clouds and it began to rain. At school we were kept inside watching a movie about Dr. Leakey digging skeletons out of the ground in Africa. After the final bell I took the bus to Fourth and Main and ran the last block home through the downpour. I stopped on the covered porch and wiped my sneakers on the welcome mat so I wouldn't get yelled at for leaving wet footprints on the floor.

Inside, the house was full of the empty hush that brings background noises into the foreground—a loud tick of the second hand on the grandfather clock, the refrigerator hum leaking in from the kitchen, the rain stammering against the roof. And something unfamiliar—a rhythmic scratching I couldn't identify but followed back toward my mother's room, not the room where my parents slept, but the one she called the "dayroom," where she kept the art deco vanity with the big round mirror, the typewriter on the yardsale desk, the Singer sewing machine, and the twin rollaway bed where she suffered through her migraines.

The door was open.

The scratching sound came from the Grundig Majestic hi-fi, which I'd almost forgotten was in there. As far as I knew it hadn't been used in a couple years, since the day I helped my father move it out of the living room to make way for his brand new Magnavox Astro-Sonic Stereo Console, which he enjoyed showing off to guests, always finding an opening for the same hokey line—that he was serving "Sinatra and Seagram's." The old Grundig's auto-changer didn't always work properly, and now the phonograph needle was stuck in that blank moat at the end of a record, scratching back and forth.

My mother lay on the rollaway bed, on her back in the blue-flowered sundress, on top of a pale green chenille bedspread. I thought she'd fallen asleep listening to the hi-fi, but on the nightstand the lamp was left on and a half-gone fifth of vodka stood uncapped in a small circle of dusty light next to an empty highball glass and a huddle of drugstore pill bottles.

Evelyn King had a warm brown complexion that showed her Mexican and Irish blood, but now her face was drained and bluish gray. Mascara ran in rivery stains down her cheeks. There was no sound of her breath. Her chest and stomach did not rise and fall. Her head drooped to one side and a trail of vomit ran from the corner of her mouth onto her neck, the smell of it tainting the air.

I didn't want to scream or cry. I wanted to show grace under pressure, courage under fire. I tried to imagine a movie, a book or TV show with a reassuring synopsis—faint-hearted kid finds dead mother's body, reacts with perfect composure, proves manhood.

I found my way to the kitchen, thinking I should call someone. The year before, my mother had redecorated. She'd painted the walls sunflower yellow, ordered a new fridge and range in harvest gold, and new vinyl flooring in a striking orange-yellow-rust pattern. I remember how proud she was when the project was finished, and how my father mocked her by wearing sunglasses to the dinner table.

The yellow plastic phone was mounted on the yellow painted wall. I stood with the receiver held away from my ear, the dial tone buzzing, and I considered the handwritten list of phone numbers tacked to the wall: the local newspaper where both my father and grandmother worked, my aunt's beauty parlor, our family doctor's office, the police and fire departments. I tried to rehearse what I would say, but I couldn't arrange a clear sentence in my mind. I couldn't imagine the words staggering out of my mouth. *Hello, this is Archer King, I just want to let you know my mother is dead.*

The square, electric Timex on the wall above the table said 4:15. Phone call or not, my father would probably be home within an hour, bustling through the door ready for a stiff drink and Walter Cronkite. Did I even want to be here then? I felt oddly embarrassed—ashamed even—to be the one who found her like this, to be in the position of informing adults of something so completely out of a child's domain. I didn't want to be the bearer of this news. But I also didn't want to be the boy who *couldn't* bear it.

I hung up the phone without dialing and drifted back to the dayroom like a sleepwalker. I slumped onto the low stool at the art deco vanity and listened to the scratching and crackling coming from the hi-fi, and in the big round mirror I saw my boyish face alongside the reflection of my mother on the bed. We were near lookalikes. She was five feet tall, I was an inch shorter. Both slender and tanned, with brown hair so dark it looked black in low light. She styled her hair like Jackie Kennedy (not Jackie Onassis), with a curved swoop of bangs above one eye; my father sent me to the Main Street Barbershop for a "regular boy's haircut" which always left me with a similar swoop.

I wasn't sure what it meant that I hadn't noticed all this before—not only the ways we looked alike, but any hint of this end. I was so clearly her son, but did I even know her? What twelve-year-old boy truly knows his mother—her dreams, her regrets, her pride and shame?

The blue-flowered sundress had two pockets thigh-high on its front. Still gazing at the vanity mirror, I caught the white flash of something peeking out the top of one pocket. Turning around for a direct view, it looked like the corner of a folded piece of paper.

I couldn't remember the last time I had willingly touched my mother. She had touched me—pushed the hair out of my eyes, turned my collar down, tried to hug or kiss me—but your average American boy knows when it's time to start keeping motherly love at a distance, especially in public.

Touching my mother's body at that moment might drive me screaming out of the room, out of the house and into the Lupoyoma streets, but I wanted to retrieve that piece of paper. I had the shy, needy hope that it might hold a clue that would help me understand. I walked around to the other side of the room, put one knee up on the bed and leaned over precariously. I grasped the corner of the paper with fingertips and carefully slid it out of the pocket without touching anything else.

It was a stationery envelope, addressed in my mother's handwriting to someone I didn't know, a soldier by the name of PFC J.R. Cole. The name meant nothing to me, but the envelope suggested she was planning to go out that day—to mail the letter if nothing else. At that time there was no home delivery within the city limits of Lupoyoma, so she would have to go to the post office or the nearest public mailbox to send the letter. Then I turned the envelope over and saw the pink imprint of a lipstick kiss.

None of this made sense. She knew I would be the first one home. I'd seen her purse and car keys waiting on the yardsale desk. Now I'd found outgoing mail in her pocket. She was clearly planning to go out. Maybe the rainclouds changed her mind. Or a headache came on and she laid down for a nap. But the vodka, the pills and the kiss on the envelope spun my thoughts off in other directions where I didn't dare follow.

The scratch-scratch from the hi-fi now seemed amplified to oppressive intensity as if someone had cranked the volume knob. I couldn't think straight. I crossed the room and lifted the needle off the record. The scratching stopped, but the silence was unnerving.

On the turntable a stack of 45s had been set up and played one after the other. I held the turntable arm suspended in the air and read the label on the top record. "*Sad Hours*," it said, in silver-gray type on a red spinning background, and I wondered if she'd known this would be the last song she ever heard, if she'd planned it that way and set up the whole stack like some grim Top 10 countdown. I watched my hand drop the needle at the beginning of the track, and sat down on the bed next to my mother, still holding the envelope.

What came out of the speakers was not my father's Sinatra, nor one of my mother's favorites like Trini Lopez or Peter, Paul and Mary. It wasn't folk or rock-n-roll or jazz or swing or country and western. And it definitely wasn't easy listening. It was like meeting someone who speaks English but with a seductive accent you've never heard before.

The bass line ambled into the room and paced the floor in a circular path with sadsack persistence. An electric guitar chimed in with jangly complaints of its own. Brushes gossiped to a snare drum and the chick-chick of the hi-hat punctuated the beat. An instrument I couldn't name took the lead—a horn of some kind that announced itself with a long, distant moan, then whined and wailed and honked bitterly. It shook its head in regret and wagged a finger in warning. There were no words, yet the unidentified horn spoke of dark days and busted hearts, of sorrow and resignation. It seemed to accuse, confess, beg forgiveness and promise a fight all at once.

Jerky film clips of shuffled memory flickered across my inner sight—the lilt of my mother's inflections as she read me to sleep when I was little, red pedalpushers and white sunglasses in the Little League bleachers, a swipe of kitchen yellow on her forehead, the scent of Aquanet hairspray hovering by the vanity in this very room.

When the song was over I wiped my eyes with a shirt sleeve and got up and turned off the hi-fi. The Grundig Majestic was a mid-fifties model in a honey-colored wood cabinet with double sliding doors that covered all the knobs and buttons when closed. The turntable was further hidden in its own drawer, which had to be pulled open for access. I closed up the whole thing with the 45s still stacked on the turntable. I grabbed the vodka bottle off the nightstand and swigged a mouthful that burned like cold gasoline, set the bottle back in its place beside the empty glass and the pills.

I took the pink lipstick envelope to my room and hid it under the bed in the Keds shoebox with my baseball cards. I pulled on a jacket and my Giants cap and slipped out the back door into the whispering rain.

PINCH HITTER

Our house stood at the bottom end of Fourth Street, half a block from where the pavement sloped right into Lupoyoma Lake. On the other side of our backyard fence was the dirt parking lot of the Lupoyoma Yacht Club, which wasn't quite as grand as it sounds and actually just a kitschy clubhouse for old Rotarians with old boats. But, beyond the Yacht Club, across Third Street, was the boundary of Library Park, a typical smalltown park with a couple square blocks of lawn populated by looming trees and wooden picnic tables. There was a dock with a diving board, a green cement tennis court, and the ivy-covered Lupoyoma County Carnegie Library.

A few summers before, I'd loosened one of the wide planks on our fence so it appeared to be solidly in place but could easily be set aside to open a shortcut to the park. Now I stepped through the gap, checking the Yacht Club parking lot for possible witnesses, my mind a tangle of shame and confusion and urgency, my breath quickened. I didn't want anyone, especially my father, to know the truth—that I'd been in the house, seen her, and left. My father was the editor of the *Lupoyoma Call & Record*. He was an old-school, self-made newspaperman who curated facts for a living and had no patience for sugar on top. A man has to look life in the eye, he liked to say. Death as well, I supposed.

And it started to dawn on me that I had possibly tampered with evidence by taking the envelope. I recognized this as the physical embodiment of what my father would call a lie by omission, but I had no intention of sharing the envelope with him or anyone else. Maybe I was protecting him, or my mother, or the rest of the family, or myself. Maybe I just wanted some piece of her all my own. Cowardly. Protective. Selfish. Bereft. All of that and more in an emotional blur, the colors run together like oil riding water.

I needed to slow down the drumming in my chest and stop the technicolor movie of the dayroom that was replaying in my head. And all the questions that came with it. The storm had emptied the park of citizens except the ducks who waddled around bickering over puddles that would soon disappear. I walked along the concrete promenade that ran the length of the park and listened to the hushing sound of the rain falling on the lake.

South of the park was the Weeping Willow Resort & Trailer Court, and I resolved to wait there to be found and notified of my mother's death. The game room at the Weeping Willow was a regular hangout for me and my buddies. I figured that was where the adults would think to look for me if I was late coming home on a rainy day. My maternal grandparents owned the place, but they were always so busy running the restaurant and the rest of the resort that we kids were usually unsupervised in the game room. We'd play pinball, feed the jukebox, drink sodas and share cigarettes stolen from our parents. If there weren't any older kids around to hog the pool table, we might shoot a game of eight-ball or cut-throat.

Timmy Bilderback and Joey Quarterman were already there, Timmy at the Pinch Hitter pinball game, Joey standing at the jukebox looking over the song selection.

"Hey Archer, got a quarter?"

I flipped him a coin. He dropped it in the machine and punched some buttons. Three songs for two bits. Joey picked *Daydream Believer* by The Monkees, his favorite band. He had an autographed photo of Davey Jones on his bedroom wall, which he got by writing to the Official Monkees Fan Club.

He moved aside and nodded for me to take my turn. Most of my favorites back then were Beatles songs. But I could still hear *Sad Hours* in my head—the echo of that strange lonely horn—and all the tiny labels on the jukebox blurred together like I was a little kid wearing my father's bifocals.

"You okay, man?" Joey must've caught the faraway look in my eyes.

I finally focused on the label for *Penny Lane* and punched in the number with Timmy now looking over my shoulder, encouraging me to "Pick a song already, dipshit." Then he ragged on Joey that Davey Jones was a homo and the Monkees weren't even a real band, and he punched in some Steppenwolf.

I'd known Timmy since the second grade, but I didn't know what he had on his walls—his parents were loud, unhappy drunks, and he never invited anyone inside.

I bought a can of Squirt from the coke machine, bummed a cigarette from Timmy and tried to act like I hadn't gone home after school and found my mother dead in the dayroom. The cue ball was loose on the green felt of the pool table, and I slung it around with my hand, trying to make three-rail bank shots while waiting for my turn at pinball.

Steppenwolf roared on. Outside my head, the scene unfolded like a hundred other forgettable days at the Weeping Willow game room. I was racking up points on the Pinch Hitter pinball machine, lost for the moment in the blinking lights and the bells and the bumps, when my Aunt Laurette appeared at the sliding glass door, peering in with her hands held up to form a tunnel around her eyes. Rainwater dripped down the door and blurred her face.

"It's your aunt with the tits," Timmy said. Even among twelve-year-old boys, Timmy Bilderback's level of sexual energy was considered somewhat obsessive. Laurette King was actually my cousin once removed. I knew her mostly from holiday gatherings or as my occasional babysitter. According to Timmy, she was a "screamin' hot piece," and I admit I agreed, but I did so in secret, her being family and all.

Mid to late twenties, trim but curvy, long dark hair ratted up on top, flame-blue eyeshadow. It's fair to say she was the black sheep of the family thanks to a teenage marriage and divorce and some other hinted failings which I'd repeatedly been assured were none of my young business. As she entered the game room I looked up and my last ball fell uncontested past the flippers. The game-over light flashed red.

She didn't look like a hot piece right then, her eyes puffy, face pale and slack. "Archer, there's been an accident," she said. I stared like an amateur actor who's forgotten a line. "You need to come with me," Laurette said, and she took me by the hand and pulled me outside. The rain was falling hard again. "Come on!" she shouted, dragging me splashing across the wet black parking lot to the shelter of her Volkswagen Beetle.

We sat in the front seats with our dripping hair stuck to our heads. She put the key in the ignition but didn't start the engine. Rain covered the windows, swirling the outside world. She gripped the steering wheel so hard her fists trembled. She released her fingers carefully, as if they fought her, and she slammed the heels of both hands against the wheel. Mascara flooded down her face. She delivered the news, crying and nearly shouting over the din of rain against cheap metal. She said my mother had mixed up the nerve pills and the headache pills and the sleeping pills. Or somehow lost track and tripled her dosage. Or maybe she'd forgotten Doc Meaney's warning not to mix her vodka with the pills. No one was sure. "A terrible accident."

I didn't know how I should pretend to react; I had no clear sense of the expectations. Doc Meaney, who was also the county coroner, had been to the house and ruled my mother's death an accidental overdose. I had to resist the urge to pour out the truth.

Earlier that summer Laurette had caught me stealing a couple Marlboros out of her purse. She'd made me light up in front of her, teased me about my cough and my inexperienced, effeminate hold on the cigarette. She gave me a mild lecture but never mentioned it to the other adults in the family. Still, I kept quiet about what I'd seen and heard in the dayroom. And what I'd taken. My face must've looked blank, no tears came.

Lupoyoma Call & Record, Friday, Sept. 19, 1969
Evelyn L. King, Lupoyoma City

Evelyn Louise King, formerly of 55 Fourth St., Lupoyoma, passed away Wednesday, September 17. She was a native of Shelter Cove, California, and a resident of Lupoyoma the past 14 years. She is survived by her husband Michael King, son Archer King, parents Edward and Mary Medina, and mother-in-law Junia King, all of Lupoyoma. Services will be held at 11 a.m. Monday, September 22, in the Chapel of the Lake at Jones & Jones Funeral Home. The Reverend Martin Jameson of St. John's Episcopal Church will officiate. A graveside service will follow at Lupoyoma Cemetery.

THE CLOTHES MAKE THE BOY

I wanted a gray suit like I'd seen my father wear. Grandma Junia drove me to JC Penney's in Santa Rosa—two hours of twisted road, dusty oak trees and September hills. It was the first time I was allowed to ride in the front seat of her 1959 Buick Electra, a decade old already but still the closest thing to the Batmobile on the streets of Lupoyoma City. Angular and sleek, acres of windshield, space-age curves, great winglike fins over the taillights. Totally cherry and always waxed and polished glossy black, with white leather seats and chrome eyebrows over the headlights at the same sharp angle as the ones Grandma Junia drew on her face.

I studied her movements closely—the rise and fall and crinkle of her full skirt as her foot switched between gas and brake, her hands moving lightly but knowingly on the steering wheel, the silver painted fingernails that matched her frosted hair. I daydreamed myself in that driver's seat, in full command of that shining blade of a car, climbing toward some heroic adulthood that would include facial hair and certainty.

She had an 8-track tape player and six or seven tapes in the glove compartment. You wouldn't find anything like *Sad Hours* in there. She wouldn't even let me play the one old Beatles tape she had. She said it was "childish and common," and claimed the Columbia House Record Club had sent it by mistake. She liked the schmaltzy Big Band dance music of her youth—Glenn Miller, Tommy Dorsey. But she also dabbled in West Coast jazz, which she assured me was "highly sophisticated." Grandma Junia had often complained that my cultural education was being neglected, and when we fell uncomfortably quiet she turned up *Take Five* by Dave Brubeck and counted the beats out loud to illustrate five-four time. "One-two-three-four-five, one-two-three-four-five." Because every twelve-year-old needs a lesson in odd time signatures on the way to buy a suit for his mother's funeral.

The boys department at Penney's had exactly one suit that almost fit me, and it was not gray. My hands disappeared into the sleeves when I held my arms straight down, and the pantlegs piled up on the tops of my shoes like rubble. Muttering into the dressing room mirror, I complained too loudly that the color was Dodger blue—clearly unacceptable for a born and raised Giants fan. Grandma Junia barged in with her arms crossed. "Archer Edward King! You will not attend this function in your worn-out school clothes. A boy your age without a decent suit—your mother should've known better! Now, this will do fine… and that's that."

Whenever Grandma Junia said that's that, she would quickly brush her hands past each other and then open them as if she had magically eliminated the grime of complexity. And when Junia King said that's that, well… that was that.

• • •

I stood beside my father, Grandma Junia and Aunt Laurette on the wraparound porch of Jones & Jones Funeral Home, a pompous Victorian on Main Street that had once been the Jones family home. The white painted floorboards glared in the morning sun. I shifted foot to foot in my Dodger blue suit and watched my father shake the hands of the men who filed by in gray and black. I surmised that my function at this function was to establish my ability to shake hands appropriately—in other words, like a man. I kept my right arm cocked in the handshake position so my hand wouldn't disappear into my sleeve, and I concentrated on shaking hands with each man—firmly, with level eyes and a straightened mouth. No crying.

My mother's parents, Pop and Molly, arrived in their old Chevy pickup. Their real names were Edward and Mary Medina but most folks in Lupoyoma knew them simply as Pop and Molly, because they'd been around so long and had owned the Weeping Willow since I was "knee high to a crawdad," as Molly would say.

Aunt Laurette hurried down the steps to greet Pop and Molly in the parking lot. Laurette had been a waitress at the Weeping Willow in her high school years, and she was the one who'd introduced my mother to her cousin

Mike King. In that way, Laurette was the original bridge between the King and Medina families.

Pop always said Molly was "ninety-five pounds of gristle and backtalk," but that day she looked shrunken and caved in, her tiny hands colorless against the black of her dress. Laurette guided her up the porch steps with a hand on her elbow. She rushed straight to me like I was a kindergartener with a scraped knee, and she pulled me close by the lapels of my suit and stood tiptoe to kiss me twice on the forehead. She was the only adult I knew who was shorter than me. She looked at my father and sighed and shook her head like she was disappointed. She started to speak, but her chin quivered, her eyes puddled, she bit her lip and looked away.

Pop came up the steps and walked right by my father as if he wasn't there. He walked toward me, I put out my hand, and he shook it strongly and gripped my shoulder with his other hand. Pop seemed twice Molly's size and his big calloused hand swallowed mine whole. He didn't speak, but he locked eyes with me and I believed this was his way of lending me strength. Molly crossed herself and went crying into the depths of the funeral home, but Pop didn't follow.

Grandma Junia was the only person who called Pop by his real name. "Edward," she said, "you're not going in to see your daughter?"

Pop shook his head. "No, not like that." He looked Grandma Junia's way, then swiveled to draw in my father's attention as well. "But you two make sure and take a good long look." He turned around, stepped down from the porch and headed back up the concrete path toward the parking lot.

"What's wrong with Pop?" I said.

"He's just upset, son," my father said.

"With good reason," Laurette said, and I thought yes, she was his daughter, his *chiquitita*, his little one.

But Grandma Junia said, "Oh hush, Laurette! As usual, you don't know what you think you know."

"Well, I only know what I read in the newspaper," Laurette said. And maybe I should've wondered what she meant by that.

When we entered the viewing chamber I followed my father's gaze across the room, where the casket was raised up on a collapsible gurney that reminded me of a sprung jack-in-the-box toy. He paused and wavered unsteadily in the doorway, lowered his head, ran one hand through his thick black hair. "Son, you don't have to look if you don't want to," he said. I was surprised. It was unlike him to offer me such a hall pass, and I hesitated at the back of the room.

But Grandma Junia said, "No, it's about time he got a grownup look at the way of things." And she steered me by my shoulders, pushing me toward the open coffin.

My mother was dressed in moonlight blue, a double-breasted woolen jacket buttoned over a silky white blouse, a string of pearls at her neck. She looked ready for church or work or a trip on a train. I took a good long look, wondering what Pop wanted my father and Grandma Junia to see. She was so still. So empty. I thought of the statues I'd pretended to shake hands with at the Wax Museum on our class field trip to San Francisco. I thought of her in the blue-flowered sundress on the rollaway bed in the dayroom. I wanted to rub her forehead like she always asked me to when she had her headaches. I wanted to listen to stories of her childhood and tell her how lovely the yellow kitchen looked in the morning.

I wanted to ask why.

Grandma Junia leaned in over my shoulder, so close that a stiff strand of her fresh-frosted hair prickled my ear. "Presumably, she's in a better place," she said, and the words smelled of beauty shop ammonia.

The recorded sound of a church organ poured out of speakers mounted in each corner of the room. I was drowning in it. My knees began to give in to the undertow. Grandma Junia finally turned me away from the coffin with a hand around the back of my neck and guided me to one of the folding chairs. The metallic cold seeped through my slacks. The organ music stopped. Reverend Jameson started a prayer and we all bowed our heads and closed our eyes.

Wet sobs broke out around me but I couldn't cry. I couldn't keep my eyes shut. I couldn't stay in that chair, that room. I heard the hi-fi scratch-scratch in my head and I was in danger of spilling out everything I knew. I rose to my feet but Grandma Junia tilted her head up and raised one penciled eyebrow. "Where do you think you're going, young man?"

I turned and fast-walked up the aisle, between the folding chairs and bowed heads, and clattered out of the room as the reverend began to read from scripture. "Brothers and sisters: behold, I show you a mystery; we shall not all sleep but we shall all be changed."

I ran through the lobby and flung open the door. I ran across the parking lot, where Pop was sitting in the old pickup. He called out, but I didn't answer and kept running and turned down a gravelly alley of dumpsters and back doors. I had no destination in mind other than escape. I ran two blocks north in the alley, a half block west up to Main Street and another block north, past Rexall Drugs, two bars and the old courthouse with the World War I cannons on the lawn. I made a right turn down Third Street, deciding I would slip through our back fence again and hide out at home. But down the sidewalk I saw the sandwich board advertising the local music store, The Music Box. I stopped, bent over at the waist, hands on knees, caught my breath.

LITTLE WALTER JACOBS

Nate Henderson was a nineteen-year-old kid whose parents owned The Music Box. He'd been considered a bit of a geek in high school, even though he played in a local rock band—the kind of guy who couldn't look cool even with a guitar in his hands. After Lupoyoma High, he'd gone to Santa Rosa Junior College to study business (and evade the draft), but he still helped out at the store when he was in town. I'd never actually met him before, but back then Lupoyoma was a snowglobe of a town, where everything seemed to be within five blocks of everything else and everyone knew the *TV Guide* version of your life story even if you'd never spoken directly to one another.

I walked in the store, approached the counter and asked Nate if he'd ever heard of a song called *Sad Hours*. Nate was a tall skinny guy with brown wavy hair almost to his shoulders and parted sharply on the side so it cut diagonally across his face and sometimes obscured one eye.

He asked who the recording artist was, and I had to say I didn't know— looking at the record on the turntable I hadn't focused on anything but the title. Nate plopped a big thick catalog on the glass countertop and thumbed through its pages, stopped and shot me a look of mild surprise.

"So, how'd you hear of this song anyway?"

"I found it on my mother's record player."

He brushed his hair aside. "No way! Trini Lopez, Streisand, or Sinatra for your dad's birthday, but she never bought anything like this that I know of."

"So, what is it?"

It turned out the horn I'd heard was actually a blues harmonica player known as Little Walter Jacobs. Nate showed me a picture beside the listing in the catalog. Little Walter Jacobs was a Black man with a hardscrabble face and big haunted eyes.

I associated the harmonica with campfire songs and Bob Dylan. I had no idea it could be made to moan and shout and protest all the disappointment of the world. Until that moment I didn't even know enough to label what I'd heard in the dayroom as "blues." Even with my mother's Mexican blood, I was basically a green white kid from the hills of Northern California. I was so white I didn't know the blues was black. I only knew it stabbed me in the heart in some way no other music ever had, and it mystified and worried me that it was apparently so meaningful to my mother.

Nate said *Sad Hours* was originally released in the early fifties and was already something of a rarity. He said that kind of blues was way out of style these days. Little Walter had died a year or so before and his singles were mostly out of print. There was just one album listed in the catalog, which Nate could order, but I didn't have the four bucks for that, not to mention I didn't even have a record player of my own.

I thought of my mother singing *Lemon Tree* along with her Trini Lopez album while ironing my father's shirts, and I couldn't help but wonder how she would come into possession—or even awareness—of such an oddity as *Sad Hours*, which seemed so out of place in her world and in our home, a musical interloper. Could Little Walter's harmonica somehow be related to the pink lipstick on the back of that envelope?

I thanked Nate for the info. He said "By the way, sorry about your mom, kid." And I left the store and headed down Third Street. I took the shortcut across the Yacht Club parking lot and back through our fence with the odd feeling that I was sneaking into my own house. I had the anxious idea to get back into the dayroom—now, while the adults were gone.

The past few days had felt like our home was quarantined with disease. I was ordered not to leave the property and not to have friends over. No one outside the family came to visit.

Grandma Junia manned the kitchen sink, dusted the living room furniture, created small corners of routine and conducted muffled conversations on the yellow phone.

My father left early for work, came home late and sat in the nervous television light with the sound down low. He rarely spoke and was rarely spoken to. He drank and watched TV with a stare like he was looking right through the picture.

Molly dutifully appeared at the front door one evening to deliver a glass casserole dish of Pop's famous enchiladas while Pop waited in the Chevy pickup parked at the curb, with the motor running and Hank Williams honky-tonkin on the radio.

At other times, Aunt Laurette flitted in and out of the house on missions ordered by Grandma Junia—to the market with a list, to the dry cleaners with funeral clothes.

And, all along, the door to the dayroom stayed closed in a forbidding way, with the adults guarding it peripherally as they went about their quiet preparations. There seemed to be an unspoken understanding that the room should remain undisturbed.

But now I stood at the closed door of the dayroom, doorknob in hand, my heart running wild and snapshots of memory flashing behind my eyes like tiny fireworks.

I couldn't seem to turn the knob. In the center of my skull I heard the staticky scratch-scratch as if the needle was still stuck at the end of that record and my mother still lay on the bed. I could not will my wrist to perform the motion to turn the knob and open the door. My body simply wasn't ready to be alone in that space again, to re-live those first minutes of knowing—and the swarm of questions, the *not knowing*, that followed.

I figured someone would come looking for me after I ran out of the funeral, and I knew sooner or later they'd look for me at home. I thought Grandma Junia would probably delegate the errand to Laurette as she had before. But I heard the low grind of Pop downshifting the old Chevy truck and the squeal of the brakes as he brought it to a halt at the curb outside.

The motor grumbled to a stop and the truck door closed with a thunk. I only had a few moments before he would make it up the walkway and through the front door.

WAVES UNDER STARLIGHT

Pop found me in my own room, sitting cross-legged on the bed. He didn't say a word, just stood towering over me and waved his head toward the door. I walked ahead, and he herded me out to the front yard.

I climbed up into the cab of the pickup and sat on the passenger side. A busted sixpack of Oly sat between us on the bench seat. Pop started the engine, opened a beer, turned the truck around and drove up the little rise to the stop sign at Main Street just in time for me to see the yellow headlights of the black hearse as it passed by toward the cemetery.

Molly was riding in front, chin up, eyes ahead. I watched the polished coffin through the long side-window, framed by black curtains. The hearse was followed by the shiny Buick Electra, with my father's stern profile in the window, Grandma Junia's frosted beehive rising up on the driver's side. I counted seventeen vehicles, headlights glowing like daystars.

Pop switched on his own lights and pulled in behind, and we followed in silence to Lupoyoma Cemetery, a few miles north of town. He parked at the end of the long line of cars, turned off the motor, and the cab filled up with quiet hesitation.

I said, "Pop, I don't understand. Was it really an accident? Why would she want to die?"

He looked at me hard while considering the question. Then he looked away, through the windshield at the acres of gravestones. "You never really know another person's why, boy. Sometimes it's hard enough to know your own."

He grabbed a fresh beer, got out of the truck, stood waiting with the door still open.

"I'll stay here," I finally said, eyes averted, tears beginning to spill onto my cheeks.

I heard him open the beer, then watched him hunt his way between the grassy graves, toward the circle of mourners, where he took his place beside Molly. I turned on the radio and listened to Merle Haggard sing a song about somebody's wings while my mother's coffin was lowered into the red clay Lupoyoma ground.

On the way back, I rode in the middle between Pop and Molly. Pop turned the radio off and none of us spoke, and I expected that would remain the tone of the day—quiet and somber with hushed voices and downward eyes.

This being my first experience with a death in the family, you'd think someone would've told me about the after-funeral party. Although I don't think the adults even told each other—no announcement, no invitations, they just knew. They didn't even call it a party; they spoke of it later as a gathering or get-together or, more formally, as a reception. I thought those were for weddings.

Pop turned the pickup down Fourth Street, and there were already six or seven cars parked on our block. Multiple women paraded from car to house, carrying great tinfoil-covered platters held out in front of their pointy breasts.

One woman balanced her offering and tried but failed to close her car door with a well-placed shove of her high-heeled foot. My father came to her rescue and relieved her of the large tray. Pop watched through the windshield of the truck. He took a breath, and it looked to me like he set his jaw for trouble. He jerked the door handle and swung the door open, but Molly reached across me and touched his arm, and he slowly closed the door. "I think we'll be going home now," she said, and she got out of the truck, stood on the curb and made room for me to get by.

Pop stared straight ahead.

Molly said, "You go on inside, Archer. Tell Laurette we're not feeling up to it, okay?"

I jumped down from the truck and ran ahead, up the stairs and into the house, through the living room full of men drinking and into the yellow kitchen full of women talking of children and recipes.

The table was covered buffet-style with the oddest assortment of food: Pop's enchiladas, Grandma Junia's apple pie, Laurette's fondue and breadsticks, one neighbor's lasagna, another's fried chicken legs, and various intimidating, inscrutable casseroles.

I grabbed a can of cream soda out of the fridge and went back to the living room, where men shook hands and poured liquor from an array of bottles lined up on top of the long Magnavox stereo cabinet. They smoked and sat and stood confidently in their suits and asked each other how business was. They spoke of Mays and McCovey and joked that the Giants were leading the division but would surely find a way to end up in fourth place where they belonged.

No one mentioned Pop and Molly. No one spoke of death. Or my mother.

Retreating to my bedroom, I laid down on top of the bedspread with the abstract pattern of overlapping circles in different shades of blue—it always reminded me of waves under starlight. I closed my eyes and surrendered to the sensation that I was backfloating in Lupoyoma Lake, staring up at the starry sky instead of the blank ceiling.

I fantasized that I would contract some strange and rare genetic condition that would accelerate the aging process of my body and mind. I would suddenly grow a wild forest of pubic hair and a bushy mustache. My voice would deepen to a baritone and I would wake up inches taller each day. Doc Meaney would have to be called in to treat my overwhelming growing pains, and I would be told there was no cure, that I would for all intents and purposes be a grown man in a matter of months. And then I would begin to see through new eyes all the things I'd been told for so long I was too young to understand.

WHAT ABOUT THE BOY?

It was running out of my mother's funeral that led to my first job in the newspaper business. Well, that and the fact that Hank Timmons had recently received his draft notice.

In 1969 Lupoyoma it was thought obvious that an adolescent boy could not be properly looked after by a single, professional man with a responsible position in the community. According to Grandma Junia, I would soon be running wild in the streets, a hoodlum with a switchblade in my back pocket and a delinquent girlfriend on the reservation south of town. I had already given weight to this theory with my "disappearing act" at the funeral.

At first, Grandma Junia answered the call to duty like a reluctant general hastened out of retirement. On school days she left work early and arrived at our house before I came home, the big Buick filling up the driveway.

She would mutter in the kitchen, rummage the shelves and rustle and clang about while I sat on the living room sofa watching afternoon cartoons: *Rocky and Bullwinkle, The Jetsons, Underdog.* I was seeking refuge in familiar comforts of childhood, and Grandma Junia briefly—and surprisingly—indulged me.

She would call me to the table around five o'clock, and my plate would already be in place, the Giants logo glass on my right, filled with cold milk. She cooked sturdy midwestern dinners that always included meat, potatoes and corn. Having lived through the Great Depression, this was her idea of bounty—as close as she came to nurturing.

She had the knack of making love seem like a favor. She was visibly inconvenienced by the demands of family and sometimes held audible debates with herself over the things she was willing or not willing to do for others.

Still, she loved me in her own tight-lipped fashion, and I believed she was trying her best to soften the blow, trying to ease my transition into life as a motherless boy. But this grim simulation seemed an uncomfortable stretch for her, and before long she made it clear it was time to re-involve myself with the so-called real world.

One evening in late October, several weeks after the funeral, my father and Grandma Junia were sitting at the oak table in the yellow kitchen enjoying after-dinner highballs and cigarettes. When I entered the room, she leaned sideways to talk to my father but kept her eyes squarely on me. "So, Michael… what about the boy?" she said.

My father took his glasses off—thick black frames with bifocal lenses—and stared down at the garish vinyl flooring and rubbed the bridge of his nose between his thumb and two fingers. He was the kind of man who was pained by not having a ready answer. Yet there seemed to be none; my mother was dead and my father a newspaperman, both afflictions apparently permanent.

• • •

Hank Timmons was eighteen, practically a kid like me. I'd met him at the funeral. He was one of several staffers from the *Call & Record* who stood in line on the porch to shake hands with my father.

"Sorry for your loss, Mr. King," Hank had said, as if he'd just learned the phrase. Eyes down, feet shuffling like he couldn't bear to stand still.

My father said, with a hint of fanfare, "Son, this is Hank Timmons. He works at the paper in the back shop." Of course, I already knew who Hank Timmons was, and my father was well aware that I knew who he was. He was a local legend—probably the greatest athlete Lupoyoma High ever produced, certainly the greatest baseball player.

I'd watched him play since he was the star of the *Call & Record* Little League team. Back then my mother volunteered as the team's scorekeeper, and when I was six or seven years old that was my introduction to the game. I tagged along and sat beside her in the small stand of wooden bleachers. I ate boiled hot dogs and grape snowcones and chased foul balls that went into the creek. And my mother allowed me to look over her shoulder and ask long strings of annoying questions. In that way I began to learn the intricacies of the game and how to record them on a scoresheet.

During those years, Hank Timmons was an absolute phenom, the personification of the old cliché, "a man among boys." He once blasted fourteen home runs in a twelve-game season, to this day the Lupoyoma Little League record.

Hank shook my hand and said, "Well, uh… sorry for your loss, bud," apparently surprised to be cued for a second performance. His wheat-blonde hair was short and uncombed. He wasn't wearing a suit like the full-grown men, just gray slacks, a white dress shirt with a tie, and his Block L varsity jacket. He looked me over. "Nice suit," he said, with a sarcastic but sympathetic nod.

"Thanks," I acknowledged his commiseration with a grateful eye roll. I had the feeling I'd just met an old friend, and I had a lot of questions I wanted to ask, like how to throw a curveball and what about those fourteen homers, but I didn't want a lecture from Grandma Junia about this not being the proper time or place.

• • •

"I understand Hank Timmons is due to report to the Army soon," Grandma Junia said, still looking across the kitchen at me in her calculating way. "It's no surprise," she said. "He should have taken his studies more seriously. It was only a matter of time before Uncle Sam came calling."

"At least he's not one of these goddamn draft dodgers," my father said. "Not a bad worker, either. He'll be missed."

Grandma Junia had a way of tilting her head down as if the movement started in her chin, and at the same time raising the Buick eyebrows slightly as she pursed her lipsticked mouth. This practiced expression was Junia King's version of a kick in the shin under the table. And in that way, with her eyes moving back and forth from my father to me, it was "suggested" that I be considered as Hank's replacement at the newspaper ahead of his leaving for basic training.

My father put his glasses back on and looked my way. "The boy's just turned thirteen," he said. "He can't even get a work permit until next year."

"Nonsense. Weren't you the same age when you started in the business?"

"That was a different time. There are laws now, and our boss won't—"

"You leave the boss to me."

My father nodded slowly, indicating reflection. "I suppose a little hard work would do him good, maybe take his mind off… things."

It was no surprise that my father thought of work as the best available grief therapy for his son—*hard work will do you good* was essentially the cornerstone of his philosophy of life.

Grandma Junia brushed her hands, "Well then… that's that."

INK IN THE BLOOD

I didn't know exactly what Hank Timmons did at the *Call & Record*. I'd only been in the back shop a few times. My father and Grandma Junia worked in the front part of the building, and I'd always entered by the door on Main Street. But that door was locked on Saturdays, so I was told to arrive by the side entrance on the cross street to begin my training as a "printer's devil." I had no idea what that meant but my father said many famous and serious men had been printer's devils in their youth, including Benjamin Franklin, Thomas Jefferson and Mark Twain.

I considered riding my old Sting-Ray to save time, even though the *Call & Record* was only a few blocks from our house, but I decided that walking there, as my father often did, was the more mature approach for a young— and serious—working man.

I passed the front door on Main and turned the corner down Fifth Street. I walked the length of the building, taking in the magnitude of the thing while carefully missing every seam in the sidewalk. From the front the building had always seemed friendly, if aging. Two stories of white stucco with wooden framed windows and doors and fake Spanish tile rimming the roof. But from the side it was stern and gray, stretching back all the way to the middle of the block and leaving the street in cold shadow. Hank's car, a beautiful fire-engine-red Mustang, was parked at the curb in the morning shade.

The wooden double doors of the side entrance were thick with black paint. I hesitated, thinking I should knock, but one of the doors clamored open while my fist was still in the air, and a voice like rustling paper said, "Come in, young man. The place isn't haunted, you know."

Percival J. Terwilliger, owner and publisher of the *Lupoyoma Call & Record*, was a tower of a man, literally and figuratively. He was quite tall, well over six feet, as tall as Pop but slender, with long legs oddly out of proportion to his torso. He was also a tower of confidence and character, respected by my father—and therefore myself—as much as any man in Lupoyoma.

Even on that warm October Saturday he was dressed in his three-piece suit, with a long-sleeve white shirt, bow-tie, and polished wingtips. He wore glasses with no frames and thick lenses that magnified his dark busy eyes. When he opened the door wider, I saw Hank Timmons nearby in dark blue coveralls, hands behind his back like a soldier standing at ease.

Mr. Terwilliger looked down his long straight nose. "Your father tells me you're ready to come work for us. You know, he started out as a printer's devil too. Trained him myself, many years ago, right here in this shop."

He looked around at his kingdom and took a sighing breath. I looked with wonder at all the hulking machinery covered in snowy paper dust. I breathed in the sweet wet smell of ink and solvent. He put out his hand, and as I shook it he said, "Welcome to the newspaper business, son. Hank here will show you the ropes."

Hank nodded as if receiving marching orders. I stepped all the way into the building, and Mr. Terwilliger brushed past me on his way out. He paused in the doorway and looked back. "You'll do fine," he said. "There's ink in your blood, you know."

"Yes sir," I said, because that was all I knew to say to that man.

But, as soon as the door rattled shut, Hank said, "Old man Terwilliger's a piece of work, eh? Back here we call him Model T. Guy's a walking-talking antique. Smells like my grandpa's closet, I swear. And how about that bow-tie? It's damn near 1970 and he's stuck in the boring twenties!" He laughed at his own wordplay and slapped me on the back. "Now, let's get to work, bud. And listen up cuz I don't want to waste time, ya hear. I'm gonna be stuck on some army base in a month—I should be cruising Main Street in the Mustang right now, chasin' tail, know what I mean?"

He turned and signaled me to follow. We weaved a path around various machines while he chattered on like a ballplayer in the dugout, pointing and calling out the names of the strange equipment. Letterpress, addressograph, bundle-tyer and more. Faster than I could process.

We arrived at a door in the wall opposite the entrance, and Hank opened it and waved his hand around in the dark until he found the chain that turned on the lightbulb swinging from the high ceiling. This was my first look at the shop closet, a cramped and shadowy space crowded with a janitorial arsenal: brooms and mops, buckets and dustpans, and a vacuum that looked like a sawed-off oil drum on wheels. On a shelf along one wall, small stacks of the dark blue coveralls like Hank wore, freshly laundered and folded so the name patches showed prominently. Vic, Stan and Hank—strong, one-syllable names.

Tacked or taped to the back of the closet door were dozens of pictures—naked women torn or clipped from *Playboy* and *Penthouse* magazines, black-and-white prints of Lupoyoma High cheerleaders in mid-air with their little pleated skirts flying up, and tourist girls in bathing suits on the beach at Library Park. "Nice, huh?" Hank said as my eyes toured the display. He pointed to one woman with large breasts barely contained by a skimpy bikini. "Look at the rack on her," he elbowed me in the arm and the heat of a blush hit my face.

Hank lifted a grungy, soiled apron off a hook on the wall and held it out to me. The thing had once been white, but now was yellowed and slick with sweat and ancient ink stains. "Here," he said, "you're gonna need this."

A FRATERNITY OF DEVILS

He handed me a whiskbroom and dustpan and led me to another part of the shop. We stopped in front of a huge mass of machinery with more parts than an illustration of human anatomy. It was five feet across and eight feet high, a tangled wall of belts and levers and switches, and wheels and gears and gauges, and handles and buttons and knobs. At the center of it all a gooseneck lamp grew straight out and hung over a big keyboard that looked like a typewriter with a thyroid condition. An empty office chair was rolled up next to the keyboard, dwarfed by the behemoth it was in position to control. According to the raised letters on the machine's nameplate, this wondrous monstrosity was called a Linotype. I assure you, if any real machine in all the world was the inspiration for Rube Goldberg's beloved cartoons, it must have been a Linotype machine.

I said, "Jesus Christ, what does it do?"

Hank pointed to a stack of five or six metal bars on the floor next to the machine. They were silverish looking ingots, about two feet long and thick as my forearm. Each one had an open loop at one end. He said, "These are called pigs—don't ask me why. They're made of lead and they go on the hook at the end of that chain there, and that chain lowers them down into a little melting pot inside the machine. The melting pot melts the lead, and the machine turns the melted lead into lines of type. Don't ask me how. Terwilliger, Vic and your dad are the only ones who know."

"My dad runs that thing?"

"Yeah, when Vic is out or busy with something else. But the important thing for you is the pigs."

"Got it. I'm in charge of the pigs, but why am I called a printer's devil?"

Hank looked at me like I was a fool for even asking. "Hell if I know!"

He had me sweep up the metal shavings that carpeted the floor around the Linotype and dump them into something called the hellbox, sort of a wastebasket where used and rejected type was collected to be melted down. It was made of scarred and darkled old wood, its four sides held together by aging metal el-brackets. Time had pried open narrow gaps at the seams, and when Hank had me carry it to the compositor's table, powdered metal spilled out like silverdust.

He taught me how to break down yesterday's pages and add the used type to the rickety hellbox. Then he led me into the room known as the forge room, or simply, the pig room. It was a dimly lit space maybe ten feet square, with a low plaster ceiling. Metal pipes ran up and down and across the walls. A gray iron cauldron squatted in one corner like a witch's brewpot. Drips and splashes of metal had cooled and hardened on the outside and clung to its belly like quicksilver in freeze-frame. The floor was littered with misshapen puddles of hardened metal, stray chunks of type, and shining splinters and powder. Inside the ducting above the melting pot, a wobbly fan went whup-whup-whup like a helicopter in the distance. Hank raised his voice, "Never-ever forget to turn the fan on when the forge is lit. These fumes will knock you out like Joe Frazier, understand?"

I understood. Even with the fan going, every breath was bitter with the stench of boiling chemicals that tightened your throat like asthma. And the heat! My own theory about the term, "printer's devil," is that it must have been the shocking heat of the pig room that brought hell and the devil to mind. I wiped my forehead with the back of my hand. "Jeez, how hot is it in here?"

Hank laughed. "It's a hundred-and-fuck!"

He had lit the gas flame on the big melting pot and dumped in some type before I arrived. He threw in a hunk now and I watched it start to melt and disappear into the leaden sea like the Titanic. He shouted over the fan, "Type lead melts at 425 degrees. 425 degrees is seriously hot, bud. Serious as a heart attack, ya hear?"

He showed me the four iron pig molds on the floor and the big iron ladle hanging from a nail on the wall. He pushed me up to the edge of the pot and coached me to use the ladle to scoop the dross off the surface and fill the molds with the liquid metal. The dross was gray scum, wet and thick as November mud. It bubbled and popped and occasionally spit into the air. I was wearing gloves, but a drop spattered my forearm and I yelped and dropped the ladle to the floor. Hank looked askance, and I showed him the new chuckhole in my arm, edged with multiple layers of cooked skin. He laughed like a goof and dismissed my wound with a wave. "Ya get used to it."

I laughed with him, ignoring the sting. I wanted to be a working man like my father and live up to the ink that Mr. Terwilliger said was in my blood. And I wanted to impress Hank, to be one of the boys, one of the crew like Vic and Stan.

My father had taught me that work was character-building duty. Hank Timmons taught me that work could be play. He made sweeping, dust-mopping, vacuuming, and even pig-making look like athletic events. He could pick up a trash can on the run, carry it outside, empty it in the dumpster and run it back to its place in less than ten seconds. He had the grace of a fine shortstop and the brute strength of a linebacker. I would never meet another man so at home, so at one, with his own body, so naturally mindful of its possibilities. He was walking around inside the best machine in the world and he knew it, although at that time perhaps in a more innocent way.

I turned off the gas, and the flame sputtered out. Hank switched off the whup-whup fan, and we left the newborn pigs to cool and harden.

I felt different walking home that day. Bigger. I was dirty and tired, damp with worksweat, and unconcerned about seams in the sidewalk. A group of geese is a gaggle, a group of crows is a murder, a group of young pigs is called a drift. Perhaps a group of devils could be called a fraternity. I'd been schooled and hazed and rightfully initiated into that fraternity, alongside Jefferson, Franklin and Twain. And Hank and my father.

I felt I had crossed an important barrier and entered the proud society of working men, where I might become tough and resilient in the face of injury and self-possessed in the face of danger and stress… and loss.

PAPER CORPSES

Working at the *Call & Record* was a bit like entering the family business. Mr. Terwilliger was the owner and publisher and had been all my life, but my father was the editor, and his name appeared right under Terwilliger's on the masthead: Michael King, Editor-in-Chief (though there were no other editors on staff). And my Grandma Junia was the office manager, or as Hank once described her, "head fussbucket." I never told him that the word was actually *fussbudget*. It seemed to fit her either way.

And it was Hank who reminded me that my mother had also worked for the paper, writing the Community Notes column for a time—those sing-song reports of local club news and wedding details, along with the self-important quotes from the wives of well-to-do businessmen, shybragging about their recent excursions to exotic locales such as Indianapolis or Baltimore. My mother had quit writing for the paper at some point, but I didn't remember when and had never bothered to wonder why. In any case, I was now the fourth member of the King family to be on Mr. Terwilliger's payroll. Ink in the blood, ink in the wallet.

On another training day, Hank showed me around the front offices. Dusty typewriters, crusted ash trays and heavy, black rotary phones. Steel desks and green leather chairs that wheeled around on battered linoleum, and oak wainscoting that was coffee brown and soaked in smoke, all of it washed in the soft light of banker's lamps.

"You sweep the offices and the halls and you empty all the trash," Hank said. "Then you straighten up and wipe down the front counter where your grandmother works. Now look, she likes it spic and span up there… and I know you know not to piss *her* off, ya know?"

I nodded with a fake somber grimace, and he snorted a laugh. He dug around in his pocket and pulled out a metal ring with three keys on it. He held them out as if performing a religious ceremony and said, "These are your keys now, bud. Front door, side door, and the morgue. Don't lose em, comprendo?"

"Morgue?" I was thinking Mr. Terwilliger might have misled me about the place not being haunted.

"Damn! I forgot to show you the morgue," Hank said, and I'm sure he saw the puzzlement on my face. "They just call it the morgue, it's where they keep the back issues."

He led me around a corner, down a short hallway, held out the keys again, and this time I accepted and opened the heavy, solid wood door. The room wasn't much wider than the hallway that led to it. It was long and narrow with floor-to-ceiling shelves on both sides, sagging with old papers, the corpses of yesterday's news. When I was done with all the other duties, I was to wash and dry my hands, then take the five papers stacked at the end of Grandma Junia's counter. Those were the copies of the latest issue that would be filed in the morgue. I would place them on the shelves according to month and year of publication, give the floor a once-over with the dust mop, and lock the door on my way out. He said not to forget, because my father, Grandma Junia and "Old Model T" had the only other keys and would occasionally check the lock.

While he gave these instructions I walked up and down the shelves fingering the old papers and peering at some of the photos and headlines on the yellowing front pages. It hadn't occurred to me that all this history would be kept in the building—much of it a product of my own family's sweat and longing—and I would have nearly exclusive access to it. And the locked door made it feel like treasure. Hank sort of tilted his head at my lingering. "This ain't a library, bud," he said and waved me out the door.

During the last days of my training, Hank followed me and observed as I went through each of the routines he'd taught me, and patiently, with his familiar teasing, he corrected my mistakes. His years as a baseball player had left him with his own fledgling coaching style, and it translated well to the back shop of the newspaper.

I had wanted to ask him about the army. The draft was on every young man's mind in those days. The war had already gone on for several years and it wasn't clear that our side was winning. The news was full of anti-war demonstrations, battle footage and flag-draped coffins. On my birthday, we'd had a small family celebration—really more acknowledgment than celebration, as it came in the shadow of my mother's death—and when talk briefly turned to the war, Aunt Laurette had taken a bold stand. "If this war's not over in a few years, I'm taking Archer to Canada myself," she said. My father and Grandma Junia had side-by-side, matching fits of indignation and condemnation. In Laurette's words, "They just about had a cow!"

In early December, I'd seen the latest issue of *LIFE Magazine* on the coffee table in our living room, the one with the story and photos of the massacre at My Lai, where U.S. soldiers had murdered hundreds of unarmed Vietnamese women and children in some sort of twisted rage. Dead babies. No heroes. There seemed to be a legitimate and frightening question whether our guys were still the good guys.

I wondered how I would do if I was drafted into the army. Hank would probably be some kind of John Wayne hero and come back with medals weighing down his uniform, but I wasn't so sure about myself. When I was eight years old, I got into a shouting match with a neighbor kid, right in front of our house. The kid punched me in the face and bloodied my nose. I ran inside whining to Grandma Junia, who was babysitting that day. She said, "We don't run from a fight in this family, young man. Now, you march back out there and stand up for yourself." She pushed me out the front door and locked it behind me. I stood on the porch, sobbing in fear and shame until the other boy laughed and walked away up Fourth Street.

Hank and I didn't discuss the army or the war, or My Lai. Hank liked to talk about girls more than anything, and I didn't have much to say about that yet. So we talked cars. Or baseball. The underdog New York Mets had confounded the experts by winning the World Series in October, and baseball fans were still chattering about it that winter.

And now that I'd turned thirteen, this spring would be my final season of

Little League. Next year I'd be required to move up to Senior League—bigger, better and faster players, regulation-size field. I was already intimidated by the prospect, although Hank assured me it was "no big whoop."

We played catch in the street on our breaks, with the Mustang's tape deck blaring oldies: Hank's tape collection was stuck in 1964—Elvis, the Four Seasons, the Beach Boys. Sometimes he would drop into a catcher's squat and give me tips on my pitching motion, and every time I threw a strike he would shout, "Bullseye!" It became his nickname for me. I liked it and it kind of fit with my first name. I'd never had a decent nickname. I hated to be called Archie, but Bullseye was okay by me.

Eventually I did get to ask Hank about the fourteen home runs he hit in his last Little League season. He acted surprised that anyone remembered, and he popped the trunk on the Mustang, rummaged around in an old equipment bag and pulled out a bat. "This is my bat from that year," he said, and he held it out to me. "Too small for me now, maybe you can get some use out of it."

"I can have it?"

"Sure, Bullseye. Might be a few more home runs in there." He winked.

At one point during one of our breaks, he finally did mention his future. He stood in the middle of the street with his arms open, the baseball in one hand and his beat-up old glove on the other. He looked around, his eyes scanning the rooftops in a way that took in the whole town, and he sighed like a kid who's outgrown the neighborhood tree fort. "I know it's crazy but I'm gonna miss this place," he said. "I'm not supposed to say it but I don't know about Vietnam. I ain't saying I'm scared. I'd just rather stay in town and work for the paper, know what I mean?"

But we both knew that wasn't an option. Hank wasn't going to run to Canada or declare himself a conscientious objector. If anything, he was a conscientious acceptor. There was really no question what the country, our families and the community of Lupoyoma expected of Hank or any of the other young men eligible to serve. And no question what most of us expected of ourselves. Regardless of Aunt Laurette.

Hank's father, Police Chief Lloyd Timmons, drove him to Oakland Army Base on the twenty-eighth of December in a blue and white patrol car with a cherry on top. From Oakland, he would be shipped who-knows-where for basic training.

The Mustang was left parked in front of the Timmons home, a two-story pseudo-colonial out on Lakeshore Boulevard. Later that winter, I rode my bike out that way on a cold sunny day and saw the car shining lonely in the circular driveway as I pedaled by. I wondered if the same guy would ever come back to Lupoyoma to cruise up and down Main Street in that beautiful red automobile.

A ROARING QUIET

Being a thirteen-year-old boy is a type of developmental limbo. I was no longer wholeheartedly the rambunctious All-American kid running the streets and fields, exploring creekbeds, hopping fences, collecting comic books, ignoring girls. But I wasn't yet a full-fledged teenager, dating cheerleaders, cruising the main drag, popping zits in the mirror and spiking the punch at school dances.

At thirteen, you're in the junior high boys room literally counting the hairs on your upper lip, or in your armpit or your crotch. You get bullied by fourteen-year-olds and you bully twelve-year-olds. You masturbate habitually, reflexively, often without conscious lust or fantasy, simply as a release of surplus hormonal energy. Your dick might suddenly spring hard just from the way the fabric of your underwear brushes up against it when you sit down at your desk. Then the teacher calls on you, and you're stuck there with your painful little boner as you try to read the Gettysburg Address aloud.

All this flourishing weirdness is turned up to an even higher volume if your mother has recently been featured in the local obituary column. Being an eighth grader with a dead mother in the newspaper is like having cancer. Nobody knows what to say but they're all sure they have to say *something*. So they mutter rote clichés about God's will and faith as strength and time as healer. One girl came up to me after art class, a girl named Robyn who I didn't know well. She had long brown hair down to her waist and all her drawings were of horses. She wore a plaid jumper in the colors of autumn and the concerned expression of a girl who has spent far too much time mothering her dolls. "God must have loved your mother very much to take her so young," she said. "He couldn't wait to have her with him in heaven." I knocked her into a bank of lockers with a huge shove and spent the afternoon in the principal's office.

Grandma Junia still came by the house most evenings and sat in the living room with my father, fretting over the many ways he wasn't taking care of himself—working too hard, not eating properly, drinking too much, skipping church, arguing with Cronkite about Nixon and the war. She brought Tupperware containers of food, and she still devoted time to lecturing me on the dire consequences of a misspent youth. "Think of your future, young man. Do you want to spend your whole life in the pig room?"

My father drank Seagram's 7 and watched TV in the evenings with the curtains drawn and the lights low. "Casserole in the fridge if you're hungry," he'd say, without taking his eyes off the news. "TV dinners in the freezer."

After the funeral, he never once mentioned my mother. Pictures of her vanished from the walls. The flowers she grew in pots on the front porch wilted and were thrown out with the trash. "He's a grown man," Grandma Junia said. "Men don't have time to dwell on these things. They have jobs and responsibilities and they just have to get on with the business of life."

As the winter deepened, a gray and cold numbness came upon me with the heavy rains and the dark empty days and nights. I took solace in the solitude of these months. I listened to the transistor radio I'd received that Christmas. Before she died, my mother had put it on layaway for five dollars a month at the Sprouse-Rietz variety store. Aunt Laurette paid the last five dollars out of her own pocket and wrapped it up in the *San Francisco Sentinel* sports section with a gift tag that said, "To Archer, From Mom."

It was big as a hardbound dictionary and had AM and FM, a telescopic antenna and an earpiece for private listening. I listened to Warriors basketball on KSFO and top-forty hits on KFRC. On New Year's Eve they counted down the top one hundred songs of 1969, and I stayed up till midnight, alone in my room, to hear the number one song announced—*Sugar, Sugar* by the Archies. I hated it, based on their name alone. And I couldn't hear anything in that song—or any one of those hundred songs—that grabbed me by the heart like *Sad Hours* on the old Grundig hi-fi.

With Hank gone off to basic training, the occupation of printer's devil ceased to be a new and entertaining distraction. I thought about the dayroom more and more, and the scratch-scratch sound and Little Walter Jacobs. Several times I slid the Keds shoebox out from under my bed, opened it and looked at the envelope I'd found in the pocket of my mother's dress. I turned it in my hands and examined its details—the blue ink handwriting, the slightly frayed edges, a finger smudge of dirt in one corner. And the weird indecipherable address to PFC J.R. Cole, a string of numbers after the name, then a string of abbreviations, Co B, 1st Bn, 5th Inf / 2nd Brig, 25th Inf Div / APO San Francisco, Ca. And my mother's maiden name, Evelyn Medina, over a return address on Rawson Road in Two Lakes, a tiny outpost of a town twenty-some miles away from our home in Lupoyoma City.

I was afraid to open it. The pink lipstick kiss on the back flap was like the flattened palm at the end of a crossing guard's arm. Do not proceed. I realized there would be no peace for me inside that envelope, and I sensed there would be a price for its contents. A trade would have to be made—some truth gained, some faith lost. I wasn't sure I wanted to pay up. Perhaps Grandma Junia was right: a man must simply move on.

I went to work three days a week.

Tuesdays and Fridays were deadline days, and I would rush straight to the *Call & Record* after school to help get the paper out the door by six o'clock. My job was to hand-stuff the B section into the A section.

You stand at a wooden counter that is approximately chest-high. The A sections kachunk off the folder at the end of the press, the sound is deafening yet enveloping. You unconsciously attune your movements to the pounding rhythm of the thing, the vibration permeates the concrete floor and thrums in your limbs. You set up two stacks of papers on the counter—A sections on the left, B sections on the right.

You open the top A section with your left hand, slide your thumb inside and widen the opening while your right hand picks up a B section and quickly slaps it into its mate. Your left hand immediately moves the finished newspaper to its own stack on the farther left. Turns of ten, stacks of a hundred. You do this two or three hours at a stretch, two days a week, all winter long—you get incredibly fast and efficient at this discrete set of precise movements, you become a human machine for those hours, and there is a kind of peace in that, a welcome numbness, a roaring quiet.

On Saturdays I was alone in the building, pouring pigs and cleaning up. Once, I sat in my father's office, in the gray chair with the green leather cushion, across from his steel tanker of a desk, and I thought about the times I'd visited him there in the past, stopping by on my way home from school to share a report card, pester a couple bucks or secure his signature on a field trip permission slip. I imagined he was sitting behind his desk as usual, and I talked to him. I asked if he remembered that time we played catch in the backyard until it was too dark. Or the time he took me fishing up Bottlerock Creek and we each caught a trout and cooked them on a low dancing fire. I asked him why my mother had died. But he wasn't there to answer.

I was paid twenty dollars a week, cash under the table. The arrangement wasn't strictly legal, but these things were not so actively policed in those days. Fridays were paydays, and Friday nights in the Lupoyoma winter usually meant deciding between a movie at the showhouse, or a basketball game at the high school. Not much else to do, especially without a car. Or a mother. I spent some of the money on kid stuff. Hanging out at the Weeping Willow game room or the roller rink. I bought a model kit at the hobby shop, a 65 Mustang like Hank's. I paid for Timmy and Joey and the giant box of Good & Plenty when we went to see John Wayne in *True Grit*. But it seemed to me there was nothing I could buy that had any lasting value.

On a late March school day when I was home alone, sick with a cold, I finally gathered the courage to revisit the dayroom. My hand trembled slightly as I turned the knob and opened the door. I sucked in a breath like I was preparing to dive under water. Of course, at some point the room had been straightened. The chenille bedspread tightly tucked and flattened. The nightstand lamp turned off. The vodka bottle, the pills, the ashtray full of pink lipstick cigarette butts all removed.

It was late morning with little chance of my father coming home, but I felt anxious that I might be discovered. The hi-fi scratching sound started up in my head again. I quickly opened the sliding doors on the Grundig's cabinet. I pulled out the turntable drawer and saw the stack of records was still there, undisturbed. I lifted the entire stack off the spindle and counted thirteen records, a baker's dozen as my mother liked to say.

Some part of me wanted to recover them as relics of history like the bones Dr. Leakey lifted from the ground, artifacts of truth. And something else in me wanted to keep them hidden like pages torn from a diary. I closed up the cabinet again, shut the door on my way out, and I took the records to my room and stashed them in the bottom drawer of my dresser under two ugly sweaters Grandma Junia had given me over the years, neither of which I'd ever worn.

RICE LIKE HAIL

I didn't notice the change in my father until an official family meeting was convened for an announcement. Grandma Junia was fond of saying I was "slow on the uptake," and there was the salt of truth in that, especially in those first months after my mother's death when I lived in my thirteen-year-old head with little attention leftover for the turning of the wider world.

The meeting was held at the oak table in the yellow kitchen, with my father, Grandma Junia, Aunt Laurette and myself present. The big announcement was that my father was engaged to marry a woman named Darlene Beverly, an advertising saleslady from Cleveland whom he'd met at a newspaper industry trade show in Las Vegas. That spring it had become common for my father to be away from home on "business trips," but I was unaware of this woman's existence until that very moment.

The below-the-fold headline was that Darlene Beverly was the mother of a teenage daughter. "You'll meet her," my father said. "She's seventeen, her real name is Barbara, but I'm told she likes to be called Billie. She's an art student at some college out there in Ohio."

Reverend Martin Jameson was to preside at the ceremony, five o'clock, Saturday, April 25, 1970, at St. John's Episcopal Church in downtown Lupoyoma. It was made clear that my attendance was compulsory, no RSVP required. Reception to follow, with hors d'oeuvres and open bar, at the Lupoyoma Yacht Club.

Darlene Beverly arrived from Cleveland a week before the wedding in a rented Ford station wagon with simulated wood trim all down the side. She was a pudgy bottle-blonde with a full face and an air of perpetual fluster. Other than a couple suitcases and a few boxes of keepsakes, the station wagon was empty. I didn't speak up but I thought, so where's the daughter?

The day before the wedding came around, and the girl had still not arrived as planned. This precipitated another kitchen gathering, which included a series of teary and frantic phone calls made by Darlene to hospitals and room-mates and police stations, and a series of skeptical harrumphs from Grandma Junia as none of the phone calls yielded knowledge of the girl's whereabouts. Aunt Laurette made cocktails, and my father took off his glasses and rubbed the bridge of his nose. Darlene talked of postponement, but my father's show-must-go-on stoicism prevailed. Even his wedding had to make deadline.

• • •

I wore the dreaded JC Penney's Dodger blue suit again, though the pants now ended at my ankles and my hands remained visible at all times. Grandma Junia wore a silver-gray skirt-suit and greeted me on the steps of the church with mock surprise at my latest growth spurt. "And who is this handsome young man?" she said in the upper register of her voice, with the Buick eye-brows rising up to the middle of her forehead.

She seated me next to her in the front-row pew. When the first notes of *Here Comes The Bride* hit the church P.A. system, she signaled me to stand up and turn as Darlene appeared at the back of the church. Grandma Junia whis-pered through her smile like a ventriloquist, "At least she didn't wear white."

I had no memories of my father dancing with my real mother. I had never seen them kiss in public or clink glasses or laugh at a private joke with their heads nearly touching. I had never seen a shine in my mother's eyes like I saw that day in the eyes of Darlene Beverly.

I flowered the wall in my Dodger blue suit, sipping syrupy punch from a styrofoam cup, watching the newlyweds and guests turning slowly to Elvis and Sinatra records played on the Yacht Club's jukebox: *I Can't Help Falling in Love with You, The Very Thought of You*. Lush and breathy songs that twin-kled and sighed in the warm April evening.

Darlene Beverly had a nervous laugh with which she attempted to dif-fuse even the slightest hint of awkwardness in social situations. At one point she hurried over and coaxed me onto the dance floor. Our arms didn't reach an immediate understanding about how we should touch each other, so she laughed and took both my hands in hers and held them out between us as we rocked side to side to the beat of *Fly Me to the Moon*. She leaned in and said, "You don't have to call me Mom if you don't want to, Archer. You can just call me Darlene."

I didn't tell her there was no chance in hell or Lupoyoma I was going to call her Mom in the first place. I didn't tell her that I preferred the rhythm of her full maiden name, Darlene Beverly, a name in five-four time. Because my father may have given her our name, but I had not.

Rumors swirled about the room like a dressed up version of the old children's game of Telephone. Wherever Darlene was not present, speculative talk of her missing daughter could be overheard. Playing the innocent, I made myself invisible in that way children sometimes can—simply by allowing the adults in the room to pay as little attention to you as they prefer—and I circulated to get the scoop.

Grandma Junia stood near the punch bowl, which was arrayed on a folding table drenched in screaming-pink crepe paper and overgrown with dusty plastic flowers. Miss Lancaster, one of grandmother's most reliable acolytes, and the very same teacher who'd sentenced me to the principal's office for bringing Robyn the horse artist to tears, ladled punch for Grandma Junia. I loitered in close proximity, imagining myself a clever reporter.

"And what's this news about the teenage daughter?" Miss Lancaster was a large and solid person. Polite women referred to her as statuesque. Some of the boys at school had nicknamed her Mancaster. In the words of Timmy Bilderback, she was "built like a brick shithouse."

"Yes, an unexpected complication," Grandma Junia said. "Frankly, we've been misled, I'd almost say hoodwinked. We were told this girl was nearly of age and living on her own. She would come for the wedding, then return to art school somewhere in the wilds of Ohio."

"Oh, an artist!" Mancaster said, straightening her big shoulders.

"Worse than that!" Grandma Junia said with one hand to her mouth, shielding the wider public from the horrific truth "We've learned she's not enrolled in school at all. And, in fact, never finished high school. She ran away from home at fifteen and lately she's been shacked up at some sleazy flophouse with a gang of these college radicals you see on the news. And now, predictably, she's been arrested!"

Miss Lancaster went silent, appropriately aghast, and I casually moved on as if oblivious. I made my way across the room, where several men clustered around the tiki bar. My father was in chummy conversation with Leslie McGoogan, the smooth and well-mannered ad man, who looked and dressed like the famous crooner Perry Como. He was a master of cardigan sweaters and sympathetic nods.

"Chief Timmons made a few calls," my father said. "She's being released to our custody."

"Oh, now you're really stuck," McGoogan nodded.

"They're putting her on the next bus—at my expense, of course."

"Fatherhood is overrated."

"And overpriced," my father said.

McGoogan raised his glass.

Over by the jukebox, Aunt Laurette and Darlene Beverly tapped their feet to Elvis and scanned song titles. Darlene's hand drifted over the glass top of the machine like a Quija board. I stood off to the side and gazed in the other direction, pretending to be interested in the old people on the dance floor.

"She's not a bad girl," Darlene said. "She's high-spirited. It's just this awful war has all the kids so upset."

"You better tell her to go easy on her politics around Mike," Laurette said.

"I just hope it's not too much, both of us moving in all at the same time." Darlene said.

"And watch out for Junia. She's the main one to worry about in this family… but you probably already figured that out."

Darlene laughed her nervous laugh.

"I'll come over tomorrow and help you get the spare room ready for Billie," Laurette said. "No one's been in there since… well, you know."

That's when it hit me that this girl was coming to live with us—once again, I was a little slow on the uptake—and the spare room Aunt Laurette was referring to was the dayroom. I must have dropped something or gone pale in the face, I don't remember, but Darlene Beverly stepped over, put a hand on my shoulder and smiled, "Archer, don't worry, I'm sure you and Billie will get along famously. She has quite a personality. Very creative and artistic and smart and… hip, she's very hip. Or is it hep?"

Grandma Junia, eavesdropping some of this for herself, sidled up with a saccharine smile and muttered just to me, "We haven't even met this girl and I'm already sick of her."

• • •

The cake was cut, the toasts were made, the bouquet was tossed over Darlene's shoulder and plummeted to the floor when Laurette sidestepped it like a falling rock. But my favorite part of the entire event was throwing the rice. I held back while husband and wife ran the gauntlet of tipsy guests who laughed and tossed the rice in the air so it fell on the couple like soft rain. I stood further away, and when they emerged from the widening tunnel of people and were almost to the getaway car, I pelted them with two hand-fuls, launched at a lower trajectory—more windblown hail than soft rain. Grandma Junia quickly stayed my arm, but not before I saw each of the new-lyweds raise a surprised hand to the sting on their cheek.

THE WINDOW INSIDE

Like many modern improvements, the Sixties were late getting to Lupoyoma County. They arrived on my street in a rattletrap Dodge pickup one drowsy evening in April of 1970. The pickup stopped in front of my house, and a girl clambered out of the cab. She yanked a faded green duffle bag out of the truck bed, slung it over one shoulder by its strap, then bounced on the curb in her bare dusty feet, waving and hollering, "Thanks for the ride, man!"

It wasn't that we were completely unaware of the changes—the new trends in music and fashion, the hippies, LSD, free love, men on the moon, assassinations, demonstrations, bombs in police stations—the multi-faceted revolution (or collapse) happening across the country. But we only saw it on television and in the pages of magazines. And in our Lupoyoma innocence we imagined that's where it would stay for the most part. At least I had imagined so... until that evening.

I was standing on the front lawn in my new baseball uniform, throwing pop flies into the air and catching them with my glove, the Willie Mays Autograph Model. Now I stood still with the glove dangling at my side as the ball fell to the grass.

The old farmer in the old Dodge waved, ground out a noisy three-point turn and headed back up toward Main Street. The girl spun around and I froze in place, measuring her in skittish glances. She had copper-red hair that curled and tumbled like stormwaves around a cheeky face. She wore a boy's white t-shirt and a patchwork skirt that looked like it was stitched by a color-blind gypsy. And to the wonderment of my thirteen-year-old eyes, she wore no bra. She strode across the lawn directly toward me with her right hand straight out. "You must be Archer," she said. "I'm Billie Armstrong. I guess I'm your new sister."

I'd never shaken a girl's hand before. It was smooth and soft, but her grip was strong.

Darlene Beverly appeared from inside, and before the screen door smacked the frame Darlene was off the porch, fussing and hugging her daughter on the walkway, pushing the red hair out of Billie's eyes and trying to hoist the duffle bag herself.

My father jogged down the steps and lightly took the bag. Billie Armstrong stood with a hand on her hip and said, "Thanks, man" with a big howdy smile.

My father said, "What happened to the bus ticket we bought?"

And Billie said, "I cashed it in, man. I only had to pitch in for gas and this guy I met at a concert last year took me all the way from Cleveland to Frisco. Saved you sixteen dollars, man. But then it took seven more rides to get up here—man, this place sure is the middle of nowhere!"

She reached into the pocket of her t-shirt and pulled out some rumpled bills. I studiously observed the movement of planets under her shirt. My father frowned at my slackened jaw, furrowed his brow at Billie. "My name isn't Man," he said. But he accepted the money, turned around and marched the duffle bag up the steps and into the house. Darlene Beverly scampered after him.

• • •

In a past life my room had been the back porch. A do-it-yourselfer had enclosed it without quite finishing the project. The inside wall of the room had previously been the outside wall of the house, and it was still covered by the dirty and faded clapboard siding. And toward the far end of the narrow room, there was a window in what used to be the outside wall. It was an aging, wood-framed, split or "double-hung" window, practically my height. On the other side of that window was the dayroom.

My father hadn't gotten around to taking out the window and refinishing the wall, but my mother had hung curtains on both sides, and the glass had been thinly whitewashed so even with the curtains open you would only see gauzy shadows and shapes. The curtains were closed now, but I knew Billie

Armstrong was on the other side unpacking her duffle bag, moving into the room where my mother had breathed her last.

I turned on my transistor radio to prepare for that night's Giants-Dodgers game. I laid out my scorebook and baseball cards on my bedspread. I had the starting lineups from both teams, plus some of the pitchers. Since my mother's death the mysterious code of symbols and abbreviations she'd taught me—the metamorphosis of pencil scratches to historic artifact—had become an important ritual

On the radio, the national anthem played and the broadcasters introduced the lineups and described the Giants' high-kicking Juan Marichal throwing warmup pitches from the mound while the Dodgers' speedy Maury Wills swung two bats in the on-deck circle. Suddenly I heard music coming from the other side of the window. A ticking rhythm, a run of bass notes, a drum fill, a raspy guitar riff, and then a low moan from some woman's gut. Horns and cymbals rattled the glass, the moaning woman began to wail and possibly speak in tongues. Maury Wills was safe at first and I had no idea how he got there.

I hesitated, thinking surely my father or Darlene would put a stop to this racket, but no one intervened and the music continued at full volume. I stomped through the kitchen and the living room and down the hallway toward the dayroom door. What I planned to say was, "whatever that is, it's too damn loud," and I rehearsed it in my head with the deep voice of my father in mind. But when I got there another song had started, and this one was quieter and slinkier.

The door was open and Billie's back was turned. She had apparently produced paints and brushes out of her duffle bag, pushed the curtains back, and was now decorating the window between our rooms with a psychedelic landscape—a pumpkin sun rising over lavender hills next to an electric indigo lake.

The duffle bag lay on its side in the middle of the room like a horn of plenty, some of its contents tumbling out on the oval corded rug. Well-worn paperbacks and old magazines. Scuffed up combat boots, wrinkled t-shirts and faded jeans. A Strathmore sketch pad, a man's denim workshirt, and yes, one white and sturdy-looking brassiere.

She began to sing along with the record. I said nothing and stood in the doorway watching the back of her as she painted the window and swayed to the music. The patchwork skirt swung with her hips like an expert dance partner. Her every movement was in rhythm—she painted, sang and danced as if they were all one thing unified by the music. I momentarily forgot my haunted memories of the room, and even why I had come to the door. I held my breath and the peachfuzz on my arms stood erect.

The song ended and I exhaled, and she turned around and caught me there. I nodded at the old Grundig hi-fi cabinet and stuttered, "That was my mom's record player."

Billie reached over and snatched up the turntable arm and rested it back on its perch. She said, "Mike, I mean your dad, said it was okay."

"Yes, but keep the volume down." My father suddenly brushed past me into the room. He sat down on the low stool in front of the vanity. I'd seen that official father-in-charge look in his eyes many times.

"And Billie, we need to talk," he said. Of course this meant he would talk and she better listen.

Billie sat down on the bed, the paintbrush now lifeless in her hand, a guarded uncertainty in her eyes. No one looked at me, so I didn't move.

"I hope you realize how lucky you are to be here right now, young lady. Personally, I believe in accepting the consequences of one's actions, but your mother's convinced me that you deserve a second chance to get your life in order. Now, I know you really don't want to be here forever, so here's the deal. When you turn eighteen, you're free to leave. Do what you want with your life. We won't try to stop you. But let me be perfectly clear—in the meantime, if there's any more trouble with the police, I won't step in again, you're on your own. Is that understood?"

She nodded like a scolded child.

My father stood. "And if you try to run away again, you just keep going, because you won't be welcome back in this house." And he left the room.

"Whoa!" Billie said. "He has that serious dad vibe totally down, man. I'm freaked out!" But I could tell she wasn't (although I thought she should be).

I left the doorway, then quickly backpedaled and leaned my head into the room. She gave me a question-mark look and I pointed my eyes toward the record player. "Oh yeah," I said, "What *was* that?"

I'm sure I had some alarmed expression, because she laughed and her red curls jostled around her face. "That's Janis, man! You don't know Janis Joplin? Oh man, you and I are gonna have a talk!" As she spoke, she barefooted back to the Grundig and, with the record still spinning, delicately dropped the needle back into the same groove she'd lifted it out of minutes before. She looked at me and wet her lips like I was a blank canvas. "We'll talk for sure, man." she said. She dipped her brush in a bottle of paint and, with the first chords of a new song, spun around to resume her work on the window. The gypsy skirt twirled in rhythm.

• • •

Janis Joplin? I was only dimly aware of her. There was no Janis Joplin on my father's Magnavox or in Grandma Junia's glove compartment. At eighth grade dances the popular girls picked the music: Three Dog Night, Creedence Clearwater Revival, awkward slow dances to The Carpenters. What did I know of Janis Joplin, except that she sounded injured?

Back in my room, the Dodgers were already leading three-zip in the bottom of the second inning. I looked at my blank scoresheet. I hadn't even finished the lineups. I closed the scorebook and tossed it on the floor. I gathered up the cards and put them back in the Keds shoebox, carefully ignoring the pink lipstick envelope, and I slid the shoebox under the bed. I turned the radio off and stood it up on the nightstand. Through the window, Janis Joplin was screaming for *One Good Man*, (preferably one that could quiet her down).

I opened the curtains and I laid down on my bed, this time on my stomach, head propped up in my hands, and I stared at the window, the shapes and the colors muted through the whitewash and all of it wavering in the swaying shadow of Billie's body. Swirling paisleys slowly formed at the edges of the landscape like distant galaxies mingled with the word *Love* written several times in a round, openhearted script. I lay there reading the window backwards like hieroglyphics from a foreign land and fell asleep wondering if I was looking in or out.

FAMILY PORTRAIT

It was Opening Day of the Little League season, and Darlene had decided it was a perfect opportunity to advance her fantasies of familial bonding. My real mother had been to every game of organized baseball I'd ever played, dating back to my first season at eight years old, and I had taken her presence for granted. My father rarely showed up, and I had taken that as a given as well. But here we were, this reconfiguration, conscripted by the nattering Darlene Beverly to trudge the four blocks of storefronts and tree-lined sidewalks to the Little League field on the grounds of the Lupoyoma Elementary School.

A couple nights before, Billie and my father had gotten into a door-slamming argument over the war. My father always gathered the family around the television when the President spoke to the nation. That night he watched from the vinyl recliner, and Darlene, Billie and I sat in a row on the obnoxiously floral couch as President Nixon announced that U.S. forces were now pushing over the Vietnamese border to attack suspected enemy strongholds in the neutral country of Cambodia. This came just weeks after he promised imminent troop withdrawal and an honorable end to the war. Now the President claimed, "We take this action not for the purpose of expanding the war into Cambodia, but for the purpose of ending the war in Vietnam, and winning the just peace we all desire."

"Liar!" Billie said, and stood up from the couch.

"Sit down!" my father said. But of course she didn't.

"It's doublespeak!" she said. "He's expanding the war to end the war? Nonsense! We're supposed to be getting out, not invading another country."

"If you'll shut up and listen—"

"I won't shut up, and I'm not sitting down. It's always the same with these fucking warmongers!"

"That's enough!" Now my father was standing as well. "I won't have that language in this house."

You can imagine the rest. More yelling. Finger pointing. The aforementioned door slamming.

And two days later on our walk to the ballpark, the tension was still sliced a little thick despite Darlene's white-picket daydreams. I strode out ahead of the group, an impatient pup on a long leash. My father and Darlene dawdled behind, holding hands like besotted teenagers. Billie caught up and fell in step beside me.

There was an awkward wait for one of us to start the conversation.

"So…" I said, with what I thought was a clever, teasing pause, "when *is* your birthday?"

I saw the hint of a smile. "August 22."

"Think you can follow the rules that long?"

She laughed. "Well, I'm a Leo—we're known for our independence."

I noticed again how that big smile spread across her face and the way a laugh would jostle her curls. "My grandma says you're a radical hippie lunatic," I said, still teasing.

"She sounds like an old crone."

"You haven't even met her. She's not a crone… what's a crone?"

"An old woman with nothing nice to say."

"Okay, she's kind of a crone." I shrugged.

But I wasn't dropping my line of questioning just yet. "Heard you were in jail," I said.

"Nah, not really, only juvey… and just for carrying a sign for chrissakes… well, and assault on a police officer so they said, but I only swung at him because he felt me up when he searched me. He grabbed my boob! Anyway I missed, never even touched him, how can they call that assault, man?"

"Jeez, what did the sign say?"

"Oh you should've seen it, I made it myself." She waved her hands around as if she was actually showing me the sign. "It had big red and blue letters that said fighting for peace is like fucking for chastity! It was beautiful! But this cop comes along and says you can't say fucking on a sign in Cleveland, so I say what happened to my fucking freedom of speech? And he says you can take that up with a fucking judge, young lady. And then some assistant D.A. wants to lock me up in reform school till I'm twenty-one! No shit! You know, the truth is your dad really saved my ass—so I don't want to fight with him, I just wanna do my time here and be on my way."

Billie Armstrong had been my stepsister for a week—I barely knew her. Although, to be fair, at the time I barely knew the girls I'd known all my life. (Hell, maybe that's still the case.) And it's true I resented her—for a swarm of reasons I couldn't even sort out. But there was also something about her that made me *want* to know her in a way I'd never wanted to know other girls. Meeting Billie was like finding a new issue of *LIFE Magazine* on the coffee table—with those big black headlines and the bright photos that shoved the world in your face—and you want to turn to the next page and the next and the next, in a hurry to take in all the possibilities.

I had no solid position on the war at the time (except that I secretly hoped it would be over before I was old enough to participate). And Billie, with all that hair-trigger defiance, scared me almost as much as the draft. I still wasn't sure if I liked or trusted her, but I wanted to keep turning those pages.

Changing the subject, I asked about her name—why Billie, and why was her last name different than her mother's.

"Well," she said, "it's really Barbara Ann Beverly Armstrong on my birth certificate—but that sounds too much like a goody-goody rich girl who sits in the front row—and my grandma's name was Barbara and I was named after her but man I'm so not like her! Except for the red hair, that is, and besides…" She was wearing bellbottoms but she did a little pirouette holding out an imaginary skirt and said, "… do I look like a Barbie to you…"

I laughed and shook my head. She could talk like a whirlpool, her hands turning in the air the entire time, and she seemed amused by the confusion it left on my face.

"… And my father's name was William Armstrong and he went by Bill or Billy—and he was an artist too—but he never married my mom because he went in the Navy and we lost him in the Korean War." She held out her hands as if revealing a magic trick. "So that's why I'm Billie Armstrong." She smiled and moved down the sidewalk in a new series of pirouettes.

· · ·

Grandma Junia was a fan of the game—in fact, she had been the team scorekeeper before my mother—but she was not one to take a leisurely stroll for pleasure (or family harmony). "Do not meander, young man; walk like you have a purpose in life," was one of her familiar exhortations. She was already at the field when we arrived, the big Buick gleaming in the parking area. She stood near the bleachers in pleated capri pants and tailored blouse and watched silently from behind her cat-eye sunglasses as we approached.

Darlene bravely took the initiative. "Junia, I'd like you to meet my daughter, Billie."

Grandma Junia slid the sunglasses down her nose and looked over them. "Ah, the prodigal stepchild," she said.

I muffled a laugh. According to Grandma Junia our family was full of prodigals. Prodigal son, prodigal niece, prodigal grandson. And now the prodigal stepchild. She apparently thought the word meant *disappointing*.

Billie stepped forward and offered a handshake. "Nice to meet you," she said, quite formally, as if she sensed the force of Grandma Junia's… uh, personality.

A limp overturned hand and "Yes, dear" was all she got in return.

Darlene had brought a Polaroid camera and managed to badger Grandma Junia into snapping our picture. I still have it many years later. We are gathered in front of the snackshack, which is decorated with a fan of red, white and blue bunting tacked up under the counter. You can almost smell the popcorn butter and the meaty steam rising off the hot dogs. There's me scowling in my baggy uniform, still in my tennis shoes, cleats in hand; Darlene is wearing her nervous am-I-doing-it-right smile and a green pantsuit, a desperate bright green that could only be achieved in one hundred percent polyester; my father is "in his shirtsleeves" as the saying went, with a can of Hamm's held jauntily in the hand he has draped around Darlene's shoulder; and then there's Billie Armstrong in her faded and patched bellbottoms, homemade halter top, big round wire-rimmed glasses with pink-tinted lenses and that wide smile framed by her waves of red hair. Barefoot of course. It is the only picture ever taken of the four of us together—this hasty lineup of cardboard cutouts posing as a family, glued down next to each other by death and marriage and varnished over with wishes and promises.

THE OLD HIDDEN BALL TRICK

Although our uniforms said *Call & Record* across the chest, we were better known as the Paperboys. It was one of those nicknames that started as a putdown but eventually became an endearment.

Our opponents for the day were the Odd Fellows, which sounded like a nickname but wasn't. They were the New York Yankees of Lupoyoma Little League. Our team had never defeated them in the years I'd played. They had big hitters up and down the lineup, and they had the fearsome Craiger Robinson, who threw faster than anyone in the league and was said not to own a smile. Craiger wasn't that much bigger than the rest of us, but anyone could see he was harder, inside and out. Nobody was in a hurry to face Craiger Robinson, at the plate or on the mound.

Needless to say, the Paperboys were not favored to win the game. But it was Opening Day— the sun busting through scraps of cloud, the grass freshly mowed after a long wet winter, the bleachers overflowing, the chalk lines flashing straight and white, the stars and stripes up the flagpole, and every underdog's dream within reach… at least until the final out.

During warmups I took my position at third base and played catch with Joey Quarterman, our left fielder. Our coach, Calvin Fish, liked to call him Joey Two-Bits. Joey wasn't much of a fielder but always a reliable at-bat, so sometimes the nickname morphed into Joey Two-Hits.

The Paperboys' starting pitcher for the day was none other than Timmy Bilderback. Timmy was short and skinny but tough as homemade jerky. He wasn't as strong as Craiger Robinson, but he was scrappy. He hated to lose.

Timmy took the mound and loosened up his arm by lobbing throws to the catcher. I threw to Joey Two-Bits and half-watched as the two small stands of wooden bleachers filled up with Lupoyomans exchanging greetings and gossip.

My father sat with Mr. Terwilliger and the salesman Les McGoogan. Darlene sat next to Grandma Junia, and neither of them looked too happy about it. I saw Billie find a spot along the top row, close to Alice Terwilliger, who had replaced my mother as the official scorekeeper for our team.

Percival J. Terwilliger had come to fatherhood somewhat late in life and his daughter Alice, at fifteen years old, was young enough to be his granddaughter. She was a tall, quiet girl with shoulder-length black hair, worn with bangs cut straight across at the eyebrows. She was an A-student who wore glasses and worked in the library after school.

Among my friends Alice was thought irredeemably plain, but I secretly found her alluring in her gawky vulnerability. In any case, Alice wasn't someone you'd automatically picture as a friend for Billie, but from a distance it seemed they struck up an instant rapport, and I wasn't sure how I felt about that.

Out of the corner of my eye I saw a flash of color and a bright red Mustang pulling into the parking area beyond left field. I stood at third base with my back turned to the plate and watched a soldier get out of the car. An excited murmur fluttered up from the bleachers as everyone recognized Hank Timmons striding toward us in his impossibly crisp khakis, pressed shirt and polished black boots, the blade of his garrison cap slicing the air.

He looked bigger than I remembered and solid as a closed fist. It seemed like the world stopped as players, coaches, spectators, vendors, umpires and even the unruly children along the banks of the creek took a moment to register the transformation of the boy they all thought they knew so well.

When Hank reached the bleachers, Mr. Terwilliger was the first to stand up and shake his hand, then my father and then Les McGoogan. The women all straightened their spines and smoothed out their clothing, even Darlene and Grandma Junia. A dirty-faced little kid ran up and saluted until Hank returned the gesture. I looked to the top row of the bleachers, where Alice and Billie stole glances at the soldier and leaned toward each other as if hatching a conspiracy.

Coach Fish checked his watch, blew the whistle and called, "Come on in, boys."

The Odd Fellows started onto the field. I was still standing there watching Hank and the crowd. Craiger Robinson walked by and said, "Get off the field, Archie." At some point he'd learned I didn't like the name, and after that he wouldn't call me anything else.

I was our leadoff hitter so I hustled into the dugout, grabbed my bat and helmet and walked out to the on-deck circle to watch Craiger warm up. Hank came up on the other side of the chain link fence. He said, "Hey Bullseye, how's it hangin?"

It gave me a little rush of pride that he bothered, and I hoped Alice and Billie were watching. "Okay," I said. "How's the army treating you?"

"Everything's copacetic," he said.

I didn't know if copacetic was good or bad. I said, "They're sending you to Vietnam, aren't they?"

"Yep, I'm home for a few weeks, and then I'm gonna go shoot me some gooks," he said, and it came out weird, like a cross between mean and funny. He was different and not different. He still had that aura of cocky mischief, but he seemed more distant and fidgety.

Meanwhile, Craiger Robinson threw his last warmup pitch so hard the catcher yowled out loud and shook off his glove to rub his hand. He didn't bother to throw down to second. The umpire pulled his mask down over his face and hollered, "Play ball."

The game came down to the sixth and final inning with the outcome still in doubt. In the Paperboys' half of the sixth, I walked, stole second base and scored on a double by Joey Two-Hits. Paperboys ahead five-four.

As we took the field for the bottom of the sixth, we were three outs away from an upset victory over our perennial nemesis. Standing at third base I was grinding my teeth with the want of it. It was only the first game of the season but I was seething with a wild sense of impending destiny, even justice. It crossed my mind that the loss of my mother, the remarriage of my father and all the other perceived impositions of my short imperfect life should entitle me to one small dream come true. I thought maybe the universe owed me, and I was ready to collect.

The Odd Fellows were down to their last out when Eugene came to the plate. Eugene was short and round and comically slow, but he could hit the ball a Lupoyoma mile—and he was Craiger Robinson's little brother.

Two down with the bases empty, Timmy Bilderback on the mound and the Paperboys on the edge of what in our young minds would be an historic upset. Eugene Robinson stepped into the batter's box and took a ready stance. Ball one, low and outside. Ball two, high and tight. Coach Fish paced back and forth in the dugout, a half-step behind his beer belly, shouting at us to stay calm. Most of the chatter from the stands faded into white noise, but I could somehow pick out Hank yelling, "Look alive, Bullseye! Look alive!"

Timmy went into his windup. I dropped into my crouch by third base, popping my glove and my wad of Juicy Fruit, chanting with the rest of our team, "Hey-batta-batta-batta-ssswing!"

The ball came off Eugene's bat with a reverberating thwack and soared toward left field like it was shot out of one of those old cannons on the court-house lawn. Over in right field, a rusted chain-link fence backed up against the Weeping Willow Resort & Trailer Court, and if you hit one into the trailers it was an automatic home run. But in left field, where Eugene's hit was headed, there was no fence at all. The grass just thinned out into hardpan, then ran into the asphalt parking lot, and when you hit one out there it was a mad footrace.

Fat Eugene is chugging hard around the bases. Joey Two Bits chases down the ball in the outfield dirt. The crowd roars to its feet. Eugene rounds second and barrels my way. Joey snatches up the ball and whirls and heaves a throw. Eugene dives face first and slides into third in a heap at my feet as Joey's throw bounces once and lands in my glove. The umpire yells, "Safe!" and spreads his arms like airplane wings. Half the crowd cheers and the other half groans.

The Odd Fellows coach calls timeout, and Eugene stands up, covered in dirt from collar to shoelaces. He's sucking air and smiling wildly in a cloud of his own dust like Pig Pen from *Peanuts*. In the crowd, fathers lean forward with elbows on knees, and nervous mothers hold their hands over their mouths the way mothers do.

Craiger Robinson is already standing by the batter's box taking vicious practice cuts… and smiling. The look on his face instantly clarifies for me who on the field is psychologically suited to the moment… and who is not. Fear strangles my chest. A big hit from Craiger could cost us the game.

I still have the ball in my mitt so I walk toward the mound and Timmy meets me halfway. He holds out his glove for the ball. I move in close and put the ball in the pocket of his glove. Then I quickly take it out just before he puts his hand in and I slip it back into my own glove. Timmy looks at me and reads my eyes, and we both say it together. "Mickey Mantle."

• • •

Six years before, Mantle and the New York Yankees met the St. Louis Cardinals in the 1964 World Series. The Yankees were in the Series practically every year back then—they were the Odd Fellows of Major League Baseball.

The Cardinals managed to win the first game but dropped the next two. In game four, the Yanks took a three-nothing lead on a single by Mantle. The next Yankee batter blooped a single to center field and Mantle loped into second standing up. The Cards' center fielder threw the ball in to second baseman Dick Groat, and Groat threw the ball to the pitcher. The pitcher fiddled with the resin bag and toed the rubber. Mickey Mantle took a three-step lead off the bag and, before anybody knew what was happening, Groat ran over and tagged Mantle out.

It was the old hidden ball trick, staple of sandlots and schoolyards. Groat had the ball the whole time! He had faked the throw to the pitcher and made a fool of the great Mickey Mantle of the invincible New York Yankees on the game's biggest stage. It stunned the fans and it stunned the Yankees. Their bats went cold, and the Cardinals came back to win that game on a grand slam and eventually went on to win the Series.

Timmy Bilderback and I were both seven years old that Sunday in 64. We couldn't get the game on TV so my father let us listen on the radio in his new Plymouth Fury. He had brought it home only two weeks before, and it was the first brand new car in my life. It was root beer brown and had space-age pushbutton controls in the dashboard.

We each stretched out on the two-tone brown and cream vinyl upholstery, Timmy lying across the back seat, me in the front. We turned up the radio, stared up at the blank, beige headliner, and discovered teleportation. We were part of the first TV generation—we thought a car radio was just Top 40 hits or background noise on a long ride to see relatives. We didn't know entire worlds could be called forth and made to shimmer behind your eyes by the sheer power of Curt Gowdy's voice. Neither of us ever forgot that day in the Plymouth or that World Series game.

• • •

I walked back to third base, and Timmy walked back to the mound with nothing but his fist in the pocket of his glove. The ump said, "Play ball!" And when Eugene took two steps off the bag, I hopped over and tagged him with my glove, then held up the ball like a white shining pearl.

Bedlam I believe is the proper word: a scene or state of wild uproar and confusion. Eugene's fat jaw unhinged. The crowd cheered and groaned and laughed. I heard a man's voice say, "What the hell?!" The umpire looked back and forth from Timmy's empty glove to the ball in my glove, back and forth again, then slowly raised his fist and made the out sign.

Eugene stamped his feet in the dirt and yelled, "No fair! No fair!" Frustration welled up in his eyes and he stood with his palms turned up to the sky in supplication to the baseball gods—or any god who might answer. But none did. Hank and the rest of the Paperboys gathered round Timmy and me, shouting and slapping us on the back. Poor Eugene yanked off his batting helmet, crumpled down in the basepath and began to cry. His brother, the fearsome Craiger Robinson, stood at home plate, glaring and pointing at me with his bat in one hand like Babe Ruth's famous called shot.

PUT ON THE GLOVES

It's a familiar ritual: each team forms its own single-file line of players, and the two lines move parallel to each other in opposite directions until every player has shaken hands with every one of his opponents. Good game, everybody says. The ceremony suggests a return to equal footing, bringing the victors down from the clouds and the losers up from the dirt. And this implies a philosophical argument about the limits of sport itself. Shake hands—after all it's only a game.

As I worked my way down the line, I could see Craiger Robinson shaking hands with my teammates—gruffly perhaps, reluctantly certainly, but dutifully at least, his black eyes mostly cast aside. When I reached him, I put out my hand and said, "Good game." He lunged with both arms straight out, slammed me in the chest and knocked me to the ground. I landed flat on my back, and Craiger straddled my middle and cocked his fist, but Coach Fish showed up in time to grab his arm and drag him off me.

The majority of the bleacher crowd had headed for the parking lot after the final out, but Billie, Alice and Hank had stayed behind and now they all ran onto the field. Alice and Billie helped me to my feet, and we were all quickly encircled by a ring of riled spectators. Craiger strained against Coach Fish's arms, his fists still clenched and a look in his eyes no one had ever shown me before—not simply childish anger or frustration, but a knowing contempt. "You cheated," he said.

A couple of Craiger's teammates chimed in, Yeah, that's right. You cheated.

Even Joey Two-Bits said, "Are you sure that was legal?"

Timmy Bilderback said, "It's a legal play, check the rulebook."

"It wasn't fair!" Eugene said, fighting more tears.

"The ump called you out, it's over, fatty," Timmy said.

"I don't care what the rulebook says," Craiger said, shaking free of the coach's hold and pointing at me. "It ain't right, and this ain't over."

"Put on the gloves," someone said, I'm not sure who, but right away players on both sides joined in. Yeah, put on the gloves. Settle it now. Put on the gloves. Almost a chant.

In those days, an adult-sanctioned boxing match was not an uncommon approach to the frequent disagreements among competitive American boys. Even at school, teachers were known to move playground shoving matches into the gym to be settled with boxing gloves. Coach Fish always kept a set in one of his equipment bags.

"Well, boys," the coach said, "you two want to shake hands and call it a day, or should I get the gloves?"

I didn't say a word. My father had often told me a man has to learn to fight his own battles, but I didn't want to fight Craiger Robinson, gloves or no gloves, not even if I had a bat and he was empty-handed.

But Craiger said, "Get the gloves."

Coach Fish looked at me. The Odd Fellows and the Paperboys looked at me. Hank looked at me, and my head seemed to nod on its own. The coach headed for the dugout.

Hank said, "That's right, Bullseye, he ain't so tough."

But Alice said, "Archer, just go and apologize." She pushed me lightly on the shoulder, and I took a step toward Craiger. "Say you're sorry, shake his hand, and let's all go home."

"This is so stupid," Billie said. "What are you even fighting about?"

"Who the hell is this?" Hank said.

"Hank Timmons, meet Billie Armstrong," Alice said, and when he wrinkled his brow, she said, "Archer's new sister."

"Stepsister," I mumbled.

Hank ran his eyes up and down Billie. "Oh yeah, I heard. The flower child jailbird."

Billie imitated his scan and put a hand on her hip, "What's it to you, soldier boy?"

Hank ignored her. "Look, Bullseye, if you don't stand up for yourself now, you'll be an easy target for every bully in town, understand?"

"What's that, your own personal domino theory?" Billie said.

Timmy said, "Hank's right, man. You can't back down."

Craiger made chicken sounds and flapped his elbows.

"Don't listen to them, Archer, you don't have to do this." Billie said.

Coach Fish waded through the crowd with the boxing gloves in his hands. He locked eyes in turn with both Craiger and me, and said, "Last chance."

"Jesus! Aren't you supposed to be the adult around here?" Billie said.

We both took off our hats and uniform shirts. Me, in my white t-shirt, winter-pale, slender and blinking in the sun. Craiger, shirtless and muscular, a full-blooded Pomo Indian with reddish brown skin dark as Lupoyoma mud, fists balled up in his eyes. He stood in the center of the ring of jostling spectators and held out his hands while the coach laced up the gloves.

"Beat his ass, Craiger," one of his teammates said.

Fat Eugene said, "You're dead meat, King. You're road kill."

Coach Fish came toward me with the other set of boxing gloves. I didn't hold out my hands. "What are you waiting for?" Craiger said.

The coach stood in front of me offering the gloves. I still didn't raise my hands. I lowered my head and focused on the damp green grass at my feet. "It takes a bigger man to walk away," my mother used to say. But it's not easy to be the bigger man when you're the smaller kid.

"He's afraid," someone said, and the truth of it cut like a stab wound.

Craiger snorted a laugh.

"Give me the gloves," I said.

It wasn't exactly a twelve-rounder. Coach made us touch gloves, then signaled the bell with a hand motion. Craiger rushed me like a mountain lion and started firing punches in a blur. I tried to cover up but he was so fast. He found holes in my defense over and over and hit me at will—in the eye and the mouth, square in the nose and upside my head. And when he landed a hard right around my belt line, I went down to my knees.

"Low blow, low blow, dammit!" Hank shouted. "Let him up!"

Craiger backed off a step, but I didn't move. I stayed down, eyes to the ground in the fetal position. I groaned and held my hands between my legs.

Hank said, "You're okay, Bullseye, shake it off."

"What the hell is wrong with you!" Billie said, and Hank backed up like he'd been slapped. She moved to stand beside me and leaned over with a protective hand on my shoulder.

Coach Fish put his hands out like stop signs. I kept up the groaning. "He's had enough," the coach said.

Craiger scoffed and turned away. His teammates attaboyed him and clapped him on the back as he yanked off his gloves and threw them down on the grass.

Billie and Alice each took an arm to help me, but I shook loose and struggled to my feet on my own. As the girls unlaced my gloves, I glowered as if still itching for a fight.

"That's right. Take it like a man." Hank said.

"Fighting doesn't make you a man," Billie said.

"Well, neither does running away," Hank said. "Running away is for cowards… and women." He winked and grinned like he thought he was teasing.

Billie said, "Wow, thanks for the extra macho on top of your bullshit."

"Oh, you're one of those commie pacifist women's libbers, aren't you?" Hank said, still grinning.

"Better than being a trained killer."

"Now, that's kinda harsh," he said. "But you know what? If it comes to it, I will kill or die for my country."

"You mean for the politicians and the fat cats."

"Whatever. Say what you want, sweetheart. It's a free country, and we're fighting to keep it that way."

"Yes, sir," she said, with a fake salute.

Coach Fish scooped up Craiger's gloves from the ground and tugged mine off my hands. He pointed toward Hank and Billie. "Maybe those two should be next." he said.

RIGHT AROUND THE CORNER

illie walked me over to the Paperboys' dugout, empty now except for scattered helmets and bats and catcher's gear. She wet the hem of her halter top in the drinking fountain, sat me down and stood in front of me to tend my wounds—a bloody nose, a split lip and a swelling eye. "You're gonna have a shiner," she said. I shivered as she wiped at the blood on my face. It reminded me of my mother's touch.

Hank and Alice and Timmy and Joey all walked over and stood outside the dugout watching my treatment through the chain link. Like I wanted an audience.

"How we doing?" Hank said, fidgeting with his garrison cap in his hands.

"I'm fine," I said, trying not to aggravate my lower lip.

Billie turned to look at Hank. "No thanks to you."

"Maybe I shoulda gave him some boxing lessons," he said.

"Like I said, fighting doesn't prove anything,"

"Proves who wins," Hank said, with a wink in my direction.

"I woulda kicked him in the balls and ran like hell," Timmy said.

I laughed, but it hurt my whole face, and I said, "You think that would've worked, Tim?"

"Not a chance," he said.

I think we all laughed then. Except Joey, who said, "That wouldn't be right." And we all laughed again.

Usually, the whole team and our opponents went for ice cream at the Weeping Willow. Close to thirty boys sweating through their baseball uniforms, pushing and shoving in line for chocolate-dipped soft-serve, squeezing six boys to a booth, yacking away like red-winged blackbirds. Mr. Terwilliger always paid the bill and sat with the coach and a dad or two, and they talked of Vietnam and Nixon and the damn protesters and the whole country going to hell in a handbasket.

I always got squished between Timmy and Joey, the three of us on one side of a booth, and we would forget the game and talk about cars we agreed were totally cherry and how many homers Willie Mays would hit that year, or the relative physical development of the eighth grade cheerleading squad.

I couldn't face ice cream that day. Most of the Paperboys headed in that direction, but Billie and I started walking home. Hank idled up alongside in the red Mustang, Timmy riding shotgun, grinning like he'd been promoted to the in-crowd. Deep Purple rocking *Smoke on the Water* on the 8-track—apparently Hank had moved on from Elvis and the Beach Boys. He stuck his head out the window. "Hey Bullseye, you and Miss Bra Burner want a ride?"

Timmy laughed, Billie gave Hank the finger, and Hank just flashed a big grin, popped the clutch and chirped the tires, and left us in a cloud of belligerent dust.

Alice caught up and said she was headed for her part-time job at the library. The three of us meandered together down the street and then into the park in the shade of the tall trees, Billie arching her bare feet like a dancer to brush her toes through the lawn, and bending over to pick a dandelion and twirl it in her fingers. "How can you guys stand it here?" she said.

I thought I knew what she was trying to say. I'd seen that look of hopeless claustrophobia on other kids who'd moved to Lupoyoma from the city.

"It's like being trapped in a bizzaro Norman Rockwell painting," she said. "Plus there's absolutely nothing to do!"

"Summer's right around the corner," I said. "It gets better in the summer."

Alice looked down shyly at the park lawn. "If you ever just feel like talking, you could come by the library."

"Not exactly what I had in mind," Billie said, but she smiled and touched Alice's arm to show she was teasing.

We fell quiet for a few moments, until she said, "Are you guys cool?"

I didn't think I was cool, and I was fairly certain no one in the world thought of me as such.

"You mean, do we smoke pot?" Alice said, and now I understood this was a special use of the word *cool* that hadn't yet filtered down to the lexicon of Lupoyoma eighth graders.

Billie looked us over. "Yeah, that's what I mean, but I'm guessing the answer's no."

"Yes," Alice and I said in unison.

"Yes the answer's no, or yes you smoke pot?" Billie teased.

Alice's cheeks lit up pink. I could see she'd already marked Billie as someone special, someone to learn a piece of the larger world from. It was in the way she tilted her head slightly and watched Billie so as not to miss a thing. And it was in the way she would glance away shyly after a few moments of contact with Billie's demanding green-eyed gaze. Of course, I noticed all of this because I was watching both girls with my own sense of nervous wonder that I was even tolerated for more than a few minutes by two high-school-age girls who seemed to be treating me, at least momentarily, as a peer.

"Well, do you know anyone who smokes pot?" Billie said.

"One time Grandma Junia said my Aunt Laurette must be a pothead because she wanted to watch the *Smothers Brothers* instead of *Bonanza*."

Billie said, "Not sure we can take Grandma Junia's word on this. What about you, Alice?"

"Some girls at school said Nate Henderson sells it. He's in a band, too."

"Well, when can I meet this dude?" Billie said.

"His folks own the music store, it's right around the corner," I said.

Billie said, "Seems like everything here is right around the corner."

Alice stopped at the bottom of the steps to the Lupoyoma County Carnegie Library. "See you later," she said, mostly to Billie and with the hint of a question mark.

"Yeah, catch ya later," Billie said.

Billie and I walked along the sidewalk that bordered the park. We crossed the street and peered in the windows of Aunt Laurette's beauty shop, the Cut & Curl, but the closed sign was up and the lights were off. She had a little apartment upstairs over the salon, but we didn't see her VW so we didn't knock. We went around the corner and up Third Street aways, but the Music Box was closed too.

I hadn't shown her the loose plank in our backyard fence yet, and I thought now was the right time. I had the guilty idea she'd earned more of a welcome from me, some sort of signal of inclusion. We headed down Third Street and then cattywampus across to the Yacht Club parking lot. I showed her how to recognize the correct plank by a certain silver-dollar-size knothole and how to fit by turning your body as you stepped through. She was bigger than me, but she managed.

On the other side, in our backyard, I stood the plank back in place, taking special care that it appeared for all the world as just another piece in a solid wall.

Billie said, "You know why that kid was so mad, don't you?"

"Craiger?" I said. "Because we won the game."

"But was that really a legal play?"

"Of course. They even do it in the big leagues."

"Seems like kind of a lie to me."

"Uh… more like a trick," I said. "Like the fence."

"Well," she said, "it wasn't the truth."

"Jeez, now you sound like my dad or something."

The truth was I already felt lousy about the whole thing—the hidden ball trick, the asskicking I took from Craiger and the fact that I took a dive to avoid worse. Craiger knew. I could tell by his dismissive wave as he turned away. He knew that punch wasn't a low blow, that my wind was knocked out but the groaning and wincing was fake, a convenient way to mask my humiliation. Like a kid who strikes out and suddenly acquires a limp on the way back to the dugout.

Fortunately, it seemed to convince Hank and the others. But now, as Billie and I reached the back door and started into the house, she gave me a streetwise smirk and said, "Oh, by the way… low blow my ass."

BRIGHTER, LOUDER

Monday morning I woke in dusky half-light to Billie shaking my shoulder and shushing me at the same time, her round face mere inches away, eyes like wet jade. I pulled back to lengthen the view and saw her red tousled hair and the extra-large black t-shirt that fit her like a nightgown, silkscreened with the Woodstock logo—a dove of peace perched on the neck of a guitar.

It took me a few sleepy seconds to realize she had somehow opened the window between our rooms and climbed through. That window had been locked and painted shut years before. I started to ask about it, but she put her hand over my mouth and whispered, "Don't go to school today. Tell the parents you're sick or something, but don't go to school."

She kept her hand over my mouth until I nodded okay, then she went back to the window, folded herself through and slid the bottom pane closed. I had no idea what her purpose was or why on Earth I was prepared to go along. She already had a power over me which I did not fully comprehend.

My father's rule was simple. Unless you had a fever—or were actually in the hospital—you were going to school. Consequently, over the years I had developed and refined the Electric Heater Fever Simulation Method. The Electric Heater Fever Simulation Method required precise timing, made even more challenging in this case by the fact that it was springtime, not the dead of winter.

I pulled the heater out of my closet, plugged it in, turned it on high, and watched the wiry coils bloom orange as poppies. It was bigger than the proverbial breadbox, this heater, but not by much—only two feet tall. Obviously, you couldn't handle it once it warmed up, so there I was, kneeling on the floor in my boxer shorts, my butt in the air and my neck stretched down to catch the heat with my forehead. Finally, beads of sweat arose and even my eyeballs felt afire. I unplugged the heater, threw on my robe, and waited for my head to cool down from emergency-room to sick-note temperature.

I didn't want my father or Darlene to see the heater or notice how warm my room was, I wanted to catch them in the kitchen or living room—neutral territory. My timing was perfect—he was knocking back a final gulp of coffee, she was halfway out the door. He saw I wasn't dressed and said, "You're running late, young man."

I let my whole body droop and said, "I don't feel good" in my best whiney voice, and I moved within Darlene's reach. Her hand shot out in an involuntary mothering reflex and landed on my forehead. I held my breath—this was the moment of truth for the Electric Heater Fever Simulation Method.

"You're burning up," she said. "Get a glass of water and go back to bed. Tell Billie to find you some aspirin."

Success! They were out the door two seconds later, and I was literally home free.

I headed straight for the dayroom and threw open the door without knocking. Billie sat primly on the green chenille bedspread, still in her Woodstock t-shirt, hands uncharacteristically folded in her lap and a strange penitent look on her face.

She started talking in a rush and her hands jumped out of her lap and danced with the words. "Archer, I didn't mean to snoop, I swear, I was just bored and I saw all those boxes marked for Goodwill in the closet and I was just looking for old clothes to try on for fun and then I saw this other box on the top shelf that looked really cool and I guess it was your mother's and I probably shouldn't have opened it but I found something you maybe don't want to see and—"

"Billie, what the hell are you talking about?"

She gave me a sheepish wince and stood up, reached under the rollaway bed and slid out a big round box—a silver and gray striped hatbox made of smooth and sturdy cardboard, with red roses printed on the lid. Billie set the box on the unmade bed and stepped away as if the thing might explode.

Based on the look on her face I shook off a flutter of dread, and I stepped over and lifted the lid on the box. Inside was a navy blue felt hat with a round crown and a wide brim. A sprig of dried flowers was pinned to a silvery hatband that was sprinkled with blue polkadots.

"It's only my mother's old hat," I said with a wave of relief. I lifted the hat from a layer of loosely crumpled newspaper used as packing material. When I held the hat in my hands I could see my mother alive. "She used to wear this when I was little," I said. "We all went to the zoo in San Francisco one Easter. My mother and father, Grandma Junia, Laurette. I remember her there, on the carousel riding a giraffe, laughing in this hat."

"It's a beautiful hat," Billie said. "But look under the paper."

I set the hat down on the bed beside the box, pulled back the newspaper and saw that it was acting as a false bottom, and hidden underneath was a scattering of white envelopes, maybe two dozen, slightly wrinkled, previously opened, and each apparently containing a letter. I pulled them from the hatbox a few at a time and spread them out on the bed.

Now I understood Billie's excitement. And her hesitation. "Did you read these?" I said, like an accusation.

"A little bit," she said, cautiously measuring my reaction.

"They're love letters, aren't they?"

"Well, yeah… how did you know?"

The envelopes were all addressed to my mother's maiden name, Evelyn Medina, in care of a Mrs. Watkins at the same unfamiliar address—1425 Rawson Road in Two Lakes—which matched the return address on the envelope I'd found in the pocket of her dress the day she died. The envelopes from the hatbox were all from PFC J.R. Cole. Some of them were marked with a red and blue striped Air Mail border and a red dragon insignia under the word Vietnam in arched, Asian-style lettering.

Coming through the door I'd told myself I was done with the ghosts of this room. Now the back of my neck was slick with sweat as if I really was feverish. Billie's presence—sketches tacked to the walls, paperback books stacked on the nightstand, various articles of clothing strewn on the floor and the psychedelic landscape in progress on the window—it all lay like a sticky film superimposed over the memory of my mother lying dead in the blue-flowered sundress on a rainy day in September.

The rollaway bed was littered with a debris field of the letters. I closed my eyes and saw the pink impression of my mother's lips and heard the scratch-scratch from the hi-fi deep in my head. The hatbox, these new letters, this true motherlode of secrets, somehow made the first envelope more real, the pink lipstick brighter, the scratch-scratch louder.

One time, when I was about ten years old, I was hunting crawdads with Timmy Bilderback along the banks of Bottlerock Creek. When I turned my head to duck under some low cottonwood branches, a mosquito somehow flew or dropped into my ear canal, then couldn't find its way out. I began to hear its constant frantic buzzing as if it emanated from my own brain. Of course, Timmy thought this was funny as hell. My mother had to call Doc Meaney at home, and he met us at his office. By then the sound of the insect in my skull was raking my nerves like a saw blade on bone. It drove me to screaming tears until the kindly doctor extracted the tiny beast with a long worrisome pair of tweezers while my mother held my head down sideways on a cold steel table.

Now, I visualized the silver roll of duct tape my father kept in the junk drawer in the kitchen. I decided to put each envelope back in the box, double-seal the box with the duct tape and stick it on a shelf in the garage behind the Christmas decorations and the old paint buckets. No, that wasn't enough. I would drop the whole box into the burn barrel in the backyard, drown it in charcoal lighter fluid and burn it all with the week's trash. I started out of the room without a word, dizzy and nauseated, thinking I would retrieve the envelope and the records from my room and add them to the hatbox as well, and then to the flames.

THAT EXQUISITE ACHE

When I entered my bedroom, I heard the creak and scrape of wood as Billie lifted the bottom pane of the window and slid it upward. She stooped to poke her head into my room and smiled her big, relentless you-know-you-like-me smile, seemingly oblivious to my inner turmoil. "So, this one letter talks about some old records he gave your mom but there aren't any records in the hatbox and I looked all through the hi-fi cabinet. Do you know what he's talking about?"

"No," I lied on reflex.

"Do you think we should look through those other boxes in the closet?"

"I think you should stay out of my mother's things."

She held up one of the letters. "Yeah but, don't you want to know what all this means?"

"What do you care? You didn't even know her."

"Well, Alice told me some people say it was suicide, and that's something I kind of understand because—"

"Who the hell do you think you are?" I went to the window to look her in the face.

Billie dropped her eyes, and for a second I wanted the words back. "I know, I know, I'm sorry," she said. "It's none of my business and maybe I should've kept my big mouth shut but look, man…" She stood and held a hand out toward the bed and the scattered contents of the hatbox like they were gameshow prizes. She looked around the room as if searching for better words, more words.

"Archer, everyone's always telling us what to do, you know? How to talk, how to think, what to wear, who to like. Parents, teachers, grandmothers, cops, whatever." She paced the corded rug, her hands tumbling through the air as the words leapt out of her mouth. "It's like you're in a movie… they hand you a script and a costume and you're supposed to just shut up and play the part. And no one even cares who you really are, man." She circled the room, brushing a hand across the furnishings—the vanity, the sewing machine, the typewriter on the yardsale desk. "And I think your mom wanted more than that, right? I mean, maybe this sounds stupid to you, but when the whole world wants you to pretend to be someone you're not, sometimes you just want to hide… or run away… like… forever."

She was near tears, and even I could tell she was talking about herself as much as my mother. I was surprised by this new side of Billie Armstrong— one without the hand-on-hip certainty I was already getting used to. Another page turned.

And I did know a little about being pushed this way and that by teachers and preachers and fathers and friends, and especially grandmothers. And it was true there were questions on my heart that could never be answered without an honest examination of the letters, the records, the envelope and everything else. Sometimes you want the truth to go away and leave you alone, but sometimes the pain of not knowing can only be relieved by the pain of knowing.

Did I work through all of this in such thoughtful detail at the time? Hell no. But I went to the dresser, and I opened the bottom drawer and lifted all the records out from under those ugly old sweaters.

"It's not stupid," I said, and I passed the records over the window sill.

"Whoa, where did you get these?" she said. "You lied, didn't you? You little asshole!" But she was laughing, and just that quickly the shadow of weary frustration vanished from her face. She moved away from the window and didn't see me pull the shoebox from under my bed and slip the pink lipstick envelope into the pocket of my red flannel robe. I wasn't sure yet if I could trust her with the whole story. I wanted to, but I wasn't ready.

By the time I tramped back through the kitchen and the living room and got to the doorway of the dayroom, Billie was already standing over by the hi-fi, shuffling through the records.

"Man, we gotta hear this stuff, I mean just listen to these titles: *Moanin' at*

Midnight, Wang Dang Doodle, what the heck is a wang dang doodle! And this one, *I'm Your Hoochie Coochie Man,* oh I think I know what that's about!" She winked and made dramatic faces and paraded around the room, acting out the labels as she read—widening her eyes in mock fear, dancing and pumping her hands in celebration, swinging her hips like a harlot. Then she stuck out her lower lip in a pouty frown. "*Sad Hours* by—"

"That one goes last," I said.

She didn't ask why, but she stacked the records on the turntable with *Sad Hours* on top and turned the on switch. My mother must have turned the same switch that rainy day, poured a drink as the music started, sat down at the vanity and swallowed the red pills and the white pills and maybe freshened her lipstick. Now I sat on the little stool myself, looking in the big round mirror, wondering how much more of the truth I was ready to know.

The needle dropped on the record with a staticky pop. The sound of a ghost moaning in the dark slithered out of the Grundig cabinet, then a guitar broke in with a gritty twang, keeping ragged time with the drummer's steady working beat. A harmonica bawled like a determined, hungry baby, and the ghostly moans became the bellowing and rasping voice of a wounded man staggering home from a crossroads bar, bent over, gut-shot. It was the man called Howlin' Wolf.

Billie said, "What *is* this?"

"I think it's the blues," I said. "I mean like, the *real* blues."

"Yeah… real," she said.

It was so real and raw it made Cream, Led Zeppelin and that whole psychedelic blues crowd seem refined and overwrought. And forget about the Archies or the Monkees and even the early Beatles—they were all fizzy orange soda pop and this was cold black coffee at the bottom of a chipped cup. The sound of dead-end alleys, broken bottles and dented trash cans, the smell of fresh puke and reefer. The words didn't quite make sense as a story—somebody's knocking on the door, somebody's calling on the phone, and the Wolf is afraid to answer but they won't go away. It's never clear who it is—perhaps a jealous husband, a scorned lover, a bill collector. Perhaps death itself, the ultimate repo man. In a desperate, rattling plea, the Wolf says to tell them he's not at home.

I loved it instantly, though not in a conscious analytical way. Rather, it seemed to release something pressurized inside me—a valve was opened and some of my awkward young angst and stifled grief hissed into the air and was dissipated like a secret gratefully told. There was something in this music that said you are not alone, your pain is real, your suffering true, and you are right that platitudes and scripted ceremony aren't an honest answer. I suddenly wanted to hear every record and every song at once, ravenous for the rush of discovery, this revelation of my mother, this spectral visitation in black vinyl and rumbling bass.

Billie felt the power too. I watched her in the Woodstock nightshirt and her bare rosy legs, standing near the hi-fi cabinet swaying and rocking to a sad ballad with her eyes closed, then reading to herself from the letters of J.R. Cole while her shoulders danced a two-step to a quick shuffle, and even breaking into a shake and shimmy to some boogie-woogie piano.

She tried to lure me to read the letters. "Oh man, you gotta see this one. This is where it all began," she said and tried to press one into my hand. I refused. I was overwhelmed by the music alone—a whirling vortex of time travel and missed opportunity. I pressed my eyes shut and pictured myself coming home from school to find my mother singing along to Big Mama Thornton's growling version of *Hound Dog* (which made the Elvis version sound like a childish novelty record). I projected imaginary home movies of my mother and myself dancing around to the raucous and defiant *Messin' With The Kid* by Junior Wells. I imagined trying to explain that exquisite ache I heard from Little Walter's harmonica—and having her nod in understanding.

"You know, when someone dies you can lose things you never even had," I said.

I didn't even open my eyes to check, but I knew Billie had heard me because she turned up the music until I felt the bass notes rise up from the floor and shiver in my chest.

QUICKSAND

We stayed in the room all day listening to the records again and again. Big Mama, Little Walter, Memphis Minnie, Muddy Waters, T-Bone Walker, Howlin' Wolf and more. We listened to all of them, then flipped them over and listened to the B sides as well. We never got dressed or turned on the TV. We forgot to eat. We smoked the longest cigarette butts we could salvage from ash trays around the house and when it got warm in the afternoon we went to the kitchen and made grape Kool-Aid, which Billie spiked with some of the gin that Grandma Junia kept in the cupboard. We brought it back to the room in tall yellow Tupperware glasses.

I sat at the vanity and refused to read the letters, but Billie chose bits to read aloud, and I was powerless to stop her. She turned the music down and walked the room, curating and commenting while the blues grooved underneath like a soundtrack, and after a while I stopped resisting and started listening to the story the letters told.

"Wow, your mom worked for Bobby Kennedy?" Billie didn't wait for an answer, but I remembered my mother being excited to be the local chairperson of Kennedy's campaign in the spring off 1968, and how she'd set up an office in a cabin at the Weeping Willow Resort & Trailer Court.

"That's how they met," Billie said. "Cole came to her office the day after Martin Luther King was assassinated. He wanted to sign up and volunteer, but listen to this—he says, *I knew I was in trouble two minutes after I walked into that cabin. I saw the ring on your finger, I knew wanting you was wrong, but the whole world seemed to be coming unhinged in those days, and there was no time for all the old rules.*" And Billie added, "Yeah man, no time for rules!"

"I'm not sure I want to hear this," I said.

I resented the way Billie seemed to thrill at the unfolding truth like an old romantic movie, and yet she managed to annoy and entertain me at the same time. At one point she parodied the voice of a melodramatic pitchman. "Presenting a heartrending true story of star-crossed love in the midst of national turmoil, with Elizabeth Taylor as the lonely, passionate Evie King, and James Dean as the troubled soldier, J.R. Cole."

It was some natural-born sleight of hand the way she mixed the uncomfortable details with comic relief so I was distracted from the mob of emotions rioting in my head—over the letters, the records, the dayroom memories, and Billie herself.

"They fell in love working on the campaign," she said. "He talks about walking all over town with her, putting up posters and signs, ringing doorbells, stumping for Kennedy. And one time they drove down Main Street during the Memorial Day parade with a big Kennedy for President banner on the side. It's like he's reliving their time together. He says, *It was the best two months of my life. But now it all seems like ancient history or a dream.*

"Oh and here's some more about the records. *I'll never forget that night we stayed in watching the news with the sound off and the blues turned up on that little record player, making plans and promises and making love and—*"

"That's enough," I said.

Billie waved me off. "Stop judging her. Try to see it from their side. In one letter he talks about coming home and it sounds like they're planning to be together. *It helps me to think one day we'll be back there on the coast with all our troubles and this terrible war behind us.*"

She shuffled the letters to find a certain passage. "He talks a lot about the war. I wish that dude Hank could hear some of this. Or your dad."

"Uh, not a great idea," I said.

"He says, *Now I see it's quicksand. Everyone has lost faith in the war but we keep fighting, hoping someone will throw us a rope and pull us out before we're sucked all the way down...* See, that's what I'm saying—Hank has no idea, talking about fighting for freedom and all that.... Cole says, *Your letters are the only peace I have, my oasis in this desert of a jungle where nothing grows but elephant grass and rice, land mines and booby traps, and rot and lies. This war is fueled on lies. The World will never even know all the lies and insanity.*"

Billie was talking with the letter in one hand, both hands fluttering around, rising and falling and circling and turning in the air, so she occasionally had to stop and relocate where she'd been reading.

"Whoa, this is intense… *Last week we stopped in a little village to drop off some food and maybe pick up some intel. Supposedly a friendly village, all women and children except one shriveled old man. A few of us were in a shack where our medic was stitching up a cut by this old man's eye. I noticed a loose floorboard, and the old man got real nervous. I lifted the board and found a stash of rifles, and now the old man jumps up and starts yelling in Vietnamese. This kid from San Diego, we call him Duke, this eighteen year old kid in-country for all of a week, who likes Budweiser and draws cartoon hot rods, he nuts up and opens fire, empties a whole clip on the old man, dude's face down in his own blood and Duke just kept shooting. Then the other villagers started running around shouting and the other soldiers started firing. I couldn't stop them. They shot everyone in the place, twenty-seven enemy casualties, down to the last screaming baby.*"

"Man…that's just like My Lai," I said.

She sat down on the edge of the bed. "He sounds sad and freaked out, it's all so wrong…" *If they hadn't caught up to us, maybe we'd be in Canada by now, together…*

"Oh no, listen to this, Archer… *One of those cops up in Shelter Cove told me it was Mike who turned me in. And, wouldn't you know it, that pig Timmons showed up at the courthouse all the way up in Eureka just to make sure they got me to sign on for this shit. I should've gone to prison when they gave me the chance. I'll never come back whole from this place, even if I don't get shot or blown up.*"

"I've heard of that," I said. "They give you a choice—go to prison or join the army. Serves him right, I guess."

"But your dad! Turning the guy in like that? Not cool, man." She shook her head in disgust.

The defensive side of the gin started talking. "Hey, my father told the truth."

"How convenient. For him."

"What was he supposed to do, just let my mother run away with some draft-dodging coward?"

"They were in love!"

"Why do girls act like the word *love* gives them a free pass for anything?"

"Why don't boys understand love is the only thing worth fighting for?"

PUZZLING NEWS

Along with the letters, we discovered some other items in the bottom of the hatbox—more souvenirs of my mother's secret history. I sat on the messed-up bed and dumped it all onto the bedspread: a child's dimestore kaleidoscope; a tiny polished abalone shell; a motel key on a beaded chain with a green plastic tag embossed with the black silhouette of a squawking crow and the words, The Crow's Nest, Shelter Cove, California; a Robert Kennedy for President pin-button; and a Polaroid photo of my mother smiling in the blue hat on a windy bluff overlooking the ocean.

We went through each object, Billie and I handling them one by one, wondering how each one might be connected to the letters and J.R. Cole.

Toward the end of the day, knowing the parents would return soon, I put everything back into the bottom of the box, covered it up with the paper, and noticed the oddly folded, slightly crumpled newspaper happened to be a page from the *Lupoyoma Call & Record*. The date was Friday, July 18, 1969.

"Right before the moon," I said, absentmindedly.

"Huh?" Billie said.

"The date on this paper," I said. "Two days before the moon landing… you know, Neil Armstrong and all that… and just a couple months before she died."

Billie closed her eyes. "I was on the roof of a dormitory at Kent State that night, partying with some friends. Someone hooked together a bunch of extension cords and brought a TV out on the roof so we could get stoned and look at the sky and watch Walter Cronkite and the astronauts at the same time. It was a beautiful crescent moon," she said, one hand reaching upward as if she could see the memory.

"I was watching Cronkite that night too, but in Lupoyoma it was like eight o'clock, and it was still light outside and hot as hell. I remember Neil

Armstrong coming down the ladder and my mother and father were out on the front porch arguing. My mother came in, slammed the screen door and stalked across the living room crying during Armstrong's little speech, then she disappeared into the dayroom."

"I always wondered if I'm related to him. Maybe my long-lost cousin is the first man on the moon." Billie said. "You never know."

"Yeah, right" I winked. "But do you think it means anything?"

"The newspaper?" She gave me a what-do-I-know shrug and set the hat on the paper, closed the box and returned it to the shelf in the closet.

● ● ●

During the winter after my mother died, I would often avoid going home to an empty house by heading for The Weeping Willow after school. If none of my friends were in the game room, I'd stop by the restaurant to visit my grandparents. Molly had a jigsaw puzzle in progress on a corner table. She'd work on it when business was slow, and when I came by she'd invite me to fit a piece or two. At first she just had the edges of the puzzle, all straight and square and connected like a frame. In the middle, separate pieces or clusters of pieces drifted, untethered to the larger reality. But slowly, over that cold rainy winter, it came together to match the picture on the puzzle box, a blue and dark painting of cobbled streets and leafy saplings in thin moonlight beside shadowy water.

Now, the picture I had to work from was in my mind—the memory of my mother in the blue-flowered sundress, lying so still, the pills and the vodka on the nightstand, the scratch-scratch on the hi-fi. But, did I have *all* the pieces? The blues records, the letters, that windblown Polaroid and the rest of the souvenirs in the hatbox. Rawson Road, Shelter Cove, Vietnam. And which pieces belonged on the edges of the picture, and which would form the center? And, of course, the sealed, pink lipstick envelope still in the pocket of my robe—where did that fit?

● ● ●

When my father and Darlene came home from work, I played the role of recovering patient and offered assurances that I could go to school the next day. Darlene made chicken noodle soup and Jello pudding, which I ate in my room thinking about the blues and the rest, especially that last letter from J.R. Cole, the quicksand letter. I didn't want to admit it to Billie, but I was disappointed my father had turned Cole in to the authorities—it seemed small and unfair. He had taught me not to be a tattletale.

But wasn't Cole wrong to run from his duty, even if the war was stupid and wrong in the first place? And was Billie right that Hank Timmons wasn't ready for what he was getting into? I wondered how he would hold up under the conditions Cole described. And how would I do if it ever came to that?

My mother was in the wrong as well, and yes, I was judging her. How could she get involved with this stranger and run away like that, leaving me behind? (Although taking me along might have been worse.) Billie was wrong too, digging through my mother's stuff like some Haight-Ashbury Nancy Drew. And maybe I was every bit as wrong as everyone else, prying into all of this while keeping my own secrets.

I couldn't finish this puzzle yet, and I couldn't connect it all to that rainy Wednesday, my mother on the rollaway bed, the scratch-scratch in my ears. In journalistic terms, I had a whole lot of who, what, when and where, but barely the beginning of why.

• • •

After nightfall I lay in bed, under the blue wave bedspread, going over my thoughts like worry beads, and I stared at the darkened window until the faint glow disappeared from under my door and the TV voices no longer drifted back from the living room. When my ears caught the throbbing hum of the house, I knew all but myself were asleep. I tried to induce my own escape by spinning my usual fantasies, but I had begun to see that I couldn't grow up by wishes and imaginary afflictions. I could be slow on the uptake but I wasn't completely oblivious.

Like it or not (and I wasn't a fan), there seemed to be a decision at hand.

I could call it a day so to speak, draw the line here and like a politician simply declare victory. That might be the sensible thing, after all. Don't wallow in the past, move on young man, the wider world doesn't care about your heart's petty bruises. Or I could continue this needy quest to finish the puzzle, to fully understand my mother's choices, damn the consequences.

I got out of bed and pulled on my robe. I stepped to the window carefully as my eyes adjusted to the dark, and I tapped lightly on the glass. After a few seconds Billie came and raised the bottom pane several inches, slowly, to avoid the noisy scrape of the wood.

"What do you want?" She was sleepy, irritated.

I slipped the envelope out of the pocket of my robe and handed it across the window sill.

"Don't open it," I said.

Billie lit a match and examined the envelope in the flickering light. "Oh my god, where did this come from?"

We stayed there at the window for what seemed a long time, whispering in the dark, our heads just inches apart like a confessional, and I told Billie the story—the September rain, the scratch-scratch, the blue-flowered sundress, *Sad Hours*, even the vodka and the pills. And wanting to burn the whole damn mess.

"And no one else knows you were there?" Billie said.

"After I left her and ran away like that, how could I tell them?"

"I don't blame you, man. I might've done the same," she said, but I didn't believe her.

KEY TO THE HIGHWAY

Early in the morning, Billie came through the window again and shook me awake. I opened one eye and she raised a finger to her lips, signaling me to be quiet. She sat on the bed kind of side-saddle close enough that I scooched away at the press of her round hip against the outside of my thigh. She dangled the envelope in her hand.

"So, are you afraid to open it and read it or what?" she said.

"No. Yes. I don't know," I said. All the suspicions raised by the pink lipstick had already been confirmed by the letters in the hatbox, but opening a sealed envelope to leer at the private words of my mother still struck me as a betrayal too far.

"I have an idea," she said. And I was afraid of that.

Of course, her idea involved the risk of serious parental consternation. She suggested I give an encore performance of the Electric Heater Fever Simulation Method and skip school again. I argued that wouldn't fly because I'd already assured the parents of my quick rebound. But Billie had a Plan B, and her Plan B would risk not only the wrath of the parents but also the Lupoyoma School District.

It was Billie who'd first taken to calling them "the parents" rather than "Mom and Dad" or "my mom and your father" or "Mike and Darlene" or anything else, because every other configuration we tried seemed to stumble awkwardly out of our tentative mouths. There was a part of me that resisted this acceptance of my father and Billie's mother as a single entity, a part that still hoped a child's hope that both Darlene Beverly and her daughter would magically disappear from my life—actually un-appear as if time could be rewound like a spool of film on the school projector.

Another part of me wanted to know more about my mother, and yet another part simply wanted to spend more time in the charged aura of Billie

Armstrong. I couldn't define or itemize what it was that drew me to her, but it was undeniable. So I got out of bed, dressed for school and made an appearance in the kitchen—sat at the table with a bowl of Frosted Flakes but avoided my father's eyes as the parents went out the door headed for work.

As soon as the Plymouth pulled away from the curb, Billie called the school office on the yellow phone and did a perfect impersonation of Darlene. "Hello, this is Archer King's mom, I mean stepmom. I'm afraid Archer won't be able to attend class today. Yes, he's still a little under the weather. The poor boy's positively beside himself to miss another day, but we don't want to chance it with this fever." All in a high sugary voice like her mom's, and complete with a few trills of Darlene's trademark nervous laughter. I was in danger of cracking up out loud the entire time.

"And now—the envelope," she said after hanging up the phone. She crooked a finger for me to follow, and I followed. In the dayroom, she made me turn around so she could change out of the Woodstock t-shirt. I faced the wall while she went over her analysis of the situation.

"You know, we could just mail it, after all that's what your mom was gonna do, but the truth is we don't even know if J.R. Cole is still in Vietnam, it's almost a year later, he could be out of the service by now, he could be anywhere, besides, who wants to get a love letter from a dead woman? And what if it's a Dear John letter? I mean, who wants to get the *kiss-off* from a dead woman, right?! Then again, he might not even know she's dead…" And Billie went on and on like that, and apparently forgot I was turned around. "Oh I'm dressed now," she finally said.

I wheeled around to see her standing with her arms out in a theatrical pose as if to say, "ta-da, what do you think of me now?" It was a look that demanded attention, pleaded for approval and defied criticism all at once. Look at me. Love me. Don't dare judge me.

She wore Oshkosh overalls with the legs cut off high as hot pants and the edges frayed just-so to create a stringy decorative fringe. She was braless again, with one strap of her overalls undone in a way that exposed the curve of her left breast under a thin tank top that was tie-dyed in swirls of red, pink and purple. That wild red hair framed her rose-tinted, wire-rimmed sunglasses, round and oversized like the ones Janis Joplin wore on the cover of *Rolling Stone*. Three inches of bangles jangling on each wrist, and on her feet combat boots with bright red shoelaces. I didn't know red shoelaces existed.

She was a magnificent alien, wondrous and unsettling at the same time. I thought of how my friends and I used to build coasters out of backyard wood and spare hardware, with wheels scrounged from broken tricycles or wagons and bristly old lengths of boatyard rope for steering reins and only our tennis shoes for brakes. You'd sit in this wobbly creation at the top of Gunderman Street, the steepest hill in Lupoyoma City, a forty-foot drop-off on one side. If you could stand the shame, you might chicken out right then—I was tempted more than once. But that was your last chance to back out. Then your friends shoved you off, and there was nothing to do but ride it out to save your terrified young life.

Billie finally laughed at the blank look on my face and dropped her pose. She held the envelope in one hand and jabbed the air with it like my blowhard science teacher strutting around the classroom with his wooden pointer. "Today we're going to play mailman," she said. "We can't deliver this letter to Vietnam, but we *can* return to sender—in a way. We can take it to the Rawson Road address your mom was using, I mean, obviously this Mrs. Watkins was helping them keep their affair secret, so maybe she's a friend or maybe Cole's mother or something and who knows, maybe Cole is there right now and we might even meet him and he could tell us the truth about your mother and the hatbox and Vietnam and the blues, the whole kit and caboodle."

I'd always wondered why the caboodle never gets mentioned without the kit, but what I said was, "That address is twenty-some miles from here. And we're not even sure how to get there."

She held up her hitchhiking thumb. "I got the key to the highway right here," she said, a nod to one of our favorite Little Walter cuts from the stack of 45s on the Grundig. And with a grin, she added, "Archer, you are a pessimist, a cynic, a killjoy."

"I prefer *realist*," I said.

NOT IN THE BIBLICAL SENSE

Billie girl-talked the attendant at the Texaco station out of a free-with-a-fill-up Lupoyoma County map, then we walked out of town on the north end while she lectured me on the rudiments of hitchhiking etiquette. Hold your thumb this way, don't turn your back on the cars, look the drivers in the eye with a friendly, open face.

I was nervous as a kid stepping up to the plate in his first Little League game, fidgeting with my hair and rocking foot to foot in the roadside dirt. Billie misunderstood my anxiety. "Don't worry, we'll get a ride."

"Yeah, hopefully before a cop shows up and we're arrested for vagrancy. Or worse, someone from town sees us and tells my father I'm standing on the side of the road like a hobo."

"Or…" she held up an instructive finger, "some weirdo might come along with a bus full of hippie girls and brainwash you with religion and drugs and group sex."

I fought off a laugh. "It could happen."

"You wish."

I relaxed a little and, when a few cars came by I tried out my hitchhiking stance, which Billie also found hilarious, barking directions and shaking her head at my awkward attempts. "Stand up straight… not that straight… oh my god, bend your elbow… and stop bouncing!"

Before long a jalopy-looking Ford Econoline came rushing toward us, filthy white, splattered here and there with blotches of rust and primer, the horn honking as it sped by. The van gradually slowed and pulled over to the side, raising a cloud of dust and rocks, until it finally smoked and skidded to a stop fifty yards past us. The passenger door swung open and we jogged up beside the van. A thirtyish man with no shirt, striped bellbottoms and a frizzy perm like Art Garfunkel sat in the driver's seat, a beer can between his legs.

"Only going up to Parker's Junkyard," he said, and we climbed in the van without knowing how far away Parker's Junkyard was, or how close to our ultimate goal.

Soon we saw it in the distance—crumpled automobiles stacked up and tottering over a faded tin fence—and Garfunkel started pumping the brakes. They finally grabbed just barely in time. Smoke rolled off the tires with the stink of burnt rubber. Gravel flew into the air and rained back to the asphalt. Billie braced herself with both hands on the dash, and I held on to the back of her seat. For a moment I thought we wouldn't stop. When we did, Garfunkel took a slug of beer, wiped his brow and looked over with a sheepish yellow smile. "Needs new brakes," he said.

We said our thank yous and jumped out to safety.

"Well, that's one way to break your hitchhiking cherry," Billie said.

We were at a crossroads, a dusty four corners of businesses that seemed content to be out of the way of modern progress. Parker's Junkyard, plus a beer-and-bait shack called Sam's, a fruit stand that was actually just a table and two chairs next to a cardboard sign that promised "strawberry's and pare's," and something called The Bus Stop Antiques & Treasures. According to the street signs, these establishments were gathered at the intersection of the highway and Rawson Road.

"See," Billie said. "Sometimes you gotta believe in what you want." As if that somehow explained our dumb luck—to have survived Econoline Garfunkel's brakes, much less to be somewhere in the neighborhood of our destination.

"We still don't know how far it is to 1425," I said.

She rolled her eyes at my defeatist attitude and started walking up Rawson Road. I followed. She stopped in a turnout and stood in the blonde dirt with her thumb out, even though there were no cars. I kicked rocks with my tennis shoes. Puffs of pale dust rose into the air around my feet like miniature atom bomb clouds. The sun scaled the sky. From the junkyard, the smell of leaked oil and gas reached us along with the winding sound of a forklift shifting gears.

In the space of an hour, a total of three cars turned down Rawson Road, and none of them stopped to offer us a ride. Meanwhile Billie talked of her travels and wisecracked how Lupoyoma County was about the worst place she'd ever hitchhiked in her long career, how she'd actually been at Woodstock and thumbed there all the way from Ohio in less time than it would probably take us to get to 1425 Rawson Road and back.

"Thought you had a plan," I said. "Key to the highway, right?" And I started walking. I was never a sarcastic person until I started hanging around Billie, and that's the truth.

This time, *she* followed me. Maybe we only walked a couple miles on that flat one-lane road but it felt like seven—trudging forward, bent in stubbornness, with the noon sun on our backs and oil stains shimmering on the asphalt.

Eventually we spotted a three-story Victorian set back from the main road, up a quarter mile of dirt driveway on a rounded hill that rose from the otherwise gentle valley floor. Exposed in the glare of the high sun, it had the look of a haunted house movie set, graying and cadaverous atop its perfect hill, watching the road through broken-glass eyes, a tongue of crumbling stairs lulling out of its double-door mouth.

Where the long driveway met Rawson Road, it was blocked by a metal gate secured with thick industrial chains and huge rusting padlocks. A dented mailbox dangled from a wooden post, only vaguely attached—a solid triple in some past game of mailbox baseball. Billie turned it around to check the street number. "This is it. 1425."

We could've climbed over the gate, but there was no way to walk up that driveway or across the bare hill without being seen. Some nosy neighbor would drive by and call the police, Billie would go back to juvey, and I'd be worked and churched for the rest of my teenage days. The place looked empty anyway, deserted, my mother still a house I couldn't enter.

The walk back toward the highway was hot and quiet. I lagged behind Billie and kicked a rock out ahead of me so I could kick it again. And again.

"Not enough cars here," Billie muttered up ahead. "Not enough cars, not enough people, not enough cool people anyway, this place is gonna drive me crazy. I gotta get out of here."

"Where else would you go?"

"Someplace where people aren't on your case if you don't fit in. People like your father and my mother. Or your grandmother—did you know she offered to take me shopping, said the store on Main Street has some new summer dresses… in the *chubby* section. That's right. Well, I don't want to squeeze myself into pretty clothes for Grandma Junia or my mom or who-ever. I don't want to be pretty. I want to be an artist. I don't want to live my life pretending to be someone else, man. I mean, look what happened to your mom."

I figured I was too young (and too male) to understand. Was my mother pretending to be someone else? Was that the why behind the pills and the vodka? Wasn't having an affair also pretending? And what was so terrible about the chubby section at Snider's Clothing? Were we even talking about clothes?

Pop once told me that a man becomes a better man when he really knows a woman. Not in the biblical sense, he said, and not in the way some people have of learning your soft spot for their own advantage, but in a deeper way of knowing that Pop said was like seeing things through another person's eyes.

"Like a meeting of the minds?" I said, because I'd read that phrase some-where and thought it hinted at something important.

"More like a meeting of hearts," Pop said.

I didn't think I would ever know a woman that way.

A THOUSAND LIVES

We stood in the dirt, thumbs out, still in silence. Now that we were back on the highway there were plenty of cars, but they roared by at high speed, kicking up gusts of hot air that blew Billie's hair back from her face. I toed the gravel. Ten minutes passed. Twenty.

"Wanna check the place out?" she said, with a might-as-well nod across the street.

The Bus Stop Antiques & Treasures occupied a repurposed gas station built of dirty white cinderblocks. A collection of rusted gardening equipment decorated the flower beds along the front of the building. The two big picture windows were hand lettered: *USED & RARE BOOKS, FURNITURE, GLASSWARE, JEWELRY, SILVER & GOLD, CLOTHING & MORE!*

A jumble of sleigh bells and wind chimes rang when I pushed the door open, but no one came running to serve us. Inside, dust floated in the sunlight slanting through the windows. Overcrowded shelves sagged with colored glassware, delicate figurines of Japanese fishermen, old cameras, old radios, odd collections of salt and pepper shakers and engraved Zippo lighters and little spoons from historic monuments and faraway states. Stacks of books clogged the aisles, straight-back chairs dangled from overhead beams, crooked paintings lined the walls. Against one side wall, racks and tables overflowed with clothing and the smell of musty cloth and leather hung in the air.

Billie headed straight for the wall of clothes. I stood where I was, next to a small counter that doubled as a glass display case for jewelry and old coins and stamps. A huge antique National cash register sat on the counter and towered over me. It was one of those big brass things that looked heavy enough to anchor a ship. I called out to Billie. "Hey, I wonder if they have any old blues records here."

"Blues records?" said the cash register. Or so I thought. Behind the counter stood a tiny old woman with a gray afro. She couldn't have been much more than four-and-a-half feet tall, shorter than my grandmother Molly. "What's a little white boy like you want with the blues?" She wore dungarees like a sailor and a green grocer's apron and stood with the poise of a dancer or maybe a judo expert.

"Wow, I love your store," Billie said, suddenly standing next to me, smiling. "It's like the world's biggest closet—full of a thousand lives."

"Well, maybe not a thousand, but I'll take that as a compliment," the woman said.

"I'm Billie." She stuck her hand over the counter.

The woman shook Billie's hand and said, "Frankie." Next thing I knew, they walked and talked right past me, arm in arm, and left me standing at the counter while Frankie gave Billie the grand tour of the premises.

I found some bins of used records against the back wall. Mostly old-people music like Liberace and Lawrence Welk and Mitch Miller. I'd want to get rid of that stuff too—so manufactured and prissy. I didn't know much about the blues yet, but I knew it was the opposite of that.

Billie flitted around the other side of the room, pulling clothes off the table and the racks and holding them up against her body in front of a cracked full length mirror. Frankie followed her around asking her blouse, bust, hips and dress size and handing her things to try.

Billie struck different poses and made faces to go with each article of clothing. Then she started the impersonations. She scurried around with a green dress and a feather duster, and in her mother's voice she said, "Oh Billie, you have your whole life ahead of you, don't waste it arguing with the world." She grabbed an old pair of eyeglasses from a shelf, put them on and took them off, rubbed the bridge of her nose and wrinkled her brow like my father in pained thought. She stood rigid behind a 1940s style jacket with padded shoulders and did a dead-on Grandma Junia, "You'll never go far with that attitude, young lady."

I laughed and laughed, and Billie turned and turned around the room like a little girl at play. Frankie said, "Where you kids from anyway?" with a hint of admiration. When I said Lupoyoma City, she looked at Billie, shook her head and said, "*She* ain't from Lupoyoma City."

Then Billie did Hank Timmons with an army uniform and a sideways garrison cap. She marched in circles. "Which way is Vietnam, Bullseye?" But she stopped and laid the cap back on the display table. She held the uniform up to her body and gave me a serious stare, "Man, I hope you never have to wear one of these."

"Oh this motherfucking war," Frankie said, with a look like she'd surprised herself by saying it out loud.

"Aw, look at this!" Billie said, right back to digging among the clothes. "Archer, come here." She held up a suit. Even on the hanger it was sharp and trim looking—medium gray, with a four-button vest and creased slacks. I walked over and stood stiffly while she took the jacket off the hanger and held it up to my back. Then the pants, along the side of my leg.

Frankie nodded at the fit.

I checked the price tag and winced. Billie held out her hand and I put all my money in it—two wadded up dollars and some change. She took the suit to the counter and dug in the pockets of her overalls to make up the difference. "You can pay me back," she said. She'd previously teased me about the Dodger blue suit in the wedding pictures and seen my embarrassment. Maybe she understood I couldn't be thirteen in that suit.

Frankie rang the sale up on the big cash register and put the suit in a paper bag. "You never answered my question, young man," she said. "Why you looking for the blues?"

I shrugged. "Seems more real than a lot of other stuff these days."

Frankie gave me a questioning look, but then smiled. She held up a hand that said wait right there, and she disappeared through a door I hadn't noticed before. She came back with a small stack of albums across her arms and plopped them down on the counter in front of me. Howlin' Wolf, Little Walter, a few others.

She said, "these were my husband's," and pointed out a framed photograph on a shelf behind the counter, a young Black man in military uniform with determined eyes and a proud chest. "I had them out for a while but they didn't sell. You take em. On the house. They deserve fresh ears."

"Did he die in Vietnam or something?" I said, thinking of her earlier curse against the war.

But Frankie said, "No. Plain old heart attack. Been three years now."

I thanked her as she bagged everything up. Billie gave her a hug, which I thought was extravagant, but Frankie clearly welcomed the gesture—the two of them had some instant connection I didn't get.

We went out the door and stood again in the blonde dirt by the side of the highway. Billie faced the traffic with her thumb out, and I watched the wind from a big truck blow her red hair back to reveal that magnificent defiance on her profile.

"You could be an artist here," I said. "The parents said you're free to leave when you turn eighteen, but you don't have to. You could change your mind."

POPPIES ON THE HILLSIDE

Seven cars and a big diesel truck whooshed by, the drivers showing no interest in picking up two scraggly, sweaty teenagers. Tired, hot, silent. I was trying to calculate in my head how long it might take to walk the twenty-some miles to Lupoyoma when we spotted another potential ride approaching in the distance. We both resumed the thumbs-out position. Then I had the sensation I recognized this indistinct hump of white speeding toward us. As it got closer, I heard the unmistakable rattle and click of a Volkswagen engine, and I said "Oh no!" and reached for Billie's arm but too late.

Aunt Laurette slammed on the brakes, downshifted, and her VW Beetle skidded to a stop right beside us. The radio was up loud, and even outside the car we could hear *American Woman* by The Guess Who. Laurette turned the volume knob, reached across the passenger seat and rolled down the window. "Archer Edward King… what in the hell are you doing out here?"

Billie froze in place with a grip on the door handle, probably wondering why this strange woman knew my name. We both peered in through the open window. Laurette, looking like some variety show go-go dancer—gold corduroy mini-skirt, white boots, a low-cut peasant blouse white and sheer enough that I could see the outlines of her lacy bra. Black hair teased up in a puffy mound and wraparound sunglasses with red plastic frames that matched her lipstick.

She took off the sunglasses to get a better look. "And who are you?"

Billie, by contrast, in worn, patched, cutoff overalls, braless in her sweat-stained tie-dyed tank top, wild wind-tossed hair and Janis Joplin sunglasses. "Um, I'm Billie Armstrong."

"Ah, of course. The newest member of our so-called happy family. Well, I'm Laurette." She reached out a hand.

"Oh, the cool aunt!" Billie shook the hand through the window, smiled her big smile, opened the car door and called "shotgun!" And she took the front seat while I was still standing in the gravel imagining my cool Aunt Laurette's betrayal at a future family gathering. *By the way, I picked up Archer the other day. Standing on the side of the road, hitchhiking. The little bum.*

Billie leaned the seat forward so I could squeeze behind and into the back. The VW motor rattled idly and The Guess Who sang on at a lower volume.

Laurette waited for me to settle, turned and looked over the seat. "Not like I never cut school in my day, you know." She flashed a quick wink, all thick mascara and her signature blue flame eyeshadow. "But, really, what are you kids doing way out here?"

I opened my mouth to say something, but Billie spoke first. "Shopping!" she said, holding up the bag from The Bus Stop. And she started off on one of her excited rambles, how much she loved second-hand stores and heard there was a great one out this way and dragged me with her so she wouldn't have to hitchhike alone, and Laurette just nodded along looking unconvinced, so Billie opened the bag and showed off the embroidery around the neck of the weird dress she'd bought, the one she said was "a far out bohemian caftan," whatever that means, and how she really dug all the cool things in the store and her line about a thousand lives, and Laurette turned back to me with this bug-eyed smile like *Is this girl for real!?*

And I saw again how Billie could talk her way right into someone's heart. Then Laurette put the red sunglasses back on, shifted into gear, pulled onto the highway and headed for Lupoyoma.

Once the VW got up to speed, I couldn't hear well, and I was still worried about Laurette's reaction to the situation, so I stuck my head up between the front seats as Billie rhapsodized over the entire inventory of the store. Meanwhile the Supremes sang *Someday We'll Be Together* with those butter-smooth girl harmonies, and the KFRC disc jockey laughed at his own corny puns, and the commercials sang of car batteries and candy bars.

"And I just loved Frankie, the lady who works there, do you know her?" Billie prattled on.

"Frankie Watkins?" Laurette said. "You don't want to get too close to her." She didn't seem to notice the way Billie and I both did a double-take on the name Watkins, could have no idea that name was on every one of the envelopes we'd found in my mother's hatbox: Evelyn King c/o Mrs. Watkins. "She's what you call persona non grata in Lupoyoma County," said Laurette.

"Oh, why's that?" I tried to fake indifference, but what I really wanted was for Laurette to slam on the brakes and spin an immediate u-turn so we could go back to The Bus Stop and interrogate Frankie Watkins.

"Well, she got busted a couple years ago… went to jail for harboring a fugitive. They say she was trying to help some draft dodger get to Canada." Laurette said.

"And they put her in jail?" Billie sounded indignant.

Laurette chuckled. "Yeah, this ain't Berkeley, you know. I'm surprised she's still around. I heard the bank took her house while she was locked up. Poor gal's living in that damn store now. And that's a risky move. Some of these flag-waving rednecks around here won't be happy till she's gone."

As casual as I could muster, I wondered aloud. "So… what happened to the draft dodger?"

"They caught him up in Shelter Cove and made him join the army. Then he ended up in Vietnam." She shook her head sadly. "This motherfucking war."

Billie sighed and threw up her hands. "That's just what Frankie said."

I withdrew into the back of the car, my mind spinning around this new information. We'd been looking for J.R. Cole without really thinking about the other name on all those envelopes. Then we'd been face-to-face with Mrs. Watkins without realizing who she was. The story Laurette told fit what we already knew. Frankie Watkins would probably know more. She might even know where to find Cole.

Up in front, Laurette didn't know what it meant to us, and Billie never let on. She just kept hopscotching from one thing to another in her normal cascade of words and busy arms, and Laurette occasionally interjected, sometimes wry and cautionary, but sometimes excited and entertained by Billie's expansiveness. They must've hit thirty topics in a twenty minute drive. Most of it went by me in a blur, muddied with the drone of the engine, the music, and the outbursts of the disc jockey.

Billie said something about Tricky Dick Nixon and ranted how Doc Meaney had refused to give her "The Pill" and called her promiscuous, then she fired off a story about a truck driver who picked her up hitchhiking and took her to see Elvis in Las Vegas; of course she did the voices of the truck driver and Elvis too, and Laurette laughed and slapped the steering wheel.

They jumped around subject to subject, story to story—boys, jobs, women's lib, more hitchhiking adventures, I only caught pieces of it. But at one point I clearly heard Laurette say, "I wish I was that brave at seventeen," and it came out kind of like sarcasm but with a touch of sadness underneath.

Billie said she'd had some rough times, too. She'd been broke and hungry, ripped off, beat up, locked up. "And worse," she said, and I wasn't sure what that meant but Laurette looked over and gave her a somber nod like she understood perfectly.

When Billie rattled on about her dream of being an artist and what a nowhere backasswards town Lupoyoma was, and how it might drive her absolutely madhouse insane, Laurette said, "Trust me, this can be a dangerous town for a girl with actual ambition, especially if you're not afraid to speak your mind."

And Billie said, "That's me all over! Big ideas and a big mouth to boot! Guess I'm screwed!" And they both cracked up laughing.

Laurette reached over and turned up the radio. "I love this song," she said. It was that *Everybody's Talkin'* song from the *Midnight Cowboy* movie that was banned from Lupoyoma theaters. Outside the car, California poppies bloomed like fire on the hillsides and the colors rushed by the side windows in a smear—green and gold and bright orange.

As we pulled up to the curb in front of the house on Fourth Street, Billie asked Laurette if she had any Midol, and Laurette said, "Cramps, huh?" and told her to check the glove compartment.

"What's Midol?" I said. And they seemed to think that was a funny question. Billie showed me a little tin container that said: FOR FAST RELIEF OF FUNCTIONAL MENSTRUAL PAIN AND ACCOMPANYING CRAMPS, HEADACHE, BLUES. It was clear they expected a thirteen-year-old boy to be embarrassed or at least uncomfortable with the mention of the menstrual cycle. And, normally, I might have been. But I don't think they got the reaction they wanted because I was too distracted by the curious idea that this particular medication claimed THE BLUES as one of the afflictions it could remedy.

I was standing on the curb and the two women were still talking, Billie hanging on the open door of the Volkswagen. Laurette said, "Anyway, if you really want a job, I hear they're looking for a waitress at the Weeping Willow."

"Oh, my dream job," Billie said.

"Hey, you don't have to make a career out of it," Laurette said. "It's part-time, minimum wage, but a girl like you would probably make decent tips."

"Yeah?"

"Think about it, let me know. I could put in a word."

I guess it was around three o'clock. The parents weren't home from work yet. We watched the VW disappear up the street. Billie handed me the bag of stuff from Frankie's store and said she was going to visit Alice at the library.

I said, "You heard what Laurette said about Frankie, right? We didn't realize who we were talking to. We gotta go back and talk to her soon as we can."

"Oh, for sure man, for sure," Billie said.

LITTLE GREEN ARMY MEN

Five o'clock came and went, but Billie wasn't back yet. Darlene Beverly was in the kitchen, cooking something I would soon be expected to eat and praise. Her cooking always smelled like hamburger in a frying pan—I swear, the woman put hamburger in everything.

My father was reclined in his chair, watching the news, wrinkled white shirt and loosened tie with a highball in one hand and a Camel burning in his mouth.

"Do you know where your sister is?" he said, when I came out to check on dinner.

Darlene stood in the archway between the kitchen and living room, eyeing me and drying her hands on a dishtowel. She had a new hairdo, a poofed-out flip so petrified with hairspray that it shook like Jello with the movement of her hands.

"Stepsister," I said. "She went to the library."

My father nodded, took a sip of his drink. "When she gets home we'll have a talk."

Instant paranoia. Maybe Laurette had ratted us out after all—for cutting school and hitchhiking out to Rawson Road. *We'll have a talk* was certainly prologue to *I'm disappointed*, followed shortly by *you're grounded*.

But it didn't happen that way.

An hour after dinner, Billie blustered through the screen door. She carried a folded newspaper under her arm and charged through the living room so quickly no one got a word out until she was no longer in the room.

"Billie?" Darlene called after her.

"I want to speak with you, young lady," my father tried to command her presence.

Darlene rose from the flowered sofa. "I'll just go see if she's okay."

I waited a few beats, then followed down the hallway at a distance that, at least in my imagination, allowed me to appear only casually intrigued.

Darlene stood at the doorway to the room formerly known as the day-room. "Billie, what are you doing?" I heard shaky confusion in her voice.

"I'm leaving," Billie said.

I gave up my pretense of equanimity and edged up to a rubber-necking position behind Darlene. Billie was dragging her duffle bag around the room with one hand, and with the other hand yanking clothing from open drawers, gathering art supplies from the vanity, grabbing paperbacks off the night-stand, and cramming it all into the duffle.

"You just got here," Darlene said and laughed her nervous laugh as if she didn't quite understand, as if she imagined Billie was packing all her belongings to go out to a Lupoyoma house party for the night.

"I need to make some long-distance phone calls," Billie said. "And I'll need a bus ticket. Or maybe I should just leave now and hitchhike to Ohio."

"Wait, wait, wait." Darlene flung her hands up in dismay. "What on Earth are you talking about?"

Billie picked up the newspaper that now lay on the chenille bedspread. She snap-tossed it like a Frisbee and some pages spun out around the room, but the front section hit Darlene in the chest and fell to the floor. She scooped it up and held the paper out in front of her. I craned my neck up and down, right and left and around her inflated hair and saw it was the *San Francisco Sentinel*, evening edition. Then I caught the huge headline above the fold: Four Kent State Students Dead as Troops Open Fire.

"The government is killing my friends." Billie said.

"Oh my God," Darlene said, eyes wide, face shock-white.

"What the devil is going on here?" My father came up from behind and pushed past me and Darlene and into the room.

Darlene's hand shook as she passed the paper to my father.

He didn't have to look. "Yes, yes, I'm aware. This is why I wanted to talk to you, Billie. Now, I don't want you to over-react. There's no reason to get emotional about this. And no reason for you to get involved."

I remained in the doorway, suddenly feeling all the tension in the room like the audience at a Lupoyoma High School production of some Arthur Miller drama. Darlene and my father hit their marks over by the art-deco vanity. Billie sat center stage on the edge of the rollaway bed, still in her cutoff overalls and the combat boots with red shoelaces. The duffle bag stood upright, leaning against the bed.

"I know people there!" Billie said, clenched anger on her face. "I was living right across the street a few weeks ago," she said. "Now four kids are dead, eleven wounded. Man, I never thought the fucking pigs would just shoot us down."

"That kind of talk will not fly around here, young lady." My father shook his head, grimly, resolutely, examining the *Sentinel* front page. "These people are criminals. They've been rioting for days. Throwing rocks at the police, setting fire to buildings, shooting at soldiers. Burning flags."

"No. Nixon and Governor Rhodes are the criminals… and people like you, always going on and on about law and order instead of right and wrong."

"Now, Billie," Darlene said, trying to tamp down the energy with a wave of her hand.

But my father was stunned. "I'm a criminal? After getting you out of jail and taking you into my home? I'm the criminal and you and these… hoodlums… are the victims? Is that right? Because I'll tell you what—I think they should've shot more of these ungrateful bastards. Maybe that would teach your whole sorry generation a lesson."

Billie turned to Darlene. "What is wrong with him!" she said. "I knew one of those girls, I met her at a party. She wasn't a hoodlum, she was just a sweet plain-jane who wanted to be a speech therapist. And now she's dead, and that's all he has to say?"

"Billie, this is what got you in trouble in the first place," Darlene said. "All this arguing. It never solves anything. You already ended up in jail once, now you want to get yourself shot?"

"They're my friends!"

"Billie, please," Darlene said.

"What do you kids have to protest anyway?" my father said. "You live in the greatest country in the world, you're wallowing in modern convenience and all this permissiveness. You read a few books and listen to some long-hair bums with guitars and suddenly you think you know better than the President of the United States? You've got the whole thing backwards. You need to grow up and see what it's like to raise a family and contribute to your community. You want to be treated like an adult? Well, adults pay their own way, for your information. And they don't set fire to their own towns."

Billie turned back to Darlene, disgust contorting her face. "He thinks buildings and flags are more important than teenage boys dying in the jungle. But I'm the one who has it backwards?"

"Mike, couldn't you just let her use the phone?" Darlene said, straining for compromise.

But my father simply could not accept Billie's questioning—much less her complete rejection—of his authority.

"You're grounded. You're not going anywhere," he said. "No bus ticket, no phone calls. You leave this house tonight and I'll have the police looking for you. Do you understand? You'll be back in juvenile hall by morning."

I'd never seen my father so close to losing his button-down cool. He had rolled up the newspaper and was strangling it in his fist. He rattled it in the air and even raised it once as if he might strike Billie. But the dare on her face, the heat of her green eyes, stopped him mid-air.

"Michael!" Darlene said, startled. And disappointed.

My father slowly set the newspaper down on the dresser.

I quickly stepped into the room and picked up the paper, unfurled it and looked at the front page for myself. The scream on a girl's face—kneeling over the fallen in terror and shock. Face-down bodies in puddles of shadow.

This gunpowder thread of death had been in the news most of my life. JFK, Dr. King, Bobby, My Lai, body bags and caskets moving across the TV screen behind breathless reporters. This felt different. The names in bold face under the senior pictures from their high school yearbooks. Allison Krause, 19. Jeffrey Miller, 20. Sandy Lee Scheuer, 20. William Schroeder, 19.

I crossed the room and sat on the bed. I looked up at my father, hoping for some peacemaking gesture to cut the barbed-wire silence. Nothing.

"It could've been Billie," I said, and I felt that reality down in the muddy bottom of my belly.

He removed his glasses and rubbed the bridge of his nose and searched down at the old brown corded rug where as a child I had mustered troops of little green army men. He shook his head, frowned, put his glasses on and left the room.

STORM CLOUDS

Later in the night Darlene went to bed and my father sat silent in the living room watching TV, the sound of Johnny Carson's monologue drifting faintly through the house. I tapped on the glass with my fingernails until Billie came to the window between our rooms.

The parents still had no idea she'd managed to open the thing—mangling one of my mother's good butter knives in the process—or that it had become our private meeting place. They merely rolled eyes whenever they saw the colorful landscape Billie had painted on the glass, and they didn't even seem to notice the latest details Billie had added to her masterpiece, including the lipstick envelope floating in the sky like a flying carpet, and a 45rpm record labeled *Key to the Highway* sprouting out of the ground, the combined effect now approaching something between Peter Max and Salvador Dalí.

Billie undid the latch and lifted the lower sash, dragged the vanity stool over and sat down.

"You really gonna leave tonight?" I said.

"No… I guess not," she said. The anger had gone from her eyes, her face was puffy, cheeks tear-stained. "What would I do out there anyway, Archer? My mom's right. I'd probably get myself arrested again. Or shot, like she said. Last thing I want to do is prove her right." She stood and paced the room, arms flailing the air. "Everything's so messed up—the war, the whole fucking country, all the killing and the hate and the lies. And it's like the people in this stupid little town can't even see how sick it is. I just don't understand."

She returned to the stool, shoulders slumped, eyes hurt and worried, arms quiet now. She pulled the pink lipstick envelope out of the pocket of her overalls and handed it to me. "Maybe you should keep this," she said, like she didn't know her own mind.

• • •

She didn't come to the kitchen table for breakfast. That shouldn't have worried anyone because she'd slept late almost every day since moving in. But Darlene stood at the harvest gold stove, frying eggs in one pan and stirring bits of leftover hamburger into a separate pan of grease-soaked potatoes, and she asked me to see if Billie wanted some. I realized this was a ruse to get me to check up on Billie, but I was craving the same reassurance.

I knocked lightly on the dayroom door and, when there was no answer, opened it slowly. "Billie, breakfast is ready."

She was asleep in the rollaway bed and didn't stir. She slept on her stomach with her arms wrapped tightly around the pillow as if she had tackled sleep itself and pinned it to the bed.

• • •

"My old man says most of them weren't even students," Timmy said. "Outside agitators. Bunch of commie pussies trying to take over America." He slammed his locker door, closed the lock and spun the combination dial with a hint of violence.

"I don't know," Joey said. "I think they're mostly just kids who don't believe in the war."

"They're not much older than us, Tim," I said. "Some of them are girls."

"A girl can't be a communist? Take a look at your sister, numbnuts."

"Stepsister. And she's more of a pacifist than a communist."

"Same shit, different pile. Fuck em. Shoot em all. Mow em down and leave the bodies as a warning." He conjured an invisible machine gun in his hands and mimed a wide arc of rapid fire, snarling the rat-a-tat sound effect through his teeth.

"Jesus, Timmy. You're a sick man," Joey said, and we all laughed like that was funny, and we headed toward the cafeteria for Taco Tuesday.

• • •

At baseball practice Billie showed up and sat alone in the bleachers. She waved and hollered encouragement when I stepped to the plate. Hank was pitching batting practice, helping out Coach Fish, who critiqued my batting stance from a seat on the dugout bench.

Noticing Billie, Hank said, "Hey, Bullseye, got your own personal cheer-leader, huh?" Then to her, "Show us your pom-poms, Red."

Billie shook her head. "Wow, so original. Smack one up the middle, Archer. This pitcher's a bum."

I took my cuts. A few misses, a couple flyballs, some grounders, one solid liner. Then I played third base while a few other guys took BP, until Coach Fish looked at the sky. A line of clouds, gray as granite, was sailing our way on a warm wind out of the west. "Better call it a day, boys. Looks like we're in for a little storm."

Billie was waiting by the chain-link gate next to the dugout. Plainly dressed compared to her usual attire. Bellbottom jeans that looked close to new. A green blouse with long sleeves. No sunglasses, no bangles, hair some-what tamed. Almost like a normal teenager.

"Guess what," she said, "I got the job."

"Uh, what? What job? What are you talking about?"

Hank strolled up and butted right in like he was being clever. "Yeah, Red, what are you talking about?" Out of uniform he looked more like the old Hank—white t-shirt and straight-leg blue jeans like every other Lupoyoma jock in those days. Popping his glove with a fist.

Billie ignored him. "Waitress. I start tomorrow at the Weeping Willow."

"Wow," was all I could get out. It seemed like a sharp right turn for her.

Hank piped up. "Nothing wrong with an honest day's work, Bullseye."

"Listen to you, pretending to be a grownup," Billie said.

"Listen to you, pretending *not* to be a juvenile delinquent."

Billie flipped him off, but with a playful sarcastic grin.

"I'll have to stop in for a burger. I'd like to see you in one of those uni-forms they have."

"Oh, gag me."

"Why? You're cute. Weird… but cute."

"What the hell does that mean?"

"I think we should celebrate," Hank said. "Got a cooler full of beer in the Mustang. Up for a little cruise?"

Billie said, "No thanks, let's go, Archer."

"You know, there's a double feature at the drive-in this weekend, my treat. Bullseye could come along, too."

"You're not used to hearing no, I guess." Billie said.

"Hey, I'm going off to war—you're supposed to be nice to me, you know? Take my mind off it all, show me a good time." He gave her one of his goofy winks.

"What's playing?" I said, curious about the possibility, although Billie shot me a glare.

"*Planet of the Apes* and something else," Hank said.

Billie scoffed. "Do you not even realize that movie's about the foolishness of war?"

"Jeez, why do you have to take everything so damn serious?" Hank said.

"War isn't serious enough for you?"

"Look sweetheart, I'm the one who's gonna be marching through the jungle in a few weeks, not you. I'm just trying to have a little fun while I still can. You know, you're cute but you don't know shit from Shinola. You think the commies are just gonna drink a Coke and declare peace like that stupid commercial?" He laughed at his own witty reference.

Billie said, "Oh man! You can't possibly believe all that John Wayne Green Beret domino theory bullshit. You're part of the military industrial complex, soldier boy. Just a cog in the war machine and you know it."

"You better watch yourself—no one wants to hear that anti-war crap around here."

"Couldn't care less."

"Like I said, cute but weird. But hey, no skin off my back."

"I don't give a damn if you think I'm cute."

"Aw, sure you do," he said. And he walked away.

I felt the first spit of rain.

• • •

After school on Friday I went to work at the *Call & Record* to stuff the weekend edition. During a break, I looked through the A-section and the

B-section and didn't find a single column inch on the dead students at Kent State. As if it didn't happen. After all, Percival J. Terwilliger wouldn't want to upset the advertisers.

But when I got home, Cronkite was covering the demonstrations and student strikes that were breaking out all across the country. The Kent State campus was now closed and occupied by armed National Guardsmen, and in San Francisco a hundred and fifty thousand people had marched that day to protest the shootings, the invasion of Cambodia, the draft and the Vietnam war in general.

My father sat in his chair, leaning forward, grievance breaking out on his face like sweat. I plopped down at one end of the floral couch, Grandma Junia sat at the other end, elegantly dragging on a Tareyton and blowing her smoke toward the ceiling with a patronizing sigh.

Ever since the wedding, Grandma Junia often stopped by after work, ostensibly to see if Darlene needed any help with dinner, but actually as an excuse for a custom gin and tonic (with four ice cubes, a squirt of lime and two maraschino cherries, sunken), which Darlene still hadn't learned to assemble and serve in such a way that forestalled complaint.

Darlene appeared with her latest attempt and delivered it to Grandma Junia. Cronkite's fatherly voice reported a clash between anti-war demonstrators and New York construction workers. Hundreds of angry little faces on the TV screen, some of them walking through the crowd holding a huge American flag spread out flat above their heads. Several men rushed past a line of police officers and began to beat up the anti-war demonstrators with fists and hardhats and even bats and iron pipes. My father stretched forward, his whole body tensed and his face screwed up like he was about to spit on someone. He pointed at the TV with his glass. "Your daughter should see this, Darlene."

He shifted to me. "You better take notice, too, young man," he said. "This is what real Americans think of Billie and her friends at Kent State. She needs to understand, all you kids need to understand, working people in this country won't put up with this nonsense forever."

"Oh, you haven't heard the latest," Grandma Junia said. "She's joined the ranks of the proletariat herself. Waiting tables at the Weeping Willow's greasy spoon… of all places."

With the words "of all places" Grandma Junia not only managed to signal her general disapproval of the Weeping Willow's clientele, their kitchen and their food, but also Pop and Molly, not to mention Billie and any other employees of the establishment. In Grandma Junia's mouth, *of all places* was a remarkably efficient phrase.

"That's good news!" Darlene said. "Isn't it?"

It was kind of sad the way Darlene directed this question to me, as if I was her best shot at finding an ally in the room. I gave her a thin smile and a pity nod.

My father said, "From what I've heard, she'll fit right in with some of the other new hires over there." He put extra emphasis on the word *other*, sort of a nudge-nudge in the direction of Grandma Junia. I wondered what he meant, but he shushed the room as the network switched to live coverage of President Nixon holding another press conference at the White House.

On our black and white TV, the President wore gray—a dark gray suit and tie, snowy gray shirt, slick gray hair, pale gray face, and a mask of somber gray sincerity. He claimed the aims of the demonstrators were also his aims. "They want peace, they want to stop the killing, they want to end the draft and get out of Vietnam. I agree with everything they're trying to accomplish," Nixon said. He promised that what he'd done in Cambodia would help achieve those goals, would hasten an end to the war.

"Now, see—the man knows what he's doing. He has a plan." my father pointed his empty glass around the room, emphasizing his point to each of us in turn. "You need to give the President a chance."

THE PROMISE OF FREEDOM

Between school and work and baseball and her waitress training, I'd hardly seen Billie for a couple days. We hadn't met at the window—she was gone too early in the morning and home too late at night. A few weeks before, Billie Armstrong was nothing but a rumor to me. Now I actually missed having her around to nudge me, joke me, guilt me, shock me into a larger view of everything, including myself, and especially my mother. And the pink lipstick envelope.

Saturday, after work, I headed for the Weeping Willow on foot. Off Main Street, I took Preacher's Alley, a narrow sloping passageway between two buildings that was popular with local kids and loose dogs as an occasional hideout and shortcut to the park. We called it Preacher's Alley because Reverend Jameson could sometimes be sighted there on his breaks, by the back door of the church smoking cigarettes (and, rumor had it, sipping from a flask kept somewhere in his vestments).

I shot straight through to where the passage dumped out on Parkview Avenue. It was a blue and soft May afternoon, ducks gabbling down at the lakeshore as I cut across the park's lawns, over to Second Street and down to the Weeping Willow's driveway. The two old oak trees guarding the entrance were leafed out green and the parking lot dominated by its usual combination of pickup trucks and Harleys. I cut through the game room, out to the big patio on the lake side and straight to the walkup window.

My grandmother Molly spotted me and called out my order without waiting. "One hot dog, plain, with nothing on it at all, just the bun and the dog." She knew how I liked it.

"And a root beer," I reminded her.

Billie brought my hot dog to the window in a little plastic basket, and the root beer in a waxy paper cup with sketchy illustrations of fishing and boating on the side. "I'm on break in ten minutes," she said, checking the clock over her shoulder. "I got something to show you." And she hustled away toward another task.

A breeze ruffled the surface of the lake and in the distance motorboats towed skiers across each other's wakes and their engines whined like mosquitos. I carried my food out on the wooden pier that extended off the patio and over the water. At the far end of the pier was a bench where I often sat to gaze out across the ever-shifting currents and contemplate my general adolescent befuddlement.

It was known as Molly's Pier because my grandmother had famously fought so hard to get it built. When she and Pop first bought the Weeping Willow, they had plans to build a new pier with a gas dock attached, but the Lupoyoma City Council didn't want any competition for the city-owned gas dock over at Library Park, where a fat cut of the revenue went straight into the city coffers.

The councilmen denied her permit application, so Molly took the debate public, showing up at meetings to argue her case and accuse the council members of abusing their power, which got her picture in the paper a few times (her head barely reaching the microphone at the lectern). She eventually found an out-of-county lawyer who filed suit against the city of Lupoyoma under the public records laws, at which point the city backed down and Molly Medina got her pier, her gas dock, and the customers that came with it.

I finished my dog and drink, Billie came halfway out on the pier, waved for me to join her. She moved crisply in the pink uniform with the white trim and the white apron strings tied in a floppy bow at the back of her waist. When I caught up, she turned and smiled that big how-do-you-like-me-now smile, and she looked like a grown woman in that tight-fitting dress with the ketchup stains on the apron and the prissy white tennis shoes, all her red hair neatly tied back, revealing her full face with a hint of sweat on her forehead. She looked like an adult, like she might look in a few years, some flash-forward Billie playing by the rules and making her way in Grandma Junia's so-called real world.

"This is gonna blow your mind," she said, and I followed her back through the game room and out to the parking lot, where she stopped next to a parked car. From the other direction, a man came walking—or rather, limping—toward us. He wore a buttoned up white shirt with dirty jeans and a white bib apron and paper hat shaped like Hank's garrison cap. Billie introduced him as Sonny, the new cook, and a "way-cool dude" who was looking to sell the dusty old car she was standing beside.

Sonny was tall with rust-brown skin, dark somber eyes, a clean-shaven, chiseled face and frizzy black hair that hung down his back in a bushy pony tail. "Heard a lot about you, kid," he said. I assumed he meant from Billie, although maybe Molly as well, and I instantly had the hope that he'd heard good things. He had a strong handshake and a deep thoughtful voice, and even in that cook's getup with the paper hat and the slight limp, a natural calm and a manly presence that left a boy wanting his approval.

He tossed a keychain to Billie, underhand like a shortstop starting a slick double play. "You got fifteen minutes." He checked his watch. "And I ain't going no lower on the price."

The car was a 1962 Ford Fairlane 500. Dull white body paint, a little chrome here and there and a few minor dings. But the interior was pristine, all of it decked out in bright red—the vinyl upholstery, the door panels, the low-pile carpet, the metal dash, the big round Bakelite steering wheel, even the foldout ashtray. "Three on the tree with a 283," Sonny said. "I bought it a couple years ago for a trip I never got to take. And I have the Harley now, so…"

The test drive was really for me. Billie had already driven the car and sugar-talked Sonny down to three hundred bucks, but he wanted half down before he would sign the pink slip, and it was going to take her a while to get that kind of money together. Still, in her mind it was a done deal and a promise of freedom to come. "Key to the highway, man—no hassles, no parents, no cops. San Francisco, the redwoods, the ocean, anywhere we want to go…"

She drove carefully but talked recklessly in her lickety-split rhythm, taking sudden detours for stories of her new worklife, complete with impersonations of the horny old fishermen and horny young waterski dudes who showed up at the cafe, and fantasies about other faraway destinations—Yosemite, Haight-Ashbury, Candlestick Park.

"We still need to go back to Frankie's." I said. "And soon."

"Yeah, for sure, but no way I'm thumbing out there again. I can pay for the car in a few weeks and you'll be out of school by then. We'll ride out there in style, man. You'll see."

When we returned to the Weeping Willow, Sonny the cook came out to the parking lot for the keys. "I better get back to work," Billie said.

"Didn't you once tell me work was for suckers?" I asked.

"I said *jobs* were for suckers, not work. Jobs, careers, the bullshit American Dream. They tie you down with rules and labels and shrink your world, man. But this is just something I need to do if I want to leave this crappy little town on my own terms and not have to look over my shoulder. I can play the game for a while—wear the costume, the whole thing, I mean, check me out, right?" She smiled a fake smile and mimed a pen and an order pad. "More coffee, sir? How would you like your eggs? Could you kindly remove your hand from my ass?"

I pretended a chuckle.

"It's really not that bad," she said. "Molly's super cool for an old lady, you know. And Sonny looks out for me with the jerks. Anyway, all I have to do is make it through the summer, get to my birthday, and then I'm free. Meanwhile, it's gonna be one helluva summer, man." She pointed at me like it was guaranteed and sashayed away humming the tune to *Key to the Highway*, patting out the rhythm with a hand on her thigh.

Billie Armstrong, tamed? Billie Armstrong, surrendered? No, I knew that uniform—or any other—would always be too tight on her. But there was something different about her that day, something changed, sharpened, something beyond the uniform—a new aura of competence and intent, the stride of someone who could see the path ahead. As Grandma Junia would say, she walked like she had a purpose in life.

But it felt like she might be walking away from me.

JAMES + EVIE

My father and Darlene were out the door early Sunday morning for a drive to Santa Rosa. Their day trips and date nights had become a regular thing—part of the piecemeal honeymoon strategy they devised because the *Call & Record* couldn't put out a newspaper without my father, or so said Grandma Junia. I was the accidental beneficiary of these outings, left on my own without adult interference more often than I'd ever been in the past.

Meanwhile, Billie was at the Weeping Willow shuttling ham and eggs to bleary fishermen and hungover bikers and dreaming of road trips in a car that wasn't hers yet. Fine, I didn't need her. My father and Darlene would be gone all day. I had the pink lipstick envelope and the gas station road map. By my calculations, I could make it to Frankie's store in an hour and a half on my bike.

• • •

I'd pedaled for what felt like an hour, and I wasn't halfway there. If you're riding in a car, a long steady incline goes by in the window almost like flat ground, but on a one-speed Schwinn Sting-Ray the same stretch of road is a thigh-burning test of manhood.

The late-morning sun climbed the sky and scorched the right side of my face. The dusty wind choked my throat and the sweet sticky smell of insecticide floated up from the pear orchards on either side of the raised road. Big diesel trucks honked by and nearly blasted me off the narrow shoulder.

There was a gravel turnout at the crest of a hill, and I pulled over, swung off the bike and toed the kickstand down, walked around to shake out my legs and prepare myself for perhaps another hour of pedaling the rolling landscape of Lupoyoma County—not to mention the trip back. I should've brought a canteen of water, should've worn cutoffs, probably should've stayed home.

A Ford van came coughing and sputtering up the road and I recognized Garfunkel's dirty-blonde head bouncing along behind the windshield. He did a double-take and pulled over, tires spitting gravel, and stopped just short of the bike. At least his brakes were working now.

He leaned over and rolled down the passenger window. "Hey man, don't I know you?"

I refreshed his memory. He said, "You look a little lost out here by yourself." When I told him I was headed to Frankie's store, he said, "Okay, so you're not lost, just late. Better throw your bike in the back, dude." He didn't say what I was late for.

He opened the passenger door and the smell of hot pizza tumbled out of the van. I rode in the front seat holding two pizza boxes on my lap. Garfunkel wore mirrored aviator sunglasses and the same striped bell-bottoms and naked hairy chest with a necklace of rawhide and wooden beads.

Leather-strapped tire-tread sandals worked the gas and clutch as the van rattled down the road and Garfunkel rattled on about how he first met Frankie a year ago when he shipped back from Vietnam with a "bitch of a heroin habit" and it was Frankie who nursed him through the horror of cold turkey withdrawals.

"She's good people. I'm gonna miss her," he said, but he didn't say why, and he didn't stop talking long enough for me to ask. We passed the junkyard and he slowed the van and downshifted, backfiring loudly as we pulled into Frankie's dirt parking lot and came to a stop next to a giant U-Haul truck with a long ramp sticking out the back.

Garfunkel said, "Bring those pizzas, man."

Strangers issued forth from The Bus Stop's front door, lugging boxes and furniture up the ramp and into the U-Haul. Garfunkel made introductions: there was beefy and sweaty Ben Parker from the junkyard, slow-moving Old Sam from the beer-and-bait shack, and shy Gilberto from the fruit stand. Turned out Garfunkel's real name was Howard, but these folks all called him Howie.

Finally I caught on. "Frankie's moving?"

"Had enough of the bullshit from these redneck assholes around here, man." He pointed at the front of the store.

Past the big U-Haul truck I saw huge spray-paint letters scrawled across the front of the store, bright orange against the dirty white cinderblock wall: *GO BACK TO AFRICA COMMIE NIGGER.*

I was startled. Yes, this wasn't Berkeley, but it also wasn't Birmingham. This was the first time I'd ever seen the word displayed so openly in Lupoyoma. Not that it wasn't tossed around in private conversations, even occasionally on the schoolyard by certain kids, but my mother had taught me this was a word that brought shame to the speaker, not their target.

The glass had been busted out of the window and the door, then swept into piles we carefully stepped around. Inside it was hot and stuffy and the store was a jumble—stacks of packed boxes, knocked-over towers of books, bare naked tables, half empty shelves, broken chairs piled like bodies awaiting mass burial, garbage bags with the arms of child-size sweaters dangling out the top.

Frankie appeared from behind the big antique cash register. She wore faded jeans and the green and dirty grocer's apron, her gray hair pushed back with a purple headband, dark arms shining with the heat. She took the pizza boxes and set them on a table, looked me up and down.

"Now, what can I do for you today, young man?"

"Well, I was here several days ago and—"

"You and that redhead girl. I remember."

I had stashed the envelope inside my shirt. I undid a button, reached in and grasped it with fingertips, but I hesitated. Under Frankie's suspicious glare, the day's enterprise suddenly seemed embarrassing, ridiculous, unexplainable.

"What's in your shirt, boy?"

I looked at the battered linoleum floor. No words came. I slid the envelope out and held it in the space between us.

"What's this?" She took the envelope, examined it closely, thoughtfully. Both sides.

"Uh, my mother died last year and—"

"Evie King, that's your mother?"

"Yes, ma'am. Was."

She looked at me warily, took a deep breath, processing the information. "Well, I'm very sorry to hear Evie passed." She tried to give the envelope back, but I didn't take it.

"You're Mrs. Watkins… aren't you."

Frankie looked down at the envelope in her hand and shook her head like people do when they're reminded how life tends to swirl around in circles. "I see," she said. "This is why you and the girl were out this way before?"

"We were looking for J.R. Cole. We didn't know you were you then."

Old Sam shambled in with a styrofoam cooler full of ice and beer and plopped it down next to the pizza boxes. The rest of the moving crew hustled in one by one. Ben Parker proved he could open beer bottles with his teeth and the men laughed and joked while Frankie shooed them out the broken door, saying "Go on now, I got business with this young man." The men drifted outside to the parking lot and Frankie turned back to me.

"What's your name again?" she said.

"Archer King."

"Well, Archer King, I think you better have a seat and tell me exactly what you think you're doing here."

We sat in old straight-back chairs at an old round table and she set the envelope down in front of her. I told how my mother died in the blue-flowered sundress and how I found her in the dayroom, the envelope peeking out of her pocket, and how I couldn't bear to tell anyone until Billie came along. "You poor child," Frankie said.

I told her about Billie finding the hatbox and the love letters addressed to my mother in care of Mrs. Watkins. She smiled when I told her how Billie and I listened to the blues records over and over that first day. She laughed about our ride with no-brakes Garfunkel, and she looked away when I spoke of her crumbling old house on Rawson Road.

"I'm just trying to find out the truth about my mother," I said.

She pushed her chair away from the table, stood up and walked outside and returned shortly with two Cokes from the vending machine. She set one in front of me, wiped the other icy bottle across her forehead, placed it back on the table and sat down. She kept her eyes on me the whole time, reading me, seeming to question my heart. Then she spoke in that weary, gravel voice.

"I called him James, and so did your mother by the way, although he preferred J.R. and had other nicknames as well. He was a Greyhound bus driver, if you didn't know. The bus don't come out here any more, but this was the end of the line then, and I used to let the drivers stay the night in the back room. Had a little cot back there and I'd bring down a plate of food from the house. But after James met your mother—well, she'd be waiting in her car when the bus pulled in and they'd go off together. It got to be a regular thing. Till he got the draft notice. Started talking about Canada. Quit his job. And then I had to stick my nose in… like a damn fool."

She took a long drink from her bottle of Coke.

"My son Daniel got drafted in 66, been up in Vancouver ever since, so I asked him to help James get settled up there. I was gonna drive him to Portland, and Daniel would come down and take him over the border. That was the plan. All James had to do was lay low until I could take a few days off. I made up a bed for him in the attic—that's how he found those records. I put them all away after my husband died, but James found them and he played some of them over and over, same as you kids."

She dug a lighter and a pack of Salems out of her apron pocket, shook one out and lit it and blew smoke toward the ceiling.

"But James, he was always in a hurry—for everything," she said. "And then that night Bobby Kennedy was shot… well, we were all… shattered, I guess is the word. You know, for a little while we really believed he would change the country, the world. And when he died, well, a lot of us lost hope. And that was it for James—he made up his mind to go right away. He bought a used car from Ben Parker across the street, and he left with nothing but a grocery bag full of clothes, some of those records… and your mother. I knew they were asking for trouble and I told them so. Nobody important would miss James Cole, but sooner or later somebody would come looking for a white lady with Mrs. in front of her name. Sure enough, a few days later, cops banging on my door." She waved a hand at the mess around us, the half-empty shop and the swept-up glass and the disarray. She gave it all an arms-wide what-the-hell shrug. "You see how that worked out."

MOTHER'S DAY

Frankie pushed the envelope across the table, and I silently read the address for the hundredth time: PFC J.R. Cole—all the numbers and abbreviations, Co B, 1st Bn, 5th Inf / 2nd Brig, 25th Inf Div / APO San Francisco. I looked at her and tapped on the envelope. "Do you know what happened to him?"

"I got a postcard once—just I'm fine, how you doing, and thanking me for helping with the letters. It was all hush-hush. He sent his letters care-of me, and I'd mail hers over at the Two Lakes post office. She was very careful—always parked her car round back when she came, so no one would see it from the road. And we'd small talk a bit. How's he doing, I'd say. And she said the war was hard on James, but she didn't say much more. Then the letters stopped coming, and your mother stopped coming, and I never heard another word from either of them. Figured James maybe died in the war. Didn't know about your mama, though."

I picked up the envelope and slid it back into my shirt. A strange dead-end emptiness hit my stomach—like an elevator dropping too fast. I felt near tears and sickness both.

Frankie seemed to pick up on my emotional state. "Look, son—your mama was a good woman, you hear?" she said. "Whatever's in that envelope, or those other letters, doesn't change that. She was a good woman, she just desperately needed something she couldn't have."

"Billie says I should try to understand because they were in love."

'Well, love is crazy, boy, and that's a fact. Love is like water in the desert. You thirsty enough, you'll crawl on your belly for it, even if it's a mirage."

I looked at the mess her store was in. "Do you regret helping them?"

"Not for a minute," she said. "You gotta stand for something in this world… or you don't stand for nothing at all."

Later, when I was already loaded up in Garfunkel's passenger seat, Frankie ran out to the parking lot shouting, "Hold on!" She came to the window of the van and handed me a record. It was a 45 in a plain-paper sleeve. *My Heavy Load* by Big Mama Thornton. She said, "When James and your mama ran off, this one got left behind somehow, and I remember it was one of her favorites, one of my husband's too." I hesitated and she said, "No, you take it. Truth is, I never cared for the blues like he did. And now it just takes me backwards in the worst kind of way."

• • •

Garfunkel pulled the van over at the corner of Fourth and Main, ran around and popped the side door, easily lifted my bike out and set it down on the sidewalk in front of me. He gave me a soul-shake. "Take care, dude," he said while our hands were clasped. "Don't do anything I wouldn't do." Which I figured was a pretty short list.

Watching him pull away from the curb I felt a tightness around my heart, another stab of nostalgia for something I'd never actually had. I wanted to know more about my mother and J.R. Cole, and why she did what she did, but the answers I needed still lay beyond my grasp. And maybe it was all a waste of time and worry in the first place. Marriages fall apart, accidents happen, people die, truth is debatable. And a man has to move on. Right?

My father's Plymouth was not in the driveway or at the curb in front of the house on Fourth Street. I dropped my bike on the weedy lawn and once inside I headed straight for the dayroom and added the Big Mama record to the stack of 45s still on the old Grundig. I switched on the turntable and dropped the needle. I guess I had some pathetic idea that listening to this last record would close the chapter that began with the scratch-scratch sound and Little Walter's harmonica on that gray Wednesday the year before. You have to understand—this was back when I still believed the past could be left behind.

The music was stripped-down naked, just acoustic slide guitar and Big Mama's rich and round, tender but tough voice. The guitar steely and slippery with a thumping bass and the whine of the slide stinging like papercuts across the heart. The lyrics forlorn, bruised, weary of the stubbornness of hope, a woman in search of rest and somewhere to let go of the heavy load of her sorrows.

The closet door was half open and for some reason I peeked in. A line of empty wire hangers dangled from the wooden dowel. Billie never hung up anything. The boxes marked for Goodwill were still stacked against the back wall, my mother's hatbox on top, looking innocent. I opened it and lifted out the navy blue hat and saw my mother laughing, eyes of mischief, riding the carousel at the San Francisco zoo. I thought again of my original plan to set the whole confusion on fire.

I set the hat and the newspaper packing material aside and inventoried the other items: the kaleidoscope, the abalone shell, the motel key, the Kennedy button and the Polaroid of my mother on a windswept bluff above the ocean. I counted every letter, held each one briefly and tried to accept that the puzzle of my mother's death would never quite be solved.

The song ended and I carried the hatbox over and pulled all the 45s off the spindle and placed them in the bottom of the hatbox with everything else—now all my mother's secrets, even the pink lipstick envelope, were in one place, ready to burn.

But as I covered it all with the crumpled newspaper page and prepared to set the hat on top, I saw something I'd missed before—a small hole cut into the paper. I unfolded the page and smoothed it out some, and there in the lower portion of page seven of the July 18, 1969 *Lupoyoma Call & Record*, was a rectangular hole, one column wide by maybe four inches deep, scissored out rather carefully judging by the fairly straight edges.

The hole was in the corner of an ad for Main Street Furniture, and I didn't think my mother had been shopping for a new couch. I turned it over to page eight, an assortment of local club announcements and social news, a few small ads. She had snipped something out of this particular page—maybe a friend's engagement notice, or instructions for entering her cookies in the county fair, or even something she'd written herself.

It struck me as odd, even hard to believe, that whatever she'd clipped out had never turned up after she died. And the mystery of it broke the spell, pierced my sense of finality and defeat. This hole in the newspaper was yet another puzzle piece, and it might connect to other pieces, which might connect to the big picture I was trying to put together. I returned the paper to the hatbox and the hatbox to its place in the back of the closet. There'd be no fire today. You can't burn away a question that's stuck in your heart.

In the kitchen I opened the harvest gold fridge and found one can of cream soda behind a Tupperware bowl of leftover spaghetti. On the wall next to the fridge I noticed the calendar Darlene had brought home from the Bank of Lupoyoma. She'd tried so hard to fill it with exciting events which she marked with red scribbles and stars. It was Sunday, May 10, and in the appropriate calendar square, Darlene's twice-underlined handwriting said "Santa Rosa!" And the tiny capital letters printed in the corner said: "MOTHER'S DAY." All day long, no one had mentioned it.

GIVE ME AN F

On Monday I swung by the Weeping Willow on the Sting-Ray after baseball practice, but I'd forgotten it was Billie's day off. I checked at the library, but Alice said she'd been there and left and I might find her at The Music Box. According to Alice, Billie and Nate Henderson had recently met and "I guess they hit it off, which doesn't make sense because Nate is a pimply nerd and, well, Billie is Billie."

To me it did kinda make sense, because they were two brainy, creative types who danced to their own odd rhythms and were near social outcasts in Lupoyoma. Plus, I remembered what Alice had said about Nate being that particular kind of "cool."

I was anxious to tell Billie all about my bike ride, my talk with Frankie, the Big Mama record, and the hole cut out of the newspaper, but when I walked into the store Billie and Nate were each leaning on the counter, Nate on the merchant side, Billie on the customer side, both singing along loudly to some folky song—something about bringing keys to Los Angeles—and when the chorus came around they sang even louder than the stereo system.

I soon learned the *keys* in question were actually smuggled *kilos* of marijuana. The performer was a young man named Arlo, son of the famous folksinger Woody Guthrie, and the record was side one of the triple-album Woodstock soundtrack, just released days before. Nate had borrowed his mother's station wagon and driven two hours through the mountains to buy a copy in Santa Rosa, because The Music Box's order was late (as usual), and he could not stand to wait any longer.

"This is too important," he said, holding up the album cover. He pushed the slash of hair that cut across his face to the side so both eyes were visible, and he adopted a fussy-professor voice. "One day it will be preserved in the Smithsonian as an artifact of the cultural revolution."

"History, man." Billie said, and that started both of them on a giggle fit. "What's so damn funny?" I said.

Billie grabbed a handful of my shirt and led me behind the counter, then through a tiny storeroom-slash-office, and out the back door of the shop into the alley. From the pocket of her denim workshirt she produced a book of matches and something even I could identify as a half-smoked marijuana cigarette. She held the joint with one hand, and with the other hand she did that trick where you bend a match over the striker and light it with your thumb like snapping your fingers. Once the rolling paper caught fire, she stoked the cherry to a glowing red with a series of little sucks, then held it out to me with that trouble-loving gleam in her green eyes. The next thing I knew I was coughing out my first hit of weed while Billie pointed and laughed and mocked my struggle to breathe.

She was dressed like a railyard hobo that day, with her too-big workshirt only half tucked into her torn and faded and patched-up jeans, but there was something beautiful in the playful tilt of her head and the bounce of her red waves of hair, the way she swayed her hips to the music and rolled a shoulder forward as she started to speak, or flung her head back when she laughed. Maybe it was because we were all high, but maybe not. Maybe it was just peak Billie Armstrong, so alive and so certain of herself and the spark of the moment. Nate could hardly look away from her and hung on every word of her monologues, which were more expansive than ever. Like me—like Alice and Laurette and even Hank—Nate wanted to turn those pages. Maybe that was part of what others feared—not just what she said, but the fact that some of us were listening so closely.

Billie responded like a performer energized by the adoration of her audience. She told hitchhiking stories, hands tumbling in the air, she zigged and zagged from one amazing tale to the next. How she'd been teargassed in the streets of Chicago and locked up in a paddy wagon. How she'd slipped backstage at Woodstock and shared a joint with one of the drummers from the Grateful Dead. How she'd picketed the Miss America pageant, yanked her bra out the sleeve of her shirt like magic and added it to a bonfire.

She rifled off quotes from Janis Joplin and Bertrand Russell and speech-ified on the wisdom of John Lennon and Betty Friedan, the courage of Martin Luther King, and the evil stupidity of Phyllis Schlafly.

She jumped excitedly to her new job at the Weeping Willow, how it was typical capitalist sexist exploitation but culturally fascinating because Molly was Irish and Pop was Mexican and Sonny was a totally righteous dude who had been part of the occupation of Alcatraz. The son of a Black man and a Yaqui Indian woman, a Vietnam vet with a leg full of shrapnel, a Purple Heart and a blue metalflake Harley, chopped and raked. She gushed on about dig-ging the whole scene and said I absolutely must come that Saturday night to see Nate's band play on the Weeping Willow patio.

"It's gonna be outtasight," Nate said.

And Billie said, "History, man." Which started another laughing fit.

I forgot all about the news I had come to share. Getting high for the first time left me quiet and hyper-attentive to physical sensation. The air seemed thick and charged, like a hot afternoon humming with insects. My feet didn't quite reach the floor. I floated across the room to some record bins and flipped through the albums, trying to look discerning and unflustered.

Over by the counter the music and talk roared on in bursts of commis-eration and exultation. Music, politics, books, news—I wasn't always sure of the categories. Vaguely familiar names and phrases flicked by.... *Blonde on Blonde... Soul on Ice... Oswald and Ruby... My Lai and Manson... Gloria Steinem... Tom Wolfe... James Earl Ray... Instant Karma... Cesar Chavez... four dead girls in a Birmingham church.* Billie and Nate swooned in tandem as if their absolute agreement on each topic was a secret treasure they'd just discovered.

In the clearance bin I found a record I wanted—B.B. King, *Live at The Regal.* I floated over and set the album down on the counter next to the dis-play of kazoos. Nate picked it up and looked it over quizzically.

"Archer's like, totally obsessed with old blues music, man," Billie explained.

"Oh yeah," Nate said. "Little Walter, right?"

I nodded, impressed that he remembered, but also happy to respond without having to actually move my mouth in a purposeful way.

"What about this?" He pointed to the record player. "Hendrix, Airplane, Santana? Heavy shit, right?"

"Heavy," I said, and I felt heavier just saying the word. I was unusually conscious of the elasticity of my face as it formed sounds. "Not real blues, though," I managed to say.

"Ah, a purist!" Nate said, and I kind of liked the sound of that. I imagined a Boy Scout patch that said Blues Purist.

Billie said, "Oh, you gotta put on side two again, Nate. I want Archer to hear *The Fish Cheer*."

In a careful, deliberate, even reverent manner, Nate removed the record from the turntable and returned it to its proper sleeve, then slid another one out, deftly twirled it to the flipside and placed it on the turntable. "Dig this," he said as he dropped the needle.

It was the infamous performance of *Feel Like I'm Fixin' to Die Rag* by Country Joe McDonald, the one that eventually got the Woodstock album banned by concerned parents (or as Billie would say, "uptight hypocrites") in respectable homes all over the country. The man had three hundred thousand kids shouting the word *fuck* over and over at the full capacity of their lungs, then he delivered the most perfect laughing-to-keep-from-crying song ever sung against the Vietnam War.

Nate turned it up loud and Billie moved behind the counter and they sang along face to face. A swelling energy—a sense of inevitable change—reverberated in the recording and in the room. It was gloriously and shockingly defiant, which cranked up my stoned paranoia.

I kept listening for the little bell on the front door, certain the music could be heard out on the sidewalk, and some tubby, red-faced man with a bad combover and a sweat-drenched suit would soon enter pointing and screaming, "I know your parents!" And, in Lupoyoma, such testimony by itself could be enough to condemn each of us to our own home version of Hell on Earth.

But Billie and Nate kept on, undaunted, joyously shouting the words all the way through to the end of the song. And when the song was over, Nate kissed her. Right in front of me, not five feet away. Not a sloppy backseat makeout kiss, but not a friendly peck on the cheek either. Rather, a sudden, impulsive, sensuous kiss that looked like a question and an invitation. Billie didn't look that surprised. Or interested. She just lightly pushed him away and laughed if off.

CURRENT EVENTS

Predictably, it took an extra week or so for the national unrest to surface at Lupoyoma Junior High, but surface it did on Wednesday, May 13. Unpredictably, Robyn the horse artist—straight-A student, student body President, yearbook editor—organized a small contingent of seventh and eighth graders to stage a walkout and declare a student strike in opposition to the war and the draft and the Kent State shootings. Robyn stepped right up to Miss Lancaster during first recess and announced the plan, then more than a dozen kids marched across the playground chanting *Strike! Strike! Strike!* with ole Mancaster lumbering after them, threatening suspension and shouting that their parents would be notified immediately.

Craiger Robinson walked off the court in the middle of a dodgeball game and joined the protest, tugging his little brother Eugene along by the arm. Joey even took a few steps in that direction, but Timmy hurled the ball and nailed him in the back. "Where you going, asshat?"

I stood still, transfixed by this little breakdown of society, this intrusion of political reality on the sacred ground of junior high self absorption.

Joey walked over and stopped next to me. "You know, Robyn's brother is in Vietnam dodging bullets right now. And, last summer, Craiger's dad came home in a body bag."

No, I didn't know.

We watched our classmates cross the outer boundary of the school and march into the neighborhood. Timmy spat on the blacktop.

• • •

Lead pressman Vic Pendergrass hit the startup button, the buzzer sounded, and the press lurched into action. He ran over to the folder and picked up the first waste copies of the weekend edition, ran around the press tweaking knobs, hurried back to the folder, checking image alignment and ink coverage. I stood at the end of the conveyor ramp and threw the waste into a wheeled cart.

The sound of the startup buzzer drew my father and Leslie McGoogan from their front offices for the official press check. They came through the swinging doors side-by-side. McGoogan said, "Big plans for you and the Mrs. this weekend, Mike?"

My father said, "I swear, she's running me ragged, Les. Movies tonight. Dinner and dancing tomorrow. No rest for the wicked, as they say."

McGoogan nodded sympathetically.

The press began building up speed like a locomotive, and my father and McGoogan stood on opposite sides of the conveyor, pulling copies off and quickly scanning for any stop-the-press errors in the editorial content or the all-important ads. When they each signed off with a nod or hand signal, their workday was done. Vic cranked up the press to full speed, and the jackhammering sound of it created that familiar cocoon of noise that shut out the rest of the world.

Vic was a short and stocky Black man who'd been a sergeant in the Navy and learned the printing trade on the G.I. Bill. He was living proof of that old saying about swearing and sailors. I'd never heard anyone curse like Vic Pendergrass. At times he made it sound like poetry.

While the press was running my job was to gather the good copies in my arms and stack them in nearby bins, hurrying back and forth so papers wouldn't back up on the conveyor. But carefully, because if you dropped an armload it could quickly turn into Lucy-in-the-candy-factory. And if you caused a slowdown or the press had to be stopped, or worse yet, if the press broke down, oh my. You'd hear, "Fuck shit piss god-dammity-damn!" And a wrench might take wing and fly across the room.

That particular Friday all went well and, after the A-section run, the press crew took a break. Stan and the new guy Don went outside to check out the chrome rims on Don's 57 Rambler. "Revlon on a pig," Vic said.

I stayed at my workstation and began slamming B-sections into A-sections. Vic turned on the shop radio and sat in the Linotype operator's chair and lit a cigarette. He smoked non-filtered Lucky Strikes that smelled like manure on fire.

On the radio a newsman said two more students had been shot early that morning during an anti-war demonstration at Jackson State University in Mississippi. At first he said "two Negro men were killed," and did not give their names. Later in the broadcast he identified them as twenty-one-year-old law student Phillip Gibbs and seventeen-year-old high school student James Green. "Men, my black hairy ass!" said Vic. "Jesus-goddamn-Christ! Couple schoolboys is more like it."

The radio said the police claimed a sniper had fired two shots at them. Therefore they unleashed hundreds of shotgun blasts that happened to kill Gibbs and Green and wound twelve other people. But no snipers were reported shot, or arrested, or chased, or identified by the police or any other witnesses. Vic threw down his cigarette and stamped it out with his work boot. "What in the holy blue fuck is happening to this country!"

• • •

By the time I headed down Fourth Street, I could see the porch light was left on although the sky wasn't dark yet—a clear sign the parents had gone out and the house was empty. On the kitchen table, Darlene had left an unnecessarily detailed note that they were off to see *Paint Your Wagon*, with step-by-step instructions on how to take a TV dinner out of the freezer, preheat the oven to the desired temperature and pull back the foil on the fried chicken at the proper time, plus a reminder to turn the oven off when the cooking was done and leave the porch light on when I went to bed. The note was signed with a big buxom capital D.

I didn't have the patience to preheat the oven. I did pull back the foil on the chicken, then dialed up 450 and threw in the dinner, went to the living room, set up a TV tray and flipped on the television. Nothing but the six o'clock news on all three channels. Just the major networks, that's all we had in 1970 Lupoyoma. Three channels of fiery columns of black smoke and roaring napalm jets and dirty grim-faced soldiers that used to be kids. Caskets and body bags issuing onto the tarmac from the bellies of planes.

Screaming demonstrations, walkouts and strikes, marches and riots. Soldiers crawling across campus lawns with rifles and bayonets ready. Police with tear gas and billy clubs and shotguns and shields. Students with signs and slogans and bottles and bricks. Working class joes with baseball bats and uppercuts. Fat greasy politicians grandstanding, namecalling, fearmongering. Everyone angry. Everyone lying. No-one listening.

"Oh, this motherfucking war," I said to Cronkite, and I turned off the television and ate my unevenly cooked Swanson's Fried Chicken Dinner in the darkening silence.

HISTORY LESSONS

Saturday, I planned to check the morgue for the July 18, 1969 issue of the *Call & Record*, hoping to find out what my mother had cut out of page 8. It probably wouldn't tell me anything I didn't already know, but I wanted to make sure.

Sticking to my usual routine, I spent the first part of the day gathering the used type metal from the Linotype machine and the composing table, dragging the full hellbox to the pig room and melting all the metal down in the big iron cauldron. I skimmed the dross, poured the new pigs and left them to cool and harden. This was the part I loved, the sweaty ink-stained hundred-and-fuck part where I was a printer's devil, not just a janitor. On these mornings, alone in the back shop, in charge of something skilled and challenging and even dangerous, I was a working man. In the afternoons I was just a peon, a drudge, the cleanup boy.

The Giants were visiting the Dodgers in L.A. that afternoon, and I'd brought my own transistor radio so I could carry it room to room and listen to the game. The Dodgers went ahead three to one in the first inning, and it stayed that way while I swept the concrete floor of the back shop, wiped down the restroom, scoured the toilet and emptied wastebaskets. Moving up front, I dusted desks, wiped down phones, mopped the linoleum and emptied more wastebaskets, the sandy baritone of broadcaster Lon Simmons following me through the dour, shadowy offices.

Games against the rival Dodgers always came with heightened intensity, even in mid-May, but this one felt bigger than usual. The Giants had lost the first two of the four-game series, dropping into fifth place in the division, three games behind the Dodgers and eight behind the first place Cincinnati Reds. This Giants team was stacked with legends like Mays, Marichal and McCovey, so the record didn't at all reflect their potential. Or most fans' expectations. My father had already written them off. "Stick a fork in em, they're done," he'd said.

But to me they were heroes. And you don't give up on your heroes. They just needed something to turn it around, and a couple wins against the Dodgers could be the spark that got them going.

When the front office cleanup was done, I scrubbed my hands with hot water and Lava soap and made sure they were totally dry. I remembered all those months ago, during my training, Hank joshing me about Grandma Junia's exacting standards and matching serrated tongue (as if I wasn't already well acquainted). She always handpicked five pristine copies to be filed in the morgue, and she didn't want them smudged by the likes of me. I grabbed the five papers she'd left on the front counter, and I went to the locked door at the end of the hallway, key in hand.

On the radio it was the sixth inning, and the Giants had just tied it up on a home run by the big first baseman Willie "Stretch" McCovey. In the seventh, they managed to pull ahead, but I didn't hear how because I was busy combing the shelves for the July 18, 1969 issue. I carefully flipped through the entire 1969 section. There should've been at least three or four copies still on file, but I didn't find a single one. It was weird, but I figured Hank probably misfiled them in the wrong year, or had forgotten to file them at all, or maybe the press broke down and for once Vic couldn't "jimmyrig the thingamajig and limpdick the bastard home."

Maybe next Saturday I would set aside time to look further, although maybe it was pointless. For all I knew, my mother had carefully scissored out a recipe for potato salad or a coupon for five percent off at Sprouse-Rietz, then simply used the pages to conceal the stuff in the hatbox in her usual tidy, organized way. Still, I kinda wanted an answer.

But on that day I didn't have time. Baseball practice that afternoon, then off to the Weeping Willow to see Nate's band and hang out with Billie. I still hadn't had a chance to tell her about my visit with Frankie, much less the missing paper, but I was hoping there'd be an opportunity that night.

In the top of the eighth inning, while I was washing up, the Giants added another run on a second blast by McCovey, and as I headed out the back shop door, they held on to win the game five to four. Maybe we weren't done yet.

• • •

Nate Henderson was the bass player and the leader of the band. He'd given the band its name, Mellow Day. He'd handpicked the players, led the practice sessions in his parents' garage and handled all the bookings, and when he'd gone away to Santa Rosa Junior College, the other members had failed to find a new bass player, or a new practice space, or any paying gigs.

Everyone knew Nate never wanted to study business in the first place and only enrolled to avoid the draft. At the time, local draft boards had god-like power. In Lupoyoma, that meant any healthy eighteen-year-old male was guaranteed to be drafted unless he was a registered college student or his family happened to have a close friend—perhaps a business associate—on the draft board. The saying was, if you have the dough, you don't have to go.

Nate didn't have the dough, so off to college he went. But in late 1969 the government held the first draft lottery, and Nate's birthdate came up number 328 out of 366. For the foreseeable future, there was no real chance he'd be drafted, college or not. He dropped out of JC, moved back to town, got the guys back together, and Mellow Day quickly reclaimed its status as a popular working band. They played poolside birthday parties for the cheerleader daughters of Lupoyoma councilmen, spiked-punch dances for the local chapter of Rainbow Girls, and the low-budget weddings of recent high school sweethearts expecting to be parents in nine months or less.

And that Saturday night they were booked to play at the Weeping Willow Resort & Trailer Court. The way I heard it, this was something of an experiment. Sonny the new cook had suggested to Molly that live music might bring in some extra business, and Billie the new waitress had supported the idea quite enthusiastically, arms waving about and such. Molly had fretted about the cost but agreed to try it once and even to consider making it a regular thing for the summer months—if all went well that night. No one knew ahead of time that it would turn out to be an historic performance. (Well, maybe Nate and Billie knew.)

BURN BABY BURN

The band was still setting up when I got to the Weeping Willow parking lot. The big Chevy station wagon that belonged to Nate's mom was backed up to the door, and Billie was helping Nate and the others lug equipment through the game room and out to the patio. Billie yoo-hooed me over to help with a large speaker cabinet. As we worked, I told her briefly that I'd been to see Frankie and had other news, and Billie said, "Oh, we need to talk, I want all the details, for sure, man." She seemed excited, promising we'd catch up later that night.

Just seeing her, I felt some of the accumulated dread of the past several days melt away. She'd swapped her waitress uniform for the muslin dress she'd bought at Frankie's store, with the colorful embroidery and a purple sash at her waist. Beads and bangles in abundance, her red hair unleashed, the huge tinted sunglasses. Some customer she'd served just a few hours ago might not even recognize her now, hands on hips, mock bragging how she was Mellow Day's official groupie, roadie and sound-chick all-in-one.

The band opened with *Light My Fire* by the Doors. Out on the patio in the warm twilight all the picnic tables were filling up and several people were in line at the walkup window. Molly had to be pleased with the crowd. Teenagers mostly, but older than me—weekenders' sons and daughters in trunks and bikinis, local highschoolers in tees and cutoffs, sitting on the benches and tabletops and standing along the railing, heads and shoulders bobbing with the beat.

I sat at a strategically located table with Billie and Alice Terwilliger. Billie helped Nate get the amplifier settings just right with a series of hand signals during the first couple numbers, then she whooped and hollered and clapped along to every song, and whirled around the patio on her bare feet. "Look at her go," said Alice.

"Crazy, huh?" I said.

"Amazing," Alice said. "So free."

Hank Timmons sat on top of another picnic table with his cousin Trey Morgan. Their mothers were sisters, but Trey and Hank were more like brothers than cousins. Grew up playing together, fighting, competing, teaming up. Same sandy blonde hair, but Trey smaller, leaner, more tightly wound, more of a ne'r-do-well, the kind who got in fights, dropped out of high school and went to work at his dad's body shop.

At the same table sat Timmy Bilderback and Joey Quarterman, slightly separate, watching Hank and Trey closely, like nerds fetishizing the cool kids. All four watched and pointed at Billie dancing by herself, and they joked and laughed and arm-punched each other.

Hank strode out to Billie and started to dance as if joining her, but she simply spun and twirled away, weaving between other dancers, uninterested in partnership, possibly with anyone, but definitely with Hank. Trey and the other boys laughed and pointed and furtively took turns on a pint-size bottle barely disguised in a brown paper bag. Hank came back to the table, jerked the bottle away from Trey and took a big couldn't-care-less swig.

Alice Terwilliger stood up in her white bellbottoms and fake leather fringe vest like one of those desperately uncool models in the teenage section of the Monkey Ward catalog. She politely but awkwardly excused herself past several dancing couples, and when she reached the front of the crowd she started to dance a few steps away from Billie, slowly and tentatively. But Billie turned and welcomed her with bright eyes, laughing and dancing toward her, and Alice broke into a big girl-party smile.

Trey pointed and sucker-punched Hank's arm. "I think you're out of luck, cousin. Looks like she bats for the other team." Hank scoffed, rubbed his arm, took another drink from the paper bag. "We'll see about that," he said.

It appeared the live music experiment was a complete success—right up until Nate stepped to the microphone and said, "We want to dedicate this next song to the students at Kent State and Jackson State who were murdered by government pigs!"

The chatter of the crowd turned to a stunned murmur. The drummer started up on hi-hat and snare, tick-tick-pop, tick-tick-pop, and the band launched into John Fogerty's *Fortunate Son*, a song that calls out the long tradition of poor boys fighting the wars that rich men start and benefit from.

As the song ended Nate pulled a piece of paper from his shirt pocket. His voice crackled as he read. "Nathaniel P. Henderson…Selective service number…twenty-eight…four…fifty-three…one-nine-seven." Some laughed nervously, some raised their glasses, a few clapped. We all knew Nate was reading from his draft card, and when he pulled a Zippo lighter out of his pocket and sparked it up, there were gasps and shouts of *oh-no!* and *don't!*

But Billie yelled, "Go for it!" And Nate touched the flame to the corner of the card and held it high for the crowd to see. And Billie shouted "Burn baby burn!"

One guy started to chant, *no more war* and others joined in. I wanted to join in, too. I gathered breath and opened my mouth, but Hank suddenly stood and started shouting *USA, USA*, knocking his bottle on the table in rhythm. Trey and Timmy chanted along, but no one else. *No more war* was drowning out *USA USA*. Hank gave a dismissive, disgusted wave toward the stage, and a let's-go jerk of his head to his table, and the four boys walked off, disappeared into the game room and toward the parking lot, to a smattering of laughter and reinvigorated chants of *no more war, no more war.*

• • •

Billie, Alice and I were helping the band load their stuff back into Mrs. Henderson's car. Sonny was there too, carrying out the heaviest amplifiers two-at-a-time. Clusters of kids still milled around the parking lot. Hank's Mustang came rolling in off First Street, glasspack muffler rumbling low, Trey sitting shotgun, the younger boys stuffed in the back seat. Hank's window was down, and he brought the car to a stop right behind the station wagon. He stuck his head out and yelled to the little crowd, "Hey everybody, party at space 19. Come on by." And someone in the crowd said, *Yeah, party down!* Hank pointed at Billie. "You too," he said. "You can even bring your commie friend Nate."

"Oh yeah, definitely," Trey said. "Bring that wuss along!" And he cackled.

"Calm down, Trey," Hank said, then back to Billie in a friendly voice, "We're gonna make Harvey Wallbangers. You should come. It'll be fun."

"I just might," Billie said, with a smirk and a hand on one hip.

The Mustang rolled away.

"I'd be careful with that one," Sonny said.

"Hank? He's harmless," Billie said. "Just blowing off steam, probably trying not to think about where he's headed in a couple weeks. I bet he's more afraid than he lets on."

Sonny said, "You never know how fear shows up."

HOW'S YOUR DRINK?

Space 19 was Trey's place, isolated at the end of a dirt driveway that branched off the main loop of the park, a seedy old singlewide that was once the caretaker's residence and now sat rusting next to Bottlerock Creek, surrounded by unruly weeds, crumbling tires and car parts. I suppose the rent was cheap.

It was just me and Billie walking out the driveway and up to the front yard. Alice said she had to go home but might sneak out later, and Nate didn't want anything to do with Trey Morgan, who he said bullied him all through school. But Billie wanted Harvey Wallbangers—they were supposed to be the cool new thing. And I'd never been to one of these local house parties. The parents wouldn't be home for hours so I thought, what the heck.

It wasn't much, really. Outside, three tourist dudes chugging beer and drooling over Hank's Mustang. In the front room, the chunky driving rhythm of some hard rock band turned up loud and distorted on a cheap little component stereo. A local jock making out with a tourist chick on a saggy brown couch flanked by milk-crate side tables. Joey Quarterman blood-eyed and splayed out on a bean-bag chair with a ripped seam, tiny white pellets spilling onto the dirty shag carpet. Timmy, already clumsy drunk, barreling across the room and banging me in the chest with the pint bottle of tequila.

I took a taste. "Jesus, that's terrible!" I took another.

"Shit makes you crazy," he said, and grinned like that was a bonus. Then, pointing at Billie, "Hey… the sister… I'm supposed to tell you… Hank is in the kitchen."

Hank hollered out, "Hey Red! Come meet Harvey Wallbanger." And Billie drifted off to join a gathering of seven or eight people in the kitchen, which was really just across the room on the other side of a counter.

I checked out the music. A fiery red album cover that said Grand Funk.

The current track, *High Falootin' Woman.* The rest of Trey's record collection was in the same vein: Led Zeppelin, Deep Purple, Steppenwolf. Some new band I'd never heard of called Black Sabbath.

Billie came back from the kitchen and handed me a can of Colt 45. "You should probably stick to beer."

I popped the top and tipped the can to my mouth. It was worse than the tequila. "What about that?" Eyeing the plastic cup in her hand. "Is that the Wallbanger thing?"

"Yeah. Pretty strong, though," she said. "Here, taste."

Sweet and smooth. Like an orange creamsicle laced with vodka. I took a triple gulp.

"Hey, don't drink the whole thing," she said.

"Whoa there, Bullseye." Hank suddenly appeared, snatched the cup out of my hand as I slurped another big pull. He handed it back to Billie. "I made this one special for you," he said. "It's got a little extra kick. Too strong for him." He looked in the cup. "Way too strong," he said. "I'll make another one for you, kid. More your speed." He headed back to the kitchen bar with Billie's cup. I gave the beer to Joey, marooned on his bean-bag island.

Trey showed up shortly with two cups and firm instructions from Hank. He carefully distributed the drinks with showy emphasis. "This one's for you, and *this* one's for *you.*" Like I was ten years old or something.

"What's with the antique flag?" Billie said.

Over by the front door, a slim jut of wall, maybe four feet wide, stuck out into the room, creating the trailer park version of a foyer. I think it existed expressly for the purpose of blocking the view to the kitchen as you entered the lovely home, so your first impression would be of the stylish wood-paneled living room. Here was this lonely expanse of white sticking out like a Stanley Kubrick monolith and decorated with a man-size flag of the United States, hung vertically and nearly reaching the crusty orange shag.

This kind of non-traditional flag display was already a *LIFE Magazine* hippie-crash-pad cliché in those days, so it struck me as unexpected here amongst the taped up *Penthouse* centerfolds and the ashtrays made of large-bore pistons. Plus, it was a forty-eight-star flag, out of date now for more than a decade.

"It's a family heirloom," Trey said. "Pretty fucking cool, huh." And we stood contemplating the flag while Trey bragged about his and Hank's grandfather, Cecil Morgan Sr., how he fought the Nazis during World War II, came home with one of those million dollar wounds and a footlocker full of uniforms and medals, pictures with his buddies, some naked lady playing cards, plus a real Nazi sword. And this big American flag. After the old man died, Trey ended up with the footlocker, traded the sword for a four-barrel Holley carburetor but kept the playing cards and the flag, which was now tacked to the wall with a couple roofing nails in honor of Hank's impending service to the good ole U.S. of A.

"But I don't expect you to understand patriotism," Trey said, staring Billie down. "You probably think your buddy Nate's some kind of hero, making a big show when there's no way he'll ever get called up his number's so high. I'd say he's a coward is what I'd say."

"Man, they sell you boys that hero vs. coward crap and you eat it up, you can't get enough," said Billie. "Pure unadulterated bullshit and you just line up to pay for it with your lives."

Trey looked about to fire off another salvo in this verbal skirmish, but Hank showed up all calm and friendly drunk, with a hand on Trey's shoulder just in time. "That's okay, Trey. Free country, different strokes and all that. Hey, how's your drink, Billie?"

"Yeah, yeah, drink up," said Trey, walking away.

"What about you, Trey? You signed up yet?" Billie called after him.

"Flat feet," Hank butted in loudly. "They wouldn't take him," he said, but then he shot us a not-really wink-wink and used his finger to make little circles by his temple.

THE WINDOW OUTSIDE

This is the part I don't remember well.

I woke up lying on the saggy brown couch. The makeout couple gone. No music, no laughing or chattering from the kitchen. Aching neck. Blurred vision. Trey Morgan looming over me, shaking my shoulder, saying something echoey and far away like *wake up kid, party's over, time to go.* He pulled me upright by my shirt. *Where's Billie,* I said. *She left….Why—what happened?… You had too much to drink, kid—go home and sleep it off.*

I couldn't get my legs under me. Trey held me up and walked me to the front door, already open to the night, pushed me out onto the stoop and closed the door behind me. Somehow I staggered down the stairs and down the dark driveway to the main loop of the park and then around to the parking lot by the cafe.

Sonny the cook was there, leaning on the old Fairlane, smoking a cigarette, talking to someone. Alice. *Where's Billie,* she said, and I said, *I don't know.* Sonny's face through curling smoke, *are you okay?… I gotta get home.*

Wait, Alice said, but I didn't.

The cafe was closed, the street empty, half a moon above. I started to cross the lawns of Library Park, tripped on my own feet by the swing-set. On my knees in the sandy dirt, an insistent whooshing in my ears. Something is wrong, I thought. I passed out and Billie just left me there? Where is she? Why was Trey in such a fucking hurry to get me out the door? A stubborn fog muffled my thoughts, like when they gave me the gas at the dentist's office. No. Like that time I took one of my mother's pills.

Something is wrong.

I rose to my feet, turned and lurched off in the other direction. If I took the back way to space 19, no one would see. I stumbled out of the park, up First Street. Took the rear entrance to the school grounds. Running across the blacktop, falling, skinned knees and hands. Cutting through the baseball field. My stomach rolled. I stuck a finger down my throat until I wretched and threw up right on the pitcher's mound. Then down into the slash of Bottlerock Creek, the water low and the banks overgrown with thorny brush.

Rounding another bend in the creek bed, a square of light above the bank. I scrambled up and found myself behind Trey Morgan's trailer, shimmering under the moon. Wet feet in muddy sneakers, bloody stinging hands, heart pounding, breath on fire.

The light came from a back bedroom window, filtered yellow through an old ratty curtain that hung slightly cockeyed leaving a thin pie-wedge uncovered in one corner of the window. I found a stray cinderblock that had settled into the dirt over the winters and was secured by weeds and time. I lifted it free and winced at the sound of the grass tearing loose and the suck of the earth. Suddenly aware of transgression and risk—trespass on my part, the threat of exposure. I placed the cinderblock on its side, an eight-inch boost. I stepped up and maneuvered my eyes to the gap where the curtain didn't cover the window.

• • •

This is the part I can't unsee.

Billie lay sprawled out on an unmade twin bed, her body limp. Her beautiful muslin dress unbuttoned and laid open to the waist, breasts exposed, the hem bunched up at her hips. Hank standing at the foot of the bed, blue jeans and jockey shorts around his ankles. White t-shirt, pinkwhite bottom, hips slamming against her. Billie's body rocked with the impact, and for a blink of time I thought she was willing, but then I saw her face. Mouth slack, eyelids fluttering half open.

"Heeeyyy," she said, one long slurred syllable.

Hank said, "Shit! She's waking up, you assholes gonna help or what?" Two figures entered my view from the other side of the room. Trey and Timmy. "Get her arms," Hank said. Trey looped around behind him and pinned Billie's right arm to the bed. Timmy hurried to the other side and pinned her left arm down, his eyes trained on Hank.

"You're on deck, Bilderback!" Hank shouted, even as he kept ramming into her.

Timmy yelled, "Hell yeah!" His eyes wild, face beading sweat, mouth twisted into a snarl, one hand mashing at Billie's breasts.

All the muscles under Hank's white t-shirt tightened, and he let go a long ugly grunt. "That's how it's done, kiddies! That's how it's done."

"Hey, no," she said. "Please. Wait." Some timid dawn in her blurry voice, head rolling side to side, eyes swimming the room, mouth opening without words.

"She's gonna scream," said Timmy.

"Joey, cover her mouth," Hank said. I couldn't see Joey but there was a beat of silence, then Hank said, "Joey, cover her goddamn mouth."

"No," said Joey's voice. "I won't." And I saw his back go out the bedroom door.

Hank hollered. "You leave, I'll kill you. Trey, go after him, don't let that little fucker leave."

All at once the scene fractured into chaos. A pounding rumbled the air like a car wreck. Knuckles and metal. A rain of glass. A distant voice shouted, "Open the door. Open the fucking door!" Trey left the room, Timmy couldn't control both of Billie's arms. She scratched his face with her free hand, drove Hank backwards with a kick to the chest. She bared her teeth and growled like a cornered animal, launched herself off the bed and staggered out of the room in a screaming, half-naked blur.

Hank stood at the door of the bedroom with an ear cocked toward the racket, not brave enough to go and investigate. Timmy drunk, confused, still grasping for arms that were no longer there.

I jumped down from the cinderblock and skirted around to a front corner of the trailer, staying hidden. Sonny the cook, on the stoop by the front door with his finger in Trey's face. "I'd go back inside if I were you, or this won't end well." And Trey stepped backward through the doorway, disappeared into the trailer.

In the moonlight a hulking shape hurried away on the dirt drive, shadowy at first, then separating into two figures, one was Alice Terwilliger, the other was Billie Armstrong, shaking and mumbling, covering her nakedness with an American flag wrapped like a blanket around her shoulders.

OUT OF REACH

I slipped down into the creek bed and careened my way back to the school grounds, climbed out behind the bleachers, sat down in the dugout on the first-base side, gasping for air, head in my hands. I closed my eyes and saw it all again. And what if she had seen me, somehow found my panicked eyes in the corner of that window, pleaded for my help and I didn't move. I could've screamed, I could've banged on the window. But I didn't. I watched in silence, confounded, dumbstruck, paralyzed, mind agape, an empty hole of time where a reaction should've been, almost any reaction, but no, just a numb fear I couldn't explain. I watched it all and didn't move.

I slapped myself across the face, trying to sober up, and it stung but also carried a charge, a stab of clarity. It felt right and I did it again. And again. But it wasn't enough. I beat myself on the forehead with the heels of my hands. I made a fist and punched myself in the mouth. But it wasn't enough.

• • •

Early in the morning, I snuck out to the kitchen and found a note taped to the harvest gold refrigerator. *Gone fishing! Just kidding, we're off to the coast for the day. Back for dinner. You kids be good. ~D.*

Grownups can be so naive.

I stared into the depths of the fridge for a long time and finally decided on a tall glass of cold milk. I chugged it down, noticed my swollen, tender lip, refilled the glass, carried it back to my room. I lay on top of the blue wave bedspread, stared at the ceiling and listened to the house. I heard the shower come on in the bathroom, so Billie had somehow made it home and into her room, apparently without alerting anyone, least of all myself. I could barely remember blundering in the back door, collapsing into bed, relieved the parents weren't home from their date.

The shower ran on and on, and I had to pee. At the bathroom door I heard her choked sobs. I didn't knock. I went back to my room, stared at the ceiling and held my bladder. My mind was still sluggish, muddled, couldn't keep up with itself, running, circling, struggling to even watch the replays, to accept what I saw, what I did. What I didn't do. Much less to ask, what now?

Sinking back into sleep, I had a dream that Billie and I were flying together. I had many dreams of flying as a boy, but in those dreams I always flew alone. In this dream, Billie and I had developed a technique that involved running right off the edge of Flat Top Hill west of Lupoyoma City. We matched the direction and speed of the wind at the exact moment that we leapt into the air. We held hands with our arms spread out like birds touching wings. We rode the wind out over the night-glimmer of the town and coasted down to the damp shore of Lupoyoma Lake like human hang gliders.

I stayed in my room all morning, only coming out when the bathroom was finally free, to piss for like a minute straight and get a bowl of Cheerios, which I ate sitting cross-legged on the blue wave bedspread.

The house was pin-drop quiet. I had checked and seen Billie's door was closed. She had drawn the curtains over the window between our rooms. No light shone through them, no shadows moved behind them. Which was fine, because I wasn't ready to meet up with her face-to-face in the kitchen and watch her stammer to explain why she hadn't gone to work and hadn't come out of her room as she usually did fresh in the morning, hands dancing, ideas bursting out of her mouth, green eyes alight. And what would I say, anyway?

I was waiting. And I was hiding from whatever I was waiting for. I knew that much.

• • •

The doorbell rang around noon. I didn't want to answer it, but I didn't want it to keep ringing. The Giants game had just started, and I was listening on the transistor radio, seeking a distraction, a retreat into the illusion of normalcy. I threw on my old flannel robe and answered the door with the radio in one hand and the earpiece in my ear. It was Alice, in a prim looking dress that let on she'd come straight from Reverend Jameson's Sunday service. "Is Billie here?" she said. I pulled the earpiece out of my ear. She looked me up and down. "Hangover, huh?" And she walked on past, leaving me to close the door. "Which way to Billie's room?"

I showed the way and lingered in the hallway as I replaced my earpiece. Alice knocked. No answer. Tried the door. Locked. "Billie, it's Alice. You okay?" A pause, then the turning of the lock, the door opening. I turned away like I wasn't interested, heard the lock click back into place.

Back in my room I sat on the floor, leaning against the wall, next to the window. Billie had drawn the curtains but hadn't noticed the window was open just a smidge. I set the radio on the floor, kept the earpiece in, but turned the volume down low. In one ear, the soothing cadences of Lon Simmons calling the game. In the other ear, whenever they raised their voices or moved close enough to the window, occasional scraps of Billie and Alice.

"They ruined my dress."

"You were half naked. I ripped that flag off the wall to cover you."

"I don't understand. Those drinks hit me so hard. I don't even remember getting home."

"Sonny drove and I walked you inside. We got lucky—Archer was asleep and your folks weren't here."

This was the final day of the four-game set against the Dodgers, the Giants having lost two of the first three. It was still early in the season, but it felt like the team was already on the edge of disaster. They really needed this game to even up the series, shore up their morale and get out of L.A. with their self-respect intact. But after three innings, they were losing two to nothing.

"How did I not see it coming?"

"It's not your fault, Billie. You need to call the police."

"In this town? What good would that do?"

"It's a crime! He should go to jail."

"I never should've come to this backwards fucking town."

If Billie did call the police, then I could tell. I would *have* to tell, wouldn't I? I was an eyewitness, the one who could back up her story. I could send Hank to jail instead of Vietnam. But she might be right about going to Chief Timmons. Or anyone else. Most people in Lupoyoma would never believe such a thing about Hank. The truth would sound like a lie. If I hadn't seen it, I wouldn't have believed it myself.

"Does Sonny know?"
"He doesn't know how far it went."
"Good. Don't tell anyone, Alice. Please. I don't want anyone else to know."
"But—"
"Just don't, okay? Swear you won't."

If Billie didn't want anyone to know, then I didn't have to tell. I *couldn't* tell. Which meant I wouldn't have to answer questions or justify my actions. My inaction. But then I would have to walk around forever like the whole thing didn't happen. Go to school, go to work, play baseball, grow up. Like I didn't see what I saw. And I would never be rid of the secret.

"But what if I get pregnant?"
"Oh my god. From one time? Don't even say that."
"It's happened before, though."
"What do you mean? Like what happened last night?"
"No, not like that, but a one-night stand, you know, and a couple months later I'm in some shady doctor's office on the east side of Cleveland. I'm not going through that again."
"What would you do?"
"I don't know, but no way I'm raising Hank Timmons' kid. No way."

Knocked up, unwed mother, child out of wedlock, bastard. Even a kid like me understood this was *Scarlet Letter* territory in 1970 Lupoyoma, a full-blown scandal in waiting. Socially acceptable options were limited to marriage or adoption, and even giving up a child for adoption was frowned on. A girl could disappear from school for months, rumors would fly, the girl would return, sad and self-conscious, classmates whispering in the hallway. Abortion was technically, just barely, legal in California, but not in Doc Meaney's office. And in Lupoyoma, single motherhood required an explanation—preferably a dead husband.

In the bottom of the fifth inning, the Dodgers pounded out six runs and I could feel the game, maybe the whole season, slipping out of reach. Not technically, not mathematically, but emotionally out of reach. The Dodgers didn't score again, but they didn't need to. Final score, eight-zero, leaving the Giants still mired deep in fifth place.

A SUMMER COLD

She managed to convince the parents she was sick, and she hardly came out of her room the next two days. I saw her Monday morning in the kitchen, barefoot, Woodstock t-shirt, puffy eyes and hair an orange bramble, pulling hot cherry Pop-Tarts out of the toaster, quickly dropping them on a plate.

I felt exposed and I figured she did too. I mumbled good morning, she only nodded. "Heard you're sick," I said, but like a question, and I guess I was hoping for some tiny sign that she wanted to talk.

She pretended to stifle a cough, looked at the plate. "Just a little bug," she said. "I'll be fine." And she took her Pop-Tarts down the hallway.

• • •

I walked to school and timed my arrival so it would be too late to hang out with anyone. During first period, we had to pick study partners for the final two weeks of preparation for the big Constitution Test, one of the scariest things in the life of every eighth grader in the country. Ninety minutes, a hundred questions and a number two pencil between you and graduation, and beyond that the imagined paradise of high school.

I caught Timmy and Joey both glancing my way, so I quickly asked the girl at the desk right in front of me—of all people, Robyn the horse artist. Joey would've been an okay partner, but Timmy would be no help—there was a fair chance he wouldn't pass the test, period. And right now I couldn't look at him without seeing the back bedroom in Trey Morgan's trailer. I wanted to punch him dead in the face, but without him knowing why.

Prepping for the Constitution Test with Robyn would be a handy excuse to avoid Timmy and Joey altogether for a couple weeks. Except at baseball. And, unfortunately, we had a game that very evening. The Paperboys vs. The Odd Fellows, round two.

This time the fearsome and unsmiling Craiger Robinson dominated our lineup. My first trip to the plate, he plunked me in the ribs. I jogged to first and stood on the bag rubbing my side while Craiger said, "Sorry, Archie, must've slipped out of my hand."

It hurt pretty good and felt like justice, a little payback for the hidden ball trick and everything else. Or maybe just smart strategy on Craiger's part, because after that I struck out twice, flinching on every pitch, bailing out and taking wild swings. Coach Fish screaming from the bench, "You're stepping in the bucket, boy. Stop stepping in the damn bucket."

We lost nine to one. During the fifth inning Timmy and Joey got in an all-out fistfight, supposedly over a pop fly that fell between them. Two runners scored while they rolled around in the grass behind the pitcher's mound. Vic the pressman was umpiring. He ran out and pulled them both up to their feet and held them apart by their collars. "You better pull your big heads out of your little asses and play ball," he said. Other players laughed, I didn't.

After the game, all of our players long-faced, hanging our heads while Coach Fish blah-blahed about playing as a team. Timmy and Joey still giving each other the stank-eye.

Robyn brought in the scorebook and handed it to Coach. I hadn't even noticed that Alice wasn't in her usual spot in the bleachers scoring the game. Turned out Alice had resigned, quit the team, no explanation, and Robyn was a last-minute sub.

I ignored Timmy and Joey and left the field with Robyn. We walked together up Main Street in the soft light of the evening. Just a boy in his baseball uniform, glove on his hand, and a girl in a plain dress, schoolbooks hugged to her chest. We made plans to get together and study for the Constitution Test. She told me the student council had booked Nate's band, Mellow Day, for the Eighth Grade Graduation Dance. I asked about her brother Ricky serving in Vietnam, and she said her family was worried they hadn't heard from him in a while.

I'd never really talked with Robyn before, and it felt good, but in a weird way that made me notice how alone I was feeling. I had so much to say that couldn't be said. Not to my mother or father or Laurette, not Hank or Billie or Joey or Timmy. Or anyone else, including Robyn.

• • •

Because of the game, I was late for dinner, but Darlene had concocted some kind of hamburger stew and kept it on the stove. She plopped some into a bowl, asked if I'd talked to Billie that day, and I said she'd made Pop-Tarts in the morning but that's all I knew.

"I'm worried about her," Darlene said. "She's hardly been out of her room and I bet those Pop-Tarts are all she's had to eat today."

"Oh, it's just a summer cold," my father said from the recliner. "Probably picked up whatever Archer had a while back."

I ate some of that stew and went to my room. The curtains were still drawn on the window between the rooms; night had fallen but no lamplight shone from her side. And not a sound.

The next day, same story, except I didn't see Billie at all, even for Pop-Tarts in the morning. I worked after school, came home in the evening, and Darlene gave me the sandwich she'd left in the fridge for Billie. She said Billie had forced down a few spoonfuls of leftover stew and gone back to bed already. Darlene and my father briefly bickered over whether Doc Meaney should be consulted. I went to my room and lay on the bedspread in the twilight gloom listening to the Giants lose yet another game. Any hope for a division championship was fading fast.

Late into the night, the game long over, I lay propped up, staring at the silent curtained window, my runaway mind conjuring half-dreams that Billie's lifeless body was waiting in the bed on the other side of the wall.

• • •

But on Wednesday I rushed home after school to check on her and found the curtain was pulled back and a slant of afternoon sunlight played on the painted window. I went around and knocked on her door and got no answer. I took the chance to open the door and peek in. She wasn't there, and I wasn't sure if that was a good sign or not.

I needed something to stop my brain from running in circles, bouncing from one fear to the next like carnival bumper cars. I went to the closet and pulled a selection of 45s out of their hiding place in the hatbox. *Mean Old World* by Little Walter, *Broken Heart* by Memphis Minnie, *You Can't Lose What You Ain't Never Had* by Muddy Waters, and *My Heavy Load*, the Big Mama Thornton record Frankie had given me. I stacked them up on the record changer and turned the selector to play. I lay on the old corded rug, staring at the blank ceiling, letting the music seep into my body.

Sometimes you just want to hear a sad song. You want to sink into that sinking feeling in your heart, lower yourself into the cool thick mud of it, gritty and dark, dirty and soothing. You want someone else's words to put shape to the feeling, someone else's voice to echo your discontent, a slide guitar or harmonica to underline it. You want the blues. You need it. Turned up loud. The bass thrumming in the floor and rising up into your limbs.

I listened to the records, maybe twenty minutes worth, then carefully put them all back in the hatbox. I saw those three boxes marked for Goodwill still stacked in the closet and I remembered how I'd forbidden Billie to go through them. Now it occurred to me that might've been a mistake.

Inside the top box I found nothing but Butterick sewing patterns and pieces of fabric. I set that box on the floor and opened the second box. And right on top was the blue-flowered sundress in which my mother had left the world—folded neatly but still on a hanger and wrapped in a clear plastic bag like it had come back from the dry cleaners.

In a horrible flash I imagined walking down Main Street and running into some strange woman wearing my mother's dress. I didn't think I could handle that. I folded up the dress, still in the plastic bag, and stuffed it into the hatbox along with everything else. Except the hat itself, which wouldn't fit back in the box now, so I put the hat on the shelf and took the hatbox to my room and stashed it deep in my closet.

Then I stood out in the backyard with Hank's old baseball bat, killing time and nervous energy by hitting apples over the fence. The apple tree had been ignored ever since my mother's death, and the result of our negligence was a collection of overripe fruit scattered on the ground, of interest only to neighborhood yellowjackets and restless Little Leaguers.

I was still there around six o'clock when Billie came through the gap in the fence in her waitress uniform. "Hey," was all she said. I faked a casual chin nod that she didn't even acknowledge on her rush past me and into the house. Definitely the shortest conversation I would ever have with Billie Armstrong, but I figured it was a hopeful sign that she'd been to work. I left the bat leaning against the back stairs and followed her inside.

On her way through the kitchen, she told Darlene she'd eaten a hot dog at work, she was tired and just needed to lie down.

"Yes, you need your rest," Darlene said. "Don't do too much too soon. You'll have a relapse."

From behind the newspaper held up in front of his face, my father's voice said, "You don't want to miss any more work."

CARNIVAL SOUP

Later, the parents were watching television, a rerun of Bewitched, the one where naughty cousin Serena turns into a hippie—possibly the corniest hippie ever portrayed—and goes to jail after a riot at a love-in. I'd seen it before, and I went to my room with the good intention to re-read something in my U.S. Government textbook.

The light was on in Billie's room, and I heard voices on the radio, though I couldn't make out the words. Nate had told us to check out an FM station out of San Francisco, KSAN, which he said was "the first radio station run by hippies." Real hippies that is, not like Serena on Bewitched. I tapped on the glass until Billie came to the window and tugged it open.

"Is that the station Nate was talking about?"

"The coolest station in the history of the world," she said, mocking Nate's enthusiasm.

"You feeling better?"

"I'll be okay." She brought the vanity stool over and sat down, smiled weakly.

I sat on the floor cross-legged, facing the window. "Ready for the big weekend?" I said.

Memorial Day Weekend was an important milestone on the Lupoyoma calendar, especially for businesses like the Weeping Willow. The unofficial start of summer on the lake, tourist families rolling into town in their campers and station wagons—the lucrative combination of bored children and dads with wallets. All in honor of our fallen soldiers, of course.

"Molly says lots of overtime," she said. "Might make enough to pay off Sonny's car."

"That would be cool. No more hitchhiking, road trips all summer like we said, right?"

"Yeah, for sure," she said, but she looked down at her lap.

• • •

The trucks and trailers started rolling into town Friday morning. A group of them passed me as I walked to school: the snow-cone trailer, the cotton candy trailer, the Tilt-a-Whirl, and then the magnificent and terrifying Zipper, folded up on the back of a truck like a giant moth in cocoon.

That year the Lupoyoma Chamber of Commerce had convinced the Lupoyoma City Council to allow the annual Memorial Day Weekend carnival to set up downtown instead of the usual spot at the fairgrounds out on the west side of town. The two blocks along the front of Library Park would be the midway, and the other attractions would set up on the cross streets. The Lupoyoma Police Department came out against the plan, with Chief Lloyd Timmons predicting unmanageable chaos, a traffic and parking disaster, drunken fisticuffs. Which at first sounded entertaining to me. But now, after everything, I wasn't quite in the same mood about carnivals, Memorial Day, or anything else.

• • •

It was evening by the time I got home from work. The streetlights were blinking on as I hustled up the steps and inside the house.

"You missed dinner," my father said, peeking out from behind the evening *Sentinel.* "You didn't miss the deadline, did you?"

I said no, we made it just on time and, seemingly satisfied, he went back to the news.

"I'll just warm it up," Darlene said, quickly up from the floral couch and on her way to the kitchen.

Even at the kitchen table, eating Darlene's terrible hamburger enchiladas, you could hear the rumble-hum of diesel generators and the buzz of chattering people as the carnival came to life.

"This is ridiculous," my father said. "I can't hear myself think."

"Oh, it's only for a few days," Darlene said. "I thought you said it would be good for the economy, for the downtown merchants."

"That was before they set up the damn Ferris Wheel in our backyard."

I said, "After dinner, I want to go check out the midway."

"You have work tomorrow," he said.

"I won't be gone long."

"Waste of time and money if you ask me," he said.

Then Darlene surprised me. "Michael, try not be such a stick in the mud for once." It surprised him too, and he retreated behind the paper.

• • •

The Ferris Wheel was set up in the dirt parking lot of the Lupoyoma Yacht Club, maybe ten yards on the other side of our fence. From our back stairs, an ever-revolving half-circle of the lighted spokes and silvery cars loomed over the fence line, climbing out of darkness one car at a time, arcing against the night sky, then disappearing, again and again.

I moved the loose board aside and stepped through the gap in the fence into a maze of wrist-thick cables running along the ground, two humming generators, a small camper trailer, and an old Ford van that looked familiar. In a sense, I was backstage at the carnival, the nuts and bolts that are always in plain sight but mostly unnoticed because the lights, the music, the talk and laughter and the smell of sugar in the air are so loud and blinding.

"Hey, what're you doing back there?" A gruff male voice, a silhouette against the light, arms waving, pointing out a path. "Come on out of there. Over this way, that's right. This area ain't safe for kids—hey wait a minute."

It was Garfunkel—or rather, Howie—and now the familiarity of the Ford van made sense. Turned out he'd worked the carnival in his younger days and he'd hooked up with some old carny friends and hired on as a ride operator. "Time for me to get out of Dodge, anyway," he said. "Might as well get paid for it."

"Tired of the bullshit, right?" I said.

He nodded. "You want a ride? First full run of the night."

"Well, I don't have a ticket."

"This one's on me."

I started to get in line, then I saw Robyn, of all people, about halfway up the line. She said, "You want cuts?"

I hesitated, and she said, "Come on, Archer, I'd rather not ride alone."

Garfunkel caught this and gave me the well-lookee-here eyebrows and a proceed-this-way sweep of the arm. Then he elbowed me as I went by and kinda whispered, "I'll stop your car at the top for a few minutes."

"Um, okay, why?"

"That's where the girls fall in love, little brother."

Garfunkel went to work loading the first customers into their cars, and I stood in line next to Robyn, looking down at the dirt, feeling like a stupid kid, thinking the talk we'd had a couple days before had possibly exhausted everything we would ever have to say to each other, the Constitution notwithstanding.

"This is my favorite ride," she said. And I finally looked up and noticed she'd kind of dressed up for the night out. White shorts and a pink button-up shirt, the tails tied in a knot below her aspirational breasts, her stomach bared to an extent that would never be allowed at Lupoyoma Junior High. And makeup, which I couldn't remember seeing on her before. Blush-colored lipstick and a touch of mascara. She had blue blue eyes that seemed lit from inside. I'd never noticed she was pretty. Not screamin' hot like Laurette, or curvy and brash like Billie, or even awkwardly endearing like Alice. Just simple and sweetly pretty.

True to his word, Garfunkel stopped the ride as our car reached the apex of the wheel, then took his time unloading and loading other riders and acting busy with the knobs and switches on his control panel.

It was quieter up there, a hundred feet in the air, the cacophony of the carnival homogenized into a din. The ride was angled to face the park and the lake, the edge of a full moon beginning to peek over the distant mountains but the water still blue-black under the night sky, a bruise on the earth. Tiny boat lights flit around on the surface like fireflies. Everything seemed so small and far away—the water, the ground, people talking, laughing, arguing, going.

I asked if there was any news about her brother, and Robyn looked out at the lake. "No, still nothing. It's been months now."

A cool wind began to blow in off the water; our car rocked gently and she slid closer to me on the bench seat. She smelled like coconut suntan oil. I wore Levi cutoffs and when her bare leg grazed my mine it sparked a tiny static charge.

"It's nice, isn't it," Robyn said. "Up here, for a little while, you're not part of it all."

"But when you go back down?" I said.

She mimed a clowny shrug. "Well… then you're back in the soup." Which made me smile. It was something we'd all heard Coach Fish say when things went from bad to good to bad again. We didn't know exactly what it meant or where it came from, but it sounded funny.

I finally apologized for that day I shoved her into the lockers. "I was just mad at everything."

She nodded thoughtfully. "I know what you mean."

After an awkward few seconds of silence, I said, "Robyn, do you still believe in God?"

She took a breath of night air. "To tell you the truth, I'm not sure any-more. But it makes you wonder… if there's no God, why do we feel guilt?"

PURGATORY ON EARTH

I tried to stay up late to see Billie when she came home from work, to hear how it went for her on the first night of the big weekend, but I fell asleep sometime around midnight. Just couldn't keep my eyes open anymore. And she wasn't up yet when I went off to the *Call & Record* the next morning.

The Giants were playing a day game at Candlestick Park that Saturday, but I didn't bring my radio to work, didn't even turn on the shop radio. I did my job by numb rote, without my usual joy or even much awareness. In the pig room I carelessly dumped a full hellbox of type all at once into the already bubbling cauldron. A splash of molten lead burned a penny-sized hole in my forearm, cooked multiple layers of skin quickly while I watched but didn't move, didn't drop the hellbox, didn't try to swipe the liquid away with my glove. I stood still and settled into the pain.

I poured the pigs, cleaned the back shop and offices, washed up, took the five clean copies of the latest edition off Grandma Junia's counter and properly filed them in the morgue. I had time that day but didn't search for the July 18, 1969 issue. I thought about it, sat down on the wooden stepstool at the far end of the narrow room, with the yellowing newspapers stacked high and close. I sketched out a systematic approach in my mind, but the task seemed daunting, overwhelming even, and more than that, unpromising.

All my life I'd put so much faith in this grand institution where the printed word was manufactured and archived, where the past was recorded and the future predicted, this factory of inky memory and promises, all of it so full of self assurance. Decades and decades of council proclamations, Rotary Club lunches, pear crop estimates, grand openings, coming attractions, births, engagements, weddings and funerals, restaurant ads, hardware ads, furniture ads and grocery ads, grapes and apples ten cents a pound. Fact after fact after fact. But, even if I located this new puzzle piece, what would it solve, what would it change? Does fact plus fact always equal truth?

I locked up the morgue and went to the broom closet, took my apron off and put it on its hook. I yanked the chain to turn on the light, closed the closet door, staying inside. I tore down all the old pictures taped and tacked on the back of the door—the magazine centerfolds and telephoto tourist girls from Library Park, the Lupoyoma High cheerleaders, and all those stupid remarks in Hank's sloppy all-caps scrawl. I ripped them off the door, crumpled them up and carried them behind the building where I dropped them into the incinerator.

• • •

The house on Fourth Street was empty yet again. The parents were out for a boat ride in Old Man Terwilliger's big Chris-Craft cabin cruiser (the three-piece tweed suit of watercraft). Another note from Darlene, another frozen dinner. Salisbury steak—the hamburger patty with better PR.

Waylaid at the Ferris Wheel the night before, I didn't have time to explore the rest of the carnival, so after Salisbury steak and a change out of my work clothes, I slipped through the fence again, and this time, in full daylight, it was easy to follow Garfunkel's instructions to walk along the fence line, around his van and all the other equipment.

A pair of local policemen were talking to Garfunkel as he stood at his control unit setting the next round of the Ferris Wheel in motion. One of them seemed to glance over at me. There was no logic to it, but a jolt of panic turned into a tight little fist in my chest as if this cop, the sun flashing off his mirrored sunglasses, could see into my growing horde of secrets.

With the noise of the carnival, and keeping my distance, I didn't hear what was said; I could only see Garfunkel shake his head no several times. The two cops each nodded, although one seemed stubbornly suspicious, then they ambled away.

My chest relaxed. I walked over all casual. "Hey Howie, what's up?"

"Bunch of bullshit. Somebody broke into the record store last night. Right away the pigs start hassling carnies."

• • •

The kiddie rides filled Third Street almost up to Main. The Tea Cups, the Helicopters, the Carousel. Screaming kids, nervous mothers, impatient older siblings. The Music Box was closed, no one around. The big picture window where they usually displayed the hot-rod electric guitars was covered with bare plywood. Glass and splinters were swept into a pile on the concrete below. Across the white clapboard wall, at an uneven angle, spray-painted in all caps, the words *COMMIE DRAFT DODGER*. Bright orange.

I headed back down the street, passed the kiddie rides again and made a right at Parkview, the two blocks of street that ran along the front of Library Park. This is where the Lupoyoma Chamber of Commerce, in all its wisdom, had decided to place the main part of the carnival.

On one side of the street, kids were tumbling and screaming and losing their pocket change on the Rock-O-Plane. On the other side, the Carousel blared its circusy horror music. In the biting sunshine of late afternoon the colored lightbulbs blinked dully. Drifts of litter choked the gutters. A congealed grime of oil and dirt clung to the belts and gears of the motors. Gasoline fumes hovered near the ground like desert heat.

It all seemed like an old toy that was dirty and broken and out of style. Maybe it was the cops, maybe the Salisbury Steak, but I felt sick to my stomach. I turned around and walked back down the street, looped around the Ferris Wheel when Garfunkel wasn't looking, and slipped through the fence into my own backyard.

Before my mother died, when I still went to church on Sundays, I remember Reverend Jameson once said Episcopalians don't believe in Purgatory like the Catholics do—as an actual place where your soul goes when you die and stays until you're purified of your sins. But, he said, just as some people speak casually of Hell on Earth when their lives are filled with misery, one might also speak of Purgatory on Earth—as a state of deep, sorrowful regret and guilt, which can only be relieved by facing and correcting the evils we have done. The good Reverend never said how long the process might take.

PEACE FINGERS

Darlene stood at the open front door in hip-hugger short-shorts and sleeveless top, oversized plastic sunglasses, everything bright green, her signature color. Topped off with that bottle-blonde Annette Funicello flip. "I'm so excited," she said, and the hairdo quivered.

Ten minutes earlier my father had said, "You about ready?"

"In a jif," she'd said.

He'd gone out to warm up the Plymouth then, and he was still sitting there now. I could see him out the window, drumming fingers on the steering wheel.

Then Darlene was flustering out the door, both arms laden with purses and totes of various sizes and who knows what unnecessary contents. "Can you get the door, Archer? Thanks, hon. Now, you're gonna be okay, right? Billie said she'll come straight home after work, so don't worry, you won't be alone all night. And don't stay out too long. You know things can get a little crazy on holidays like this. Have fun and stay away from firecrackers, I know how you boys are. And we'll see you in the morning at the pancake breakfast. Okay—toodles!"

Yes, she really did say "toodles." I closed the door before she could say anything else. My father gripping the steering wheel, staring straight ahead, no doubt with great concentration restraining himself from leaning on the horn. It was perhaps an indication of how Billie came by her own verbal capacities.

It was Sunday afternoon, and this time Old Man Terwilliger had given my father the keys to the Chris-Craft for an overnight excursion. But the boating privileges came with a catch: my father would fill in for Terwilliger as pilot in the annual lighted boat parade, flying the *Call & Record* banner, after which he and Darlene would attend the big *schmooze-fest* (Laurette's term) at the Lupoyoma Rotary Club. Only then would they be free to set anchor somewhere offshore for a romantic night under the stars in this wooden castle on the lake.

The Plymouth Fury pulled away from the curb out front, and I went back to my room, my transistor radio, and the Giants, who were playing a double header against the San Diego Padres. I pulled out the old scorebook and scribbled through the games, a familiar comfort, and somehow a way of being alone but also connected. To my mother, of course. And my father. And Alice and even Robyn now. In the first game, Mays, McCovey and Bobby Bonds all homered, McCovey twice, and the Giants won handily six to one. In the second game, the Giants scored seven times in the fifth inning and held on to win seven-six. They had clawed their way back to fourth place. The beginning of an historic comeback? Hey, you never know.

• • •

Before she left the house that day, Billie had also left me a note, torn from her sketch pad and scotch-taped to the window sill on my side of the wall. Her handwriting looked like her, the letters rounded and full or curvy with the arms stretched out at odd angles. *Come to the cafe at 7:30, got a surprise, B.*

So bidden, I headed out after the Giants game, by way of the carnival. I would have cut through the park, but the lawns and picnic tables were already crawling with people claiming territory—spreading blankets, unfolding lawn chairs, and strategically placing ice chests and strollers, everyone vying for a view of the upcoming boat parade and fireworks display. By comparison, the meandering crowds on the midway were much less threatening.

I ran into Alice Terwilliger in front of the Tilt-a-Whirl, which was tilting and whirling directly across the street from the library. She said she too had received an invitation from Billie, although by phone instead of paper. *Come by tonight, I got a good spot for us.*

"It's gonna be packed," I said. "Maybe she reserved a table on the patio."

We agreed to walk together, and I thought about asking Alice why she quit as team scorekeeper, but I figured I already knew, and I didn't want to open that five-pound can of worms, as Grandma Junia might say.

Further down the midway, we were spotted by Timmy Bilderback, tagging along with none other than Trey Morgan, who stood at one of the sucker games pitching baseballs at fake milk bottles. Timmy tugged at Trey's shirt and pointed our way. We kept walking.

"Hey there, sweetheart," Trey called. "What's your hurry? You can't slow down and say hello?"

Alice smirked. "I don't think so." We walked on.

"Alright, I see how you are."

"Stuck-up," Timmy muttered. In his white tee and 501s he looked like a mini-Hank Timmons.

"Well, if it isn't the redneck's apprentice." Alice said. And we stopped.

Trey put a calm-down-I-got-this hand on Timmy's shoulder. "Where's Billie, your hippie girlfriend then? She's a helluva lot nicer than you."

Timmy grinned, petulant, arms crossed, a well-manufactured look of invincibility.

Alice didn't answer. Neither did I, struck dumb by jumpcut memories flickering in the drive-in theater of my mind—Billie's eyelids fluttering, Timmy wrestling her arms, his face a primal snarl.

"Well, you tell her Hank's looking for her," Trey said. "We're having a big sendoff tonight at my place after the fireworks and all. He ships out tomorrow, you know. She oughta come by. We're getting a keg and we're having Wallbangers again, too. She likes those."

"And quaaludes!" Timmy said, loud enough that Trey gave him the shush sign, but sarcastically, indulgently.

It was all a big joke to them, and I was seething inside but didn't say a word. I wasn't afraid of Trey, even with his tough-guy sneer, his shoulders cocked back and tense, oily jeans and black t-shirt with cutoff sleeves, the curled brim of his ratty Texaco ballcap tilted up like a let's-take-this-outside challenge. But I had to pretend I didn't fully understand, like I didn't get the insinuations about Billie and quaaludes and the rest. Everyone knew I'd been at the trailer and barely stumbled home, but no one knew that I was looking through the back window later that night. And I hoped no one ever would.

But Alice didn't have to play stupid. "Yeah, booze and pills, that's the only way you'll ever get laid," she said.

Trey grinned, cold and unfazed. Alice waved a hand dismissively, turned and started walking away.

"Hey, Timmy," Trey said. "How many hippies does it take to screw in a lightbulb? …Three. One to screw it in and two more to share the experience." He laughed at his own joke.

We walked. Trey spoke louder.

"Timmy, what's the difference between a hippie and a trampoline? …You take off your boots when you jump on a trampoline."

"Good one, Trey!" Timmy said.

Alice stopped and turned and moved toward Trey, arms wagging a big smarmy double peace sign like a wacky Nixon impersonation. Then she slowly turned her wrists and morphed the peace signs into fuck-you fingers.

Meanwhile, Timmy slipped a firecracker from his pocket, lit the fuse with a Zippo and threw it down on the ground between us. Blam! Alice and I and some other folks nearby all jumped and put hand to chest. It was then I noticed the slash of orange paint on one of Timmy's sneakers. I had an upset feeling in my stomach again, an angry roiling more like bees than butterflies.

But Alice started walking away, and I hurried to catch up. "Come on," she said. "I think I'd like to find Billie before Hank does."

And I forgot myself and said, "Yeah, me too."

THE PICTURE OF CERTAINTY

Down at the end of Parkview, the midway built to its gaudy crescendo—the Flying Bobs with the big stereo speakers booming out the swampy guitars of *Run Through the Jungle* by Creedence, and the mighty Zipper towering over the street, riders screaming into the sky. The crowd was thicker here, older teenagers and twenty-somethings milling around, talking fast and loud over the music, sucking on cigarettes. A constant stream of cars crawled by on First Street, and a stream of people poured down the sidewalk, all headed toward the park, the lake, and the Weeping Willow.

Alice wore bell bottom jeans and a wildly colored paisley blouse with puffy sleeves like a musketeer. She had her father's long legs and marched ahead in determined strides, weaving this way and that, around and through the clumps of slowgoers like a slalom skier, and I struggled to keep that blouse in sight.

The Weeping Willow's parking lot was choked with cars and motorcycles, some of them run up over curbs and onto the grass and sidewalks. A single lane of traffic crawled around the circular driveway in a futile search for parking, but they were all forced to follow the line around and then back up toward Main Street.

The big picture windows of the cafe allowed a line of sight through to the patio, already swarmed with people. Clearly there was no picnic table reserved for us or anyone else. The cafe itself looked empty, the lights low, the entrance locked, and I didn't understand why. But Alice knocked on the glass and Billie popped out of a hallway, scampered over, unlocked the door and opened it. "Quick, get in here," she said. We slipped in and she shut the door behind us. "We're closed. I mean, look at all the people out there! Molly said close at seven, *before* it gets out of control and man was she right, no way we could keep up, it's insane!"

Alice and I sat at one of the tables in the middle of the empty dining area. Outside, the last rays of the sun lit up the backs of the crowd, and all their chatter merged into a murmur as if we were underwater in a fish bowl. I could just make out the occasional announcements coming from the big PA system over in the park, pumping up anticipation for the boat parade, promoting tomorrow's pancake breakfast, reminding folks this was the last night to enjoy the carnival.

Somewhere in the kitchen KFRC was dialed in on a radio, and *Get Ready* by Rare Earth played as background music. Billie and Sonny were busy cleaning up, wiping down this and that, putting dishes and supplies away. Then Sonny sent Billie to our table with some leftover hot dogs and a basket of fries. She seemed in fine form, dancing to the music, twirling into the dining area to deliver the food with a trademark Billie Armstrong flourish. Behind the counter, Sonny caught my eye and gave a slight jerk of his head like *get a load of that, ain't she something.*

"So, what's the big surprise?" Alice said.

It turned out Sonny was going to let a few of us up on the roof to watch the parade and the fireworks, just him and Billie and me and Alice, and Nate was supposed to show up, too. "It's gonna be way cool from up there!" Billie said. "But don't tell Molly!"

"And don't fall off!" Sonny shouted from the kitchen, and we all laughed together.

The sun disappeared below the roofline, the shadows spread over the crowd and, inside, the dining room lights glowed warmly on our faces. I was struck with a great sense of relief that Billie would be fine after all. She was moving on. And everything else would eventually work out, too. I would finally get the answers my heart needed about my mother's death. My father and I would reconnect. Robyn and I would ace the Constitution Test. The Giants would come back to contend in the Western Division.

Then the front door of the cafe clicked open and Hank stepped inside in full dress uniform, PFC Timmons, at ease, hands behind his back, feet apart, chin up, chest raised, hard as a granite cliff. The picture of certainty.

In the stunned quiet, I heard the radio crackle and The Four Tops singing *It's All in the Game*, a fifties oldie updated in that smooth Motown style—killer bass line, angel harmonies, that top-down cruising main street sound.

Billie emerged from the kitchen carrying a tray loaded with soft drinks. It took me a second to absorb the look on her face as she spotted Hank; was it shock, anger, wonder? Yes, all that and horror. Dread and horror. Her hands went limp and opened like a trap door, the tray crashed to the floor, drink cups toppling, rolling, dark foamy soda bleeding out across the linoleum. She turned and ran back up the hallway by the kitchen.

Alice scrambled to her feet and went after her, leaping over the mess.

"We're closed," Sonny said, coming out from behind the counter. He walked slowly, deliberately, stepped past Hank and locked the cafe door.

"I just wanted talk to Billie," Hank said. He seemed momentarily caught off guard by Sonny's approach. For a second I thought he might've come to apologize, and I wished desperately that he would, imagined him hat in hand, eyes welling, asking forgiveness.

"She don't wanna talk to you right now," Sonny said.

"She told you that?" Now the two men stood face-to-face.

"Lucky for you, that's all she told me."

Hank looked at the linoleum and a hint of a cocky smile played at the corner of his mouth. "Well then, how about a beer while I'm here?"

Sonny paused, a little surprised at Hank's brashness. "You're under age."

"Aw, give a fellow soldier a break."

"That uniform don't make you a soldier in my book."

Hank didn't acknowledge the insult. "It's okay, the cops around here don't mind," he said.

"I know who your father is."

"Yeah. He knows you too."

Alone at the table, hot dog and fries forgotten, I watched it all like a television show, wondering if the two men might come to blows. Sonny was a big dude, a biker, a combat vet, what Grandma Junia would call a rough customer. You knew just looking at him that he knew how to fight, even with a bum leg and a paper hat. I played it out in my head. They take it outside to the Weeping Willow parking lot. Sonny knocks Hank to the ground with a right cross, then straddles his midsection, holding his head up to beat him some more, like some movie sheriff gone feral.

But Alice emerged from the hallway, scowling at Hank.

"What's wrong with her?" Hank said, jerking his head toward the hallway Billie had disappeared into.

From my seat at the table, I was the only one who could see her lurking in the shadows halfway down the hall. Listening, cowering.

Alice stared at Hank with a hard look of disbelief. "What the hell do you care?"

"Hey, it's my last night in town," he said. As if that implied an obvious set of obligations on our part. "I gotta be in the parade, but we're having a party at Trey's later and…"

"You want to invite Billie to another party at Trey's?" Alice said. "Man, you have some nerve."

"Why not?" Hank said, pretending he didn't understand where all the tension was coming from. But underneath, a hint of caution in his tone.

Alice shook her head. "She told me what happened the last time, Hank."

"Told you what?" he said, like a challenge. "She was so out of it that night, I bet she doesn't remember a thing."

"She remembers."

He hesitated for what looked like a worried moment, but then he actually grinned. "So what? I never heard her say no."

Which I knew was a lie.

"She was practically unconscious!" Alice said.

"So? We all had a little too much to drink, got a little carried away, big fucking deal. She was having a good ole time till you showed up and freaked her out. Running her down the street like that."

"Are you for real? She was having a good time? Wow."

Hank shrugged. "Whatever."

"We could tell someone, you know."

"Yeah? Who you gonna tell? Nobody in this town's gonna believe her."

I stood up. My mouth was probably halfway open. I intended to speak. I intended to tell everything. To bear witness.

Sonny stepped over to the door, unlocked it and held it open. "We're closed," he said again and he gave Hank a look like *go now if you know what's good for you.*

With the door held open, the crowd noise spiked louder and sharper. A Harley Davidson roared in the parking lot. Car horns honked. The smell of exhaust floated in.

Hank smiled, turned to go out the door. "Party starts after the fireworks," he said, pointing eyes at Alice. "And, oh by the way, tell her we want our grandpa's flag back."

Sonny closed the door behind him, locked it again.

"Are you fucking kidding me," Alice said to no one. "I don't even know what to say to that."

Billie hurried out with dishtowels, kneeled and began to clean up the mess. "I'm sorry," she said, like she'd done something wrong. Her hands shook and Alice kneeled to help. *Everything Is Beautiful* by Ray Stevens started up on KFRC, that corny intro of kids singing part of *Jesus Loves the Little Children.* Sonny went to the kitchen, snapped off the radio, returned with a mop.

Luckily, no one attempted to explain the situation to me. Maybe they assumed I knew or would see it as a run of the mill boy-girl spat, maybe they didn't consider me at all. I was still of that age where adults and even older teens sometimes ignored my presence, assuming the troublesome details of their grownup lives were beyond my comprehension.

"The parade's about to start," I said, and sat down.

UP ON THE ROOF

own the hallway on the right were the two doors to the restrooms, marked *INBOARD* and *OUTBOARD* respectively, which had thoroughly confused me as a little kid. Toward the end of the hall, a left turn up a narrow stairwell led to a tiny, hot and stuffy attic which squatted right over the kitchen and served as Molly's office. We all carried cups of soda up the stairs—except Sonny, who brought a small cooler of beer. He showed the way and opened a window for us to duck through and step out on the roof.

This part of the roof was flat with a grainy rubbery surface. It had apparently started out white, but that was some time ago. Sonny had furnished the area with some colored lawn chairs and a few coffee-can ashtrays. Our little beach in the sky.

Nate showed up and whistled from the parking lot till Sonny spotted him and sent me down to let him in—with a stern reminder to make sure and lock the door afterwards.

Twilight edged toward night. Everyone was quiet at first, subdued after Hank's ambush visit. Alice and Billie moved two chairs and sat apart from the rest of us, huddled close and low-talking.

Nate updated us on the vandalism at The Music Box and the Lupoyoma Police Department's so-called investigation. Chief Timmons had taken a quick tour of the damage and said right away it looked like the work of some drunk and rowdy carnies. Nate showed him the bright orange words on the front of the store and asked if that looked like carnies. And Timmons said, "Some of those guys are veterans, you know, maybe they heard about your little stunt the other night. You made that bed yourself, young man." Nate said his parents didn't burn anything, they didn't deserve this. Timmons said, "We'll file a report and ask around, but the carnies are a tight bunch. Hard to get a straight story out of that bunch."

"That was it," Nate told us. Timmons got in his car and left.

"It wasn't the carnies," I said, and that came out with surprising authority.

"How do you know that?" Sonny said, and I told about running into Timmy and Trey at the carnival and the orange spray paint I saw on Timmy Bilderback's shoe.

Nate said, "So, you think Timmy did it?"

"He's just about mean enough," Alice said.

"Yeah, maybe," I said, "but I went to school with Timmy since first grade, and he can't spell for shit." That got a couple laughs.

"He follows Trey around like a stray pup now." Alice said.

"Well, I went to school with Trey, and he's dumb as a bag of hammers," Nate said, and that got more laughs.

"So, think about it," Sonny said. "Who do they both look up to?"

And Billie said, "The cops won't do shit if Hank's involved."

They all grunted and sighed and nodded in some sort of group shrug. I sipped root beer from the waxy cup with sketches of fish and ski-boats and imagined what I would've said to Hank when I stood up with my mouth open in the restaurant: what's happened to you, what's wrong with you, who are you? Or simply, I saw you. But no.

Nate brought other news as well, and this hit me in the gut; a friend of his had been killed in Vietnam, a boy he'd known since the first grade. Two soldiers in uniform had shown up on his family's porch that day. He was just nineteen years old. His name was Ricky Withrow.

"Oh man, that's Robyn's brother," I said. I was standing near the edge of the roof and nearly lost my balance, closing my eyes to a wave of shock.

"That's right," Nate said, "He does have a little sister about your age."

"Jesus, I can't believe it. She's been really worried about him."

"You okay, Archer?" Billie said.

"It's so wrong."

"This motherfucking war," Sonny said, and there was another round of grunts and nods.

The parade started up and I let myself be distracted by the unfamiliar view from the roof—out over the bobbing, nattering heads of the patio crowd, across the shallows of the lake to the lighted boats putt-putting by in a line with lights glowing and banners flying.

For the first time, I noticed it was the same sad little parade as the year before, and the year before that, my whole Lupoyoma life. Rotary Club, Lions Club, Yacht Club, Cub Scouts, Boy Scouts, Girl Scouts, 4-H, Grange and Future Farmers, the Chamber of Commerce and the Junior Chamber of Commerce, the VFW, American Legion, and on and on. As each float was announced over the PA, the occupants waved like desperate pageant contestants and the rowdy crowd cheered and jeered according to their allegiances.

Nate had scored a pint of Southern Comfort somehow, and he walked around the roof spiking our sodas. Sonny popped another can of Hamms. I got the vibe that he didn't want to play chaperone or cop, but he did shoot me a look when Nate poured some of the liquor into my cup, a watch-yourself look that suggested caution.

Percival J. Terwilliger's cabin cruiser was the last boat in the parade and one of the biggest. My father and Darlene stood in the cockpit behind glass. Strings of red, white and blue Christmas lights hung from the deck railing. A single white spotlight shone on a figure standing at the rear of the vessel—Private Hank Timmons saluting the crowd like he was posing for a recruiting poster. The final image of the 1970 Lupoyoma Memorial Day Lighted Boat Parade.

There was a mix of establishment applause and anti-war boos from the crowd below and a moment of tense silence up on the roof. Sonny shook his head, crushed an empty beer can in his fist. Nate stood and gave a mock salute. In a loud preachy voice, he said, "God Bless America and all the ships at sea!" Some folks down on the patio overheard and laughed.

We laughed too. Except Billie. Sitting ten yards but a million miles away and staring out at the lake, she said, "I gotta get out of this place," her voice hollow and resigned.

I felt the hunger of the darkness, how the many colored lights twinkled so hopefully on the boats, but in a wider view the lights were so small and the night swallowed the world.

Billie and Alice went off to the bathroom together like girls do. They took turns folding themselves through the window of Molly's office and headed for the stairwell and the *INBOARD* sign. They didn't come back for a while.

The big barge the fireworks were launched from had been tugged into place in front of Library Park a hundred yards out on the water. Sonny stood up from his lawn chair. "Show's about to start. I better go check on those girls."

Eventually all three of them clamored back through the window and onto the roof, Alice and Billie talking excitedly, Billie waving a piece of paper, arms flailing the air like normal Billieness. "Freedom!" She said. "I hold freedom here in my hand!"

"Is it a joint?" Nate said. "If it is, spark it up!"

"No, silly, it's not a joint. It's the pink slip to my car!"

"We will not be sparking it up," said Alice.

"Yes, don't set important paperwork on fire!" Nate said.

"Wow, so you paid if off?" I said.

"Not quite, but Sonny said close enough for now."

"But remember, I'm not giving you the keys tonight," said Sonny. "Tomorrow, when I know you're sober."

"In that case, let's party!" Billie snatched the bottle from Nate, took a big slug and handed it to Alice. Turned out Nate was the one who produced a joint, handed it to Billie and she lit it up with her one-hand matchbook trick.

The patio crowd murmured impatiently, and out on the lake dark figures moved around on the barge, prepping the fireworks show. We pulled all the chairs back together in a semi circle and sat in the mostly dark passing the joint around.

When Billie passed to Sonny, he said "You're definitely not getting the keys tonight." And he passed it along after taking a short hit.

"I guess you'll be leaving Lupoyoma now," Alice said, wistful, as if it had just sunk in.

Billie sorta pshawed the notion. "Well, not yet, not until I'm eighteen anyway—I don't wanna piss off the parents."

The first firework sounded off. The low pop of the launch, the crowd's sudden inhale, the airy whistle as the rocket climbed the sky, then the gunpowder crack and the shower of yellow-red stars lighting up the drifting clouds. And in the flash I saw how Billie's face had transformed. There were new plans in her eyes, maps and highways and calendars, and she seemed to be nodding in rhythm to an inner voice.

The crowd cheered and oohed and aahed, and I took a hit from the joint and drank root beer Southern Comfort from the waxy cup. It wasn't horrible.

A BIGGER LIFE

Sonny drove us home in the Fairlane, and at first I wondered why, because the streets were choked with cars and pedestrians leaving the park and the carnival. We could've walked home more quickly. But he pulled up in front of our house, parked at the curb, got out of the car and handed Billie the keys—in exchange for her promise not to drive anywhere that night.

"I promise, I promise," she said and nearly knocked him over with a big long hug and even a kiss on the cheek. "Thanks… for everything."

Sonny started to walk away, stopped, turned and pointed at me. "Hey, don't be in such a hurry to grow up, kid. It's not all it's cracked up to be."

"Same with being a kid," I said.

• • •

First, we raided the fridge, pulled out some leftover chocolate cake. That was Darlene's other specialty. Anything with hamburger—no, *everything* with hamburger. Or cake. Layer cake made from a box with frosting out of a can. My real mother made it from scratch, beat the frosting in a big metal bowl and let me lick the spoon. Darlene's cakes always came out dry, but we had the marijuana munchies and didn't care. We ate big hunks of cake at the kitchen table with our bare hands and laughed about how bad it was.

Still stoned and tipsy and tired, with over-full stomachs, we headed off to our separate bedrooms. I'd just walked in when Billie slid open the window and poked her head into my room. It was what she did late at night when I wanted to sleep and she wanted to talk. I sat cross-legged on the floor and she dragged the vanity stool over by the window sill. She'd let her red hair loose after work and now it jumbled around her face. On the radio, low in the background, the KSAN DJ promised to play the Beatles' *Let It Be* album in its entirety and segued into the first track.

"She tries though, you know, man?" Billie said. "She's trying so hard with your dad. I mean, even her cake is desperate to please, right? But I see now it's just cuz she's worried things won't work out… after all, they never have, with her other guys that is, and I guess I only made it harder all these years, me being me, you know. And maybe she just wants to feel okay where she is for once, like the bottom isn't about to fall out at any moment. I don't even think it matters to her if she's not super happy, she's just sick and tired of starting over."

I nodded, not really knowing what to say. I admit I'd never thought too hard about how the world looked through Darlene's eyes. I'd resented her as an intruder and usurper. I'd dismissed her as a hapless weakling and even pitied her the way she was caught between the rock of my father and the hard place of Billie Armstrong. But I'd never really empathized with her, and I'd never before heard this kind of understanding coming from Billie either.

"Hey, I almost forgot…" she held up a wait-a-second finger, stepped out of the frame of the window for a moment and returned with her leather-fringe purse. "Look what I brought home!" She reached in and pulled out the Southern Comfort bottle, still about a quarter full. She unscrewed the cap, took a sip and passed it through the window with a smile and a wink. That mess of red hair lit by lamplight, the pink and white waitress uniform, the rose-tinted sunglasses, John and Paul singing *Two of Us* on the radio.

She stood up, hands outstretched in front of her, palms up, trying to grab the right words out of the air. "My mom doesn't want me to make the same mistakes she did, which I get, but she has this 1950s postcard in her head and it's two kids and a station wagon, PTA meetings, cocktails and fondue, the neighbors for dinner and a man who can hold a job, and I mean like the same mind-numbing soul-killing job for forty fucking years. I don't give two shits about any of that, man. My life ain't gonna be her do-over."

She was drunk-stoned rambling, but there was something more—a swelling energy, a rallying to self, a reclamation of power. She paced back and forth behind the stool, still in my view through the window frame, her voice rising, arms churning the air in swoops and circles, turns and tumbles.

"I don't want normal. I want more. If I wanted normal I'd stay here—this town will normal you to death. I want weird. I want daring. I want art and music and books and dreams and joy and struggle and winning and losing. And love. And that's the whole problem, right? I want more and some people are afraid of that. Because what would that say about their little cardboard cutout lives? My mother, your grandmother, or that puffed up soldier boy. I know you think he's some big role model like everyone else does—"

"I never said that."

"—well I'm telling you he's not and people in this town have no idea, someone needs to take him down a peg or two and maybe I'll do that myself before I leave—you know, eventually, whenever. And when I do leave the parents will probably say I'm throwing my life away. But I don't care. I won't let anybody shrink me."

Her hands came to rest at her side and she sat back down on the stool, took a breath of satisfaction and a slug of Southern Comfort.

"You're bigger than all of them," I said.

She broke into a teasing frown. "Are you saying I'm fat?" She shook her finger at me. "You better take that back."

"You know what I mean."

"Yeah, thanks." she said. "You're one of the good guys, Archer. You're one of the few I'll miss."

"I'll miss you too. Turns out most of my other friends are assholes."

She laughed, handed me the bottle, and I took another drink. John Lennon sang *Across the Universe* on the radio.

"I suppose you were right when you said that's what my mother wanted too," I said. "A bigger life, something more than normal."

"But for her it was already too late," Billie said.

MY TRICK MEMORY

Years later, in 1989, my Giants finally would finally win the National League pennant, securing their first World Series appearance since I was in kindergarten. The 89 Series was famously interrupted by the Loma Prieta earthquake, which hit Candlestick Park on live television shortly before game three was scheduled to start. It's still one of the most indelible moments in the history of TV sports.

Or is it?

For decades, whenever that event came up in conversation, I would share my where-were-you-when story thusly: I was watching in my tiny studio apartment above the newspaper where I was then employed. When the picture began to shake and flip and then disappeared completely, I started cursing at the TV, sure that some miscreants at ABC had somehow screwed up the feed and I was going to miss the entire game due solely to their incompetence. I'll never forget it. I can still see the room, me sitting on the edge of the bed, the paint-peeling coffee table and the 29-inch RCA television, one of those big old tube models with the rounded back, thing must've weighed sixty pounds, I swear. Indelible.

But it's totally wrong. For some reason it was not until thirty years later that it finally clicked in my brain that I didn't even move into that apartment until 1991. Somehow I'd gotten it all mixed up with something else. For thirty years.

Memory is a trickster. It sugar-talks you, feeds your pride, cheers you on. It stalks you, bullies you, laughs behind your back. It cons you, betrays you, abandons you and hides your secrets in the lies it tells. You are born of it and when it dies you die. You don't choose what you remember any more than you choose who you love.

· · ·

This is the part I might have imagined.

I awoke in deep shadows, half drunk, half asleep, half-dreaming that I was standing under a waterfall. I blinked my eyes open and found Billie next to me, side-saddle on the edge of my bed. "It's okay," she said, and that could have been part of the dream, too. Her hair was wet and tangled in loose damp curls around her face and on her bare shoulders. She wore a white full slip, and dusty light washed in from the window and played on the folds and highlighted the lace trim against her chest.

She leaned forward and brushed hair out of my eyes and kissed me on the cheek. "Archer," she said, and she shook her head slowly as she said it and pronounced my name in a way that spoke of more than the moment. There was something wistful and nurturing in the sound, as if it contained a full sentence within the one word—as if, instead of just my name, she'd said, "Archer, I'm afraid for your heart in this world." I had the weird sense that I was dreaming but *she* was awake and had climbed through the window in the drunken night to invade my dream. She seemed to read this confusion in my eyes, and she said again, "It's okay."

She stood and moved to the foot of the bed, and now I realized I hadn't quite made it under the covers when I finally sank onto the bed. And I hadn't quite undressed. I lay on top of the blue bedspread with the abstract wave pattern, in t-shirt and white boxer shorts, my Levi cutoffs scrunched up at my ankles, roadblocked by my tennis shoes.

"Let's get these off," Billie said. The light danced on the white slip and I saw the form of her body underneath like smoke in a glass. She tugged each of my shoes off and set them down silently on the plank floor. My cutoffs slid past my feet and fell out of sight.

"I'm sorry," I said. And I wished she could understand what I was referring to, what my apology, my regret, my sorriness encompassed. How big one sorry could be.

"Shhh," she said, with her lips pursed. Then I felt the tickle of her fingers curling inside the waistband of my underwear, and she slid them down over my hips, past my knees and into the thin air beyond my feet. She held her slip up with one hand as she climbed onto the bed and straddled me on her knees. I lay in the folds of the blue bedspread, heavy and ponderous, still floating between a watery dream and the dry land of consciousness.

I reached for her, but she nimbly caught my hand in the air and returned it gently to the bed. She looked deeply into my eyes then, in my most conscious moment, with a look sad but sure, a bittersweet half-smile on her lips and a teary sheen in her eyes that I read as grim resolve.

She slid a hand down my stomach and found me hard, moved up and lowered herself onto me. The folds of the white slip puddled on my belly and thighs as if I was swimming in her. My hands remained at my sides, my arms spread out on the bed supporting my floating body.

She closed her eyes and tilted her head upward and to the right as if she was trying to catch the lyrics to a song drifting in from another room. I never took my eyes off her. I stared, gaped, dwelled. I spotlighted her in the dusty light. I inhaled the scent of her soap and sex and shivered at the scratch of lace where the hem of the slip brushed my stomach. I listened to the rusty whisper of the bed springs. It was all over before I could identify its nature or purpose, before I could guess its why.

When she turned her face back to me there were tears on her cheek like tiny baubles of light. She took my head in her hands and leaned over and whispered one more time, "It's okay, Archer," and kissed me on the forehead. She climbed off the bed and for a moment the moonlight sparked her red hair like a flame and set the white slip aglow. She looked like a candle moving away toward the dark. The moment gone, her shadow ducked back through the window to her room. I heard the wooden scrape of the window sliding shut. The light went out.

BATTING PRACTICE

This is the part where she fought back.

I woke suddenly to some noise, a thud or something else that goes whump in the night and leaves quiet behind. All was darkness and the low hum of the civilized world. And this time I sat up, fully awake. I listened to the dark and strained my ears for information. From the kitchen, I heard the Timex wall clock tick away a minute. The harvest gold refrigerator chanted om in its stately meditations. No other sound.

I slid out of bed and stood naked on the rough plank flooring. Felt and sensed my way toward the window. Knocked one of the model cars off the sill—hopefully the red Mustang. My eyes adjusted and shapes of darkness announced themselves—edges defined by degrees of shadow. Some promise of dawn whispered timidly on the glass.

Billie had come to me through the window and gone back the same way, that memory was at least fresh if not certain. I tugged and slid the lower pane up, grimacing at the creak and scrape of the wood, not wanting to wake her, but needing to check on her, needing to test reality.

I stuck my head in and saw my mother's old clamshell travel clock on the nightstand next to the rollaway bed. Three a.m. it said with its glow-in-the-dark hands giving off just enough light to reveal the crumpled twist of empty sheets. Across the room, the other window, which faced the narrow sideyard, had been left slightly up, perhaps to invite the night air.

I thought I heard the thunk of a car door closing. I hurried on my cutoffs, a t-shirt, and Keds with no sox. I went out the front door and there was the Ford Fairlane still parked at the curb under the streetlight. It was empty, or at least Billie wasn't behind the wheel. But her duffle bag lay across the back seat, and a tug in my stomach said she was packed to leave Lupoyoma City that night, for good. Forever.

There was nothing moving on Fourth Street. I went back in the house and tried the dayroom door. It was locked from the inside. I went out onto the back stoop. The three-quarter moon was now high and yellow in the west, lighting a path across the yard. The loose plank had been moved aside and the gap in the fence left open.

I wriggled through the fence into the same old dirty, empty parking lot of the Lupoyoma Yacht Club, Garfunkel and the Ferris Wheel now vanished, presumably on to the next town. I crossed the street to the edge of the park lawns and searched out at the shadows, unsure what I was hoping to see. One voice of me suddenly felt exhausted with dread and wanted only to return to the blue waves of my bed, to backfloat into heavy sleep. Another voice was frantic with the desperation of abandonment.

The carnival had evacuated, packed up and gone like it was married to the wind. The park lawns lay down in patterns of rectangles and connecting paths, trampled and dimly faded in the wake of the crowds, littered with crumpled paper cups and balled up food wrappers. The air was still and warm. In the dark absence of the music and the machines and all the mad chatter of the carnival, the slurp of water meeting the shore seemed impolite.

But ahead, in the aura of one of the park lights, a silhouette in the shape of a young woman was moving quickly across the lawns. I kept my distance and followed the shape I assumed was Billie, which cut across the park on a diagonal line, straight for the Weeping Willow archway, pulling away like a bus I couldn't catch.

When she stepped out under the streetlight in front of the archway, it was her, no question—patchwork skirt, tank-top, combat boots, and my baseball bat in her right hand, held like a club. I didn't yell out; the quiet and the darkness seemed to rule the night. I began to jog at first, thinking I could catch up to her before she did whatever she planned to do with that bat.

Inside the Weeping Willow, the world talked in its sleep. Transformers hemmed and hawed on telephone poles, midges gossiped under streetlights. Electric fans prattled next to windows, fathers snored in tents, and a breeze off the lake whistled in the willow trees.

Billie marched up ahead, down the middle of the one-lane blacktop, then turned up the long driveway to Trey Morgan's trailer. She marched, and I scuttered along, leapfrogging between the shadows of trees on the edge of the lane, never close enough for her to hear my steps.

Hank's Mustang was parked in front of Trey's trailer, the red paint job shining in the moonlight. Billie headed straight for it, and I hid myself behind the trunk of a huge oak tree.

As she reached the Mustang she lifted the bat from her side. She coiled up the entire force of her body and smashed the bat down into the middle of the car's windshield. The impact made a sound like popping the top on a shookup can of beer. Pwoosh. Then a crackling sound like the crumpling of brittle paper.

I froze against the tree. I almost called out to try and stop her, but the door to the trailer burst open and Hank suddenly stood on the front stoop—tan khakis, no shoes or shirt, fly open, wavering like a sleepy boy.

"Jesus Christ, what the hell," he said, and then, "Oh no. You bitch. You little bitch." He started down the porch stairs.

"Stay where you are." She took a big swing at one of the headlights and it popped and shattered, shards of glass splashing to the dirt. She brandished the bat like a warning.

Hank stood still. "That's enough goddammit!" Then more calmly, like he was the rational adult on the scene, "You're making too much out of this, Billie. Just put the bat down, walk away and there won't be any trouble."

"No, Hank. You're not getting off that easy."

He looked to his left and right as if searching for a witness. Or a weapon. Billie wound up for another smash, but something inside the Mustang caught her eye, and she checked her swing. She reached in through the driver's side window, pulled out Hank's keys, the *Playboy* bunny charm dangling from the ring. She jingled the keys in the air.

Hank clenched his fists and sucked in air like smelling salts. "I'm warning you, don't fuck with me."

Billie rested the bat on her shoulder with one hand and walked down the length of the car. You could hear the key cutting a deep gash into the paint job, the red paint flaking away.

"That's it." Hank said. He leapt off the stairs and bounded toward her, but in the shadowy moonlight, he must've stepped on some of the headlight glass. He cried out and went down to a knee.

Billie slipped the keys into the pocket of her skirt, turned and started running away.

"You fucking whore," Hank hollered after her. "I'll kill you, goddammit!"

She ran back the way she came. Hank stood, quickly tested his foot, and started after her like a stud relief pitcher called in to snuff out a late inning rally—measured strides, chest out, fists pumping.

I held my breath and flattened myself against the crusty bark of the oak tree as each of them pounded by in the street. He would catch her eventually. Hank could probably run for an hour at that speed, even with the cut. Billie could not.

I followed them, lagging behind, shadow to shadow again, not running but fast-walking and sometimes jogging, but never making enough noise to turn Hank's head. Blood churned at my temples, a wet drumming pulse shot through with static, a sound like the recording of an unborn baby's heartbeat.

Billie ran through the parking lot, under the oak tree archway and cut across the street. I could tell, even from thirty yards behind, she was headed for Preacher's Alley, and Hank was gaining fast.

I picked up my pace, Billie disappeared up the alley, then Hank. I heard a sharp, short scream and then a scuffle and thump and what I heard as a grunt of surprise, followed by a wooden clatter. I thought she'd either dropped the bat or thrown it aside. I pictured it cartwheeling down the concrete passage and rolling to a stop against one of the buildings. Maybe she thought she could run faster without it. Maybe she threw it at Hank to slow him down.

Some semblance of relief hit me that this bat I had spent so many hours with should be cast out of this particular game. It was part of Hank and part of me, and I didn't want it to be part of this. Right then I wanted to go down to the shoreline and hit rocks out over the lake, and listen to the sound of the stones punching holes in the water. I didn't want to wear a gray suit or play in the big leagues or know any woman's secrets. I wanted to stand by the lake and play ballgames in my head.

I took several more quick strides across the street and turned into the opening of the corridor. I saw the cowering shape of Billie rise from the pavement and stagger out onto Main Street. She did not look back.

Hank stood near the end of the passageway, wobbly on rubber legs, and this time he heard me and jerked his head around. He pivoted to face me and pulled his head back as if sizing up the unexpected. His face all a question and the yellow moon over his shoulder.

A SIZE 9 WORLD

Late in the morning, it was Chief Timmons himself who kicked in the dayroom door with his big black boots, the wooden door jam cracking and splintering like a lightning-struck tree. And that startled me awake and into instant panic. I tugged on my robe and ran around to the front room where Laurette, Grandma Junia and my father stood in shock while Darlene screamed, "What is happening! Don't you need a warrant! Mike, do something for God's sake!"

And, before we all followed Timmons and two other officers into the dayroom, it was Laurette who took me by the shoulders and delivered the news, as she had in her VW the day my mother died. "Hank is dead and Billie is missing," she said. And once again I had to pretend to Laurette that I knew nothing, was not a witness.

I hadn't actually been in the dayroom since Wednesday afternoon when I was listening to the blues records. Crossing the threshold now, I struggled to believe that was just four days ago, because something astounding had happened in there. Across the far wall, on both sides of the painted window, Billie had designed, created and assembled a display that was something like a collage but it was more than that. I didn't know the term "mixed-media" at the time, but that's what it was.

There were clippings cut from the *San Francisco Sentinel*, *LIFE Magazine*, and even the *Lupoyoma Call & Record*—a grim assortment of headlines, pics and passages tacked and taped and pasted to the walls, angled and jumbled and sometimes overlapping. King, RFK, Nixon, Agnew, Woodstock, My Lai, Apollo 13, the breakup of the Beatles, Kent State, the Hard Hat Riots, the Student Strikes, Jackson State… as if the past few years of history had been vomited on the wall, all of it arranged in a shape that suggested an angry tornado.

Guardsmen Fire on Rock Throwers; Protests Close Campus; Mayor Praises Police… A grainy photo of a beer-bellied policeman waving a pistol and pressing a boot to the chest of a bloodied protester lying in the street… *Students Boycott Across U.S.; Cops and Marchers Clash…* A large bright picture of three cops in riot gear on a campus lawn, little clouds of tear gas hanging low in the air…

… An article titled *Tragedy in the Heartland*, much of the type painted over in black swaths like government censorship, except selected quotes… *I want to sit down and throw up… Is this my future—getting killed or seeing my friends getting killed… We had to shoot, maybe it'll wake these thugs up… You get an order to clean up a latrine; you do what you're told…*

… A village on fire. A family's home. Dead children piled up beside a dirt road. A headline says *Americans used to bring us candy and medicine…* right next to big ads for Chevrolets and cigarettes, Scotch whiskey, color televisions and life insurance… A busty woman in a crochet mini-dress, the tiny caption alongside her leg identifying her as *Eileen Feather, Leading Figure Authority.* The huge boldface headline: *SUMMER IS A SIZE 9 WORLD…*

… And in the middle of all this, draped over the window, a man-size forty-eight-star American flag, hung upside down and splattered and dripping with blood-red paint like someone got their head blown off in that room with a shotgun.

"Oh my god, Billie," Darlene said.

Laurette gasped and wrapped an arm around me from behind in an anguished, protective hug, and I leaned back into her in solidarity, commiseration, my mouth hanging open.

"I knew that girl was trouble from the get-go," Grandma Junia huffed. "I said so, too."

My father took a good long look around the room, arms crossed, gave it all a tight-lipped nod, turned and walked out without a word.

Chief Timmons stood still, in a narrow-eyed staredown with the wall, especially the defiled flag, one hand balled up in a fist, the other wrapped around the handle of his pistol, his jaw muscles clenched so tight I thought he might break teeth.

My father came back into the room grim-faced with drink in hand. "I warned her," he said.

Grandma Junia said, "I gather this display is intended for us… some sort of political statement." She pronounced *display* with withering disdain.

"It's a work of art," I said, but nobody listened.

"Frankly, it's alarming," said Grandma Junia.

"Can't you see she's suffering?" Darlene said.

Timmons said. "I want all of you out of this room. I don't want anything touched. I want this room sealed, boarded up, off limits until I can get a detective in here."

From the Lupoyoma Call & Record, May 27, 1970

Soldier's Body Found, Female Suspect Sought

A badly beaten body, identified as that of Floyd Henry Timmons Jr., 19, of Lupoyoma City, was found Monday by city and county police officers. The deceased was located in a narrow drainage corridor between two buildings in the downtown area of Lupoyoma City. Police believe it is the scene of a homicide. A baseball bat, believed to be the murder weapon, was also found at the location.

Timmons, a private in the U.S. Army, was last seen Sunday evening, May 24, at a relative's residence at the Weeping Willow Resort & Trailer Court, where he'd attended a going away party held in his honor, prior to his reporting for transport to Vietnam.

The victim's car was located in front of the residence Monday morning, apparently vandalized. Timmons was not present in the residence, and a search was initiated by law enforcement. A male juvenile found asleep in the residence reported witnessing an earlier altercation between the victim and a female identified by the juvenile.

The Lupoyoma County district attorney has issued a warrant for the female, Barbara Ann Armstrong, 17, of Lupoyoma City. The suspect is also known as "Billie" Armstrong.

Jones & Jones Mortuary & Funeral Home is in charge of arrangements, with the funeral set for Friday, May 29, at their facilities in Lupoyoma City.

ODDS AND ENDS

We all had to go to the funeral, for appearances if nothing else. The too-familiar porch at Jones & Jones, my father in his gray suit, straining to show respect (and self-assured innocence) with as many solemn handshakes as he could distribute throughout the gathering. Grandma Junia flashing her superior frown in a swanky black outfit from another era— pleated skirt, brimmed hat with a half-veil as if she'd been widowed again. And poor Darlene, all but dragged along, her red-eyed shame hidden behind dark sunglasses, desperately holding onto Laurette's arm with every step.

"She's got some nerve showing up here," said Miss Lancaster, her imposing frame tented in black chiffon.

Half the town was there: Mr. and Mrs. Timmons, of course, the chief in full uniform, glaring as we came into the chapel as if we were all suspects. His broken wife crumpled in a folding chair, sniffling into a handkerchief.

Half the town was there, but half the town was not: Old Man Terwilliger (but not Alice); Leslie McGoogan and the rest of the *Call & Record* staff (minus Vic Pendergrass); Coach Fish and some other Paperboys (Timmy, but not Joey); a few former classmates (Trey Morgan but not Nate Henderson). Not surprisingly, other no-shows included Pop and Molly, Sonny the cook, Craiger and Eugene Robinson. Also Robyn Withrow, who had already been to one funeral that week, and no doubt one was enough.

$\bullet \ \bullet \ \bullet$

Meanwhile, the police had been searching everywhere for Billie Armstrong, now portrayed as a dangerous radical bent on political violence and wanted for the murder of a United States soldier. The FBI was called in and set up checkpoints on all three of the roads leading out of Lupoyoma County. They swarmed the house, crime-taped the dayroom and snapped hundreds of pictures in there. They even picked through the Goodwill boxes, impervious to Laurette's feisty objections.

They found the duffel bag in the Fairlane, dumped out the contents and took pictures of Billie's eclectic wardrobe scattered on the lawn, including her underwear and the largely neglected bra. They even confiscated her sketchpad to pass on to some psychiatrist in San Francisco.

Sour-faced skinny-tie FBI agents lifted her paperback books by the corners of the covers as if the words inside might be contagious. *Siddhartha, Mrs. Dalloway, On the Road, The Bell Jar, One Flew Over the Cuckoo's Nest, The Feminine Mystique. The Autobiography of Malcolm X* — that one really got them scowling and pursing their lips.

They searched every inch of the car, but it was clean; she hadn't had time to leave any evidence in there besides the duffel, and the car was still technically registered to Sonny, so they didn't impound it. The keys were in the ignition and, days later, Sonny would show up and drive it away.

Other agents were busy checking out Billie's relatives and childhood friends in Cleveland, and raiding her old crash-pad near the Kent State campus. They questioned Darlene, Laurette and Alice, and Molly and Sonny, too. I heard they gave Nate a real hard time, threatened to prosecute him for burning his draft card, but he knew his rights and there was not much he could tell them about Billie anyway.

And they questioned me, especially about the bat, branded as the murder weapon, and they took my fingerprints because they'd found three sets on the bat and were able to match Hank's and Billie's, but wanted to confirm the others were mine. I told them over and over I'd gone to bed and slept through the whole thing. "I barely knew her," I said.

"Well, she was your sister," the FBI guy said.

"Stepsister," I said. "We really didn't get along."

When Laurette mentioned The Bus Stop, the detectives thought they finally had a lead. Rumors flew out the door and within hours everyone in Lupoyoma knew the traitor Frankie Watkins had helped Billie Armstrong escape, maybe even helped kill the Timmons boy. The agents all hurried out to Two Lakes and interrogated what was left of the Four Corners crew: Ben

Parker, Old Sam, and shy Gilberto, but they all agreed Frankie had gone out of business and left town well before the dates in question. Apparently they never mentioned me. Or Garfunkel.

Disappointed, the FBI guys came back to our house and packed up. Billie had vanished without a trace and they were out of ideas for the time being. "She's in the wind," one of the agents said, all dramatic like a bad TV show.

Once all the cops were out of the house, my father and Darlene began to quarrel. She wanted him to search for Billie himself, maybe find her and talk her into turning herself in, get her a good lawyer and on and on. But my father said, "I told her I wouldn't intervene on her behalf again. I warned her."

"Michael, this is different," Darlene pleaded.

"She's caused enough trouble for this family already. I wash my hands of the whole affair." He turned to me. "Now, I want you to clean up that room and take that garbage off the wall. I don't want to see it again, is that understood?"

That night, I tore it all down, put all the paper clippings out back in the burn barrel, but I wasn't sure what to do with that bloodied old flag, so I folded it up flat as I could and just barely managed to stuff it into my mother's hatbox, still stashed in my closet.

• • •

Sunday, two days after Hank's funeral, the Paperboys met the Odd Fellows for the third time that season—the much ballyhooed (and now dreaded) "rubber game."

Once again it came down to the final inning, the final at-bat. The Paperboys were losing five-four and down to our last out against the fearsome Craiger Robinson. Timmy Bilderback worked a walk, and I somehow managed a grounder to left field that literally disappeared in the unmowed grass and was ruled a double. Dead ball. Time out. Timmy stood at third base and I stood at second, the potential—if highly unlikely—tying and winning runs.

Craiger's brother Eugene jogged out from his position at shortstop and found the ball. He picked it up and started back in. Craiger ran out to meet him halfway, took the ball and gave his brother a don't-worry-I-got-this pat on the shoulder. He walked back to the mound, pawed at the dirt with his cleats, stared in at the catcher. Like a good shortstop, Eugene held up two fingers and reminded his teammates, "Two down, two down."

Timmy took a long lead off the bag at third, lowered into a half-squat and began dancing side to side, arms stretched out and hands shaking like some mad crab boogeyman. Even I was annoyed at the distraction.

Vic the umpire picked up his chest protector, pulled the mask down over his face and waved for the next batter, Joey Quarterman, AKA Joey Two Hits. We can still win this game, I thought. A clean base hit would score Timmy from third and give me a chance to race home with the winning run.

Joey dug in and took his stance. Vic hollered, "Play ball!" and lowered into his crouch behind the catcher. Craiger toed the rubber and began his windup. I took a short lead toward third, my heart drumming a syncopated six-eight rhythm.

Like a ghost, fat Eugene Robinson suddenly appeared beside me, pulled the ball out of his mitt and tagged me on the hip. "You're out!" he yelled, and he held the ball up high and white for all to see. "You're out! You're out!" he kept saying, and he did a little dance, jumping round and round in the blonde infield dirt. The old hidden ball trick.

Craiger turned and showed me his empty glove. And a thin, satisfied smile.

● ● ●

Over the following week, Robyn and I met twice to study, and on Friday the entire eighth grade class at Lupoyoma Junior High School sat in the cafeteria and took the Constitution Test. Then we all went home to worry. But a week after that, on Friday June 12, we stood in line, heard our names (even Timmy Bilderback) and walked across the stage to receive our diplomas from the chairman of the school board, the ubiquitous Doc Meaney.

I wore the gray suit that Billie had picked out for me at Frankie's store, and afterwards I even struggled through three minutes of slow dancing with Robyn the horse artist of all people, while Nate Henderson and Mellow Day struggled through the chord changes of *Color My World* by Chicago.

And the day after that, I came home from work to find Darlene hoisting her suitcase and a couple overstuffed cardboard boxes into the back seat of Laurette's VW Bug.

Laurette said, "If your father asks, I'm taking Darlene to her cousin's in San Francisco. Although I wouldn't be surprised if he doesn't ask."

"I'm sorry it didn't work out, Archer," Darlene said. She gave me a quick peck on the cheek, eyes brimming. The Volkswagen went up the street, and I went up the front stairs and into the empty house.

Billie Armstrong had crashed into my life like a psychedelic wrecking ball. On the way out she left a jagged splintered hole. It was almost three weeks since the night she disappeared, the night of Hank's death, and all that time my whole life seemed to hang on the edge of a cliff along with hers. If she was caught, I'd told myself, I would tell the truth, or some of the truth, at least the part that would help her, protect her, save her. That's what I'd told myself to feel brave and not feel the fear of actually having to follow through. But she hadn't been caught, might never be caught, and I might never have to choose what to tell or what not to tell.

FLAG DAY

"Whoever knowingly mutilates, defaces, physically defiles, burns, maintains on the floor or ground, or tramples upon any flag of the United States shall be fined under this title or imprisoned for not more than one year, or both." — *1968 Flag Protection Act (found unconstitutional by the US Supreme Court, 1990)*

"The flag, when it is in such condition that it is no longer a fitting emblem for display, should be destroyed in a dignified way, prefera-bly by burning." — *American Legion U.S. Flag Code*

I dug the hatbox out of my closet, pulled out Grandpa Cecil Morgan's forty-eight-star flag. In my mind, in my heart, it was no longer a fitting emblem of the ideals it was intended to represent. It was defiled in spirit by the actions of Hank Timmons, even before it was used to cover Billie Armstrong's half-naked escape, and even before its last service as part of her artistic farewell to Lupoyoma and our "family."

Now was the time to retire this flag in a dignified way, and I decided in the same moment to add my mother's blue-flowered sundress to the cere-mony as well. I threw several lit matches into the burn barrel until the old news clippings caught and the flames began to grow. I lowered the flag in slowly as the fire climbed its folds.

After I dropped the last corner, I took the dress out of the plastic and held it up by the hanger, let it unfold to full length and took a good long look. I looked at the pocket where I had found the lipstick envelope. That day, I'd been so overcome, so confused, I'd never even thought to check the other pocket.

Now I reached in and my fingers recognized the touch of old paper. Old newsprint...

Lupoyoma Call & Record, July 18, 1969

Lupoyoma Man Killed in Vietnam

Private First Class James R. Cole, U.S. Army, of Lupoyoma City was killed in action (KIA), according to a recent report issued by Army command personnel at Nha Trang Air Base in Vietnam. Private Cole was shot when his patrol unit came under heavy fire while securing a Vietnamese village controlled by enemy forces. The 25-year-old soldier had been serving in Vietnam since September of last year. Private Cole had moved to Lupoyoma County in 1968 from his former home in Pacheco, California. He is survived by his mother, Althea Yberra Cole, of Nogales, Arizona. Members of his unit reported that Private Cole was killed before the rest of the unit was forced to retreat, and his body has not been recovered. No funeral plans have been announced.

A GRITTY STONE

For a few shining moments, I was sitting on top of the mean old world. I had recently been awarded the 2010 Pulitzer Prize for Commentary, the highest honor a lowly newspaper columnist can receive. To celebrate (and to reap the PR benefits), the *San Francisco Sentinel* hosted a lavish banquet in my honor. Publisher Daniel Lockhart, a pudgy red-cheeked man with disheveled prematurely-white hair, stood at the front of the Gold Room at the Fairmont Hotel in a wrinkled seersucker suit and read from three-by-five index cards. "Ladies and gentlemen, please welcome San Francisco's favorite contrarian, the Working Man's Thinking Man, Archer King."

I stood up to moderate applause, strode to the lectern and shook Lockhart's fat sweaty hand. I gave a short speech which began with the well-worn tale of the wise old editor who changed my life in the early days of my career by informing me that I was far too arrogant, judgmental and undisciplined to make it as a straight newsman—therefore I was promoted to columnist.

Throughout this recitation I was distracted by the gaze of a woman standing at the back of the room near the baroque wooden doors. She seemed out of place, a little too businesslike and refined for the newspapering crowd, sipping red wine and leaning lightly against the wall as if she'd wandered in by accident and stayed to study the natives.

She had dark auburn hair that fell to her shoulders in loose curls, and she wore a brown tweed blazer over a matching knee-length skirt. Medium height and build, but not medium attractive. In fact, beautiful in a certain dark and guarded way. Clearly younger than I, late thirties if I was forced to guess out loud.

Her eyes were unabashedly focused in my direction, and even while speaking I briefly imagined she was attracted to me and would make her intentions known later in the evening—such is the monkeying mind of the

American hetero male. But I quickly realized her look was too discerning, too penetrating and questioning. I was being sized up, but not for romance or sex, and not for business either. And, after all, what else is there?

All of that winked through my mind as I doled out the wise-old-editor story and a few other pre-fab laugh lines, then segued to a more elevated tone with a quote from Thoreau: "It takes two to speak the truth; one to speak and another to hear." I salted in a line of kissass about the superior acumen of San Francisco readers, then I returned to my table, my ribeye, and my tumbler of bourbon.

I was seated at a round table draped in white linen and glimmering with silver and crystal, the opulence of the scene tarnished only by the presence of myself and my sodden compatriots—wizened old section editors and beatup beat reporters, the same jaded wretches I usually drink with, albeit in friendlier, shabbier (and cheaper) locales.

There was a distracting flurry of activity as a waitress delivered another round of drinks on the *Sentinel's* tab, and a gaggle of gladhanders and sycophants (all arch-rivals or staunch critics before the Pulitzer) vultured around the table with drinks in one hand and phones or business cards in the other. They lined up for handshakes and selfies and clapped me on the back and hinted at future alliances, or dalliances, or both. When the sea of them finally parted I noticed the woman in brown tweed had left the room.

• • •

I woke up at home with one of those hangovers that craves the safety of walls and shadows, yet I was reveling in it perversely. I had a plan: a celebratory breakfast of strongman coffee, pork chorizo and eggs, plus orange juice, bourbon and a Percocet, followed by a criminally indulgent shower long enough and hot enough to threaten the environment, and an all-day *Godfather* marathon with intermissions of ill-advised processed food and nod-offs in the La-Z-Boy.

I wobbled out of the bedroom in pajama bottoms and t-shirt, navigated to the stereo and cued up some Jimmie Vaughan vinyl at low volume—laid back and blue and just a little coarse, like fine-grade sandpaper to smooth out the morning's edges. I scrambled up the chorizo and eggs and fed myself out of the skillet, standing at the big bay window facing Lincoln Way and Golden Gate Park. I watched the sunlight climb the misty trees across the empty morning street. San Francisco always looks so clean in the sun, even to me. I chased the chorizo with the bourbon and the bourbon with the OJ, and I began to muse on future prospects. After the Pulitzer and some love from the national press, maybe I'd get a fat syndication offer from the *Chronicle* or the *Post* or, in my fanciest dreams, the *New York Times*.

Then my damn phone went off with the ringer turned up way too loud, juddering my still aching head. I barely got through *hello-who-the-hell-is-this* before a woman began to speak in a measured, solicitous tone. "I'm sorry to bother you at home, Mr. King. My name is Valentine Jones. I enjoyed your remarks last night at the Fairmont. I wanted to talk to you, but I didn't get a chance."

"Ah… red wine and brown tweed at the back of the room?"

"I would've introduced myself, but you seemed preoccupied. I didn't want to spoil the fun."

"Nonsense, you should've stopped by my table. You're not in the newspaper business, are you?"

"I'm an attorney."

I laughed. "Well, I'm already divorced, so I know all about how attorneys can spoil the fun."

"I'm not a divorce attorney, Mr. King. However, I am calling about a legal matter."

"Am I being sued?" I threw in another chuckle.

Valentine Jones did not laugh. "No, actually I was hoping you'd be willing to talk to me about your involvement with the Billie Armstrong case."

I paused longer than I wanted to. I walked toward the kitchen with the impulse to pour another drink. No one had pestered me about Billie Armstrong for several years. Most of the press and law enforcement had lost interest in the whole thing, and some even presumed Billie was dead by now. "Look, Ms. Jones, I don't know how you got this number or who told you different, but I'm afraid I really can't help you. I've told the police—and the FBI, and everyone else—everything I could, over and over."

"Yes, I've read your previous statements," she said. "But I think you can help me… and so does Ms. Armstrong."

Again I paused, suspicious of the implications. "Has she been captured?"

"No, but she's tired, Mr. King. She's been a fugitive most of her life—forty years on the run from a charge she doesn't deserve. She's tired, and she's ready to turn herself in and have her day in court. She thinks you might know something that could help clear her name, something you *didn't* mention to the police back in 1970. Or since."

I poured two fingers of bourbon and took a slow, fortifying sip. This woman was fishing, and it was too early in the day, and I was too hungover, or perhaps already too boozy to nibble politely. "Are you accusing me of withholding information?"

"Not at all," Valentine Jones said. "My client will surrender to the authorities soon—within the next several days—and I'd like to meet with you before then, voluntarily if possible, to discuss your eventual testimony."

"What the hell does that mean—voluntarily if possible?"

"Mr. King, I know the two of you were close at one time. She was your sister, after all. I'm hoping that still means something to you. But, if necessary, you can be compelled to testify."

"Look, Ms. Jones—Billie Armstrong was my *stepsister* for about a minute, a long, long time ago. And testify to what, exactly? You don't know what you think you know, and neither does she. I'm not even convinced you are what you say you are. How does a wanted fugitive suddenly show up out of the blue with a slick, pushy lawyer like you anyway?"

This time *she* paused. "Sir, I'm her attorney… but I'm also her daughter."

I knew with a newspaperman's instinct that Valentine Jones was telling the truth. I knew by the way the sound of it sank like a gritty stone in my gut. After all the years of hope and dread, the past had finally and truly come calling. And I could not spit a word.

Outside the bay window, the famous San Francisco fog crawled up the street and smothered the sun. I watched my finger tap the red button to end the call—gently, as if my hand was tip-toeing backwards out of the room. I turned off the phone and placed it face down on the kitchen counter, drained the glass of bourbon, went to the bedroom and swapped the pjs for a pair of khakis, a hoodie and some slip-on sneakers. I grabbed my wallet and keys on the way to the door, pulled the hood up around my face and walked out into the gray city day.

THE PERSISTENCE

Perhaps you've seen the video of my arrest later that night. I was told it went semi-viral, another disease upon the disease that already is the internet. I was handcuffed by one of San Francisco's finest and digitally immortalized by a pixelheaded tourist kid with a smartphone and a sideways Dodgers cap.

The video appeared above the clever title: Prize-winning Writer DUI'd and TKO'd. The footage opens with a wide shot of my brand new Cadillac CTS, run aground, cockeyed and high-centered on the concrete island in the middle of Lincoln Way—mere blocks from my home. I stumble out of the car, leaving the door flapped open. On the Bose stereo, Howlin' Wolf is growling out *Moanin' at Midnight*.

A dashboard warning bell dings out of time. Red and blue lights spin and strobe in the night. You hear a quick woop-woop from a siren. The picture jiggles as the camera zooms in, the officer walks into the frame, asks if I'm alright, sweeps the beam of his flashlight across the interior of the Cadillac. It's after midnight, but I say, "Good evening, officer." I lean on the Caddy, a study in casual debauchery.

My original plan was simply to catch my breath in neutral territory so to speak, a favorite bar in the Outer Sunset called Remo's. A dark old place of smoke-stained wood, red tuck and roll and a pool table under a beer light. A working man's dive long past its peak earning years, where two strangers drinking in silence at opposite ends of the bar are actually engaged in a form of male bonding, and a fresh drink can be ordered with nothing but a chin nod.

Just a couple stiff ones in the cool and understanding shadows—to relieve the tightness in my chest, organize my synapses and consider next steps. Of course Valentine Jones was right—I knew things I'd never told the authorities (or anyone else) back in that summer of 1970. Or since. And some of what I knew might help clear Billie Armstrong's name. But I also knew it wouldn't be that simple. Not for me. And not for Valentine Jones or her client.

"License and registration," the cop says. I pull my wallet out of my back pocket and fumble it to the ground, then manage to pick it up and hand it to the officer with a hapless shrug. Asserting my rights, I slur out a refusal to take the field sobriety test. The cop nods, unperturbed. My chest expands as if I've scored a minor victory. He's not impressed. "Mr King, I'm placing you under arrest for driving under the influence. Please turn around and place your hands behind your back."

I begin to sputter bitterly. "God damn you," I say. "Showing up out of nowhere… after all these years… like a fucking ghost? God damn you, Billie. Not now." My arms stretch out as if I'm being unjustly martyred. The cop calmly spins me around and tries to gather my hands but I yank loose and start firing punches at the hood of my own car. A solid combination, a right and left jab followed by a hard overhand right that shoots pain throughout my body like I've been tased.

The cop tries again to corral my hands, but I whip around and take a wild swing in his direction. Fortunately, I miss by a mile, lose my balance, and down I go, ass-first, tailbone smack against the curb. I'm lying on the pavement for a ten-count, and he just shakes his head, helps me to my feet and snaps the cuffs on. He shoves me to the patrol car, stuffs me into the back and slams the door.

You see my face through the window, the whirling lights bouncing off the glass, my mouth in a holler. My voice now distant and faint and the tone shifted to righteous self recrimination. You only hear snatches of my lament—some garbled nonsense about "the persistence of truth." Meanwhile, Howlin' Wolf is still moaning the blues in my Cadillac.

TWO CAGES

spent the next two nights in a holding cell until the County of San Francisco got around to properly booking me. I didn't complain. I didn't call a bailbondsman or anyone else. I didn't want any help, and I didn't want any questions. But I didn't know about the video yet.

I was released on my own recognizance Monday morning, narrowly escaping a public arraignment and most likely a black-robed lecture about the point-two-five I'd racked up on the Breathalyzer. In return for my release, I was required to sign a paper accepting a later date with the court, at which my attorney could appear in my stead. My California Driver's License was confiscated, and I was issued a piece of paper to serve as a temporary license, good only until my court date.

There's a whole lotta woulda-coulda-shoulda to be heard (or said) in the drunk tank at your local jail. I would've been better off if I hadn't gone to Remo's. I could've saved a lot more than money. I should've known Valentine Jones wasn't going away on the strength of my whiskey'd obstinance. But woulda-coulda-shoulda just means you didn't. Or so I was taught.

It was six Benjamins to get the Cadillac out of the impound lot. The shallow indentation I'd left in the hood wasn't as impressive as the swollen red knuckles on my hands, but at least the knuckles would heal for free.

I should've hit myself in the face instead of punching my car. That's the way I would've handled it as a kid, but as an adult I'd learned to divert my flares of self disgust to inanimate objects. Through the years, I'd built a small, expensive collection of damaged treasures—a Martin guitar with a gaping splintered hole left by a thrown bottle; a laptop with a spider-cracked screen after a tailspin flight across the bedroom, the sheetrock scar covered with a framed Edward Hopper print; and now a fist-sized dent in the hood of my Cadillac that would probably hit my wallet for a grand at the body shop.

I was right about one thing. Hanging up on Ms. Jones had only pissed her off. When I got back to my apartment and my phone, there was a string of texts ranging from a polite suggestion that we'd been disconnected, to a heated disparagement of my fundamental moral character. Except for the one jagged detail—that she was Billie Armstrong's daughter—I would have called my own lawyer and stepped out of the path of these flames.

But the truth is, I had it coming. I'd had it coming for forty years. I'd almost convinced myself that it was all behind me. You can run through life dogged and headlong, arms pumping, determined to outrun your ghosts, but the bastards keep pace without breaking a sweat.

• • •

I had it in my head that showing up at the *Sentinel* that morning would provide some cover once the arrest inevitably became public knowledge.

My colleagues and my bosses (and their bosses) would be inclined to dismiss the entire episode given that I'd come to work so soon afterward and appeared to perform with my usual shaggy competence. In future conversation I would shortside my Breathalyzer results by at least half and suggest the whole thing was a typical example of nanny-state overreach. The pinstripe overlords would nod sympathetically and interest would quickly subside.

And I imagined, during this perfunctory appearance at the office, I would call Valentine Jones. Now that I was sober, humbled, and somewhat unnerved by the prospect of her hunting my secrets, I had to apologize for hanging up, and I had to try to negotiate a compromise.

Yes, I had information I'd been withholding for decades. Yes, I wanted to help. But. I had my own ass to cover, and I was feeling a bit of a chill back there. Surely an experienced attorney like Ms. Jones would understand my desire to protect myself from any possible charges or damaging public exposure. (Hopefully she would never have to know I was trying to protect her as well.)

And, given a little more time, I would have called and tried to work something out. I swear. But, as it happened, Valentine Jones and Billie Armstrong had other plans.

• • •

I wasn't required to show up at the *Sentinel* Building on Union Square. I was technically an independent contractor—that's how it's done these days, to save the faceless shareholders the cost of a benefits package. At least, that's how it was done at the *Sentinel*.

But they'd given me a tiny office in the corner of the newsroom, a space no bigger than a walk-in closet up in Pacific Heights, with no windows and a front wall of glass that exhibited me like a zoo animal. Here is the legendary Ink-stained Wretch, one of the last alive in captivity. And the digital children on the other side of the glass finger their devices and stare at their celebrated analog ancestor, and they imagine this heritage somehow ordains them as principled journalists rather than clickminded typists mushed by dollarhearted tyrants like Daniel Lockhart.

It wasn't like I was in the office every day. A lot of a columnist's job is in the head and the feet, and the eyes and the ears. I had to move around and listen and watch and eat and drink The City. And the rest of the job—the writing and polishing, the fact-checking and bureaucratic politicking—could be done electronically from almost anywhere. But there was always something about being in the newsroom that quickened my inky blood—the ringing of phones, the squabble of reporters' questions, the tap-tap of keyboards. It all seeped into my glass cage and diffused into a comforting hum.

I'd been with the *Sentinel* fifteen years. People said good morning when you came to work, they'd nod or wave, the intern from j-school might stop by with donuts. After the Pulitzer was announced, even the strangers said hello. But that morning, the day after my two-day incarceration, there was not a word as I made my way through the newsroom, not a word. All eyes were riveted to screens or notepads, or squinting officiously into desk drawers—a veritable gauntlet of performative bustle, with a smattering of what I could have sworn was suppressed laughter.

I still didn't know about the video.

I wasn't two seconds in the Aeron chair behind my desk when Tom Monihan walked into the room without a knock. He shot me a Spock-like eyebrow and closed the door slowly and carefully as if he didn't want the click of the latch to wake up a suspicious wife.

"You got a serious pair of stones, King," he said. "I did not figure you showing up today."

Monihan is a tall, ponderous Black man with a shaved head and gray goatee. He'd been managing editor at the *Sentinel* long enough that he was the one who hired me. And we go back even further—he was the "wise old editor" in the story I told at the banquet, though the line was a bit of a private dig, as he's only a few years older than I.

"You might want to disappear before Lockhart finds out you're here," he said. "A couple days to cool off and he might not fire your ass."

I gave him a clueless what-the-fuck shrug.

Monihan pulled his head back in disbelief. "Damn. You haven't seen it?"

He moved behind the desk and rolled my chair aside with me in it. He commandeered my mouse and stood at the computer rapidly clicking here and there on the screen.

My eyes caught up to the cursor when the YouTube homepage appeared and Monihan clicked the play button on a "trending" video posted by some kid wearing a Dodger hat in his profile pic.

THE FELLOWSHIP OF MEN

Monihan said, "You're a goddamn star," with an odd mix of both doom and glee in his tone. "Oh, this part is great!" He pulled the corner of the video window to expand the picture. There I was, stumbling, slurring, ranting, punching my car in the face like an idiot. Monihan shook his head, cackling and pointing at the screen. "Jesus H. Christ, Archer. What the hell got into you?"

I hung my head and rubbed the bridge of my nose between my thumb and two fingers. They say even bad publicity is good publicity, but I wanted to slap myself. "Are you sure Lockhart's seen this?"

Monihan's nod was accompanied by what I took to be an expression of fascinated pity. "That new advertiser called, too. They've seen it… and they're pulling out."

With the Pulitzer buzz as an added selling point, Daniel Lockhart had personally wrangled a big-dollar deal with the local Cadillac dealership. They were ready to dedicate half their print budget to take the entire page next to my column twice a week—a significant chunk of revenue for the *Sentinel*, plus some bottom-line bragging rights for Lockhart at the next board meeting. I had helped soften the ground by buying the beautiful new automobile I was now seen punching out on YouTube.

The video itself was something I could live down in time, but shanking this Cadillac deal was a major transgression. Here I'd been having all those sexy *New York Times* daydreams, and now I might have to kiss Lockhart's fat corporate ass just to keep my job at the *Sentinel*.

"And what's this—more of your shitty karma?" Monihan said, but now he was looking out at something beyond the glass wall. I followed his gaze and found Valentine Jones standing across the newsroom in a double-breasted navy blue power suit. She spied a lane and began to cut through the rows of reporters' desks, those dark auburn curls dancing around her face and shoulders and a showdown stare hardening as she approached my door.

I'm sure Monihan guessed she was just another irate subscriber, come to read me her personal riot act for some perceived slight to her religion, political party or some other newly-minted cultural identity—it would not be unprecedented. I am, after all, a professional shit-stirrer. As she reached the door Monihan opened it with an exaggerated bow and flourish, a flash of mock courtesy that seemed to acknowledge the mounting comic absurdity of my morning. He grinned with teeth. "May we help you, ma'm?"

Perhaps this sounds like a disappointing display of schadenfreude by the man I consider my oldest friend. But the truth is men sometimes show intimacy in this way. The confidence to needle your friend at his low points and thereby rub his nose in the brutal realities of fate (and the futility of all complaints), well, that indicates a high level of male fellowship.

But, on this particular morning, my good fellow had no way of knowing that he was holding the door open for a handgrenade launched in the direction of my life. Perhaps Valentine did not know, herself.

She came into the little room and filled it up by the way she stood in front of my desk with her fist wrapped tightly around the handle of a brown leather satchel. "I won't be ignored," she said, glaring down at me in the Aeron chair. "One way or another you're going to answer some questions."

She had her mother's jade green eyes and the same hand-on-hip stance. The shock of recognition blurred my vision. For decades I'd spotted Billie in crowds even though she wasn't there. At baseball games, on television, at concerts or carnivals. A hint of boldness in the swish of a skirt, some wry mischief in a jostle of red curls, an accidental facsimile of that defiant but playful hand on hip. Now her daughter stood in front of me, the echo of all those fretful sightings.

I tried to muster an unperturbed smile. "Tom Monihan, meet Ms. Valentine Jones, attorney at law."

He apparently saw this as an entertaining plot turn. "Well, King, with your mouth I always thought you'd get fired… and/or sued someday. Not on the *same* day, though." He gripped her hand. "Nice to meet you, Ms. Jones. Now, are you suing this reprobate, or are you stuck defending him?"

"Neither… just yet," she said with a cruel tease of a look slanted my way. "Today I'm just a delivery person."

She reached into her bag and Monihan said, "Oh, perfect—it's a subpoena isn't it? King, I think you're about to get served."

TRIANGULATION

Perhaps Valentine Jones came to the *Sentinel* with that very moment scripted in her head. If so, the fact that Monihan was present to witness her performance must've made it all the more satisfying. In any case, she reached into the leather satchel and, with a parody of Monihan's earlier flourish, produced a cell phone. "I have a message for you, Mr. King… it's from Billie Armstrong."

She was clearly playing for dramatic effect, but she couldn't possibly have planned the next few minutes of the scene. The name Billie Armstrong meant nothing to Tom Monihan at that point, but the glass door to my office had quietly opened behind him, and Daniel Lockhart had leaned into the room just as the name tumbled past Valentine's lips—causing Lockhart's mouth to spring open like a cash drawer ringing up a sale.

"Billie Armstrong? The fugitive Billie Armstrong? Is that who you were mumbling about in that ridiculous video? *That* Billie Armstrong?"

Valentine couldn't have known that Lockhart would show up at that moment, ready to berate and possibly fire me over the YouTube video and the Cadillac account. And nobody in the room could've known he would recognize the name Billie Armstrong.

Lockhart had been Publisher of the *Sentinel* for all of three months, during which he'd never set foot or head in my office until that moment. He'd given me a fat-fingered handshake and a plaque that night at the Fairmont. He'd called me Archie—and I hate that. The office gossips had him pegged as a hatchet man for the profit wolves at Westland Media, with a mission to slash payroll and sell the paper—or wring it dry of every last dollar before parting it out. But with the mention of Billie Armstrong he'd suddenly morphed into some true-crime nerd whose DVR was probably crammed with old episodes of *America's Most Wanted*.

He stepped the rest of the way into the room, clicked the door shut and peered at me and Monihan. "If either of you is in contact with, or has knowledge of the whereabouts of Barbara AKA Billie Armstrong, I need to know about it. Now."

He said it exactly like that: "Barbara AKA Billie Armstrong," as if it was all one flowing name, as if he'd heard it that way a hundred times. Then finally he looked at Valentine. "And who are you?"

She offered her hand. "Valentine Jones, attorney for Ms. Armstrong."

Lockhart accepted her offer the way many men shake hands with a woman—light and loose with his palm turned up slightly, a lady-shake. "Daniel Lockhart," he said. "I'm the publisher here. Now, what's this about a message?"

Valentine played it cool as a TV poker shark, tapping her phone a few times while aiming a prim, in-charge smile at Lockhart, who held his hand out, expecting the phone but cast his eyes toward Monihan. "This could be a huge story, Tommy. She's one of the last of the Sixties radicals still on the loose. No one's heard from her in decades."

"Oh, she's not that big of a story anymore," I said, a feeble attempt to dampen Lockhart's gathering enthusiasm.

"The message is for Mr. King," Valentine said and held the phone toward me.

Lockhart frowned, pocketed his disappointed hand. I took the phone, searching Valentine's eyes, and I thought I saw a dew of sympathy there, but with a hard undercolor of brinksmanship. She'd caught on that Lockhart's excitement meant extra leverage, and she was happy to press her advantage.

The message app was open to a short exchange between Valentine and a person identified only as Mom.

Will he come?

Heading to his office, will ask again.

Tell him to be at Molly's pier at sunset tonight.

Molly's pier??

He'll know.

I read the messages twice through, Valentine watching in silence with questions—and demands—in those eyes. A child's hope, a woman's warning.

Something in me gave way then. A wave of fatigue broke over my body, and I slumped into the Aeron chair, my head lolling back. I stared upwards at the dozens of gnats trapped in the fluorescent light fixture, all corpses except one desperate scurrier who had temporarily forestalled his inevitable reckoning.

Lockhart lifted his chest and crossed his arms across his pale blue Oxford shirt and the Jerry Garcia tie he thought would ingratiate himself to San Franciscans. "Well?"

"She wants a meeting." I said.

This opened up new calculations behind Lockhart's eyes. "An interview? Perfect, we'll get someone assigned right away."

"My client wants a chance to tell her own story." Valentine said.

"Your client is a fugitive, wanted for the murder of an American soldier. The *Sentinel* won't play soapbox for some wild-eyed manifesto."

"No manifesto, Mr. Lockhart. She's planning to turn herself in—"

Lockhart cut her off, "That's huge," he said. "It's front page—a jailhouse confessional with anecdotes showing the hardships of life on the run… this is gold. Gold with legs."

"No confession. She's ready to stand trial if need be, but she'd like the public to hear the truth before the courts and the…uh, less scrupulous press." She had stared straight at me on the word *truth*.

Lockhart was getting the drift and was not entertained. "King, how in the hell are you involved in this anyway?"

I shrugged and sucked in a deep breath, stalling.

"My client is aware of Mr. King's reputation for unflinching honesty," Valentine said. "I'm authorized to offer him, and only him, an exclusive interview." She was one sharp kid, running interference for me while deflecting Lockhart's question and selling the proposal to him at the same time. And she knew this triangulation would back me right into the corner where she wanted me. In an odd way, I was proud of her.

Lockhart huffed, pressed his lips together, stroked his chin, but appeared to resign himself and switch gears. "Where exactly would this interview take place?" he said, already figuring the overhead costs, I'm sure.

I shook my head to signal an emphatic need-to-know status on this information. Lockhart the publisher would aid and abet a fugitive to sell newspapers, but I wasn't sure Lockhart the true-crime aficionado could be trusted not to blab to the authorities or anyone with a camera and an audience.

He waved it off. "Never mind. I don't care." Then he turned to Monihan. "Look, Tommy, I want a series on this, three pieces minimum. Pull the files on the original crime. King will do the one-on-one to get Armstrong's story. We'll balance that with a sidebar on the official law enforcement version. And have someone on the news desk ready to do play-by-play on her surrender and any future developments."

"I'll send a shooter with Archer, too." Monihan said. He'd been standing over by the door, his head following the back and forth like a tennis match, obviously enjoying my discomfort, although with no idea what they were getting me into.

"No photographers." Valentine jumped in.

Lockhart steamed out another exhale. "Okay, no pros," he said. "But we need something more than file art, so King gets to shoot one good mug on his phone."

She considered, then assented with a nod.

"Any other conditions, Ms. Jones?" Lockhart was one of those leftover men who simply could not pronounce the term Ms. without a note of condescension.

"No video, no audio recordings. And, obviously, no police. Or anyone else. Just Ms. Armstrong, Mr. King, and myself."

"It's all on you then, Archie." Lockhart gave me a go-get-em slap on the back.

The conversation had seemingly rushed right by the point where I had a choice, but I threw up a desperate last shot anyway. I said, "Look, Dan," because at the banquet, as if doing me a huge favor, he'd told me to call him

Dan. So now I said, "Look, Dan, this Armstrong thing sounds like good copy and all, but it's really not my beat. My contract clearly stipulates that I'm an independent opinion columnist and not obligated to accept reporting assignments."

"Contract, my ass. You get the fucking story or you're done at this paper, Pulitzer or not. Understand?" And he blustered out of the room.

KNUCKLES

The Pulitzer Prize for Commentary: "Archer King, *San Francisco Sentinel,* for his controversial and thought-provoking, yet colorful and down-to-earth columns on the tension between society's professed values and the reality of human frailty."

Translation: I get paid to call fuckup and bullshit on the highest and mightiest of individuals and institutions. Hey, it's a living.

A tangential observation: all secrets come wrapped in shame.

I once wrote that the Golden Gate Bridge was a beautiful and sad monument to the marketing power of America's perverse work-ethic nostalgia, the way the history of the thing is always sepia-tinted and awash in glorification of the many Depression-desperate men who risked—and eleven who lost—their lives so that bucolic Marin County could be colonized by Market Street money changers, the Coastal Miwok Indians could be further displaced, and suicide dramatists would have a place to make a scene. This was not a popular assessment, and letters to the editor poured in to the *Sentinel* offices for weeks.

Controversy drives single-copy sales, but perhaps my words were a bit harsh, and perhaps colored by personal antipathy. I had not been on the Golden Gate Bridge since the day I moved to San Francisco to take the job at the *Sentinel.* On that day, with The City glittering across the Bay like a giant blank page, I told myself I would never go back the way I'd come. I'd left too many sinkholes and culdesacs of memory on that side of the bridge.

Yet now I found myself stuck on the thing, with no clue why all northbound lanes were at a standstill at 2:40 on a Monday afternoon. The minivan in front of me had an old Bush-Cheney sticker plastered on its bumper, and I had the urge to ram it with my already-dented car. Hemmed in on all sides, I couldn't even see the ocean. A Muni bus rumbled in the lane on my left, the exhaust warping the air and the cloying smell of diesel crawling through the car vents. To my right, a tow truck pulling a rotting Winnebago that was probably some unfortunate's home earlier that morning. In my rearview, a UPS guy checked his watch. Again.

If possible, I would've made a u-turn, which I'm pretty sure would be highly illegal on the bridge. I was rage-gripping the steering wheel of the Cadillac, hunched forward on this forced march toward the past, spun up like an old speedfreak, running on compulsion and defiance, jonesing to self-harm by cutting into my oldest emotional scabs.

Or was I wrong; is there nobility in this sort of surrender? Honor in the alchemy that transmutes secrets into news? Can wrongs be righted, coward-ice redeemed, damages compensated, debts repaid—with truth as currency? Monihan said, man-up brother, this is the smart thing to do. Valentine said it's the right thing to do for Billie and your own peace of mind. Lockhart said just get it in print. Did the truth even matter?

There was a compression of the traffic, a tightening of the screws of antic-ipation. The Bush-Cheney minivan moved two feet. I released the brake pedal and the Cadillac glided forward, our bumpers now close enough to sever a leg between them. The UPS guy honked his horn, trying to change lanes as if he knew something—perhaps from his higher perch he could see the edge of an opening ahead.

And when the way was clear and this artery started to pump cars again, I would be carried across the bridge and spirited backwards through my own history. I would speed north on 101, noting the exit signs for Petaluma, Santa Rosa, Cloverdale, chicken towns, cow towns and lumber towns that are now off-ramp bedroom towns with strip-mall wine bars and the mere ghosts of the pop-and-mom newspapers where I had cut and sharpened my teeth—now all swallowed up by Gannett or Westland or another media Godzilla. And fur-ther north, beyond where the freeway narrows to two winding lanes, I would turn inland to drive up and over the hills toward Lupoyoma, the wellspring of my discontent, though I could not fully explain my reasons, even to myself. I drive the Cadillac, but what drives me?

I laced my hands and popped my bruised knuckles as the traffic inched forward. Recently I'd read about an experiment in which researchers MRI'd people cracking their knuckles, and tiny sparks of electricity showed up on the images—lightning bolts inside the crooks of your fingers. We are walking, talking worlds, each of us a complex system connected to the impossibly vast universe of systems. We are living, breathing planets, racked with storms we don't understand. And we are laughably inaccurate forecasters of our own weather.

The minivan finally started moving—steadily, slowly, not yet five miles an hour. The Muni bus coughed and shifted into gear. Only now did I notice the murmur of talk radio babbling from the stereo. It had been on since I started the car, but I'd been so far in my head that it receded into the sonic distance like an argument in the next room. Now I heard some self-righteous politician who expected me to believe the U.S. invasion of Iraq had something to do with my personal freedom, and I turned off the radio.

I hit the start button on the CD player. The same mix-CD that was playing when I got arrested, the selection of old blues I hadn't listened to in years, long stored in the closet along with the splintered guitar and the cracked laptop. The CD player whirred to life, a piano pounded out an intro, a harmonica jumped in with a ragged growl and the snare drum hit the backbeat, Little Walter Jacobs started singing about that key to the highway.

With the volume cranked I could almost see Billie Armstrong, standing by the side of the road with her thumb out. She is 17 years old, a blurry Polaroid vision of untamed red hair, that cheeky smile, those flashing green eyes, hand on hip—the feminine embodiment of candlefire.

For the moment it was forty years ago in my head, but as I reached the north end of the bridge, I checked the reality of the Cadillac's dashboard clock—3:30, approximately three hours until the sun would set on Molly's pier. I could still make it… if I still wanted to.

OLD FRIENDS

In the passenger seat rode another artifact retrieved from the closet—my mother's old hatbox, with the silver and gray stripes and faded red roses printed on top. Before I left my apartment, I'd ransacked the closet and found the hatbox, stuffed behind old shoeboxes and file boxes and other boxes of life's leavings.

The hatbox contained important time-travel accessories: a child's kaleidoscope, a polished abalone shell, the Crow's Nest motel key, the Kennedy for President button, and the photo of my mother smiling in the blue hat on a windy bluff overlooking the ocean. You know the rest: the pile of letters from Vietnam, some crumpled up newspaper pages, and the pink lipstick envelope, after all these years still unopened. I had the childish notion that Billie and I should open it together.

Somewhere on the back side of the rolling Mayacamas Mountains, just shy of the Lupoyoma County border, the steep road got narrower and windier, the chuckholes bigger and deeper, the asphalt cracked and gouged in spots and warped and bubbled in others, October oak trees shaggy with moss, beer cans and burger wrappers mixed into the rocky slide debris that sometimes extended into the traffic lane. The metal sign marking the county line was freckled with rusty bullet holes.

Lupoyoma County is the only county in the entire state of California without a single mile of railroad track—nobody who's ever been there was in that big of a hurry to return.

I first got out in 1975, won a fancy scholarship to a private school, but eventually I found college interfered with my wanderlust (and some of my other lusts). In 1980 I ended up back in town when Pop died of the cirrhosis and Molly needed help for a while. I came back to help her, but I was also in sore need of help at the time, broke and road-weary after a couple years rambling up, down and around California and the rest of the West, young, dumb and full of Kerouac.

I came back to Lupoyoma for Molly and myself, and I stayed until breast cancer took her in the summer of 84. Those were some of the darkest years of my life, but I owed her and Pop. They had taken me in when I couldn't live on Fourth Street anymore. Knowing your father's secrets is not necessarily the precursor to a healthy adult relationship.

• • •

I hit the valley ahead of schedule, pulled in for gas at a new place on the south end of town. Ran my card and started the pump. There was a rough looking chopped Sportster parked in front of me, primer gas tank, cracked leather seat, balding tires. Out of the mini-mart strolled Timmy Bilderback. Long stringy blonde hair shrouding his face. Gray hoodie zipped up against the autumn air, threadbare jeans, no chaps, dirty Nike knockoffs, not boots.

"Well, what the fuck? Somebody die or something?"

"Didn't expect to see you either, Tim."

"Why? Were else would I be?"

"Oh, I don't know. San Quentin?"

"Funny guy. So, what the hell are you doing around here?"

"Family business," I said.

He only nodded, like I get it, you ain't sayin'. He looked at my car. "New Caddy, huh? Must be nice." It wasn't exactly a compliment and he didn't wait for a response, just swung a leg over the duct-taped seat, stomped on the kick starter, revved it up loud and roared off.

I turned north on Main Street and counted the chain stores and fast-food joints that now occupied the fields I once roamed. A few scattered leftover vacant lots with fading for-sale signs. But the center of town much as I'd known it—a patchwork of late 19th century and early 1960s building spurts, every corner filtered through snapshots of old memory, like holograms projected through my eyes. I made the right turn at First Street, toward the shoreline of the big lake. Pulled into the Weeping Willow parking lot heart-struck by that cliché sense of a shrunken world. Even the vast blue-green of

Lupoyoma Lake somehow seemed smaller than I remembered.

Back in the late 70s when, for various reasons, tourism started to dry up in Lupoyoma, Molly finagled a liquor license and turned the cafe into more of a bar and grille, heavy on the bar. Sonny the cook became Sonny the bar manager. And when Molly passed, Sonny inherited the whole shebang, the bar and grille and the entire Weeping Willow Resort & Trailer Court—rightfully so, given that I was a strung-out barfly at the time (but that's another story).

• • •

Valentine Jones stood in the parking lot next to a well-worn Toyota pickup raised up over some chunky off-road tires. Not what I expected. I parked a space away, opened the door and slowly unfolded out of the Caddy.

"We're early," she said, looking at the phone in her hand. "Billie's not here yet."

The sun was low in the western sky, veiled by thin clouds but not set.

Her eyes swept the area beyond the parking lot, taking in the scenery of cabins and trailers and trashy cars, and she seemed to be putting something together in her head. "This is where it all happened isn't it?" she said. "I've only seen it in her paintings."

"Paintings?" I asked. But she ignored me.

"According to my mother, I was conceived in this town. She used to tell me it was a teenage hookup, a one-night stand and then the guy got drafted and died in Vietnam. Said she didn't even know his last name. No pictures, no letters, no trace. I only learned the truth a couple months ago when she started to feel like the FBI was closing in. That's when I first heard of Billie Armstrong. And Hank Timmons. And the rest. You know the rest, though, don't you? At least she thinks you do. And she said if she was right, you would stand up and tell the truth. That's your brand, right—fearless truth-teller?"

"Well, I'd like to think it's more than just a brand."

She gave me a skeptical nod like we'll see about that, then she took another long look at the setting. "So, where's this mysterious pier?"

I was relieved at the change of subject, unsure of what Billie thought I knew, or how she thought I knew it, or what she may have told her daughter.

"Pier's around back," I said, "Fortunately, we can cut through the bar."

The glass was all tinted now, you couldn't see in—or through to the patio like in the old days. A beer light glowed in one window, but the closed sign hung on the door.

Then the door swung open and Sonny stuck his head out. "Well, long time no see, kid."

"Nice to see you too, old friend."

We shook hands. His black hair had gone salty, and he'd gained a little beer fat around the middle, but his dark eyes were clear and steady as ever and his handshake just as firm.

"I knew you'd show," he said.

"Sounds like you know more than I do."

He gave me a slow mulling-it-over kind of nod and turned to Valentine Jones. "Nice to finally meet you in person."

They shook hands. "Thank you for agreeing to do this," she said. "I understand the risk."

I hadn't previously thought to wonder how Sonny was involved in all of this. More and more I was starting to feel like I was just a passenger on an unnamed carnival ride.

We went in and the first thing I noticed was that real down-home dive-bar stench, not of poured alcohol ready to be sipped (or tipped or slugged or shot or chugged), but thirty-some years of exhaled alcohol, drunk once and then released into the contained atmosphere as exhaust and trapped there with a permanent tobacco stink in some sad inversion layer, a beer and whis-key smog belched out of fleshy smokestacks with rheumy eyes and mottled teeth. Dank shadows loitered at empty cocktail tables on the edges of the room like ghosts of blackouts past. Buzzy electric light fell across the aged wood and twinkled like Christmas on the hips of liquor bottles. I never felt more at home.

"What's your drink these days, Archer?"

I hopped up on a stool. "Maker's, neat."

Valentine interrupted. "Is the pier through there?" Pointing at a door in the back wall, looking at her phone again. She didn't wait for an answer, went out the door, but came right back in. "I don't see her," she said.

Sonny put the glass of bourbon on the bar in front of me. "Sun's not down," he said. "A few more minutes till dark."

Valentine nodded. "Comfort and Coke, then."

Sonny poured himself a draft and stayed behind the bar. The three of us sipped our drinks and waited. He and I manufactured small talk. How's business? Seen any of the old gang? What happened to that old Ford? Valentine went to look out the back door every few minutes.

Like a weird echo of the ancient history of this room, the front door swung open and Timmy Bilderback stood in the doorway looking all satisfied with himself.

"Bar's closed on Mondays, Tim. You know that." Sonny said.

Timmy glanced at the drinks on the bar. "Don't look closed to me."

Sonny didn't miss a beat. "Private meeting. Invite only. Trying to keep the riffraff out."

Timmy fake-laughed, looked at me. "Seems like you failed."

"Alright, what can I do for you, Tim?" Sonny, so calm it sounded like a warning.

Timmy, unruffled, took a stool between me and Valentine's neglected drink, laid two bucks on the bar. "Cold Bud I guess. Just wondering what's going on, ya know. I mean, seems like old-home week in here. We all go back aways, we should catch up." His attempt at a sarcastic smile was undermined by his missing teeth.

Sonny opened a bottle of Budweiser, set it down on the bar and slid it over in front of Timmy.

Valentine, standing by the half-open back door, looked over her shoulder and finally noticed our uninvited guest. "Who's this?"

I said, "Valentine Jones, meet Timmy Bilderback."

"Timmy Bilder… uh… where have I heard that name?" Then she made a face like she remembered. "Why is he here?"

"Well, whoever you are," Timmy said. "I just came in for a beer and a chat with some old friends, that alright with you?"

I said, "We haven't been friends for a long long time, Tim."

Outside, the sun dipped behind the mountains and the day began to melt into deep blue.

Valentine turned eyes back to the doorway. "There's a light," she said. "I see a boat."

THREE DRINKS AND THE TRUTH

Sonny walked down the bar and picked up the bottle in front of Timmy. "Time for you to clear out, Tim. Like I said, private meeting."

Timmy said, "I ain't going nowhere. You'd have to drag me out kicking and screaming. I want to see who else is coming to this shindig. Besides, I ain't done with my beer."

Sonny started to come around the bar.

"No," Valentine said. "I know who he is. He stays." And she went out the back door again.

I didn't move. I stared into my glass of bourbon and thought again of all the times I'd seen Billie's face in the faces of strangers in cafés and bars, or her red hair flashing in a crowd, her hips swinging up the street and disappearing around a corner. The many Billies that were not Billie. And now the familiar hope and dread flooded me heart to stomach. I *hoped* to detect a flicker of the old fire burning in those green eyes—consolation if not reprieve, a sentence of time-served for my guilt-ridden conscience. I *dreaded* the prospect of cold bitterness in a face mapped by years of gray worry.

Timmy shook a bent cigarette out of a rumpled pack of Kools and fired it up, all the while eyeballing me in the bar-back mirror like some movie psychiatrist lighting his pretentious pipe. He was enjoying this.

She wore a white peasant blouse and a stone-washed denim skirt that flared out above black tights and Birkenstocks, and if I'd seen her across the street in some other town, I might not have recognized her. Her hair still tumbled in waves around her face but the waves had turned silver. I might have thought she was just another middle aged hippie woman that you could see in any Northern California bookstore or coffeeshop, or at the city council meeting speaking out for a lost cause. But when she entered the room and smiled at me with one hand on her hip—even though I was hoping to see it—I was shocked at the effect. There was a churning in my mind and the blood rushed up to my face. Unseen in the dim light of the bar, I may have blushed.

"I knew it!" Timmy said. "Billie fucking Armstrong. I got to thinking, big city writer Archer King, been shit-talking Lupoyoma for years, all of a sudden he's back in town? Something's up. And I was right. Oh yeah, I was right, shit's gettin' close to the fan now!"

Close up, Timmy was pitted and withered to an extent I hadn't noticed before. He looked older than Sonny, who had about dozen years on him. He was concentration camp thin and sallow gray, the complexion of wet ashes. I recognized the look, the toll of long-term drug use. I'd been pretty far out there myself back in the lost 1980s when it seemed the whole population of Lupoyoma County was wired to the gills. I ran across Timmy a couple times back then, spotted him across a parking lot or a barroom, pretended not to notice and left in the other direction. The legacy of that era was divisible into three categories. There were those who died, and they were too many. There were those who wised up, got clean and moved forward. And there were those who never stopped drugging but somehow stayed alive, all the while dying in front of you. That was Timmy.

"Bilderback, Timothy, juvenile," said Valentine, stepping forward. "Key witness, according to the files. I don't know why it didn't click immediately."

"Who the hell are you again?"

"I'm Ms. Armstrong's lawyer." She stood behind the pool table, hands on the rail in a commanding way that transformed the barroom into a courtroom.

He coughed up a laugh. "Well, I got nothing to say to you… except your client's in big fucking trouble when they catch her ass. And they will. Soon. Real soon. Everybody knows she killed Hank, and they're gonna lock her up and throw away the fucking key."

"Actually, most of the evidence is circumstantial. You were the closest thing to an eye witness. Now it's been forty years, and you have a criminal record of your own and a court date later this month as I recall—possession for sale, isn't it? Yes, I can't wait to get you on the stand."

Timmy paused for a split second, but he never was one to back down.

"I ain't afraid of you," he said. "I know what I saw that night."

"And what was that, Mr. Bilderback? Pretend you're under oath now."

"No big deal—I was in the living room at Trey's, asleep on the floor. I heard some kinda commotion—glass breaking, Hank shouting. I looked out the window and saw this crazy bitch swinging a bat around. I went to get Trey, but he was passed out cold. When I looked out the window again, Hank and her were both gone, and I thought well, show's over, and went back to sleep. Then in the morning, bunch of cops showed up. I told them, same as I'm telling you."

"You were spending a lot of time at Trey's then, weren't you?"

"Yeah, so what?"

"You were also there on a different night—the night Ms. Armstrong was raped."

I felt Billie's eyes on me, measuring my reaction, and I figured there was no point in pretending surprise. Now that the truth had entered the room, it might soon be calling my name.

"Don't know nothing about that," Timmy said.

I said, "You remember, Tim. It was the night Nate's band played on the patio, the night Nate burned his draft card."

"I went home early that night, the party was still going when I left."

"I don't think so," I said. "You were bouncing off the walls. Too much tequila. You weren't going anywhere."

"You're the one who passed out on the couch," Timmy said.

"Yeah, wonder why."

"Well, I was stone cold sober," Sonny said from behind the bar. "And I saw you ducking down the hallway when I came in."

"I don't care what you saw, I don't know nothing about no rape."

"Oh yes you do," Billie spoke up. "You know because you were in the room. You and Trey held my arms down." Her voice was firm, but she was still standing over by the back door like she might want to escape.

Timmy forced a laugh. "No one in the world will believe a word you say." He pointed like his finger was a weapon. "You'd say absolutely anything to save your ass."

Valentine said, "According to the police report, there are other potential witnesses. Trey Morgan, of course, and the Quarterman boy—"

"Trey wouldn't give you the time of day—if you could even find him. Ran off to Idaho last year, joined some fucking militia, gets off on walking through the local Walmart with his AR-15. And Joey Quarterman bought the farm fifteen years ago, OD'd thirty feet out his own back door, face down in Bottlerock Creek with a fucking needle still in his arm."

Being reminded about Joey's death made me thirsty, and I signaled Sonny for a second drink. Joey never came clean to anyone about the rape far as I know. I suppose he had his reasons. Like me. But one day, a couple years after the headlines, I was sneaking a smoke on the hill behind the high school foot-ball field, and Joey walked up the dirt path, stood next to me, lit a cigarette, kept his eyes on the field below and said, without preamble, "You know, I don't blame her." I knew what he meant, and we never spoke of it again, but I knew it was eating him up. Like me.

Sonny filled my glass and left the bottle on the bar in front of me, sighed and crossed his arms. "I found Joey sitting out on the pier that night crying and shaking and hugging his knees, apologizing out-loud to God. Wouldn't even look at me."

"Well, I ain't coppin' to shit," Timmy said. "Like I told you, I wasn't there. I don't care what any of you say, especially this murdering commie bitch."

"I wasn't thinking of Trey or Joey," Billie said. She came a few steps further into the room, and that perked everyone's ears up. "I think I saw someone else that night, someone who maybe witnessed the whole thing… through the window."

Timmy said, "What? What a pantload! What are you even talking about? You were practically un…" Realizing how close his foot was to his mouth, he shut up.

My heart started running in circles. I poured myself another drink, my third. I took a twenty out of my wallet and started to lay it on the bar. Sonny held up a hand and said, "On the house."

Valentine looked as shocked as Timmy. "I think I'm gonna need another, too," she said.

Timmy knocked the heel of his empty beer bottle on the bar. "How bout me? I could use another beer over here."

"You pay in advance," Sonny said.

Timmy sneered and laid the money on the bar.

"We all know I wasn't just drunk," Billie said. "But, even so… there was a moment when I looked across that room and I swear I saw a pair of eyes flash in the corner of the window," she said. "Someone was there… and I think I know who."

A ten-thousand-pound silence hung over the room as Sonny poured Valentine's drink and set the glass quietly on the bar. The ice cubes rattled as he stirred in the Coke. Valentine came and picked up her drink, took it back to the pool table as Sonny slowly went to the cooler, fished out a Bud, popped the cap off and set it down in front of Tim.

Billie seemed to be stabbing me with her eyes. I felt everyone was waiting for me to say something. Or maybe it was only me who was waiting for me to say something. Waiting all the years.

I slammed my empty glass down on the bar, and everyone flinched.

"Oh, what the hell," I said. "You're a lying son of a bitch, Tim." Something solid in my tone alerted him, and he spun around toward me. I faltered for a moment, realizing I'd just dipped my toe in scalding water. Billie seemed to encourage me with a tilt of her head. I locked on her. "It was me, goddammit. In the window… the eyes you saw… it was me, alright?" In Billie's face I saw a quiet knowing. And grateful relief.

I turned back to Timmy. "I saw what Hank did and I saw you help, Tim."

"You're full of shit, King. Still making up your little stories for the newspaper. No one's gonna believe that crap. Like, why didn't you tell the cops back then? Hell, why don't you tell them now? You gonna tell the whole world you watched your sister get raped and you didn't do a thing about it? Yeah, put that in your big city fishwrap."

"Archer—you saw?" Valentine said, and the question doubled as an accusation, first against me, and then against her mother. "Mom, why didn't you tell me this before?"

"I wasn't sure," Billie said. "I had to be sure. That's why we came."

I braced myself with my hands on the bar. I searched Billie's eyes again. I hung my head. My own eyes brimmed, my defenses tattered.

Billie seemed to read my anguish. "Archer, you were just a boy," she said. "All of thirteen."

Valentine had a different take. "But why didn't you ever tell someone… how could you—"

The cops exploded into the room through both doors at once and were suddenly rushing everywhere in their bulletproof vests marked S.W.A.T. in Helvetica Extra Bold, yelling and pushing, their weapons drawn and zip-tie handcuffs at the ready. My legs were kicked out from under me with no warning, I heard my knees crack on the linoleum and the pain shot up my thighs. I was slammed to the floor with my head turned to the side, looking over at Billie's face in the same position. Those fierce, wet jade eyes.

RAINING IN MY HEART

The county had built a new correctional facility several years before, out among the bare hills north of Lupoyoma City. When inmates are released, there's no ride to town, no bus, and no public phone. Sticking to the paved streets it's a five-mile trek into town in whatever weather the sky is offering that day. The officers who processed me out returned my phone, but the battery was dead. The rain started to fall the moment they ushered me out the front door. I stood in the parking lot staring at the black screen on the phone, then I started to walk.

From behind me I heard Sonny's voice. "Hey, hold up." Apparently, they had processed him right after me. I stopped. "Got a phone?" he said.

"Dead," I said, "You?"

"Stashed back at the bar."

I started walking again.

"Maybe they'd let us make a call at the reception desk," he said.

"I'm not going back in there."

"Long walk in the rain," he said. "And the wind."

I said, "At least it's not cold." Then the rain and a chilly wind came harder, seemingly on cue. I had left my sportscoat draped over the passenger seat in the Cadillac, which was still parked in front of the bar. The knit polo I was wearing did not qualify as rain gear. We walked together, each with our heads down and our eyes on a few yards of pavement in front of our feet. We walked out to the road that leads back to Lupoyoma City. A few cars went by but we didn't try to hitch a ride. Who would stop for two sopping-wet old men who had obviously spent the night in jail?

The shortcut to town led through Lupoyoma Cemetery, over the back fence and down a brushy hill to the football field behind the high school and so on, shaving a couple miles off the trip. I didn't want to go. The cemetery held nothing but dread for me. I never got out of Pop's truck at my mother's burial, and I'd never been to the place since.

We walked through the open gate, an arching wrought-iron gothic assembly anchored on both sides to squarish concrete pillars topped with big winged lions. The main road sloped up at a steady incline between rows and columns of headstones and monuments nestled in a wet carpet of grass. I said, "I haven't been here in a long while. Seems funny it happens this way."

"Maybe it's time," Sonny said, as if he understood. He looked toward a walkway to the right. "She's down that way if you want to see her," he said.

"How would *you* know?"

"Well," he said. "You get old in a small town like this, you spend a lot of time at the cemetery." He chuckled. "I literally know where the bodies are buried."

The sun slipped through the tattering clouds and the rain slowed to a bright sputter. The breeze carried that gritty smell of fresh rain on oily asphalt. It was the first time I got a good look at him outside the gloom of the bar. He had to be in his mid-sixties by now, but he looked lean and tough as a game bird. Wrinkled and dark, and despite the slight limp, steady on his feet. Brown carpenter's pants and a shortsleeve henley, that long frizzy ponytail streaked with gray. He turned down the path and I followed until he stopped and pointed with a nod of his head, then looked away, I assumed out of courtesy.

EVELYN MEDINA KING… OUR 'EVIE'… 1938-1969. My mother's grave lay modest and cold, a slab of concrete where a rectangle of lawn might have grown, a small bronze plaque set into the ground rather than a headstone. Not one flower. She was buried next to Pop and Molly, their legal names, Edward and Mary Medina, revealed there for what might have been the first time to many people who'd known them for decades.

Grandma Junia was buried in a different section, closer toward the crest of the hilltop, with a proper headstone in the shape of a cross, granite with chiseled lettering, all prearranged by her, I'm sure. I stood at the foot of her grave and quickly brushed my hands back and forth. "I guess that's that."

Sonny walked ahead, picking a way around and between graves, never walking over them, never violating that old superstition. He did not hurry, and I forgot that we were supposed to be taking a shortcut. At each graveside we visited, Sonny stood at a respectful distance, hands folded loosely in front of him, eyes on the ground or toward the distant hills.

There were two empty plots next to Grandma Junia's. I knew one of them was reserved for my father, and it wouldn't remain empty for long. He and I had parted on the worst of terms all those years before. And we hadn't talked in a long time, but I occasionally heard news of him through Aunt Laurette. He was sick and bitter with lung cancer now and dying in the house on Fourth Street. Laurette had drifted into the difficult role of caregiver. She regularly pestered me to visit, and I regularly resisted. Now I looked at his future resting place, weighing guilt against resentment and arriving at futility.

"One of these was supposed to be your mother's," Sonny said, diverting my thoughts, "but Pop and Molly wouldn't stand for it. I guess by now you know why." This last thought came out like a question.

"I knew they blamed my father for her death, and I thought I knew why." I said. "But sometimes it seems like I never really knew any of them. How can it be that you spend all that time with people and don't know who they are?"

"They never really know you either," he shrugged.

"Except for Billie. She could see right into me, although I could never know enough about her. Drove me crazy."

Sonny said, "Hah! She's a botheration alright."

"Why'd you stick your neck out for her, anyway?" I asked. "You only knew her for a few weeks a long time ago."

"I know what it's like to have a small town turn against you," he said.

We were almost at the fence.

"What about Hank?" I said.

"Wasn't sure you'd want to see that one," Sonny said, with a look full of memory. I nodded, and he led me back up the slope a short way, to a grassy spot surrounded by a low concrete wall.

FLOYD HENRY TIMMONS JR... PVT US ARMY... LOVING

SON… 1951 - 1970. The sun broke through the clouds and landed on the white marble headstone like a spotlight. Two tiny American flags on tiny wooden flagpoles were stuck in the manicured lawn. I nearly spat out the bile that rose to the back of my throat. I swallowed, took a sighing breath and closed my eyes against the threat of a more visible reaction. I didn't think Sonny saw, but there were a few silent seconds before he walked on.

On the back side of the slope, Sonny weaved a path that generally headed toward the corner of the cemetery, where we could jump the fence. He stopped at one point to retie the laces on his work boots. I stopped as well and by chance noticed the plot beside me. Another small bronze plaque set in the ground. No flags here.

JAMES R COLE… PFC US ARMY… VIETNAM… 1942-1969.

Sonny raised an eyebrow at the look of recognition on my face. "Somebody you know?"

I hesitated. "No. Just a story I read in the newspaper once."

In my head I heard the gravelly sound of Elmore James singing *The Sun Is Shining (Although it's Raining in My Heart)*. But I was hearing the song for myself rather than the dearly departed. Whatever I thought I knew about Evie King and the blues and J.R. Cole would always be just a story in the newspaper. Or a letter, or my own mind. *Of course it matters what you believe,* Billie had said once. But I wanted more than belief. I wanted the truth. And you can't talk the truth out of the dead. Maybe that's the loss I was mourning that day as much as any of the souls buried on that hill.

Sonny said nothing else about Cole's grave, and we walked on. We followed the slope down to the wire fence and climbed over and made our way through scrub oaks and brush, down the old dirt path worn into permanence by highschoolers trudging up for a smoke or a makeout tryst, then down to the wet glistening football field and across the rest of the school grounds.

When we finally reached downtown Lupoyoma City we walked along Main Street, past the houses and stores and offices that were the landmarks of my childhood, and eventually we reached the old *Call & Record* building, now converted to a health food store after the paper had moved to a new building on the south end of town. I stopped and peered into the front win-dows and saw my own reflection.

Sonny stopped too, and considered the building with his hands in his pockets. Then, as we approached the Fourth Street intersection, he stopped and looked down the street toward the lake, and he said, "Laurette still comes by the bar now and then. When she can get away. It's been hard on her taking care of your father."

"I'm not sure I see the point in showing up for one last argument with him." I said.

"Hey, no judgement," Sonny said. "Point is, I know *she* would like to see you."

I let that suggestion fall and kept walking up Main Street.

THE EDITOR'S LAST CORRECTION

The Giants were in the National League Championship Series against the Philadelphia Phillies, and I had missed the first couple games sweating out that two-day hangover in a San Francisco jail. By the time Sonny and I made it to the Weeping Willow parking lot, game three was about to start, and I was going to watch every pitch, hell or high water, as Pop would say. And damn the rest of the world.

I sat at the bar, sipped my way through a couple beers and a couple bourbons, watching on one of the big screen TVs. My old "friend" Craiger Robinson, now Sonny's right-hand man, was tending bar. We clinked bottles and swapped Little League war stories and what-you-been-up-to-since-way-back-when stories.

I knew there was a small, albeit unconnected, cadre of people who were at that very moment in a butt-clenching hurry to see me, question me, order me, threaten me, but I'd left my dead phone in the Cadillac, and no one in the bar except Sonny and Craiger knew who I was. I was drinking incognito, and that was good, because I needed time *not* to think.

The series was tied one-one after the first two games in Philly. A win in their first home game could be crucial for the Giants. And they delivered. Starter Matt Cain threw seven strong innings, and Javiér Lopez and closer Brian Wilson slammed the door on a three-nothing victory. The Giants were up two-one in the NLCS! I wondered if my father was watching.

• • •

I had the bothersome idea that I should probably get back in touch with the rest of the world. I sat in the parked Cadillac and started the engine to charge up my phone.

The great Howlin' Wolf, came blasting out of the stereo singing *Moanin' at Midnight*—that pained and gutwrenched roar of his, like a man pouring whiskey on his own stab wound. Somebody's knocking on his door, and he does not want to answer.

When enough juice reached my phone to bring it back to life, the thing went off like a clock store at the top of the hour. Repeating triplets of chime-ding-bloop, chime-ding-bloop. I let it all tally up like a slot machine jackpot: seventeen text messages, nine voice mails, twelve emails and six Facebook messages. Then I yanked out the charging cable and threw the phone over my shoulder. It bounced off the back seat and thumped on the floor. Meanwhile, Howlin' Wolf's phone is ringing off the hook.

I should've known what was coming.

After all, I knew I'd missed the deadline for the Billie Armstrong story. By now her arrest and mugshot were already hitting front pages and cable news everywhere. There would be a series of questions from Tom Monihan, turning into demands, leading to outright begging and finally a profane tirade. There might be an email or two from Daniel Lockhart himself, containing some threatening legalistic googlymoogly about contractual obligations and the company's recourse for breach.

And I knew Billie had been transported to a federal facility in San Francisco and was being held without bail. The pair of FBI agents who questioned me in jail that morning had filled me in on that while making it clear that, although I was being released, I remained a "person of interest" for possibly aiding and abetting a fugitive, and I could easily be in the same situation as Billie if at any time I chose not to cooperate to their satisfaction.

Lastly, I knew of course that Valentine Jones would be expecting to hear from me. I knew she would want me to sign an affidavit and agree to testify in court if necessary, plus she would probably want to talk to death the secrets that had poured out in the bar.

Not now, I thought. Not right now.

I put the car in reverse and backed out, turned the stereo up and drove under the arch of oak branches and out of the Weeping Willow. Howlin' Wolf came in for the big finish, saying not to worry, Daddy's going to bed.

I'd always thought that was such a bizarre non sequitur—but now it struck me as accidentally prescient. I'm a rational man. As I've said before, I am not a believer. I have no faith in faith. And I won't try to be on both of sides of that fence by claiming to be "spiritual but not religious." I've been in barfights over such things. And yet I can be as superstitious as an old third base coach. I pay attention to certain signs—musical omens and portents—that others would call coincidence. The right words in the right song, blasting out of the right stereo speakers at the right time, can briefly take control of my state of mind, my car, and thus my life.

• • •

The yard at the old house on Fourth Street was a sad mess—the lawn overrun and the walkway threatened by a gang of dandelions and their weedy associates, the rosebushes in front of the porch all thick and tangled and thorny Medusas. Aunt Laurette sat in the old wicker chair on the porch puffing on a cigarette.

She saw it was me climbing out of the Cadillac, and she screamed and waved and threw down her lit smoke and hurried down the steps. "Archer King, I swear, your ears must be on fire! I was just talking about you." The years had stripped away her figure and she was now a small thin woman with a big hairdo that was not naturally black. She wore a tight leopard print blouse with white skinny jeans that emphasized the sticks she had for legs. Still sporting her trademark blue flame eyeshadow.

She met me on the sidewalk and gave me a long-lost kind of a hug, stepped back and looked me up and down. "Boy, you look like hell," she said. She gave me a wink like the kind she could always embarrass me with in younger days.

"I was in town…" I said, and I looked down and toed at a dandelion in the seam of the sidewalk. "and I thought maybe I should see him."

"Well, I think you should," she said and patted me on the arm. "But I'm not sure he'll agree."

"What do you mean?"

Laurette winced like she wanted the words back. "I mean he might not know who you are. The hospice nurse is with him now, he's unconscious a lot, and even when he's awake he's confused… and he can be a cranky pain in the ass."

I didn't respond, unsure if I was disappointed or relieved.

"We're talking days, maybe hours now," she said.

"Got anything to drink?"

She shook her head at my obvious dissipation and waved for me to follow her up the stairs and into the house, through the old wooden screen door with the screen peeled back from the frame in one corner. She held a finger to her lips and whispered, "Wait here."

The curtains were closed and the stale dim smelled like cigarette smoke and mildew and piss. I heard muffled voices drifting up from the back of the house and then my father hollering in a voice almost unrecognizable. "I said no visitors! Make them go away, goddammit! Fucking ghosts. Don't let them in my house." Words spat out in gasps between hacking gurgling coughs, words like ground up rocks shot out of a cement mixer.

Then the nursing and shushing voices of the two women. A duet of calming reassurance.

Laurette came back, shrugged an apology and waved me into the kitchen, signaling me again to keep quiet. She wiped the dust out of two glasses with a dish towel and poured in some Seagram's 7. "He says a lot of weird shit these days," she said.

We sat and sipped whiskey and spoke in hushed tones among the litter of pill bottles and paperwork piled up on the table. When the coughing quieted down, Carla the hospice nurse came out and stood by the front door with a pack of cigarettes and a lighter. She was a plump Mexican woman with wavy hair and beautiful eyes dark as a tall glass of Guinness. "I gave him another shot, he will sleep now," she said with a sad careful smile, and she stepped out to the porch.

Laurette stubbed a cigarette out in the overpopulated ashtray. There was a cardboard file holder, the kind with accordion folds, propped up on one of the empty chairs, and she lifted it to the table and flipped open the cardboard lid. She pulled out a small manilla envelope, maybe six by nine inches, and set it down in front of me. It had my name written on it. Just my first name, in black felt pen, in a spindly shaky hand.

"My inheritance?"

She didn't laugh. She lit a new cigarette, aimed a stream of smoke at my face. "One day I heard a crash," she said. "And I ran in there and found him on the floor over by the file cabinet. He was holding that envelope, and he told me to be sure you got it after he's gone. But who the hell knows when I'll see you again, so…" She left me at the table and took her drink and cigarettes out to join Carla on the porch.

I poured another inch of whiskey and opened the envelope. I was expecting some sort of legal document, but inside was a single folded piece of cheap typewriter paper like I remembered from my early days in the offices of the *Call & Record*. I unfolded it and saw a U.S. Department of Defense logo and a block of type in fading black ink. In effect, these were my father's final words to his son.

US ARMY PERSONNEL COMMAND, OAKLAND CA

OFFICIAL PRESS RELEASE

DATE: JULY 13, 1969

Private First Class James R. Cole, US Army, a legal resident of Lupoyoma City, California, is considered missing in action (MIA) according to a recent report by Army command personnel at Nha Trang Air Base. PFC Cole was on duty when his patrol unit came under heavy fire while securing a Vietnamese village which was believed to be controlled by supporters of the North Vietnamese army. Members of his unit reported that PFC Cole was hit by enemy fire and immobilized before the rest of his unit was forced to retreat. It is currently undetermined if PFC Cole was taken prisoner by enemy forces.

HE SAYS YOUR NAME

I read through it three times. Maybe more. And all the handwritten revisions in my father's small, tight printing. True, the booze was not enhancing my faculties, but this was a lot to process, well-lubricated or not. I understood what the document meant on the surface—MIA *not* KIA. It took the extra reads to recognize the terrible unavoidable implications: that my father had rewritten an official government press release and published a fake obituary, all in some desperate attempt either to hold on to my mother or punish her.

I already knew he had arranged for J.R. Cole's arrest and coerced enlistment into the army; that was clear from the letters in the hatbox. I knew Cole's obituary had fed her depression and led to her death, accidental or not; the scrap of paper in her dress pocket told that story. But it was *true* they'd committed adultery. It was *true* he was a draft dodger. And I believed it was *true* he'd died in Vietnam. But now I knew my mother had been killed, even if indirectly, not with the truth, but with my father's lie.

And he'd planned to keep this from me until it was too late for a confrontation. Too late for accountability. A deathbed confession on the cheap. I went to find him, ready to rage in and shake him awake, make him pay up by showing him the contempt he deserved.

He was laid out in the dayroom. It was the biggest space and the closest to the bathroom, the logical location for all the deathwatch paraphernalia— the motorized bed and the oxygen concentrator and the hanging drug bags and blinking boxes. No room for the old Grundig hi-fi. The bed pushed up against the wall where the window between Billie's room and mine had been. He had torn the window out and sheetrocked over the hole. There was no sign it had ever been there.

I stood in the doorway and studied the shrunken shape in the bed, his gray-yellow face. I listened to the wet-rattle rhythm of his breath and watched his eyelids flutter and his mouth grasping for air. At the same time I saw my mother in that bed with a cold washrag on her forehead. And Billie sitting cross-legged in a patchwork skirt reading Betty Friedan out loud.

The front door was open and Laurette and Carla were out on the porch, murmuring in low voices. A motorcycle grumbled by in the street. I went to the kitchen, slumped down into a chair and poured another drink. I folded up the press release and returned it to the manilla envelope.

Laurette came in. "Well?"

I said, "Do you remember what you said at my mother's funeral?" She looked at me like I had a bad haircut, but I went on. "I remember Pop was all pissed off, and you said he had a good reason, and Grandma Junia said you didn't know what you were talking about. Then you said—"

"Boy, that's some powerful old shit you're dredging up," she cut me off. "But I do remember. I said, I only know what I read in the newspaper."

"You were talking about J.R. Cole, weren't you? His obituary."

She said, "Now, how do you even know that name?"

"Well, we never told anybody but, right after Billie moved in, we found some letters in the dayroom closet."

"I see," she said with a nod that I read as resignation. "So, way back then you knew about Cole and Evie—your mom—uh, carrying on?"

"And we knew he was the draft dodger you told us about when you gave us a ride that time, the one Frankie Watkins got in trouble over. And how they tried to run away to Canada but my father made sure Cole got arrested and forced into the army."

She let out a long sigh and poured herself another drink. "Yeah, that's all true. Your father thought it would break them up, and then Evie would just get over it somehow. Like magic. But love don't work that way. She was blind crazy for that guy, and there wasn't a damn thing Mike could do about it. Sending him off to the army just pissed her off, drove her further away. But when they sent him to war—well, she kinda went off the deep end after that. That's when the yelling and the headaches and the pills and the drinking all got worse. I guess you kinda figured out the rest. Broke her heart clean through's what it did."

"And that's what you meant at the funeral?"

"Yep. Your father would never admit it, and neither would Junia, but if I'm being honest I'd say that's what killed her, one way or another."

"Grandma Junia knew?"

"Hell, Junia's the one who got the draft board to look into the poor guy's status in the first place. But Pop and Molly knew the whole story, too, and that's why Pop was so mad. He blamed your father mostly. And I think, in secret, your father knew it was his fault. And it tortured him."

"Well, it was his fault! And it was a fucking lie. Turns out Cole didn't even die in Vietnam—at least not then. And for all we know he's walking around above ground at this very moment."

"Archer, what the hell are you talking about?"

I slid the manilla envelope across the table next to Laurette's ashtray. "Read it now or read it later when you're alone, or when he's passed, I don't care, but I shouldn't be the only person alive who knows this shit."

"Okay. I'll read it. Later. I promise. But listen to me, whatever it is, you can't keep letting the past eat you up," she said. "You gotta find a way to move on."

She lit another smoke and we went out on the porch with the nurse. No one said anything for a few moments. It was late afternoon, and the sun was still high and sharp in the west and flashing off the chrome on the Cadillac. October leaves skipped down the street on the breeze.

I downed my drink and set the empty glass on the porch railing. I shook Carla's hand and said, "Thanks for your help."

"He says your name in his sleep," Carla said. "Morphine dreams."

"Well… that's something," I said, and I kissed Laurette lightly on the cheek and walked down the stairs. At the bottom I turned and looked back. "What was he like—Cole, I mean—did you know him?"

"No, I never met him. Pop and Molly did, I guess, but I never even saw a picture of the guy."

CHASING GHOSTS

I stopped at Main Street Liquors and bought a pint of Maker's and set it in the passenger seat next to my mother's old hatbox. In my mind I saw myself all those years ago by the burn barrel in the backyard, holding up the blue-flowered sundress by the hangar, checking the other pocket and finding the J.R. Cole obituary. I remembered reading that scrap of paper and thinking I had finally found the truth—when I had only found the mask of a trick, a crime against the truth.

But what was I doing with my own secrets? Lowballing for Billie's freedom—and my own redemption—by telling as little as I thought I could get away with.

I opened the hatbox, thumbed through and found the Polaroid snapshot of my mother next to the ocean in the blue felt hat with the silvery band and the blue polkadots. She stood on the edge of a cliff, facing the camera at a three-quarter angle, the coastline curving northward behind her. The wind was gusting and she held her hat on with one hand while her hair blew around her face. Her smile was shy and cautious but real. She was lovely, and not just in the usual sense of that word as a bland synonym for pretty or charming, but in a truer sum, meaning *as in love*.

At the bottom of the hatbox I found the key to Room 24 at the Crow's Nest Motel, and it flashed me back to all those fantasy road trips we dreamed of when Billie and Sonny first made the deal for the Fairlane. As a young man, I'd made it to some of those destinations. Hitched out to Chicago and hung around the blues clubs. Drifted up the coast to Canada and down the coast to Mexico. Made the seven hills of San Francisco my backyard. But I never did get to Shelter Cove, despite my curiosity about my mother's history there. For one thing, Shelter Cove is one of the most remote towns in California, sitting on the edge of the serrated Pacific coast at the end of a narrow twisting road

that is the only way in or out. For another thing, I knew I would never be able
to think of it as anything but the last place my mother was happy.

I slid the sunroof open, hit the down buttons on all the windows, cranked
up the stereo, and pointed the Cadillac out of town. I drove, fueled by whiskey and impulse. And the blues. I kept the engine rhooming and the wind
roaring through the car. I drove north out of town and west on the highway,
speeding past Parker's Junkyard, the only business still operating at the corner
of Rawson Road.

I was thinking about the shortcut Sonny and I took through the cemetery and wondering who bothered to buy and mark the empty grave of a man
who hadn't in fact been killed—my mother, my father, someone else? And if
J.R. Cole had somehow made it out of Vietnam alive, where was he today
and did he ever think of my mother and Shelter Cove and blue polkadots on
a silver hatband.

By the time I got to the coast, it was dark and I was wildhearted drunk.
Can you drown anger, regret and disillusion with whiskey? I was giving it a
go. I stopped to replenish my supplies and ask for directions at the general
store, which fortunately had a liquor section. "Just stay on this road and look
for the big neon crow," said the old guy behind the counter.

I turned in when I saw the sign and parked the Caddy near the office. Out
beyond the parking lot of the motel, I caught moonlit glimpses of tumbling
water, heard the ocean scolding the rocks. A young woman with multiple
facial piercings and purple highlights in her hair ran my credit card and gave
me the key to Room 29. She looked concerned at my beat appearance—no
shower or change of clothes after the night in jail, unshaven and blood-eyed
from too little sleep and too much drink. She handed me a flyer for the local
pizza place and said, "Here, mister. They'll deliver to your room."

I lugged my overnight bag, the hatbox and the new bottle upstairs to my
room. I poured bourbon into a plastic cup, used the room phone to order a
large pizza, then stood on the balcony looking down at the parking lot and
the blue neon crow with the red neon letters that bisected its body, saying
"The Crow's Nest," pulsing on and off like an electric heart.

• • •

That night and the next day and then another night are stitched in threadbare memory. Sockfooted late-night trips to the ice machine. Mad dreams infiltrated by raving infomercials and colorized westerns. Wandering empty streets in thick nightfog that somehow manifested a color that could only be called dark white. Stumbling upon a Gen Y bacchanal—a menagerie of twenty-somethings who all looked like the motel clerk. Freakshow piercings and acres of tats, work boots and flannel shirts, all in a cloud of kush smoke as thick as the fog. Three dreadlocked white dudes on guitar, standup bass and banjo, playing what I estimated to be male feminist punk bluegrass. A big-legged gal with a head of black patent leather hair was dancing on the wooden deck in extravagant twirls. I showed her the Polaroid and asked if she recognized the location. She laughed and danced away.

One thing I do remember clearly. Room 29 was the last room at the far end of the two story building. Bringing in my "luggage" that first night, I passed Room 24 and noticed a light on. The next day, Wednesday I guess, somewhere close to dinnertime I think, I happened to be making my way back from another supply run, and a white-haired couple came out of 24. Relaxed-fit jeans and orthopedic shoes. Matching immaculate white fisherman sweaters. They passed me in the parking lot on the way to their Prius and I nodded and said, "Evening." They smiled and they both said good evening and held hands like second-honeymooners.

I watched from the balcony as the old husband backed the Prius out, turned on the headlights and drove out into the foggy twilight. I went to my room and took the old room key out of the hatbox. I strolled the balcony down to Room 24 and casually checked in all directions. The key slid right into the lock and it clicked open with a slight turn. I slipped inside quickly.

The Crow's Nest must have been a fairly new establishment in 1968 when my mother and J.R. Cole were here. Now, in 2010, there were signs it had fallen into disrepair over the years and then recently been refurbished. The architecture had that early Sixties, rectangular, skinny-tie and loafers feel, but the new paint job was teal and coral and white, something you might expect from a second rate decorator hired out of Marin by some Silicon Valley cashouts.

I thought maybe this moment was why I came to this diminutive nowhere by the sea, to be in this space with the ghosts of my mother's madness. But standing there in the middle of the room brought no peace or understanding. It was just a pastel motel room waiting for its rightful occupants.

The white hair Prius couple were tidy and organized. Before they checked out, the woman would probably straighten up, strip the bed, and pile all the dirty towels in an orderly mound on the bathroom floor. The man would still leave a ten for the maid.

ROOM SERVICE

On Thursday, I woke to someone knocking loudly on the door of my room. I thought, that better not be the maid again. I'd already told her I didn't give a damn about clean sheets and towels, and I'd made goddamn sure the do-not-disturb sign was hanging on the doorknob. Besides, I looked at the digital clock on the nightstand and the red numbers said 7:15. I frankly had no idea if it was morning or evening. Last I knew I was watching game four of the NLCS on this shit 22-inch flat screen. The Giants and Phils were tied up five-five after eight innings. Guess I passed out. But whatever—the maid should not be knocking on my door at 7:15, a.m. or p.m.

I hollered out, "No housekeeping. Do not disturb, comprende?"

"Open the door, Mr. King." Definitely not the maid's voice. I didn't remember stripping down to my boxers, but oh well, I wrapped up my half naked body in a twisted clump of bedding and opened the door.

Valentine Jones pushed me back into the room and slammed the door behind her. She was clutching a piece of paper, waving it in my face. "This is a subpoena!" She was leaning forward, red-faced. "You are hereby ordered to appear in the U.S. District Court of San Francisco on Tuesday, October 26, 2010. In case you've lost track, that's five days from now."

"Well, at least I have time to get dressed." I said, directing her eyes to my rumpled outfit.

She looked around and took in the room. Empty bottles, dirty clothes, damp wadded up towels, grease-soaked burger bag, half-open pizza box with a curled up slice of pepperoni and sausage sticking out one side. My mother's old hatbox open in the middle of the undressed bed, its contents strewn about. A shameless tabloid news show on the television squawking about some baby-daddy's oxy relapse.

"Jesus, Archer, what are you doing in here?"

"Hiding. Or so I thought, how the hell'd you find me?"

"Really? That's your first question? You better be glad I found you, I'm probably the nicest person looking for you right now besides your Aunt Laurette."

"You met Laurette?"

"Sorry to be the one to tell you, but your father passed away last night."

"Not exactly unexpected," I said, but I sat down on the bed.

"Is that why you disappeared?"

"I came up here to visit my mother," I said, and I suddenly felt the spiritual weight of all the oil-slick food washed down with off-brand bourbon and the fetid nightmares induced by all-night TV. I handed Valentine the Polaroid photograph. "More like a memory of my mother."

She did a little bit of a double take. "She was lovely," she said.

"You gonna let me get dressed or what?"

She turned the back of her gray pinstripe pantsuit to me while I found a pair of jeans and a wrinkled t-shirt on the floor. "I don't understand," she said. "You ran away up here to drown old sorrows? Did you even stop to think about all the people you left hanging? Laurette, your editor, your boss, me and my mother. Don't you check your messages?"

I flipped open the top of the pizza box with my foot. "Ah-hah!" I said. "I've been looking all over for that!" I rescued the TV remote from the box, wiped off some cheese and clicked off the gossipmongers. I stood up and tugged on yesterday's jeans.

"This hasn't been easy for me either," I said.

She spun around to face me. "Funny," she said. "From what I can see, running away and hiding in a bottle is the easiest thing in the world for you."

I ran down the story about my trip to the graveyard, and the "visit" with my father. I told her I decided I'd rather be here with the memory of my mother than back in Lupoyoma City waiting on the porch for my father to die. For the son, the father is often the man you're trying to live up to and live down at the same time, for your whole life. I told her about the J.R. Cole press release, and what it meant.

"Now the bastard's dead," I said. What am I supposed to do with that?"

"Well, you could you spend five minutes of your life thinking about somebody else. I'm really sorry about your father, mother, the whole tragic tale, but while you've been hiding, my mother's been in jail with a first degree murder charge hanging over her head—and you're probably the only one who can help her."

I sat back down on the bed with a limp sock in one hand, temporarily speechless, mesmerized by predicament and hangover. Simply getting dressed threatened a gauntlet of challenges to my diminished coordination and cognition.

"So yes, I get that you're going through a difficult time. But look at yourself. You're a drunken coward."

That kinda blew my hair back, whiplashed me, and I let it hang in the air while I searched for a pithy defense. "Better than being a cowardly drunk," I said. "No one likes a cowardly drunk."

"Really? Another joke? What the hell is wrong with you? You think sarcasm is the answer to every problem?"

I gave her a nolo-contendere shrug. "Not really, but I believe they come in the same bottle."

She didn't laugh. She frowned and took an edgy calming breath, she went to the window and yanked back the curtains, stabbing the room with bladed daylight, and she stood with her back to me, looking out the window.

"When I told her I was coming here to arrest you, her first instinct was to protect you. She said you were just a kid then and there was so much you didn't know. She was ready to give in, take her chances without your help, but I'm not letting you off that easy."

"Wait, wait, wait. Arrest me for what?"

"There's a sheriff's deputy waiting in the parking lot. I will have him take you into custody if I have to." She shook the paper at me again. "I have the authority to detain you as a material witness to a criminal proceeding."

"Look, I'm willing to sign an affidavit."

"Not enough," she said. "The feds smell PR honey all over this. They want an indictment and they're not backing down over an affidavit. You're going to have to testify."

"In open court?"

"If it goes to trial, yes. But, if we're lucky, maybe the grand jury drops the charges, or at least we plea bargain down to manslaughter and she gets a suspended sentence—no trial. That's best case scenario."

"Worst case scenario?"

"Worst case we go to trial, the jury believes Tim Bilderback, and my mother spends the rest of her life in prison."

I sucked in a huge breath and exhaled slowly, trying to absorb the full weight of what I'd just heard and what I was about to say. "Okay. I'll comply. No need for the cops. I've already spent enough time in jail for one week. But, really, how did you find me here?"

She shook her head with a bemused smile jostling the dark hair around her face. And she stood with a hand on one hip and said, "You really don't know where you are, do you?"

I picked the last stale piece of pizza out of the box on the floor and tore loose a bite, chewed laboriously. Valentine winced.

"Put that down, it's disgusting," she said. "Finish getting dressed, I'm buying breakfast."

PELICAN, CROW, DOLPHIN

Valentine cross-examined my eyes a few times to double-check my commitment before she waved off the deputy in the parking lot, then we got in the Cadillac.

The restaurant was called The Lost Pelican. It was everything you would expect from a typical smalltown grease and gossip joint. Full of hubbub and clatter, with saucy waitresses named Fran and Jo, and the owner named Smitty or Red or Mac. The booths upholstered in sky blue vinyl and packed mostly with locals not tourists. You could tell by their practical, workworn clothes, the mud caked on their shoes, and their unimpressed postures.

An oldtimer named Buck lumbered in ahead of us and sat at the counter and ordered "the usual." He hunched over his coffee in Carhartt overalls and gave the weather report. "Chilly this morning," he said, and he blew breath across his cup. "Don't expect this fog'll burn off."

A previous occupant had left the sports page of the *Eureka Times-Standard* on the table. I learned the Giants had pulled off a six-five victory in game four against the Phillies, thanks to a three-hit day from rookie catcher Buster Posey and a walk-off sacrifice fly from Juan Uribe. I had missed Uribe's heroic blow, passed out chin to chest, but now we were up three games to one, just a win away from a trip to the 2010 World Series.

What I didn't expect from The Lost Pelican was its secondary purpose as an art gallery. The walls featured paintings of local scenery, each booth with a separate piece mounted above the table. The subjects were commonplace: seascapes, boats, a lighthouse, weathered houses and outbuildings, standard postcard fare. But the style was distinctive and consistent across the six or seven pieces. Vibrant and luminous colors with a quiet energy—low voltage splashes of deep rusty red, electric blues, and rich lively greens. The lines were loose and not always confined by the shape of a particular subject. This produced the effect of a vibrating instability of the forms, suggesting hidden connectedness across false or tenuous boundaries.

The other unexpected thing about this cramped little cafe was that everyone there seemed to already know Ms. Valentine Jones. Customers tramping in and out, the waitresses, even Buck and Smitty or Red or Mac—they all addressed her simply as Val, and they all said hey or howdy, and wanted to know about somebody named Barb. *How's Barb doing, Val? Tell Barb we're rooting for her, Val. Tell her we love her, Val.*

"What's that all about?" I said, sliding into one of the vinyl booths.

"You really haven't figured it out?" she said.

"My grandmother always said I was slow on the uptake."

"And apparently she was right."

"So, why does everyone know you in this place?"

"Because I grew up here."

I looked around some more—at Valentine and the paintings on the walls, and an inner dawn came up on what she was saying. "Barb." I said, letting it sink in.

"Starting to make sense now?" she said. "Isolated, tiny town left off most maps, where everybody thinks they know everybody? Nobody here ever guessed who she really was, not even me. Read the signature on the painting."

On the wall next to our table, a dark seascape of a small boat on a stormy sea, signed, B. Jones.

"Yeah, Barbara Jones," she said, leaning toward me with a low voice. "To folks in Shelter Cove, that's who my mother is, no matter what the papers say."

"Barbara Jones," I repeated, in numbstruck monotone.

"It's all over the television, too. Haven't you seen the news the last couple days?"

"I've been avoiding it like the plague," I said. "Baseball, infomercials, old movies. Anything but the news."

She mocked me with a sad headshake. "You have major issues, mister."

• • •

After breakfast, we circled back to the Crow's Nest, and I packed up and checked out. The fog had lifted despite Carhartt Buck's forecast. Valentine had flown in to the local airstrip in a friend's plane, so the plan was to drive back to San Francisco together in my car. She said there were a couple of stops we needed to make first, and she sat in the passenger seat and talked and pointed me left and right until we turned down a one-lane street called Dolphin Drive.

The blacktop quickly turned pockmarked and gravelly, and the road got narrower and narrower until it shrunk down to a scrabbly path that came to a dead-end on a ledge overlooking a black-sand beach. She told me to park and I did. "There's something here I think you should see," she said.

I stepped out of the car into a déjà vu. This looked a lot like the spot in the old Polaroid where my mother was standing on the bluff in her Easter hat. I had searched for it in the drunken fog a day (or two?) before. I had walked (staggered?) the coastline for I don't remember how long with the photo in my outstretched hand, holding it up to the live scenery, trying to get reality to match the picture. Nothing looked right, and then night came on and I stumbled into the big-legged woman at that blurry house party, after which I gave up the whole besotted quest.

But now I went to the car and got the photo out of the hatbox, and I hurried back to where I'd just been standing. I held the photo in my hand at the end of my arm like a nearsighted man… and it fit. Everything clicked into place like the last piece of Molly's jigsaw puzzle. A gust of wind pushed the hair out of my eyes, and I flinched at the touch. I didn't understand it, but I knew this was what I had come to Shelter Cove for. It wasn't in Room 24, it was out there on the ledge all along. It was a glimpse of my mother's wild runaway love for J.R. Cole, the joy on her face in the photograph, the fleeting knowledge that a moment is right and true. And for some reason I needed to physically connect with it.

Valentine had been leaning against the Cadillac, silently observing, and I'd nearly forgotten her presence until she cleared her throat. "Thank you," was all I could muster in response.

I walked to the car, put the Polaroid back in the hatbox and closed the lid. Valentine was waiting in her seat when I slid behind the wheel. I looked over and said, "I'm ready." I had some grand feeling buzzing in my chest like I was bravely going into battle.

But Valentine said, "One more stop."

THE BOY IN THE WINDOW

There was another series of lefts and rights before Valentine directed me to a dirt turnout in front of a battered little house that sat back from the street on a minor hill terraced and cultivated into what was now a weedy garden. From the street I saw the wooden stakes leaning this and that way and leafy yellowing vines run amok, snaking around rotting tomatoes and gigantic zucchinis. Around the garden a balding picket fence was bedecked with surprising little sculptures or conglomerations of found materials—bottle caps and broken glass and driftwood and abalone shells and rusted hamster wheels and who knows what else. The house itself was a simple affair, what the oldtimers called a "salt-box," the pale blue paint beginning to fade.

I followed Valentine up the steep wooden steps and onto the wood-floored porch. "I promised her I would bring back some clothes," Valentine said. Inside, she quickly excused herself and left me in the front room at loose ends. The room was maybe twelve by twelve, not much of a "living room" by today's standards at all, more of a "parlor" or "sitting room" as it might have been called when the house was built.

There was a certain patchouli and tofu aesthetic that was inescapable. Eclectic and definitely vibing toward the thrift-store school of earth-friendly decorating. Franklin woodstove in the corner. A well-tread Persian-identifying rug with a mandala pattern dominated by deep red and sporting goldenrod fringe. A beat-down sofa in burgundy velveteen with big rounded armrests. Hundreds of records—a long line of old vinyl albums on the floor under a shelf holding a turntable, an honest to timewarp Girard turntable in like-new condition. Vintage McIntosh amp and Advent speakers.

Through a doorway into an adjacent room, I noticed a painting. Originally, this next room was probably a second parlor, but now each wall was chest-deep in dark wood bookshelves absolutely brimming with books. Hard-backs and paperbacks of every size, scrunched together, some stacked on their sides and some piled on the floor, homeless.

Normally, the first thing I do when faced with a stranger's library is examine the contents at length. What can't you learn about a new acquaintance from tilting your head to read the spines of their books? What you *can* learn is whether you might ever wish to learn more. And in a way this Billie, this grownup fleshed-out Billie, was a new acquaintance, although one I had day-dreamed of meeting for many years.

But I was distracted from the books by the striking power of the paint-ings hung on the walls above the bookshelves all around the room. They were clearly hers, clearly in the same style as the paintings at The Lost Pelican—the rich colors of the forms not quite contained by their sharp black outlines, cre-ating a live-wire pulsating effect of universal but fragile connectedness across the illusion of individual sovereignty.

Everything in these rooms worked as evidence of a personality, a heart, a soul that had stayed the course. There was a part of me that felt ashamed at the fealty she had shown to her vision through the years, and under the threat of capture, while I had squandered most of my principles to see myself sparkle and sputter in the eyes of others. I was merely a blustery headline, but Billie had managed to live her truth, even in hiding.

Besides the singular, arresting style of the paintings, I recognized the forms themselves as a dreamer recognizes the details of past dreams that invade a new dream as if they are memory, although memory of a separate timeline that only exists in the dream world. "Dreamality," Billie had riffed one sunwashed morning long ago, sitting like a yogi on the green chenille bedspread.

Here was the Ferris Wheel, the top half of its circle rising above an old faded fence, the cars all empty but for one small and indistinct person stuck at the top of the arc. Here was Molly's pier stretching out toward the middle of the lake, the backs of two seated figures in silhouette against the moonrise. This whole room seemed to be a museum to those few weeks that Billie spent in Lupoyoma City. The Ferris Wheel, the pier, the ballfield. The Watkins place and Frankie's store. The Fairlane and the Weeping Willow, Molly's pier, Trey Morgan's trailer, Preacher's Alley. All represented here in the shimmering shapes and dark earthy colors of her heart, a combobulation of elements that spoke of love and pain and processing.

I stood frozen before one large canvas when Valentine came into the room without saying a word, as if the room itself tended to hush its occupants. The painting that transfixed me was maybe three feet by four and unframed. It depicted the window between our rooms at the house on Fourth Street. This painting was brighter than the rest of the work, except for the window itself, which was streaked blue gray like a thunderous evening sky and darkened even more by the deep blue silhouette of a slender childlike figure apparently trapped on the other side of the window, one hand raised to the glass.

"Do you think this is enough?" Valentine said, and I looked over and saw the full-size suitcase she had packed for Billie. She held it in front of herself with both hands and leaned backwards to counter-balance the weight of the thing. I recognized this was my cue to help, to take the suitcase out to the car, or at least to signal that I was available to do so. But I couldn't move. I stared into the painting and saw May 1970 and the haunt of all the years since.

Finally Valentine said, impatiently, "Are you ready?"

"I think I might need a lawyer," I said.

There was a blank pause, a stutter in the air.

"You don't need a lawyer just to testify to the grand jury," she said. "Just answer the questions truthfully and it'll be fine. With your testimony and Billie's testimony, I believe we have a good argument for self-defense."

I looked at the boy-like shadow in the painting, with his hand raised to the glass as if somehow the life on this side of the window was off limits to him.

"It wasn't self-defense," I said, but Valentine had left the room.

I caught up to her on the porch, still lugging the fat suitcase stuffed with Billie's clothes. I stood there, with the late morning sun raising the dew off the shaggy front-yard garden, and I looked out to the blue line of the ocean in the west, but my mind's eye stayed on the blue-black shape of the boy behind the window in the painting.

"One time when I was a kid," I said. "I asked my grandfather, Pop—everyone called him Pop, and a six-pack and a rocking chair always turned him into a philosopher—but once I asked him, 'Pop, what does a man know that makes him a man?' And Pop said, 'Boy, a man knows the difference between shoveling dirt and hitting hardpan.'"

"What the hell is that supposed to mean?"

"It means I need to see Billie."

PREACHER'S ALLEY

This is the part that could ruin me.

The bat lay on the ground in the space between us. Moonlight struck the fat part of the barrel. Hank loomed almost as a silhouette, standing with the moon over his shoulder and his features muddled in shadows. A cool drop of sweat slid down my nose and I wiped it away.

"Bullseye, where'd you come from?"

I didn't answer.

"Did you see," he said. "Did you see what she did?" He steadied himself with a hand against the wall. "Hey, bring me that bat, okay," he said, and he waved "come here" with his other hand like he was calling me off the pitcher's mound to discuss strategy.

He stood twenty feet away, but I still felt his hand on my shoulder—that light, firm grip of a coach focusing your attention. "Bullseye, come on. We gotta catch her. Did you see what she did to the Mustang? The Mustang, man! She stole my keys too—we can't let her get away. I gotta report for duty." He winced and wavered and looked dizzy drunk. "Man my head hurts," he said, pressing the heels of his hands to his temples with his eyes shut tight.

My head hurt too. I was sober now, but a headache had come on during all the running, and the pain drummed behind my eyes. I took a step toward the bat and saw Hank flinch as if he had a momentary thought that he might beat me to it. But he relaxed, leaned his back against the wall, and I took several quick steps and picked up the bat. I held it loosely in my right hand and let it hang down beside my leg.

"Give it to me," he said, uncertainty rising in his voice. He took two steps with his hand out. His long shadow reached my feet.

I raised the bat with both hands and he stopped. My voice trembled and cracked. "I know what you did, Hank."

"What're you talking about?"

"I know you raped her."

"What? That's a fucking lie."

"No it's not. I was there. Outside the trailer that night. I saw the whole thing through the window. I saw."

He rubbed his forehead and looked at the ground for a response. Turned his face up to me with a false smile and open hands. A swath of blood colored the side of his face. "Aw, we were just having some fun, Bullseye. Free love, right? You seen the way she struts around." He even winked.

"All that time I thought you liked her. But you didn't like her—you just wanted her. Like some kind of trophy."

His smile twisted into disgust. "Okay… yeah, that's right. And you know what, a real man takes what he wants. Now give me that bat."

He took another step and I raised the bat higher and shook my head, "No, Hank," I said. "Stay back." Tears and sweat stung my eyes.

"Well, look at you—all of a sudden you're some kinda knight in shining armor? You're gonna play hero?" He jabbed himself in the chest. "I'm the hero here."

"You're not my hero."

"Fuck you then. I'll take care of her myself." He turned and headed for the far end of the alley, where Billie had escaped.

I caught up in three quick steps and swung at his legs. He yowled and went down and rolled over and I held the bat over him, ready to swing again. He made a move to get up and I hit him in the leg again. He struggled to his feet and seemed unsteady but kept his eyes leveled on me. I backed up a couple steps and cocked the bat just like he'd taught me. Knees slightly bent, hands up, back foot loaded. I held the bat high and my hands shook with a rush I'd never felt before—some lethal cocktail of adrenalin and rage.

"Aw, Bullseye, you're gonna ruin everything," he said. He balanced on one foot and winced when the other one touched the ground. His shoulders dropped, and he shook his head in what looked like surrender.

Then he lurched toward me one big step and launched himself for a flying tackle. But his back foot slipped and he fell in front of me on his hands and knees and I swung the bat and heard his skull crack and saw his head snap to the side. His arms came out from under him like broken table legs and his body followed his head onto the concrete. Blood gathered in the gutter and gleamed in the moonlight.

And I ran.

Pop said, "Boy, there's no telling another person's why." I look at these flickering memories behind my eyes, and they're like jumpcuts from a movie of another person. A character I don't know any better than the other characters—Billie, Hank, my own father and mother, J.R. Cole. I'll never know why the boy in the movie does what he does in this scene. Even though I watch it over and over again.

EITHER, OR

It took most of the five-hour trip from Shelter Cove to finagle a media pass to the Federal Correctional Institution in the city of Dublin. Valentine drove the Cadillac while I made a series of glitchy calls whenever my phone could muster a two-bar connection as we sped down Highway 101. As her attorney, Valentine could see Billie almost any time she wanted. Not me. Fortunately, I'd once written something favorable about a gal who knew a gal whose girlfriend was the lieutenant who could sign off on inmate interviews; otherwise it could be two weeks of questionnaires and signatures to get in the place.

We arrived around four o'clock. FCI Dublin was nominally a low-security facility out at the edge of Bay Area suburbia in the long shadow of Mount Diablo. Still, it was a federal prison. I was ID'd, questioned, patted down, wanded, and made to empty my pockets like I was boarding an international flight.

We were told to follow Correctional Officer Gonzales, a giant in black uniform, various implements of control bulging his pockets and hanging off his belt. We fell in behind him, and he led us through a maze of hallways and buzzing doors, my field of vision reduced to his massive back, like driving behind a huge semi at night. He ushered us into a narrow and sunless cinderblock room that hoarded the cold like a tomb. A glass wall and a line of visiting booths down one side. Without a word, Gonzales directed us toward a pair of stainless steel stools at one of the booths. Then he pointed gravely toward the far wall where large stenciled lettering said *KEEP HANDS VISIBLE AT ALL TIMES* in all caps spray-painted in black on the white cinderblock. I took my hands out of my pockets and sat down.

Valentine took the stool next to me. Gonzales stood in the corner and stared directly at me, unremitting and unapologetic, hands folded at his waist. The fluorescent light tubes flickered overhead, and the light blared off the stainless steel and the white cinderblock. The room smelled brightly of disinfectant.

A door buzzed open on the other side of the glass and Billie walked in. Cliché orange jumpsuit, oversized and rumpled, with the sleeves and pantlegs turned up a fold. Her silvered curls somehow matching the brushed stainless steel furniture. She looked at Valentine, but Valentine's eyes pointed at me, and Billie sat down across from me with a tentative smile.

She picked up the clunky black phone receiver, and I picked mine up and held it in a ready position. But neither of us spoke. The moment was still and full and well-lit, unlike the rush and dim of the meeting at Sonny's bar. Face to face, not across the room from each other. A focused box of space, defined by the booth dividers and the frame around the glass. Yet another window between us, each seeing the other as if under a spotlight.

I searched her eyes, her face, the tilt of her head, the lines of her shoulders—for a report, for signs, for the story of all the weary years which I thought must be written there, as surely as they were written in the shadows and lines on my own face and the spidery veins in my eyes.

Then she laughed. And I laughed too.

"I'm sorry," she said.

"I think that's my line."

"I know you didn't want to be involved in this."

"It's okay. I want to help."

It shamed me that she probably knew Valentine had to track me down in Shelter Cove with a subpoena. I wanted to blurt out, *I'm an asshole.* I'd rehearsed it in my head. But, deflecting as usual, I said, "I saw your paintings."

She smiled. "I saw your video."

She already knows I'm an asshole.

"I saw myself in the window."

"It's not realism," she said. "It could be you, but maybe it's another part of me. Maybe it's both of us somehow."

I nodded, and I remembered all the indefinite lines that made her forms seem less than solid, always in transition or transformation, border-crossing, mingling, becoming.

"I was a long time just trying to put the past to rest."

"I get that," I said. "I keep trying to drown it with words and bourbon. Hasn't worked yet."

There was a pause while neither of us found the courage to laugh.

Billie broke the silence. "Val said you had questions."

"Oh, just a hundred or so," I said, straining to keep the mood light, but Billie kept an even gaze on me, serious and attentive.

I said, "Maybe this is not the time," and glanced in the direction of Valentine.

"Maybe not, but here we are." Billie met her daughter's eyes with the kind of calm resolve I could only envy. "Val, I know this has already been a lot for you. I'm sorry I had to hide so much for so long."

Valentine had an oh-what-now question mark on her face. She seemed to guess we were headed into rooms she didn't want to see.

I tried to be delicate. "Well, uh, I guess, you know... I've never been sure exactly what happened that night."

"At Trey's you mean?"

"No, not *that* night. The night you left... before you left... in my room."

She sighed, looked down at the battered floor, spoke quietly. None of her old trademark windmilling of hands and arms, no waterfall of words like used to tumble out of her mouth. "I had to leave, Archer. I had to get out of that place. And I was so afraid I was gonna be pregnant... from what happened with Hank. The timing was right, wrong, whatever—the moon and all. And it happened to me before from a one-time thing—which got taken care of, but I don't wanna talk about that... I had to leave. And I only came to your room to say goodbye. But then... if I *was* pregnant by Hank, I didn't want anyone to know. I didn't even want to know. Do you understand? I was so afraid I wouldn't be able to love my own child. Now she lifted her eyes and looked steadily at Valentine. "I *chose* not to know," she said. "Do you see?"

I saw that look I remembered, the one that said don't dare judge me.

"Yes, I see now," I said. "Thank you. All these years I've never even been sure it happened, much less why."

Valentine's face said, I can't process this avalanche of shit all at once. She shook her head in confusion, frustration, overwhelm.

"Are you saying you two…"

Billie looked her steadily in the eye. "I hope you can understand."

"Okay, well, I just want to get this straight," Valentine said. "A few months ago my mother was a beloved artist, wildly popular in a small community. Then I find out she's actually a fugitive radical wanted for murder. Next she's a victim of sexual assault who acted in self defense, and I am the child of that assault. But now you tell me the murdered rapist might not be my father after all, is that right? And this man here, this piss-poor excuse for a man I've been chasing all over the state, he might be my biological father? Christ, I might prefer the dead rapist."

"Valentine, sarcasm is the lowest form of wit," Billie said.

"I don't need Oscar Wilde right now, Mother. What I need is a paternity test." There was a loaded moment of silence.

"That's fine," Billie said. "It took a long, long time, but I'm not afraid anymore."

The three of us shifted and stretched and straightened our posture on the steel stools, an undeclared cease-fire.

I swept my eyes around the room. Imagining prison life for myself, I'd always had the romantic notion that I would study and meditate and condition my body with the discipline of a monk, then walk out with a mission like Malcolm X or the Count of Monte Cristo. But underneath I had the terrifying vision I would be beaten by masochistic guards and sodomized by gang leaders with shaved heads and tattooed eyelids.

Valentine took a deep breath to refocus, but her words still came in stabs. "In any case, what we really need to know right now, Mr. King, is what you're prepared to tell the grand jury on Tuesday."

Then the big guard's radio barked and chattered in bursts of static and garbled talk. Billie leaned forward with her arms on the cold stainless steel counter that ran under the window. "We might not have much time," she said, as if I should get to the point.

Gonzales answered his radio, "Copy that." He looked at his watch.

I blurted out, "I was there, Billie."

"Yes, you said that at Sonny's bar. You were the eyes in the window," Valentine said, impatient.

A loud buzz went off like a fire alarm on Billie's side of the window and began to pulse in four-four time, braying like an out of tune saxophone.

Billie said, "Aw, shit! Lockdown."

"No, not at the trailer," I said. "In the alley that night. I followed you."

The alarm vibrated the inside of my ears.

"Wrap it up!" Gonzales said.

"Archer, what are you trying to say?" Billie said.

I heard heavy boots pounding the hallway outside the room.

"Hank was still alive."

The metal door on Billie's side swung open and another officer came through, a bulldog of a woman with a clipboard.

"Armstrong! Now!" The bulldog barked and held the metal door open, waiting. Gonzales left the room, and the door on our side clunked and buzzed shut behind him. Valentine and I were locked in.

"I gotta go," Billie said, and she stood up and scooted her stool backward with her foot.

"Wait! There's something else," I said.

Officer Bulldog wasn't interested. She grabbed Billie's arm and pulled her toward the metal door, stretching the phone cable to full length.

"What is it?" Billie said, but the phone slipped out of her hand. She looked back chin over shoulder as she was dragged through the doorway.

"I killed him," I shouted into the phone, but it was too late. Billie couldn't hear.

Valentine heard, though. And she stood up in a rush and backed away from me like I was on fire. She steadied herself against the far wall. "Oh my god," she said, eyes wide.

The metal door stayed open on its own for a second, then began to swing shut. Billie disappeared into the line of orange bodies being herded down the hallway. The branging pulse of the alarm hammered in my head.

Valentine crossed the room in three steps. Her hand met my face like an exclamation mark. The woman slapped with Barry Bonds handspeed. My head jerked hard to the side and I dropped the phone. All her years of feeling abandoned tremored in her eyes and in her hand. She slapped me again, and I lost my balance and sprawled on the cold cement. The stool screeched across the floor as I went down. That tang of Pine-sol fumes hit me in the face. The alarm pounded on.

"*You* killed him? And then you kept your mouth shut while the whole world blamed her? She's been running and hiding for forty years while you drink up the proceeds of your own arrogant bullshit? Mr. Truth-teller?"

I sat up with my legs spread out on the cement. The alarm finally stopped. The step and rustle of officers double-timing and the hiss and chirp of busy radios continued on the other side of the door. Valentine paced the length of the room, away toward the door, then back to me sitting on the floor. She stood looking down on me, my own personal karma delivery person.

"So, what you're telling me now is you're either my father, or you're the man who killed my father. Jeez, maybe I don't need a paternity test. Because, frankly, either way, fuck you."

She began to sob. I pushed myself up off the floor and sat back on the stool. I hung my head and stared between my feet at odd stains left on the cement over the years, indelible blemishes of time in shapes like Rorschach inkblots. I saw spiders and dragons and boats on fire. She stepped closer and leaned over me. "Fuck you, fuck you, and fuck you!" she said, and jabbed her index finger close to my face with rhythm. I looked up and saw mascara pouring down her cheeks. The metal door buzzed and clunked and swung open. Officer Gonzales filled the doorway.

THE TRUTH AMONG MEN

Valentine did not say another word to me as Gonzales escorted us out of the building. In the parking lot, she retrieved her purse from my car, pulled out her phone and immediately called a taxi. I waited to make sure her ride showed, then I crawled into The City in the Cadillac along with rush hour traffic and the late afternoon sun.

Game five of the National League Championship Series was already a couple innings old when I hit the freeway. The Giants had a chance to punch their ticket to the World Series with a win, but it was not to be. During the season, broadcaster Duane Kuiper, had dubbed the team's style of play "torture baseball" because of their many late-inning nail-biter wins and some frustrating losses of the same character.

The moniker stuck and the team maintained that M.O. right down to the final day of the season. They were following the same pattern in the NLCS, missing the opportunity to finish it off at home. Now, after a four-two loss, they would head to Philadelphia, where getting that last win would likely be much tougher. It all seemed so fitting.

I got to my house, parked the Caddy in the garage, stopped in the foyer to check my mailbox. Four or five days of shreddables crammed in there. I felt a tingling fatigue like an opiate come-on as I plodded up the stairs. I got through the door and went for the bourbon, first things first. I wasn't hungry. I wasn't sleepy or sad or angry or even afraid. I was rumpled outside, wrung out inside and some new kind of numb all over. I described this to myself as the peace of surrender.

I walked my glass of Maker's over to the stereo and pushed play, starting with something blue and familiar. *The Best of Little Walter*, which opens with the jaunty *My Babe*, followed by *Sad Hours*, that wonderful wordless conversation between Little Walter on the harp and Muddy Waters on guitar that brings to mind shadowy images of two men drinking after hours, talking regret at a wrongside bar. And still takes me back to the dayroom.

I sat in one of the leather recliners by the big bay window with my glass close-by on a side table, and I stared out across the street to Golden Gate Park where the glow of the westering sun lit up the tops of the eucalyptus trees like candles against the dusk.

The doorbell buzzed, and I really didn't want to get up, but I thought it might be Valentine. It turned out to be Tom Monihan. He came in rubbing his shaved head like he does when things get awkward. He said he didn't expect me to be home, said he'd left a shit-ton of messages on my phone and where the hell was I the last five days.

"I thought I might be leaving this outside your door," he said, and he handed me a cardboard filebox full of the personal stuff from my office.

"So, I'm fired?"

"Missed the deadline, no story, no show, no call. That's fired in my book."

"I'm sure Lockhart wouldn't have it any other way."

He nodded confirmation, and I offered him a drink. We sat in the matching recliners looking out the bay window at the twilight falling on the street and the park. I told him the story of the five days since I'd left San Francisco to interview Billie. I told him the truth. About the five days.

I poured us both another drink. Then I told him the rest—that I had killed Hank Timmons with the same baseball bat Billie had smacked him with before making her escape. I was practicing saying it out loud, relating the factual details in order— he did this, she did that, I did something else. I realized I was implicitly asking for editorial advice, but he offered none.

Monihan was my oldest and closest friend. Perhaps my only friend. We'd spent a lot of time together over the years, checked off all the boxes on the male bonding questionnaire. Camping, carousing, road trips, hangovers, romantic triangles, bail money, every etcetera in the book. His reaction was stone-cold x-ray vision. "Long time to live with such a hard secret. That probably explains why you're so fucking tough on the world. And yourself."

"I made a lot of wrong calls," I said.

"You were just a kid," Monihan said. "And he had it coming."

"Doesn't change a thing," I said. "A man has to look life in the eye. Right?"

Monihan rubbed his bristly head. "You gonna tell the whole thing to the grand jury?"

"I don't know, man. I hope I can."

Across the street the eucalyptus trees were turning into black silhouettes against the purple nightfall. On his way out the door, Monihan pointed at the cardboard filebox. "There's an envelope with your severance check," he said. "And the Armstrong story we ended up running, if you're interested."

I rummaged around in the box a bit. There wasn't much in there: the two-volume *Oxford English Dictionary* that Robyn gave me when I left for college, a baseball signed by Willie Mays, a framed photo taken the night I jammed blues harp with the great Buddy Guy in Chicago, assorted books and papers, and the engraved plaque the Sentinel gave me to celebrate the Pulitzer.

The severance was decent—more than my contract called for. Probably a bad PR move to dump a prize-winning loudmouth writer and not throw in some go-away-quietly bucks. Of course, when Lockhart signed the check he didn't know I would be at the federal courthouse the next day. He only knew I'd managed to cost him a bucket of ad revenue and some brown-nosed phone calls.

A newspaper, or rather a section of a newspaper, had been quarter-folded and slid in between some books. I pulled it out and saw the headline. "Fugitive Captured After Decades On The Run." Dateline: Lupoyoma City.

Most of the piece read like standard wire copy—straight, boilerplate skimming material. "After more than forty years as a fugitive, time ran out Tuesday for Barbara Ann 'Billie' Armstrong… anonymous tip… arrested by the FBI and local authorities…The 1970 crime attracted national attention… known anti-war protestor… The victim had enlisted in the U.S. Army… Armstrong is now held without bail… grand jury review… first degree murder charge…" Blah blah de blah.

But the final paragraph hit like a punch in the face.

"Also detained at the scene of Armstrong's arrest, although subsequently released, were former *San Francisco Sentinel* columnist Archer E. King, and Lupoyoma City resident James R. (AKA 'Sonny') Cole, the owner of the bar where Armstrong was taken into custody. Sources say both men may have aided Armstrong's efforts to avoid capture, but the U.S. Attorney's office declined to say if either would face charges in the future."

I laid the newspaper down next to my drink on the side table and buried my face in my hands. "I should have known," I said out loud to no one. Turned my face up to the ceiling, laughed at the muddy convoluted truth.

BLUE INTERLUDE

There's an old blues tune called *Sufferin' Mind*, written and recorded by a New Orleans player named Eddie Lee Jones, who went by the stage name Guitar Slim. He had a few big hits in the early 1950's, but a short career. Some folks live life at a faster tempo and Guitar Slim drank his way to a Louisiana cemetery before his thirty-third birthday.

He was an innovator who pioneered the use of amplifier distortion and influenced later rock-n-roll greats like Jimi Hendrix and Stevie Ray Vaughan. Legend has it he was one helluva showman, known to dye his hair with wild bright colors to match his equally colorful suits. They say he turned every knob up to ten and used a guitar cord hundreds of feet long so he could walk out the front door of the club and play in the street for the moving, honking world.

Unfortunately, not a single piece of video and only a few photographs of Guitar Slim exist today. He isn't one of the bluesmen best remembered by the public, but he left these words that I remember well.

So, if I have any wisdom… you know that you will find
that life means nothing to you when you have a worried mind
So forgive me for what I do… cuz' I just live on with a sufferin' mind

The blues is the foundational truth of American music. It's the trunk of the tree that grew from the roots of Africa, Appalachia and the fields and churches and juke joints of the South, and seeded everything else from country and rock-n-roll to jazz and hip hop. From the Mississippi Delta to Memphis and New Orleans. Up to St. Louis and Chicago, down to Texas and out to the West Coast. And finally to Lupoyoma County in the luggage of a soldier named Watkins.

Another American songwriter, a man named Michael Franks, wrote a song called *White Boy Lost in the Blues* to express his own attraction to the form. And that song's success over the years testifies to the wider truth of its title. It sure rings all the way home for me. I was a thirteen-year-old white boy in a drowsing backroads town in 1970 Northern California. The blues hit me like a slap upside the heart—an instantaneous love at first twang that felt taboo, unearned, illicit, and yet exhilarating and undeniable.

I'm not trying to pawn myself off as an expert. I haven't read everything ever written on the music or the history, or heard every record ever made. I'm not well-versed in whatever the academic scholars think they know about the blues. I don't claim to know fatdoodleysquat about what the music means to anyone else. I know what it means to me. I know I've been lost in the blues since the day Billie Armstrong opened up a hatbox full of my mother's secrets, fired up the Grundig, and dropped the needle on the Howlin' Wolf.

Down the many years since that moment, I've played at playing the blues, on harmonica and guitar, and still I have no idea how to play any song, any progression, or even any single lick just exactly right. And I think that's how it has to be.

In the blues there's no such thing as just exactly right. In the blues, cleanliness is not next to godliness—it's not even on the same street. All you need are three chords and a scar on your heart. Beyond that, it's your holler. The blues is ragged-right like this column of type. Like a serrated knife that'll cut ya bone deep. Don't worry too much about what it means. Just make it feel.

> "For, while the tale of how we suffer, and how we are delighted, and how we may triumph is never new, it always must be heard. There isn't any other tale to tell, it's the only light we've got in all this darkness."
> — *James Baldwin, Sonny's Blues.*

Tell em your heart. That's all it means.

MERE MOMENTS

In the morning, I cooked chorizo and eggs and ate out of the skillet, standing by the bay window and watching the traffic lurch by on Lincoln Way. I enjoyed the second-story view of hands clenched around the tops of steering wheels, restless fingers drumming, anxious to achieve the next car length. I showered and shaved and dressed in a gray suit and tie—not in a hurry, but in the relaxed rhythm of someone who's already made a difficult decision and now has only to go through with it and live with the result.

Down in the garage, I felt around behind the driver's seat and finally found my phone. I turned it on and deleted every message from Monihan and Lockhart. Irrelevant. I read the latest message from Valentine. She wanted to meet at the front entrance to the courthouse at 10:30, a half-hour before the grand jury would convene. I used the phone to deposit the severance check to my bank. No way I would give that prick Lockhart the chance to stop payment. I took the yellowed, wrinkled lipstick-kissed envelope addressed to J.R. Cole out of my inside breast pocket, scratched out the address and wrote the Weeping Willow address off to the side, then slipped the envelope back into my jacket.

• • •

Valentine wore a knit gray skirt suit over a cream silk blouse. I spotted her from the side as I came toward the courthouse entrance. She was unmistakeable in her upright, on-guard bearing, with her dark hair falling in loose curls to the middle of her resolute back. She was beautiful in a way that drew you toward her right up until she turned her eyes on you. Then, if you were paying attention, you might see the danger signs around her heart. If she was in fact my daughter, I hoped that knowledge wouldn't always be a disappointment to her.

She saw me and when I got close enough, she offered a perfunctory, straight-lipped nod. She didn't exactly apologize for her reaction at the prison, but she pushed my chin to one side with a brush of her fingers and checked to see if she'd left a mark on my cheek. Satisfied that she hadn't, she grimaced a sheepish smile and gave me the my-bad shrug.

"I had it coming," I said.

She nodded in full agreement.

I took a deep breath. "So, what's likely to happen?" I said. "You're going to ask me questions, I'm going to say what I say, then what?"

"First off, I won't be asking the questions. Defense attorneys aren't allowed in the room. And there's no judge. There's the prosecuting attorney, he's there to make the case that Billie should be indicted. But he didn't subpoena you, the grand jury subpoenaed you—because in preliminary discussions I argued you had relevant information. So, the grand jury foreperson will ask the questions, then you'll get your chance."

So, is old Rusty the bailiff going to handcuff me on the spot and drag me away to solitary confinement?"

She laughed a little. "No, this isn't TV" she said. Even if the prosecutor wants to press charges, You're not getting handcuffed on the spot. I think."

"You think?"

She threw up her hands. "I'm a small-town defense attorney. Like I said, they don't even let us in the room."

"You might've shared that detail a little earlier," I said.

"Sorry."

"No, I'm the one who needs to be sorry around here," I said.

"I'll get to see Billie for a few minutes before she goes in," she said. "She's nervous. She's not sure what to expect."

"Tell her not to worry."

"You'll tell them the truth?"

I showed her a grin. "I'll give em what they need."

She gave me a head tilt that said she just hadn't figured me out yet.

"What will happen to her?" I said.

"I expect she'll go free." Valentine said.

I think that's when I stopped clenching my jaw.

She checked her watch. "You should go upstairs and check in," she said, and motioned me to follow her into the main lobby, where we stopped in front of a bank of elevators.

I pulled my key ring out of my pants pocket. "Just in case I don't come out of there—"

"Stop," she said, "that's not necessary."

"These are the keys to my car and my house. The Cadillac is parked in the garage on Turk Street, level B." I reached into my jacket and pulled out the envelope. "And please, get a new stamp on this, and put it in the mail as soon as you can."

She looked at the worn old envelope with J.R. Cole's name and the changed address.

"It's already forty-some years late," I said, and she still looked puzzled. "Show it to Billie, she'll understand."

Valentine nodded, leaned in and kissed me on the cheek. "Good luck. And thank you."

"Luck, hell. I'm definitely gonna need a lawyer."

"Yeah? Do you know any good ones?"

"I'm not sure," I said. "Might be one in the family."

The bell dinged and the elevator doors opened, and Valentine nudged me forward with a hand against the small of my back. "I'll be up later," she said.

I walked in and pushed the button for the third floor.

I found the designated courtroom, where a bailiff was stationed at the coffered double doors, checking credentials and identification. It wasn't Rusty. It was a teacherly Black woman with short white hair and a doubting smile. Dark blue uniform with gold trim, and a peaked cap with a black shiny visor. Her brass name-tag said Washington, but she introduced herself as Marietta, and when I told her who I was she checked her list and told me to sit down on one of the wooden benches that lined the hallway. "When the jury is ready for you, I will come out and call your name," she said.

The bench was polished oak, long enough for a dugout bench or a church pew, and the thought of church reminded me of Reverend Jameson, and my mother lying dead in the coffin at Jones & Jones Funeral Home. "We shall all be changed," the reverend recited, and that rang my heart now like a moment of truth.

When we speak of the truth, why do we speak of mere moments?

Because that's all we get.

Bloop. A text came through from Valentine. "Coming up in the elevator now." Ding! The elevator doors opened and Officer Gonzales clomped out like a wall dressed in black, with his grim on-duty frown. Behind him came Valentine, straightbacked and battle-ready in her tweedy gray lawyer suit.

Next to her, Billie, somehow looking like a brash teenager on a sunny day by the lake. Sky blue wraparound skirt, a white blouse with embroidered lace, silver curls jostling on her shoulders. She saw me and stopped in the hallway and smiled like summer, with a hand on one hip and a brave flame in her eyes. The one and only Billie Armstrong. A woman like a trick candle.

The big double doors rattled and clunked, and Marietta Washington appeared. She held the door open wide. "Mr. King, it's time."

EMBER AND ASH

The day after I testified to the grand jury, the Giants took game six of the NLCS thanks to an eighth inning home run lashed over the right field wall by Juan Uribe. I watched it down at Remo's with a well-oiled crowd of fellow die-hards. Yes, I took a cab there and back. They went on to win the 2010 World Series in five games, their first in my lifetime. I watched the final out at the old house on Fourth Street while in town to settle my father's estate. In spite of everything, I wish we could've watched that game together.

Now I live there. I sleep in the dayroom and once in a while Robyn Withrow, of all people, sleeps with me. "We're old, not dead," she likes to say. I cook chorizo and eggs for breakfast and we sit in the old wicker chairs on the covered porch and discuss our aches and pains and the frailties of faith. I no longer hear the scratch-scratch in my head. Occasionally, I fire off a column for the *Call & Record*, where Alice Terwilliger is now the editor and publisher. But, I admit, I don't trust my opinions as I once did.

At my age, funerals have become a staple of my social life. Laurette and Sonny are gone. Nate Henderson, Craiger Robinson and Tom Monihan, too. And Billie died this past summer on her seventy-third birthday, August 22, 2025. Like Frankie's husband, a plain old heart attack, perhaps the only part of Billie Armstrong's life that could be considered plain. Her ashes were buried at a hilltop cemetery in the town of Mendocino, where she'd enjoyed the last years of her remarkable life after the feds dropped the charges.

I was not charged either. There was doubt among medical experts that the deceased would have survived the initial blow from Billie even if I hadn't come on the scene. In the end the grand jury seemed to agree it took both of us to kill Hank Timmons. There was no way for the prosecution to make a winnable case out of the puzzle, and that was that.

Valentine Jones went on to a successful career with a firm in Southern California. We stay in touch but we've never been close. The past remains a barrier—a canyon full of jagged questions. But when Billie passed, Valentine called me with the news and asked if I would be willing to take a DNA test.

At Billie's funeral, I met my granddaughter. Her name is Ember. I don't know if her mother realizes how perfect that is. I wore a gray suit. Ember wore a summery floral print dress without a care for gloomy tradition. Wavy strawberry blonde hair dancing about her shoulders on the ocean breeze. She is fourteen years old and already has some of her grandmother's swagger in the tilt of her head and the spark of dreams in her hazel eyes. And she is brash in that disarming and familiar way. Walked right up with arm extended, shook my hand and said, "I'm Ember, I guess I'm your new granddaughter."

It was Ember's idea to set aside small portions of Billie's ashes for close friends and family to take and spread or keep as they chose. I drove home with the velvet drawstring pouch sitting in the passenger seat of the Cadillac, sunroof open, windows down, that old blues CD blasting on the stereo. I stopped at Main Street Liquors and bought a pint of Southern Comfort, took it down to the Weeping Willow and out to the old bench at the end of Molly's Pier. I sat on the bench and cried and toasted, and I opened the little velvet pouch, emptied it into my hand and held the ashes there for just a moment before the wind came up and carried her away.

When I was a child the pier was sturdy and freshly painted. Local boys considered it an important rite of passage to dive off the railing, knife into the water, kick down and return from the depths with a handful of muddy proof that you had touched bottom. But Lupoyoma Lake is ancient, its bed layered with silt and sifted to a soft fineness by the ages, and as you rose from the darkness toward the milky green light at the surface, the mud in your hand slithered like mercury and slipped between your fingers, and when you broke back into the world and gulped air and shouted and opened your fist to show your truth, there might be nothing in the palm of your hand but a tiny sandy puddle.

The End

ACKNOWLEDGMENTS

This is the part where I say thank you.

This book wouldn't exist without the support and encouragement of many people, especially those listed below. They are teachers, writers, readers and confidantes. And friends. They have each earned my sincere gratitude during the twelve years this book was a novel-in-progress, sometimes a novel-in-doubt. Thank you.

Joshua Mohr, because I'd squandered away a significant portion of my youth and vitality on foolish distractions and thought maybe I'd missed my chance at this dream. But you convinced me I hadn't.

Gail Ansel, R. Cathey Daniels, Tracy Hill, Megan McDonald, Simi Monheit, for reading, commenting, gossiping, sharing, cheerleading, listening and commiserating through it all. Aren't you tired of this book by now!?

Leslie Wahlquist, for your generous hospitality and all the great talks over wine and whiskey about writing and books and art and politics and life. So often the book took a leap forward during my DIY retreats at your home.

Carole Stivers, for your sound advice, and for nudging me toward more clarity with your sharp eyes and thoughtful questions.

Coleen Cobbs, for being reader, cheerleader and counselor all in one.

And Jacqueline Dufrain, for never once questioning the dream.

ARCHER'S BLUES

If you have hungry ears and want to dig into some of the great blues music mentioned in the book, here is a small sampling.

('Archer's Blues' is available as a public playlist on YouTube Music)

Sad Hours / Little Walter and His Nightcaps
1952 / W. Jacobs / Checker Records

Moanin' at Midnight / The Howlin' Wolf
1951 / Carl Germany / Chess Records

Wang Dang Doodle / Koko Taylor
1966 / Willie Dixon / Checker Records

I'm Your Hoochie Coochie Man / Muddy Waters
1954 / M. Waters / Chess Records

Spann's Stomp / Otis Spann
1966 / Spann / Vanguard Records

Key to the Highway / Little Walter and His Jukes
1958 / Checker Records

Hound Dog / Willie Mae "Big Mama" Thornton
1953 / J. Leiber, M. Stoller, J. Otis / Peacock Records

Messin' with the Kid / Junior Wells
1960 / London / Chief Records

Mean Old World / Little Walter and His Nightcaps
1952 / W. Jacobs / Checker Records

You Can't Lose What You Ain't Never Had / Muddy Waters
1964 / McKinley Morganfield / Chess Records

Broken Heart / Memphis Minnie
1953 / M. Minnie / Checker Records

Sufferin' Mind / Guitar Slim
1955 / E. Jones / Specialty Records

My Heavy Load / Big Mama Thornton
1966 / Thornton-McDowell / Arhoolie Records

The Sun is Shining / Elmore James
1960 / E. James / Chess Records

Juke / Little Walter and his Night Caps
1952 / Little Walter / Checker Records

HELP SUPPORT INDY AUTHORS

If you enjoyed this book, please consider posting a review on Amazon, or Goodreads, or your favorite social media. Better yet, just tell your reader friends how much you liked the story. Every little bit helps and is sincerely appreciated. The old cliche is absolutely true: The best advertising is word of mouth! And, as always, thank you for reading!

ROY DUFRAIN JR

is a writer and musician who grew up in the hills of Northern California and spent much of his work-life in the newspaper and magazine business. He now lives in North Alabama with his wife and a precocious goldendoodle named Andy. He is a graduate of Sonoma State University, and the Continuing Studies Novel Writing Certificate Program at Stanford University. *The Blues and Billie Armstrong* is his first published novel.

roydufrain.com
facebook.com/rdufrain
bloodwaterbooks.com